Caught in the Act

Sex and Eroticism in the Movies

Caught in the Act

Sex and Eroticism in the Movies

David Shipman

ELM TREE BOOKS
London

This book is dedicated to all those
who enjoy sex in the cinema –
or anywhere else

First published in Great Britain 1985
by Elm Tree Books/Hamish Hamilton Ltd
Garden House 57–59 Long Acre London WC2E 9JZ

Copyright © 1985 by David Shipman

Book design by Trevor Vincent

British Library Cataloguing in Publication Data

Shipman, David
    Caught in the act: sex and eroticism in the movies.
    1. Sex in moving-pictures – History
    I. Title
    791.43′09′09353   PN1995.9.S45

    ISBN 0-241-11403-9

Typeset by Rowland Phototypesetting Ltd, Bury St Edmunds, Suffolk
Printed and bound in Great Britain by
R. J. Acford Ltd, Chichester, West Sussex

Contents

Introduction

Movies did not last much more than a few minutes in the 1890s and an embrace was almost all they had time for. Later, the motion picture camera learned to peer through keyholes, which may be why the nickelodeons appealed to those who liked the peepshows on the seaside promenades. Romantic love had long been a preoccupation of the stage but the cinema added a prurient note, leaving audiences to speculate on what exactly occurred between the cuddling couple in the railway carriage as their train went through a tunnel; or what thoughts passed through the mind of the shoe-store assistant when his customer raised her skirt a little higher than necessary.

The movies soon learned to tell a story, borrowing from the comic and risqué situations of vaudeville. When it was clear that narrative was what the public wanted they offered the love stories of history and antiquity. Those film-makers with a less elevated view offered transcriptions of Victorian melodrama, tales of rape and ravishment – or, at the other end of the scale, simple love stories, starting that polarisation of screen sex which was to be maintained till the permissive age. And there were others again who, realising that this was a dynamic new form of mass communication, wanted to instruct and reform. These entrepreneurs came up with stories that were harsh, topical, crusading, of vital importance to every member of the audience: but the 'white slave' boom didn't last long, and it was back to the tales of rape and ravishment.

Then came the film-star, the idol, the bathing beauty. It is difficult for us to imagine the awe in which these were held; how eagerly awaited was the idol's next appearance. We're brought up now constantly bombarded with images glowing from the box in the corner of the living-room: idols, ankles, kisses – we've seen them, even if knowing not their significance, before we've learned to read.

Early film-makers quickly realised that the revelation of an ankle was an easily-recognised symbol, for except in desperation nice girls didn't; on screen an ankle certainly never failed to ignite passion in the male beholder. It is more difficult to say how the audiences felt, because those who wrote about movies in those far-off days seldom admitted to sexual passion. The many lyrical writings on Garbo do not neglect her erotic fascination but it is not, rightly, separated from her beauty and acting ability. If, however, it was implied that making love with Garbo was the ultimate it could not be suggested that five minutes with Clara Bow might be fun. Garbo was a great actress and not in the titillation business, as was Clara Bow; and there was little serious writing about Clara Bow.

It is easy enough to speculate on Miss Bow's effect on red-blooded men of the time – it wouldn't have been very different from that of Marilyn Monroe on men in the fifties, if only because public morality, on the surface at least, had changed little. Cole Porter wrote 'Anything Goes' in 1934 to demonstrate how far they had moved since a glimpse of stocking was looked on as something shocking, but it took another thirty years before Anything really Went. You certainly didn't learn the facts of life from going to the picture palace. These were learnt in the school yard and any girl who let a boy go further than a kiss was irretrievably lost. You learnt about life from the Sunday papers and checked in the dictionary for words you had never encountered beyond the printed page. And sex in the movies was indicated by a slowly-closing bedroom door.

We and the movie-makers took a long time to emerge from that long Victorian twilight when, to use the most famous and ridiculous example, the piano legs were covered. Emancipation was expected to come during the Roaring Twenties and again after the Second World War, but on neither occasion were the movies of much overt help. The cinema had always looked to the theatre and novels to provide it with a lead, but it remained kicking and screaming against any honest depiction of sexual behaviour till well after the former had broken down taboos, and then it only caved in because commercial pressures dictated. The film industry, as long as it was prosperous, pretended to dislike sex, but once the chips were down it found that it loved it. By abandoning the Production Code in 1968, after thirty-four years in which it had been the firm custodian on all matters of movie morals, the industry went haywire, and there was so much humping and screwing on our screens that one longed, after all, for that slowly-closing bedroom door.

It was about this time, too, that the cinema's past began to become available to a new generation. Watching old movies confirmed what we already knew, that popular cinema was almost entirely reliant on the star system; and the stars were subjected to rigid typecasting. So if a player first attracted attention because of a saucy smile, an amorous wink, a leer, even a display of flesh, those were the features they were expected to utilise in their days of stardom. The amount of sexuality in any given film depended on the star's image. This was true until the 1970s, when star power finally faded, except for a period in the early 1930s: because of the Depression attendances fell and those cinemagoers who remained loyal responded to the growing honesty with which many matters were handled. It could be said that sex had a fairly good run on the screen till 1934, when the rules of the Production Code were implemented.

Although I cannot ignore that factor, this is not a history of movie censorship, for several already exist. And since so many facets of sex in the cinema have been extensively covered elsewhere this does not seek to be an exhaustive survey. It is a book about popular cinema which chiefly means Hollywood; at the same time the text deals with some 'fringe' movies and many more from Europe because they have been admired or influential (one of the reasons why I have had to exclude the Japanese cinema is that very few of its manifold stories of geisha life have been seen in the West). I have tried to reflect the cinema's proportional

approval of heterosexuality *vis-à-vis* homosexuality, and because it was never my intention to be comprehensive I decided to exclude movies on homosexuality made by homosexuals, which for complicated but inexplicable reasons seem to me dishonest, as well as movies directed by women in which after a while the female players begin to lose interest in their menfolk and take to kissing each other.

I have wanted to write about some of the films I have seen; I have wanted to write a book from primary sources. This book is about those aspects of sex which film-makers managed to show while pretending they a) weren't b) were acting in the public interest c) were condemning immorality d) were urging social reforms e) were expressing moral indignation f) were only reflecting 'real' life g) were only giving audiences what they wanted h) were bowing to the star's whims i) were bowing to the wishes of the star's fans, and j) all of these things.

David Shipman

1.

Peepshows and White Slavers

The Kiss (1896) is one of the most celebrated of the first films. The players are a couple past their first youth, May Irwin and John C. Rice, who are discovered whispering sweet nothings to each other and looking mighty pleased about it. Rice breaks away and strokes his large moustache before moving in for the kiss, which he subsequently repeats. *The Kiss from the Widow Jones*, to give it its full title, was made for the Edison Company under the supervision of Edwin S. Porter. The play, *The Widow Jones*, had achieved a certain notoriety when it had toured America, but what was apparently acceptable on stage was not when magnified on a screen – or not, anyway, to one Herbert S. Stone, a Chicago publisher who fulminated against it in one of his periodicals.

We know this from one of the earliest of screen histories, *A Million and One Nights*, by Terry Ramsaye, first published in 1926, and one of our few written sources for this period, which may be why *The Kiss* has retained its fame. Scientists and sociologists had noted the birth of movies, but since these were an attraction at carnivals, fairgrounds, music halls and the like, they were not treated seriously. They were not respectable.

It was not clear, at the time of *The Kiss*, whether the future of the new medium lay in projected images on a screen or being watched by individuals in the Kineto-scopes or Mutoscopes which were, to those who frequented them, merely a streamlined version of the peepshow or the slot-machine. The most famous feature of the slot-machine was 'What the Butler Saw', which

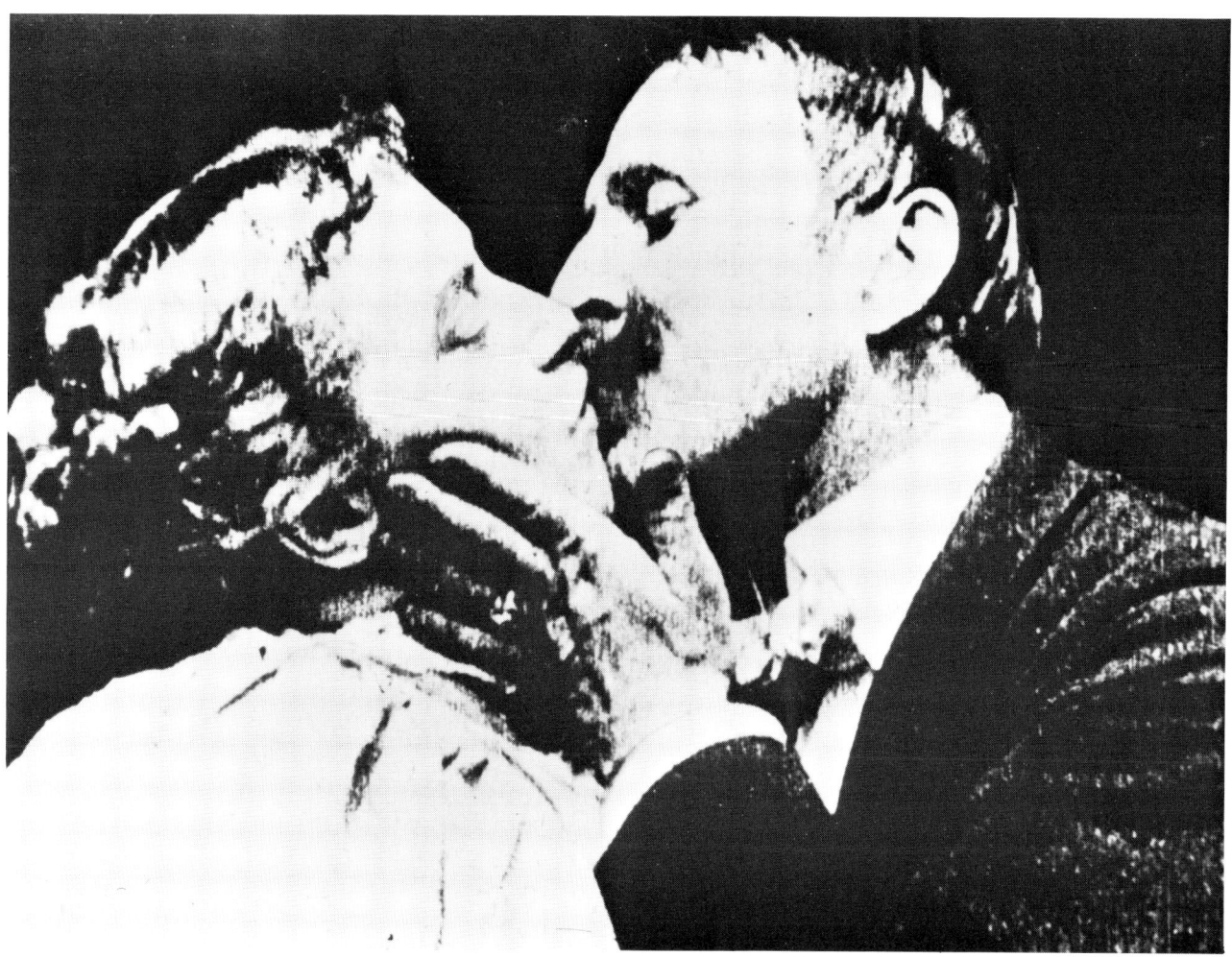

The screen's first kiss from the play, *The Widow Jones*, with May Irwin and John C. Rice. Many people were scandalised, making this an early example of matters permitted on stage but thought unfit for the cinema.

could still be viewed on British seaside piers as late as the 1940s. Since films had not yet used narrative there must have been many other kisses and peeps through keyholes at this time, as well as records of rather daring vaudeville acts, usually of dancers in *déshabillé*.

Few films of this period survive, but many of those that have are of sexual anecdotes, suggesting that there was a larger demand for these prints than for those on other subjects. Further, American, British and French film-makers were duplicating each others' brightest ideas, for audiences were no longer content to watch a mere embrace. A kiss, for instance, in a railway tunnel was far more titillating. While it may be discreet before and after the train enters the tunnel, the audience might imagine any amount of ardour during the time in the dark. I have seen two British versions of this subject and half-dozen examples of the keyhole films, none of them showing anything more spectacular than a couple chastely embracing or a woman in her (often voluminous) petticoats. The later versions are more sophisticated, as in *A Search for Evidence* (1903), produced by Biograph, in which can be seen some gamblers, an attempted suicide and a domestic scene before the film's climax, in which a man and a girl are discovered by someone whom we suppose to be his wife.

As the narrative film developed, so did the urge to moralise, even if the majority of the stories are lighthearted. Erring husbands were always found out, though their sin was seldom more than a smile, and the wives were invariably armed with either a rolling-pin or an umbrella. Wives were also tempted, many having lost their husband's passion in favour of Wall Street, but the merest hint of temptation would make him see his mistake. Widows were something else, jolly and/or predatory, but prone to ill-considered choices till that last-minute revelation – that the suitor was a) engaged b) married c) a flirt d) a bounder e) penniless f) a drunkard g) a confirmed bachelor unlikely to change his ways h) a criminal i) a widower with countless kids j) mean, and the owner of a large mansion without servants . . .

Film-makers approved of women who went out to work, perhaps because, like themselves, they regarded them as breaking new ground. The store clerks and stenographers are demure, seldom encouraging husbands with roving eyes. In contrast the temptresses always have time on their hands, and their heavy make-up should have been warning enough: they are never plain nor ever successful. Professional temptresses are much luckier, usually picking up the first men to whom they speak, but they then steal from him – after slipping him a Mickey Finn – so that we condemn them for being criminals rather than for being prostitutes. They are not named as such, since intertitles were not yet common, and the client is just as likely to be punished, for having been unprincipled enough (or stupid: this is the country rube/city slicker tale in another guise) to accept the woman's invitation in the first place.

These tales of prostitutes seem to have disappeared quite quickly as the new industry sought respectability, but as films grew longer – from two-three minutes and from a reel to two reels – the comic subjects hardly

changed. When the narrative film arrived in 1903 the initial subjects were crooks and criminals. Audiences discovered new thrills in seeing them apprehended and as they tired of that, film-makers turned for inspiration to the criminals of the 19th century, many of whom had trod the boards in simulated dramatised form. The next step was to raid the old melodramas – the broken home, the forced abduction, the unwilling alliance: the rapist carrying off the innocent and the lecher tempting her. These latter were recognised – at least, by those who had attended theatres – less by their actions than by their appearance, which probably included both a moustache and a silk hat. The traditions of Victorian melodrama were incorporated into the plots of the new medium and, amazingly, were to hold sway till the cinema bowed to the permissive age. The rules were simple (in the comedies the sporty widows and such were seldom too intent on their purpose): the male was the aggressor; women were either respectable or 'fallen' – that is, designed to be either wives or mistresses. If the latter, they were always punished, though they might be allowed a last-minute restitution if they had put up a good fight or manifested an inordinate amount of remorse. In the archetypal stage melodrama the landlord took the heroine instead of rent, and the movies merely modernised the situation: the intending ravisher became a factory manager, a mine-owner or a party host, while his intended victim was a secretary, an employee's wife or the new maid.

Typical of these films is *The Mill Girl*, produced by Vitagraph in 1907. The boss is attracted to one of his employees, but she repulses him. He goes to a low dive and hires two thugs to attack the girl's sweetheart who easily vanquishes them. Next day the boss sacks him, and again tries his dastardly tricks on the girl. She flees, to a factory deserted because it is on fire. The boss grabs her again, too demented by lust to notice the flames. She faints and the boss wanders away crazed, presumably to perish in the conflagration. Her boyfriend rescues her, lowers her to safety – and they are reunited amidst their fellow workers.

Screen rape received great impetus when D. W. Griffith perfected the technique of cross-cutting to enhance the climaxes of his films. The primitive crime films made before he became a director had understood the importance of showing both the rescuer and he, she, or it about to be rescued. We cannot complain of the sameness of Griffith's climaxes, since too few of his 450 one- and two-reelers survive. For the same reason we cannot say how often an attempted rape provided the climax. There are two in his most famous film, *The Birth of a Nation* (1915): halfway through Miriam Cooper is threatened (which is why her brother forms the Ku Klux Klan), while at the end it is Lillian Gish who is in danger. Griffith had received his training in the theatre touring the sticks in melodramas, and these were to influence his work long after critics had begun complaining that his films were old-fashioned. Sometimes it seems that he was unable to make one without an attempted ravishment at the climax – and he never permitted the rescuing hero to arrive too early or too late. Credibility gives way to suspense, as in his war story, *Hearts of the*

World (1918), when no amount of exploding shells can prevent Erich von Stroheim from wanting his way with Lillian Gish.

The First World War was a godsend to the film industry since the beastliness of the Hun could be safely exploited: indeed, making war turned out to be a diversion disguising his true intent, the ravishing of the local women. Even in the fiercest propaganda he could not be successful because women were sacrosanct, even in Europe. American film producers and moviegoers were not entirely happy with such offerings as *The Mill Girl*, for the behaviour of the boss was clearly, if not demonstratively, un-American. Fortunately, there were the classics – the famous lovers of history and legend, such as Romeo and Juliet, Paolo and Francesca, Paris and Helen – which had the advantage that the darker, greater passions were not only long ago but far away. That was important, for in most time-hallowed tales sexual desire was not always thwarted, and that created, if you will pardon the pun, a whole new ball-game, since the film's denouement could not be predicted. All the same, in the extant versions of the classic tales which had begun to pour from the studios at the beginning of the century the clinches are very chaste, but that may be because the movie companies hoped to attract to them a better class of spectator, i.e. those who had previously thought moviegoing beneath them. By now producers knew they were involved in an industry that was rapidly expanding, but as nickelodeons gave way to the grander buildings called cinemas they yearned for respect.

The first producers, like their successors, wanted to have their cake and eat it. The first pornographic movies were being made in South America, to be bought abroad by wealthy private collectors and the owners of European bordellos. But for the cinema the depiction of physical love was unthinkable and/or punishable by a prison sentence. For those who devised the plots of movies, the dilemma was simple: courtship and marital love, although liable to misunderstandings, was not in itself as dramatic (or as enticing to audiences) as illicit love. That, however, could only be shown within convention, the chief of which was that it had to end badly – if not for all concerned, certainly for the female protagonists.

While film-makers in several countries pondered upon ways of presenting reputable variations on this theme, one Danish producer made a series of films devoted to men's darker lusts. In 1907 Ole Olsen presented *The White Slave*, in which an advert in a newspaper is brought to the heroine's attention by her father; she goes for an interview conducted by a middle-aged woman, who charms her. She says goodbye to her father and also her boyfriend, whose parting gift is a white pigeon in a cage. In an unspecified, presumably foreign city she is dressed in a lace négligé before realising her fate, and is locked in her room. While a party goes on downstairs she writes a note and fixes it to the pigeon, which is despatched to Papa. He and the boyfriend arrive with the police and the partygoers are carted away.

The expression 'white slave trade' was a euphemism,

acceptable on cinema posters while promising titillation. The theory was that the victims were either charmed into leaving or abducted against their will and then starved or imprisoned until they succumbed to a life of prostitution. In fact the operation was a great deal more sophisticated than that in Olsen's simple little film. The girls selected were usually desperately poor and the promises of wealth awaiting them on arrival abroad quite considerable; on landing in the unfamiliar and hence frightening foreign city they would not be met as promised, but the 'organisation' would send an apparent stranger to help them out of their desperate plight, which meant that there was only one way in which they could earn money to eat and find somewhere to sleep.

These were not facets Olsen chose to use when he remade the film more elaborately three years later, with the international market in mind. The French company, Gaumont, had started a series of supposedly realist films which were so successful in the US that they had been emulated by Vitagraph. It was at this market that Olsen aimed *The White Slave Trade* (1910), directed by August Blom. At twice the length of the earlier one-reel film, this has an identical plot line but more detail. The foreign city is easily identified for there is a painted Big Ben outside the girl's window, though the street scenes look nothing like London. The chief 'improvements' are: the girl receives a first client, whom she tries to strangle; she gets a note out via a complaisant maid; and she agrees to go to the party, where she recognises her boyfriend posing as a customer. The rescue and escape are more complicated affairs, involving Scotland Yard, which also featured in the dozens of similar films which followed, for Olsen had been right in estimating an international success.

Indeed, many of the later films concentrate on the rescue, with plots similar to other cops-and-robbers tales, since only so much could be shown of prostitution. The orgy in *The White Slave* looks not unlike tea at the vicarage – admittedly a rather merry one – except that the women are smoking, which was not then socially acceptable. The party in *The White Slave Trade* takes place in a more ornate room, there are more male guests and a few of the girls have removed their frocks but are still wearing mountains of petticoats. In the obligatory bordello group scene in Olsen and Blom's *The White Slave Trade's Last Big Job* (1911) even the wine glasses are absent, and were it not for a couple of lecherous middle-aged gentlemen we would not know why (in this case) the heroine has been kidnapped. No matter what the duress, she will never succumb. Since such perils were supposed to be lurking in all big cities, these tales were thought to be relevant and of course moral, though that was only achieved by limiting the options open to the victim, for she could not be shown enjoying her predicament or risk audience frustration by dying – the *only* alternative to rescue.

The Danes' other contribution to world cinema at this time (apart from their sea stories) was the circus drama. The milieu was important: circus-folk and bohemians obeyed different rules to those of the bourgeoisie, as well as providing more colourful prey for lecherous aristocrats than the upstairs maid. As the century entered its second decade film-makers everywhere had begun to understand their audiences: in adopting the bogeyman of Victorian drama, the wicked landlord, they had found a threat understood by the proletariat, and as cinemagoers consisted largely of the latter it was appropriate to show them as honest and hard-working but at the mercy of a dissolute and lazy upper class. That Olsen's company specialised also in tales of philandering among the aristocracy is due to the fact that such stories were especially popular in Russia, which was one of the most lucrative markets for Danish pictures. Thus as dukes and diplomats pursued bareback-riders and artists' models, their wives, neglected and sexually deprived, began to play the same game, taking advantage of idle grooms and artists bereft of models. Emma Bovary may have committed infidelities, but women as sexual predators were rare in Western literature. One may be found, however, in *The Great Circus Catastrophe* (1912), directed in Denmark by Eduard Schnedler-Sørensen. The lady in question is the star attraction of a circus, which is joined by a penniless count. She is soon practising her wiles on him in her hotel room, but the hotel catches on fire and that puts paid to that. He is so in thrall to her, however, that he gets drunk and goes to do his dangerous stunt in that condition, despite the pleas of the ballerina who loves him truly. The circus hero of

The Four Devils (1911) is spotted by a wealthy lady who is also a blatant seductress. Invited to her mansion, he allows her arms to twine around his neck as they share a bottle of schnapps, but it is he who takes the initiative in leaving the room, to be followed by her. Audiences must have known what they planned to do, which in my experience makes this movie unique in early cinema. (And, yes, they are punished: she by his growing indifference and he when his wife lets him fall during their high wire act, before plunging to her own death.)

Although we do not see it, couples did make love in other Danish movies: how, otherwise, the high proportion of unmarried mothers among the heroines? These are not the victims of vile seducers but, in the tradition of Scandinavian literature, those who have loved not wisely but too well. If I anticipate slightly here it is because such was often material for the Swedish writer Selma Lagerlöf, whose novels provided the source of two of the finest films by her fellow countryman, Victor Sjöström. In *The Girl From Stormycroft* (1917) the trouble really starts when an engaged man befriends an unmarried mother, and in *The Ingmarssons* it is caused by a groom unable to retain his continence till the wedding night. These are movies of psychological complexity, and thus some way away from the Danish tales of seduced and abandoned heroines – unfortunate beings who will be deserted by the weak, parent-

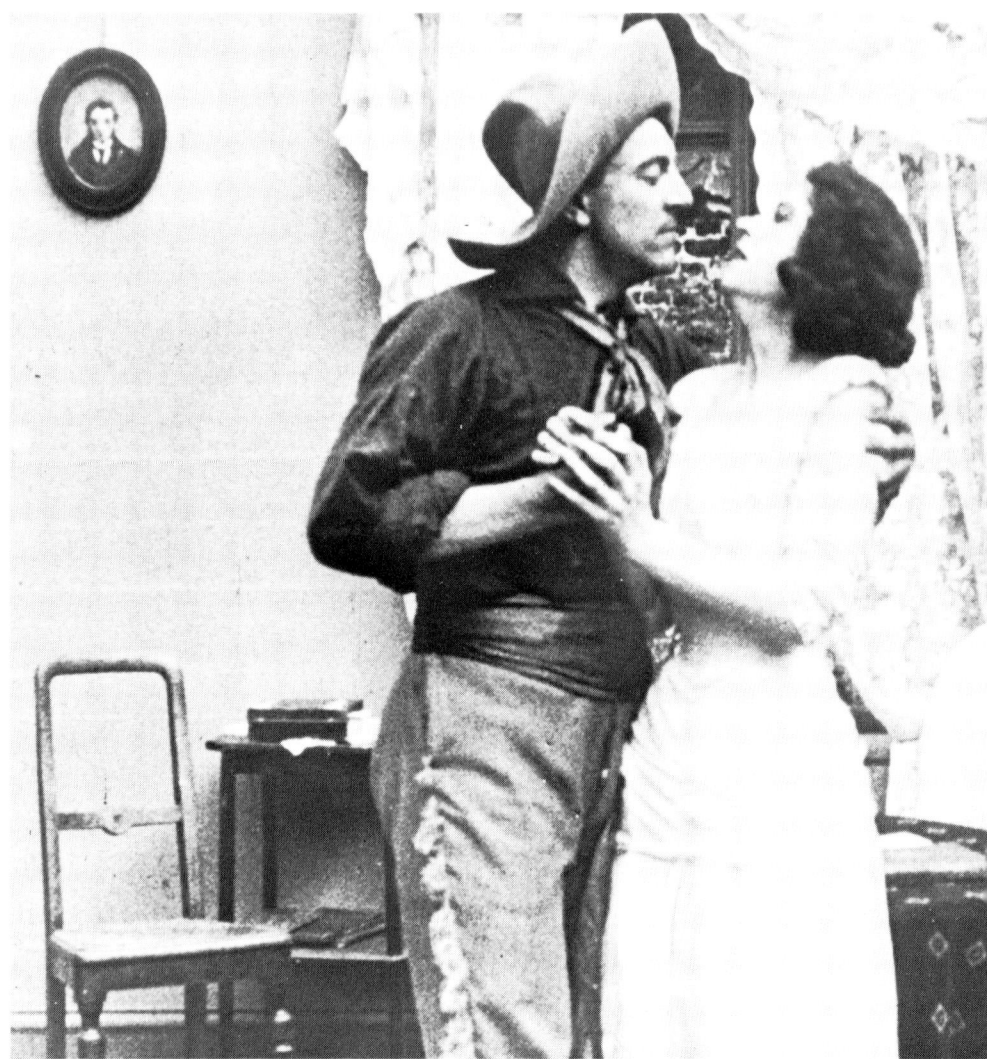

Above: Smyrner's Candy Store in *Traffic in Souls*, and it is certainly respectable enough – as is its owner, a prominent reformer. Secretly, however, he runs a chain of brothels, and here is his agent (William Cavanaugh) plotting to get the heroine (Ethel Grandin) from one establishment to the other. Her sister (Jane Gail) obviously has doubts.

Left: Asta Nielsen, the screen's first wicked lady, often gave her favours away and then found herself forced to sell them. Most of her vehicles made her more sinned against than sinning. This scene from the first of them, *The Abyss*, shows that instant which would lead to a long career of dallying on the primrose path.

dominated true love and either go mad or die in child-birth, or both.

One such did live to tell the tale, but only in the most degraded circumstance, and that was Asta Nielsen who, in *The Abyss* (1910), began a long career in which she inevitably paid for one mistake – usually the same one – of confusing lust with true love. In *The Abyss* she is attracted to a circus performer who, miraculously divining this, climbs a ladder to her room and has her promising – after one kiss – to go away with him. To him she is only, as Beatrice Lillie put it, a passing fancy, but his kiss leaves her breathless – as her handsome engineer fiancé, who is prepared to forgive her, discovers after he seeks her out in theatrical digs. When he sees her again she is playing the piano in a beer garden: he sends the manager a note to say that he wants to see her, and her seducer interprets this as a request to be one of her 'clients'. The film had an astounding effect on world audiences and it took Miss Nielsen and her writer-director husband, Urban Gad, to Germany, where he made the very similar *Die Arme Jenny* (1912). Jenny is the daughter of caretakers of a luxury block of flats, among whose inhabitants are Reinhold, a rotter. When he invites her out she goes in borrowed finery, but he disapproves of that and he soon provides her with a series of snazzy outfits which bring truth dawning to her parents, who cast her out. Unwillingly Reinhold takes her away with him, but he flirts with other women and she leaves him. 'The working girl also has honour' says an intertitle, but this one obviously has no money, for it's step by step into the abyss again. The earlier film ends with Nielsen being led away by the police; this time the wages of sin bring news of Reinhold's marriage, twelve years later, which causes her to walk out into a snowdrift. In the many variations which followed Miss Nielsen usually met death at the end.

The popularity of the Danish movies on the White Slave Trade had not gone unnoticed by the American film industry. It did not feel obliged to follow suit in this instance, however, as it had also noticed how many of these movies had had to brave the wrath of the countless local censorship boards. It was useless to point out to the censors that the message was moral and the films of a condemnatory nature, for this was an era when Authority believed itself to have a parental duty to keep the uneducated and unsophisticated in that blessed condition as long as possible. The popular press was still in its infancy, and it was thought, probably rightly, that those who attended the pernicious nickelodeons were illiterate. Certainly in America the growing immigrant population did not, by and large, read the newspapers. For those who did, the press carried sporadic reports on international attempts to stop the trade in prostitution. The reader will not need reminding that this is the oldest profession: its growth in the second half of the 19th century is bound up with the increasing concentrations of the population in the cities. Whether or not the Victorian wife disliked making love her husband, if wealthy enough, kept another establishment primarily for that purpose. The *demi-monde* was not invisible – nor were the stews. If whoring was a wholly acceptable pastime for rich young men, those that made them happy did so from desperation. The concentration of wealth was all at one end: that was one reason so many men emigrated from Europe, often leaving their womenfolk behind. Transatlantic fares were relatively cheap and it was not difficult for the unscrupulous to find poverty-stricken women to follow them to fulfil, whether willingly or not, the natural need of man, doubtless increased by the nightly intake of booze. Those without families or unable to read had few ways of spending their evenings other than in drinking.

In 1899 an international congress was held in London in an effort to agree on measures to curb trading in prostitution. It was followed during the next decade by another in London, and others in Amsterdam and Paris. Investigations into prostitution in Chicago and New York culminated in a Grand Jury inquiry under John D. Rockefeller Jr, published in June 1913 as the Rockefeller White Slavery Report. That proved an inspiration to George Loane Tucker, an actor and director with Carl Laemmle's Imp Company. Since Laemmle had refused to sanction a feature on the subject Tucker began work clandestinely and had in fact left to take a position in Britain before the film was completed (at a cost of $5,700). Jack Cohn edited it, and it was he who showed it to Laemmle, offering – on behalf of Tucker and their fellow conspirators – to reimburse him the cost if he refused to distribute it. After some initial hesitation Laemmle booked it into Weber's Theatre in New York, describing it as a '$200,000 Spectacle'. It was an instant success, is estimated to have taken over $450,000, and led to a number of imitations by other movie companies.

Seen today, *Traffic in Souls* (1913) is respectable and responsible, but not exactly brimming with conviction. To an extent it is a film about hypocrisy, since the brothel-owner, Mr Trubis (William Welsh), is a prominent member of society and a big wheel in the 'International Purity and Reform League'. After showing the operation at work – the madames pay the go-betweens, who communicate with Trevis by dictaphone or through his agents – the film gets down to the nitty-gritty: a country girl is met off the train by one operator; two Swedish girls, on the quayside, by two others. These three unfortunates are locked away, threatened, and then put into pretty frocks while we worry about the fate of the heroine's sister, who has disappeared. The two girls work in a candy store owned by Trevis, but after the heroine is sacked Trevis's wife gets her a job as his secretary; the last section shows how she and her policeman boyfriend trap him. There is no indication that her sister will succumb, though the treatment gets rougher every time she refuses to accept the proffered gown and she is about to be whipped when the cops eventually break in.

Unlike the Danish films, the brothels in this movie are seen to be dank, dark and poorly furnished – places not even the randiest fellow would want to visit. There is no dancing (except in a café where one of the villains wines and dines the girl he hopes to dupe). The title may have promised titillation, but what audiences actually saw was a thriller with a moral ending. Retribution! Trevis's daughter loses her fiancé, 'The greatest society "catch" of the season' and later she goes insane; his wife dies of grief and he commits suicide. An intertitle informs us that there are another 50,000 white slaves in the US.

With the profits from the film Laemmle built Universal City, and thus there grew from an exploitation film one of the great continuing studios of Hollywood history.

2.
Diva into Vamp

In France Sarah Bernhardt committed her Marguerite Gautier to film for posterity – or what was left of the piece after it had been reduced to two reels. It is difficult to think of this stagey *La Dame aux Camélias* (1911) as bringing an erotic theme to a wider public. Certainly Bernhardt brought people into the cinema who had hitherto despised it; and it is the story of a courtesan who returns to her 'protector' in order not to jeopardise society's opinion of the man she truly loves. Equally surely there is little in this record to show why Bernhardt had enslaved and moved theatregoers on

several continents; but it was those who emulated her in Italy who were responsible for a new breed of glamorous heroine.

These were the *dive*, so-called after their counterpart in opera, the diva. They are also known as the *divismo* actresses, for the word *divismo* covers the genre – melodramas in which the stars adopt statuesque Mucha-like poses in overstuffed rooms while driving men to destruction. Some of them came from noble families, while others were the mistresses of the aristocrats who financed the film industry – and who in some cases they

The death of Marguerite Gautier, Sarah Bernhardt, in *La Dame aux Camélias*. Her Armand is Lou Tellegen, who was to have a successful Hollywood career before committing suicide.

married. They include Francesca Bertini, the most admired and renowned, Lyda Borelli, Lina Cavalieri, Maria Jacobini, Alda Hesperia, Pina Menichelli and Italia Almirante Manzini. They entered films between 1907 and 1913, and the first of them were famous by 1910. Until the vogue for the *divismo* films waned at the end of the second decade most of them made over a dozen films a year – almost all of which have disappeared. Their credits show the traditional *femmes fatales* of literature and the classics, including such modern heroines as Pinero's Mrs Tanqueray and Feydeau's Amelie. In general, however, they seem to have suffered and laughed less than have been intent on seducing the susceptible males around them. These ladies played opera singers, countesses, diplomats' wives, socialities; men have committed suicide for them before the action begins; they leave their husbands and take lovers while others conspire against them, all in a bubble of scandal to be resolved in a spectacular finale – a fire, a flood, a theatrical performance. Only a few sequences survive of *Serpe* (1919), but they are riper than those complete films that I have seen. A countess

The Italian *diva* Francesca Bertini, giving an idea of the dominant powers these heroines were said to possess.

(Francesca Bertini) tells a young violinist 'My father killed himself because you denounced him: I shall denounce you in revenge', whereupon he becomes her slave. In her apartment she keeps a portrait of his last mistress so that she can mock them both. In one scene she lies on a circular silk-covered divan, dressed in white with pearls on her brow and ostrich feathers at ner neck; she looks gloatingly down on him, extended on the floor, lolling against the couch, eyes closed, in white tie and tails, a champagne glass held limply in one hand. She exults in her power over a male so consumed by passion that he has drunk himself into lethargy.

The woman as predator, as the dominating figure, the man in subjugation: this is a situation virtually unprecedented outside the Delilahs, Shebas and Cleopatras, outside tales of princes in thrall to courtesans. That it became so entrenched in Italy at this time may be due to the matriarchal nature of its society. Perhaps something in the Italian character made these women as attractive as they were powerful, and they certainly reflected – if only by chance – the concern about woman's new place in the new century.

That was not what attracted William Fox to a film of the same genre, although admittedly *A Fool There Was* (1915) was one of the many new feature-length films being made in the US based on popular plays. It remains as blatant a copy of the *divismo* films as was *Traffic in Souls* of its European prototypes. Its theatre origins conveyed a qualified respectability, while the quotations from Kipling (the title is taken from one of his poems) served to underline the moral – in any case inescapable – that adultery does not pay. It is the man who suffers, while she – 'a notorious woman of the vampire species' – is not required to atone for her sins (in Italy she sometimes did). The actress concerned was Theda Bara, who although in fact born in Cincinnati was said to be of mystic origin, chiefly Oriental, while the film itself infers that really sinful sin was a European phenomenon. Though the setting is mainly the US, the woman's name is not given, thus obscuring her nationality; she first exercises her wiles on her victim on a transatlantic liner and he is first seen 'fallen' in a European garden that we may suppose to be hers. He is a decent American – a social reformer (like the hypocritical brothel-owner in *Traffic in Souls*) and it is the greater tragedy, therefore, to be the plaything of this un-American woman who, returned to New York, is unrepentant in ostracism and so brazen as to mock him before wife and child: 'Kiss me, my fool' she commands, reducing him to jelly – a step on the way to complete disintegration. Surprisingly he does not become a drug-addict, since the weak and wicked men in movies took as easily to drugs as to rape. Disappointingly, the vamp's motive turns out to be revenge – on the wife, who snubbed her in reel one. However, adultery and drunkenness were concomitants, and the guests at the parties in the Bara mansion heed not the empty bottles as they dance and play wicked card games. Freed from the constraints of home life, of religious observance, of etiquette, men give themselves over to boozing – which, the film implies, becomes habitual when the social pressures outweigh the freedom.

The success of the movie was such that there came into being Fox Studio, which endures today as 20th Century-Fox. It also made Miss Bara a star, until she bowed to public indifference and retired in the early 1920s. At the end Fox tried to change her image, but the problem was that of all the screen's early wicked ladies: she was required to vamp, enthrall, enslave, seduce – but as a star she needed to be likeable. Her actions, frankly, were unlikely to endear her to Mr and Mrs Joe Public, who knew little of such matters even if, on the first occasion or so, they were fascinated. The fan magazines, now growing in numbers, could assure their readers that the Baras of the movies were at heart simple little housewives never happier than when baking apple pies. Miss Bara was the first example of a star who, in the end, was neither one thing nor the other: the fan magazines presented her as a vamp who was wifely from time to time or vice versa, while in her movies she vamped till the last reel, when she suddenly and unexpectedly went through a complete character change, which could not be quite wifely. For her and her myriad imitators there began an inordinate number of conversions, reformations, repentances, renunciations and pleas for forgiveness, as the devisers of movies sought to make these miscreants sympathetic, whether or not their fall from grace was their own fault (which it usually was). As the courtesans – Camille, Carmen, Cleopatra – made their way to the screen, they were required to be popular and sympathetic. The impetus again came from the stage, following the tradition which maintained that Nell Gwynn was the only known likeable royal mistress: her counterparts were painted and haughty till their fancy was caught by some handsome guardsman or peasant boy, revealing themselves to have undreamt-of reserves of generosity and simple-heartedness.

These ladies came to the screen by public demand, which had decided long ago that vice was more interesting than virtue. If audiences were intrigued by the corruption of the virtuous and the once-only-but-damned-for-ever, how might they react to the ladies who longed to be corrupted and damned – and having achieved both, thus continued to enjoy themselves? Only their sex was allowed the choice: the stronger sex, being stronger, was noble or dastardly, with no semblance of emotion between – unless, that is, he has imbibed too much. The curse of drink, like the erring servant girl, was no myth to the proletariat: that the two were often in conjunction is evident from the popular press, and movies only reflected common prejudice in showing alcohol as a menace to all men, dastardly or noble. Villains in any case were bound to misbehave, so the schemes and/or ravings of a drunken villain were incalculable; they drank to increase audience tension. Heroes drank only in a moment of weakness, understanding for the first time their baser desires – which circumstance would prevent them from realising.

Between the hero and villain was the weakling, and whole tracts were devoted to him. Miss Bara's prey in *A Fool There Was* is one such, but at least he went to damnation in sexual ecstasy. The weakling always spent the first reel as a good man and his path to perdition depended on what started him off in the first place. As

Theda Bara as Salome, minus a veil or so, dancing in the 1918 film of that name.

like as not it was not a woman, but just as often it was a dropped postal order, a geegaw left lying around, or an unwanted pocket watch. At this time, and perhaps since the Industrial Revolution, the very many very poor must have wondered how they might feel if they could acquire a little of the immense wealth of the very few; and many a three-decker Victorian novel had detailed the reversals always attendant on that moment of temptation. The theme was old-fashioned, if still topical, when Cecil B. De Mille dug it up once more to use in *The Whispering Chorus* (1918). The title refers to the inner voices which dictate our actions, and the action which sets our sad sap hero on his road to doom is a spot of gambling. His cuffs are frayed, but his wife has enough money for a new dress. Who knows that a spot of luck won't allow him to buy her two new dresses and a new coat for himself? Before long he cooks the books; and disappears. As befits the wicked, he goes from bad to worse. He is soon too disfigured, too drunk and too poverty-stricken to think of the opposite sex, while his deserted wife has met and married a handsome and wealthy congressman. Where to next? An opium den, of course. Infinitely few picturegoers could ever have been in an opium den, but weaklings in movies ended up there, right into the Talkie era.

The usual end for sinners and weaklings was suicide – but only after a last-minute realisation that they were not good enough for this world. Since those who got themselves pregnant without benefit of marriage fitted into either or both of these categories you didn't expect to see them alive at the fade-out either. Pregnancy was never caused by rape or ravishment, or by any male unfit to father a child: it never happened to vamps and apparently it could only be caused when the heroine yielded under pledge of marriage. Such promises were not always made by the lascivious or already married, but the girl was unlikely to be of the same social standing as her seducer, so there was always someone standing by to prevent the match – and it was just as likely a sister or aunt, to explain by her own example why she could not enter his world. By implication, it served her right for believing, even subconsciously, that her body provided a passport to a position for which she was unfitted. She could do so only unsullied, and audiences never tired of watching wealthy scions falling in love with girls from the slums. There were occasions when the situation was reversed; but if a girl could move upward only on the strength of her looks, a poor boy needed to be very hard-working, to have a brilliant mind and to have – in the last reel – the approval of his fiancée's father.

I cannot think of any version of the Cinderella story in which the amorous couple anticipate their wedding night. To have done so would have damned them in the eyes of God and the moviegoer. At the same time the unvarying moral code would not, for the sake of profits, always dictate the course of the stories. Film-makers could not rely indefinitely on the self-righteousness of audiences, nor on their acceptance of the invariable ending – Paying the Ultimate Price. Besides, the cinema was becoming a pastime for the whole family, and while it was known that servant girls and such liked a good cry their boyfriends did not. Likewise families seemed not to want to leave cinemas with their faces bathed in tears. Or so the producers believed.

Fortunately for this belief the unswerving screen morality was reinforced by the growth of the star system. While European audiences thrilled to the exploits of the mature Miss Nielsen and the Italian *dive* their American counterparts were more likely to be watching adolescent girls in gingham. American film producers had been reluctant to name their players because they feared that they would demand more money and command more power – and the actors, by and large, were people without claim to either, having little or no reputation or prior thespian experience. When a rival company filched 'The Biograph Girl' from the company of that name, a publicity stunt revealed her to be Florence Lawrence, and at the same time the names of other popular players became known to the public as the companies fought for their services. This was an important factor in the struggles for studio supremacy, and an uncongenial one for the combatants, who resented the increased salaries which they were, nevertheless, so ready to pay. An actor with a stage reputation, such as Maurice Costello, was another matter, and as the battle between the companies intensified it attracted other renowned theatre performers, notably the 'Famous Players in Famous Plays' which Adolph Zukor offered to motion picture audiences. The movie producers, with their parvenu thinking, ardently believed that movie audiences would welcome the idols of Broadway, but if these enjoyed seeing white-haired William H. Crane in

the title-role of *David Harum* (1915), one of his most famous parts, what did they make of the portly and equally venerable DeWolf Hopper (a Gilbert and Sullivan veteran) scampering around in the title-role of *Sunshine Dad* (1916) – and now recalled, if at all, as the first husband of the gossip columnist Hedda Hopper, who married him when a very young chorus girl?

If Miss Lawrence herself was in her twenties, her rivals – who included Mary Pickford, the Gish sisters, and Blanche Sweet – were in their teens, and the rest often seemed to be, certainly when compared to Zukor's middle-aged and often paunchy Broadway stars. Despite this, other producers followed his lead, but of this influx only the energetic Douglas Fairbanks and John Barrymore were to have substantial careers in movies. After an initial flurry of interest most of their theatre colleagues returned from whence they came, with few regrets on the part of moviegoers. In fact, they were over-age at a time when almost all the leading men were on the ripe side.

Maurice Costello was in his thirties when he entered the new medium, as were Fairbanks and Barrymore. Both of them, however, were younger than such established draws as William Farnum, Dustin Farnum, Earle Williams, Thomas Meighan, Henry B. Walthall and William S. Hart (the oldest, at forty-five). They were the first heart-throbs, and that gives us pause if we consider audience tastes of the time, for these gentlemen could never have been mistaken for the patrons of movie houses. The age of emulating movie stars in dress and manner was just beginning, as was the custom of wearing sports clothes or casual wear (at least for the working classes; the gentry had always had the appropriate furnishings for their pastimes). No man of any social class would be seen out of doors without a hat and when he changed from his work clothes it was usually into a three-piece suit and a shirt with a stiff detachable collar. As the first male movie stars also sported hats and three-piece suits they made themselves into authoritarian figures with their spats and monocles, their canes and their gloves, which were carried in summer. (The latter might be thrown aside for a spot of fisticuffs, but they could not be retrieved without some delicacy.) And of course white tie and tails for the evenings – even Hart, in his non-Westerns.

The most accessible of these stars must have been Fairbanks, with his high spirits and his air of recklessness. Although in life he dressed in a manner befitting the uncrowned king of Hollywood, he had a more plebeian image in the films which carried him to huge popularity, wearing the Norfolk jackets, cloth caps and plus-fours of the well-heeled but not fancy young man. He also appeared in his underwear, which was permissible, for his vehicles (before he turned to swashbucklers) were comedies: but there was all the difference in the world between clowns like the Keystone Cops losing their pants, a stable of vaudeville routines, and a handsome and vigorous fellow like Fairbanks parading himself in crisp white underwear and black silk socks and garters. At the beginning of *The Nut* (1921), he is bathed and dressed mechanically which although a comic routine may also have been done as a turn-on for the ladies, who seldom witnessed such things. Later, undressed again, he finds himself in the street and, not unnaturally, he is fearful of being arrested for indecency. The way out of the predicament comes when he spots a team of long-distance runners and he simply whips off his garters and joins them – an almost inconsiderable action, but one not lost on audiences at a time when virtually all civilised men held their socks up with what the Americans call garters and the British suspenders. For the transformation is enormous: without his garters Fairbanks has become macho, a sportsman, an athlete, while a moment earlier he had been, if slightly comic, a lecherous – 'indecent' – bedroom figure (one of the deleted scenes of von Stroheim's *Foolish Wives* showed a husband in his underwear so excited by observing his wife in his shaving mirror that he attempts to rape her). Those women admitting (if only to themselves) that they found men sexually appealing would have found both apparitions attractive, while the metamorphosis itself is in keeping with a time when a man may have worn shorts and bathing-trunks at the seaside but would not have deemed it seemly for any woman to see him in his underwear, even his wife. (Sheilah Graham told me that

Scott Fitzgerald had no inhibitions as a lover but he never permitted her to see him naked.)

If it is true that a man loses much of his dignity without his pants, that was in keeping with Fairbanks's constant deflating of the romantic image accruing to him. At that time, except in slapstick, a bare-legged fellow was rare. Within a few years, however, most leading actors appeared at one time or other in their undershorts, and not necessarily in comedy. Fairbanks was a show-off and an extrovert, and like today's actors probably didn't turn a hair at having to disrobe in public, but till this became common (in the mid-1920s) it must have been a traumatic experience for the more timid actors.

Matters were different for actresses, who in the pre-movie era had long posed for photographers displaying much shoulder and bosom. In this age of otherwise copious attire, a glimpse of ankle was standard titillation. If its owner pulled her skirt high enough, she was at best a flirt and at worst a hussy – whatever, an ankle was not a common sight; nor did most male spectators get a chance, in life, to admire the bodies which disappeared below the low décolletage of actresses and society ladies. Historical costuming allowed for more of the

The sex appeal of Douglas Fairbanks lay in his immense charm and bounding vitality. After achieving fame as a ne'er-do-well in comedies he turned to swashbucklers. This is one of the most exciting of them, *The Gaucho* (1927). The senorita is Lupe Velez.

torso and other limbs to be on view, but the camera never lingered. Cecil B. De Mille was responsible for much historical disrobing, some bathtubs and ladies in négligés, as we shall see later, but at this stage it may be said that although he allowed us glimpses of Gloria Swanson's naked back (getting into her tub) her *déshabillé* wear was so shapeless as to conceal her contours. Many others would certainly have followed De Mille's lead, but shortly after he made these films hemlines began to rise radically and for the first time in recorded history man could admire women's lower limbs as he went about his daily business. Undoubtedly the popularity of Mack Sennett's bathing beauties helped towards this enfranchisement, but these ladies were more potent in stills than scampering about the sands in the flickering Silents. The stars were posed for glamour, but bathing-suit pictures were still a decade away; and it wasn't till the late 1920s that moviemakers acknowledged that the men in the audience liked watching their favourites in silken hose or other undergarments.

So although female nudity had always been more acceptable than men in the buff the cinema failed to take advantage of the fact and surprisingly the female spectator was altogether better catered for. Her favourites played prizefighters and Orientals in loin cloths, and ripped off their shirts when the duelling became heated. John Barrymore, like Fairbanks, did not mind exposing his body. Both appeared in tights in their swashbucklers, if seemingly castrated: we know from graffiti appendages to subway posters that this is an area for controversy but it was not so for movie producers, who for over fifty years denied the fact that there might be anything within that area. A venturous (or homosexual) costume designer might try to get away with an occasional codpiece, but most were required to stuff it all in and smooth it all out; and the unfortunate actors were so constrained that it is a wonder that they managed to swash a buckle as blithely as they did.

We shall never know for sure whether the ladies enjoyed the spectacle of these lithe figures, because they never said so publicly. It was acknowledged that women fans mooned about their screen idols, but the pretence was still maintained that women were interested in neither sex nor male sex-appeal. It was retained from the 19th century to at least the Second World War, so that Tallulah Bankhead knew that she could still shock when she said, in the 1960s, that one of her reasons for going to Hollywood thirty years earlier was 'to fuck with that divine Gary Cooper'. Without such guidance, we can only examine the early screen idols as historical artefacts. Only thus can we tell their sexual, as opposed to romantic, appeal. The men were never seen near a bed with a lady. To the fair sex they were always chivalrous. Their kisses were ardent rather than passionate. And they were too important as stars, as ikons, to fall heir to temptation – at least as far as the flesh was concerned. The exception is Hart, who established himself as an honest enough exponent of the West. He became known as the Good-Bad Man. The plots of his films were much of a muchness, variations on the theme of a bad man reforming for the love of a good woman and,

since he was bad, he was permitted to dally with a woman of like kind on his way to conversion.

Most Westerns of the period harboured a hussy or two in the saloon, an establishment 'thriving on the shame of women and the evil in men'. The line is from *The Deserter* (1916), but – historical fact aside – the shameful saloon ladies may have become acceptable with *The Spoilers*, filmed two years earlier. The exigencies of the plot, which was based on Rex Beach's popular novel, required one. The lady concerned had been a girlfriend of the hero, and from the look of her now she isn't the one to stop at a kiss. Furthermore, she wants him back, but he is only tempted for the teeniest second, having eyes only for the dewy, upright heroine. *The Spoilers* takes place in Alaska, a gathering place for the rough and tough of both sexes, as in the West. The West was where rugged types turned up, and rugged types often had a past. This was what was known as the 'Sowing Wild Oats' syndrome, permitted to outdoor men but not to city slickers. And might not a man who had once fallen from grace not tumble again?

These tempting women who lurked in the beer-hall and gin-palace usually had vestiges of once great beauty. Life had toughened them – in contrast to the winsome schoolmarms (they are seldom anything but) who descend from the stagecoach. The fact that these demure things had got to the West in the first place was supposed to denote courage and character, but I doubt if any would have survived without the support of Mr Hart or some other strong, comforting cowboy. They are objects of derision for the saloon girls, who will lose their men to them – and who sometimes, having compared their own carnal desires with true love, will make the great sacrifice. It is surprising how many of them got in the way of the villain's bullets. As I said, bad ladies were expected to come to a bad end.

In the case of *The Spoilers*, Cherry Malotte (Kathlyn Williams) is paired off with the heroine's black sheep of a brother, both of them now reformed. Cherry and the vamp of *A Fool There Was* were sisters under the skin. Both were modern Carmens, but with an unwritten book of rules on survival. No matter how evil she, or how fleshly feeble her prey, the temptress could not experience a love which would be consummated – not this time round, anyway, for it was, as it turned out, True Love, and everyone knew that True Love and sexual intercourse were incompatible. Well, no: it was all a misunderstanding. Having been thrilled by her glamour and sinful demeanour for several reels, audiences discovered that her motives were basically pure and that she had been blackmailed into vamping, hating herself for so doing, and only able to reveal her true self at the fade-out.

It is almost impossible now to watch the vamps at work. Of Miss Bara's thirty-odd films only *A Fool There Was* survives; her imitators have been hardly luckier. It is much easier to see the films Mary Pickford made during this period, but is that because more prints were struck? Or did posterity all but lose Miss Bara because her films were screened so often that they wore out? Glancing at the titles I do not think so. I cannot, for example, imagine her a convincing Juliet. Also, despite

Mary Pickford and Charles 'Buddy' Rogers (whom she married after divorcing Douglas Fairbanks) in the most delightful of her adult roles, in *My Best Girl*. The butler knows something she doesn't: that Rogers is not just a co-worker 'borrowing' the boss's house, but the boss's son.

many attempts to change her image her career was fading by the early 1920s, while Miss Pickford's was going from strength to strength. But the truth may not be as clear as has always been thought: Miss Pickford was approved of, written up, admired. Mothers took their daughters to see her. What sort of person would admit to admiring Miss Bara, whatever the last-reel revelation? Her appeal may have been exclusively to men, who probably didn't care for the dainty charms of the gingham-clad heroines, but would they have dared to say so? This polarisation (which became traditional in the Western) was meant to appeal to the two sides of man's nature – the pure, which he was most of the time, and the impure, which he was for five minutes every other Thursday (unless he had been drinking, in which case it was every Thursday).

Loose ladies not only gave movies a bit of ginger, but they could be relied upon to demonstrate their inferiority to the dimpling heroines. The plot of Griffith's *True-Heart Susie* (1919) depends on Robert Harron's preference for store-bought Clarine Seymour over homespun Lillian Gish – somewhat ungratefully, you may think, since Lillian paid for his education, enabling him to go to the city and meet the 'fast' Clarine. Harron soon learns the error of his ways, which serves him right: Lillian stays pure and loyal, while Clarine refuses to cook or clean, in the process changing from one sort of slut to the other, neglecting clothes, make-up and a comb. We can blame Clarine on Miss Bara. Most of the critical writing on this movie concentrates on Miss Gish's exquisite performance, but how many men in the audience would have traded her cooking for Miss Seymour's performance in bed? My question presupposes that we find loyal little women, adept at housekeeping, less attractive than ladies who wear lipstick and loll about the house reading movie magazines. Well, movies had already conditioned audiences to that view: anyone who wed for glamour rather than character could expect to come home and find his bed unmade and his supper uncooked. You might think Mr Harron so sexually fulfilled that he doesn't really notice, but that would be presuming a structure of sexual values – and sexual values, when it came to practice, simply didn't exist. In movies, that is.

Miss Bara's imitators included Barbara La Marr, Virginia Pearson and Louise Glaum, none of whom could be mistaken for Miss Pickford, even on a dark night. I have already said that the fantasy fodder provided by movies served better the women than the men. The ladies could not only dream about being loved by their heroes but could identify with the dainty heroines and thrill to the gowns and exploits of the vamps. The men identified with Tom Mix and William S. Hart and enjoyed their adventures; but the screen view of women was so polarised that it isn't till the advent of Clara Bow that they found the sort of girl for stepping out with on Saturday night. Significantly, Mary Pickford is most attractive at that time, in *My Best Girl* (1927), playing someone of her own age; but till then audiences had found her most appealing playing children or teenage girls. If they, the audiences, had subconscious paedophile instincts, so be it, but the Pickford movies

often jar today – especially when, in the last reel, she grows up in order to marry the Daddy-Long-Legs figure she has admired in the other five. She was required to play these roles only by her own greed: as her own producer she might have persevered in playing adult roles instead of returning to short skirts each time the public failed to respond to her as a grown-up. I yield to no one in my admiration of Lillian Gish, but I do think her waifs have a very limited sex appeal. I pass by the madcaps and tomboys who came in during the second decade – Mabel Normand, Priscilla Dean, Pauline Starke – in a certain bewilderment, and move on to another waif, Janet Gaynor – in fact a throwback, for she began playing the role in the mid-1920s, at the time that Pickford and Miss Gish turned to more challenging parts.

The waif is such a persistent figure in Silent cinema that we cannot ignore her. Like the wicked landlord, whose prey she becomes, she comes from Victorian melodrama. Sometimes unwed mothers were waifs, which is why they become waifs, having been turned from hearth and home by a righteous father. Unscrupulous landlords had existed but waifs were figments of imagination – if only too real to those who knew of the prevalance of child prostitution, often caused by the advantages taken by the mendacious and voracious on the poverty-stricken. The waifs represented those who survived with their virtue intact, more or less. In Griffith's *Way Down East* (1920), based on a 19th century barnstormer, Miss Gish is promised marriage by the landlord figure, who after having his way with her then doesn't want to know. Penniless, she and the babe go from pillar to post, and audiences doubtless feared that she would succumb, taking the desperate way to earn a living. Waifs, after all, have to eat, but I cannot think of any precedent (in an American film) for Miss Gaynor in *Seventh Heaven* (1927) admitting that she had 'sinned' in the past – though, mind you, she has a sister who beats her and they were starving at the time. She is also French, and puritan America could believe anything of decadent Europe. (And prurient America was aware of 'Frenching' and 'French kissing'.) In *Street Angel* (1928) Miss Gaynor is a Neapolitan and the reason for her 'fall' is a sick mother. This was another vehicle for Miss Gaynor and Charles Farrell who (as a later generation would say) shack up together, as in the earlier film; but Frank Borzage, directing again, has taken even greater pains to emphasise the purity of their love. They have separate rooms. He is embarrassed at seeing her straightening her stocking top, and is puritanical about other women: 'That kind have only themselves to blame' he says, which is why she doesn't tell him about That Night. In actuality she had noticed a street girl while worrying about paying for Mama's prescription and had approached a few men, who had ignored her. So she stole instead, which is why Mr Farrell tries to strangle her – the last of her many, many sufferings: but, it is implied, these spring less from the theft than that impure impulse.

It is hard to believe that moviegoers did not find the waifs old-fashioned, too numerous and, by this time, tiresome. The truth is otherwise: both films were out-

Though *The River* (1928) no longer survives intact, it is one of the most memorable of the realistic sex dramas which Hollywood turned out towards the end of the Silent period. The thesis of most of these is that the relationship between the sexes is at best difficult and at worst dangerous. In this case Charles Farrell, right, is an innocent country boy enamoured of the experienced Mary Duncan, whose lover, Alfred Sabato, has just returned to reclaim her.

standingly popular, and Miss Gaynor headed the popularity polls which began about this time. Following the fashion of the time, Fox's publicists came up with an epithet for Gaynor and Farrell, 'America's Favorite Lovebirds', perhaps prompted by Gaynor's petite stature. Farrell bulked large and it may have been the contrast in their sizes which made them probably the most popular of the several romantic teams of the time – destined to breach the coming of Talkies but to fade soon thereafter, mainly because Farrell's voice was much less virile than his appearance. Sometimes Miss Gaynor showed her knickers, which the more certifiably sexy stars seldom, if ever, did: it's a particularly odd thing for a waif to do, and can only have been done with executive approval, perhaps to endear her to male spectators. Until proved otherwise I shall continue to believe that the following of the dewy-eyed Silent heroines was restricted to the distaff members of the audience, dragging their menfolk away from the shoot-em-ups of the cowboys.

The best possible reason to admire Mary Pickford is that she is the first self-made woman millionaire in history – probably the first of her sex to become immensely rich other than by inherited wealth or through the endowments of a husband or lover. Conceivably many wealthy women had become richer from speculation or investment before her time, but Miss Pickford not only managed to amass her fortune very soon after it was accepted that women should go out to work (other than service), but she did so very publicly in a very glamorous industry. Her bargainings with executives were notorious and, if not known to all her fans, might have been guessed by them. She was an inspiration, literally, to feminists and indeed all women. Perhaps they were fascinated by the dainty Mary on the screen and the businesslike Mary behind it.

3.
Sexual Advances

As the Armistice was being signed, in November 1918, the producer-director Maurice Tourneur was previewing his latest film, called simply *Woman*. In the prologue a couple quarrel and the husband reflects upon the opposite sex, with examples of same, fat, frowsy, grotesque and beautiful. Then we are whisked back to Ancient Rome for the antics of the Empress Messalina (Flora Revalles), frequenting back street dives, picking up willing centurions en route. Finally she goes too far, to

'the crowning infamy of a bigamous marriage to the prefect Silius', which means, as far as we can see, togaed extras lolling on sofas. Two more segments show woman as betrayer (Heloise and Abelard, and a Southern girl and a Yankee soldier) while the other, based on a Breton legend, is a curious piece about basking seals which turn into beautiful maidens by night. A fisherman captures and marries one, who is perfectly happy till one day she catches sight of her fur coat, hidden in a trunk. Doubt-

Gloria Swanson and Wallace Reid in *The Affairs of Anatol*. Stars in négligés were not yet common, but De Mille recognised fashion and glamour as prime factors in Swanson's appeal to her fans.

A quite extraneous flashback sequence from De Mille's *Manslaughter*.

less if this had been a Talkie we would have heard the 'Oik oik' as she returns to the pod. An omnibus film like this would not have seemed odd to audiences still accustomed to one- and two-reelers of differing content. The material of this is suspect, till the end, when the four stories are explained by an intertitle – 'The woman was a slave before the slave existed'. History had always shown woman as fickle, feeble and all manner of untrustworthy things. It had taken a war to realise that the 'society butterfly' could be enticed from her drawing room and we see her at the front, in factories, helping in hospitals, and, as Edith Cavell, being led to her death.

You may think the film a curious way of paying tribute to women, but its final point is well made: the War had entirely changed their own and many men's thinking about women. And so did movies. In backwoods dramas there remained an inordinant number of girls unprepared for the perils attendant on accepting a warming drink by the fireside, but the city woman was more knowing. She is at her most attractive in the comedies of Cecil B. De Mille, modelled on the European plays by Somerset Maugham and Arthur Schnitzler – in fact, De Mille filmed one of Schnitzler's plays, *The Affairs of*

Anatol (1921), which promptly turns the subject on its head. Nevertheless the women in De Mille's movies returned the sex to a world from which they had been banished by the Baras and Pickfords – the real. Well, real enough: the decor was sumptuous, and usually included a double bed. De Mille's women knew the facts of life; they knew how to use their bodies to get their own way, though not necessarily by going to bed with men; they did not want to stay at home; and they sometimes pictured themselves as the courtesans of history – or so we may suppose, from De Mille's disconcerting habit of suddenly dropping in a flashback, set in Ancient Babylon or somewhere warm, where he could get his heroines into a scanty and revealing series of silks and jewels. The flashbacks are examples of De Mille's opportunism, as are the heroines' bathtubs, which were beginning to appear in all his movies. No matter: he could be a stimulating film-maker during this period and the prevailing hypocrisies about sexual matters are compensated for by some truths elsewhere.

He was influenced by his success with *The Cheat* (1915), one of the least truthful movies ever made – as far, anyway, as the tribulations of the heroine are con-

Obviously De Mille was influenced in *Manslaughter* by the rape of the Sabine women. Such commercial ploys were common in De Mille's movies and by this time audiences expected them.

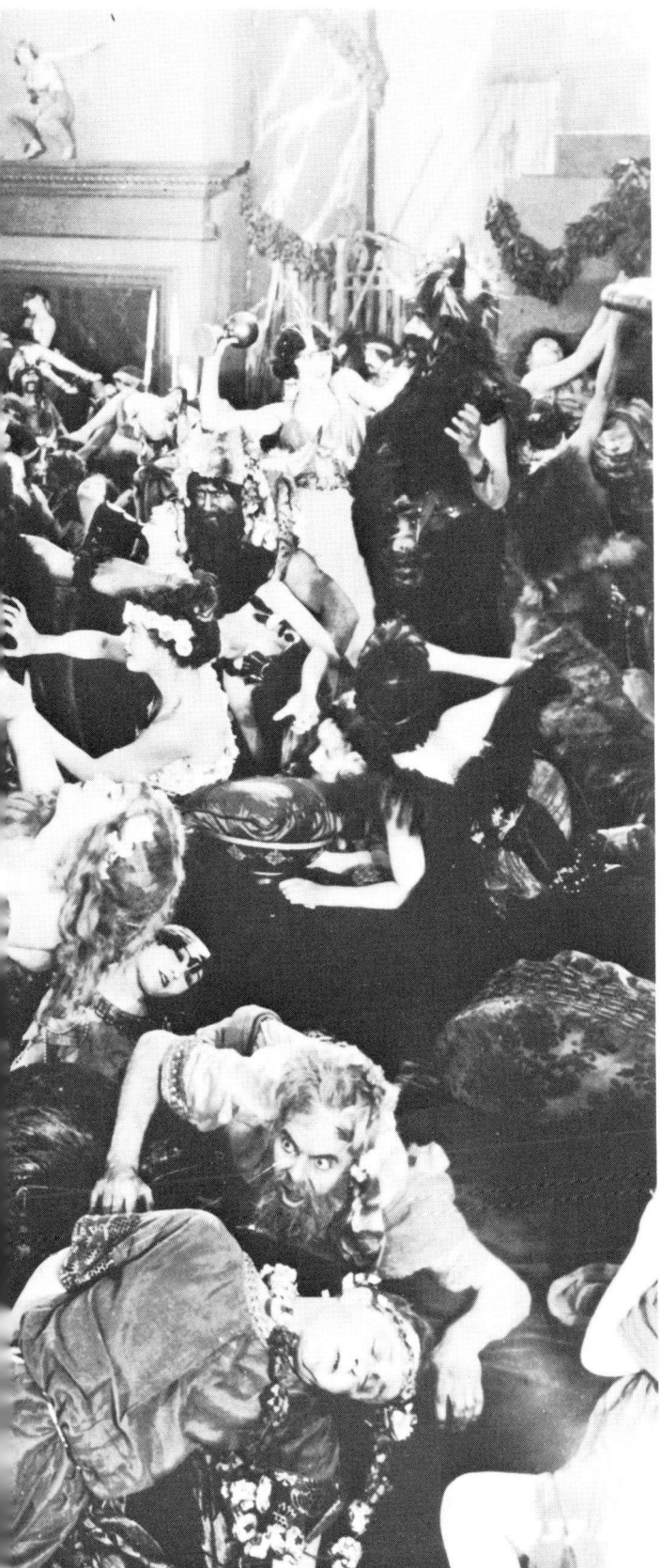

cerned. The portrait of high society wasn't very flattering and that established a pattern which remained for twenty years. Audiences never tired of pompous bankers with dowdy wives, though sometimes those bankers were sugar daddies with cuties in tow, and sometimes the middle-aged ladies, inevitably gross, had indecently young husbands; all couturiers were effeminate and all artists and musicians were wild-eyed, long-haired and usually foreign. In the midst of these types De Mille set his discontented wives being tempted by middle-aged roués and neglected husbands whose eyes strayed to pretty little midinettes who were not always aware of what they were doing. Not having thought it through, they assumed that flirting was rewarded with jewellery and furs: those who knew that a heavier commitment would be exacted were ruthless in their pursuit of such pressies, but they also came equipped with delights the wives knew not of – lacy lingerie, a record of the latest jazz tune, 'Hindustan', a drink (on other occasions a perfume) labelled 'Forbidden Fruit' and, to denote real decadence, a leopard skin or so lying around the apartment. Consummation was only implied so that happy endings were possible, proving that no one suffered in vain. *Don't Change Your Husband* (1918) and *Why Change Your Wife?* (1920) are companion pieces, in which those who have gone through divorce and remarriage live to regret it. As sanctioned by the Church, these spouses do get to sleep with a couple of attractive people of the opposite sex – which may well have been one more than most members of the audience: in any case the success or failure of these marriages is not decided in the kitchen but in the bedroom. Divorce was then rare, scandalous and open only to the immoral rich, which may be a further reason why spectators were titillated by these movies, while at the same time finding them remote from their everyday experience.

De Mille's principal exponent of female sexuality was Gloria Swanson, who was both sympathetic and glamorous, an ideal personification of the restless, postwar generation with its more liberal attitude towards women. As her wardrobe and her starring vehicles took her further into the realms of fantasy so her hold on her public increased; and when there was a sudden falling off in her popularity she had the good sense to turn to playing working girls. As far as glamour was concerned, she had a rival at her own studio, Paramount, in the dark and sensual Pola Negri, brought across after her success as Carmen and Madame Dubarry, which were directed in Germany by Ernst Lubitsch with a lighter touch than was customary in historical spectacle. On the strength of these Mary Pickford invited Lubitsch to California to direct her as a warm-hearted and impetuous senorita, but that was one of her adult roles to which the public didn't respond. Lubitsch turned to a series of marital comedies with plots not unlike those of De Mille's, but different in tone, set in much less fearsomely decorated boudoirs and drawing-rooms. Their background is Europe, which till the advent of the flapper became almost exclusively the setting of all American films with a high sex quotient. And it was a very simple Europe: a stock shot of the Eiffel Tower or the Houses of Parliament established the locale, while all exteriors were

filmed in the studio, in streets and gardens so anony-
mous that they might be in any city in the Western
hemisphere.

If Lubitsch acknowledged a debt to De Mille, his
philanderers and coquettes were never on the brink of
suffering, as Miss Swanson sometimes had been. Sex
was not something to be ardently sought by the frustrated and the dissatisfied but a game to be played by
sophisticated people with nothing better to do with their
time. On several occasions Lubitsch used Adolphe
Menjou, who became for the new decade, the 1920s, the
male equivalent of Negri and Swanson, impeccably
attired and with little ambition other than his appearance and enjoying the company of the opposite sex.
Unlike the ladies, he is unscrupulous in his pursuits
and, also unlike them, he may be having several affairs
simultaneously. He belongs to all the best clubs, those
for gambling, those with private rooms for dining tête-à-
tête and even, surprisingly, those which provide elegant
ladies with the accommodation. Whether married or a
bachelor Menjou's conduct hardly varies – and he would
surely have infuriated all female spectators were it not
for his sense of honour and the charm with which he
invests his characters; and if he was, on occasion, made
to see the error of his ways, it was not with deep anguish
but a shrug.

Adolphe Menjou in *The Marriage Cheat* – clearly hoping to
be forgiven by his wife.

Pola Negri had been appearing in German films for five years when her portrayal of a French courtesan turned her into an international figure: indeed, American critics were so enraptured by her *Madame Dubarry*, below, with Emil Jannings, that the Hollywood studios were in rivalry for her services (Paramount was the winner). Before leaving, she played another historical seductress, *Sappho*, left, but – as you can see – in a modernised version which gave her admirers not usually associated with that lady, i.e. men – in the persons of Albert Steinrück, left, and Johannes Reimann. The title of the first was changed to *Passion* for American audiences in an attempt to disguise its German origins (the First World War had not long finished), while *Sappho* became *Mad Love* – but conceivably in this case so that there would be no misunderstanding.

Rudolph Valentino, far left, when he first enflamed the hearts of women the world over, in *The Four Horsemen of the Apocalypse*. He was not always as macho as this, as the picture from *The Young Rajah*, above, shows. The lady is Wanda Hawley, while it is Vilma Banky being mawled in *Son of the Sheik*, centre. The three pictures indicate why there was no unanimity over Valentino's looks, dress and acting; most men were unimpressed.

However, the male star most people associate with the 1920s is Rudolph Valentino, whose exploits were far more exotic than Mr Menjou's. Like Menjou, he lived his life exactly as he pleased, but as a libertine and gigolo rather than as a man of the world. Even his clothes proclaim his attitude: he is not so much well-dressed as draped, so that no matter what covered his body – silk shirts, three-piece suits, gloves, spats, pearl pins – it was always evident. He achieved stardom in *The Four Horsemen of the Apocalypse* (1921) playing an Argentinian playboy who redeems himself in the War by courage and death. Thereafter the Valentino image varied as much as his performances, depending on who was guiding him at the time – June Mathis, the producer who had elevated him to star roles in *The Four Horsemen*, his lesbian wife Natacha Rambova, or the producer J. D. Williams, who took over after Rambova had almost ruined him. By turns Valentino was an indolent adventurer who swept women off their feet, a cad who turns out to have been maligned by enemies, and a romantic but ruthless dare-devil. At his worst he projected an intensity born less of passion than neurosis and narcissism; at his most appealing he was graceful and boyish. Perhaps his female fans wanted to mother him, or perhaps they didn't really fear his masculinity, despite the rape in *Son of the Sheik*. In that film and its predecessor – *The Sheik* – he fulfilled many a woman's fantasy of being hauled off to the desert and wooed under the stars. The East, at a time when few people had ever been out of their home town, let alone abroad, was very mysterious; and foreigners, an unknown quantity outside fiction and movies like this, were obviously exotic. Their manners and morals were not only different from those of the boy next door, but so exciting as to be spine-tingling. Many prefer to fantasise about those who if encountered in life would prove no sort of sexual danger, from 'gentle' stars like Van Johnson to androgynous ones like James Dean – in a line which culminates perhaps in the cross-dressing, heavily-made-up pop stars of the current day. In dreams, after all, anything is possible: Valentino's caresses would not lead to any act that might be construed as infidelity, so he is not really a threat. All the same . . .

If in my mind's eye I think of the typical moviegoers of the 1920s as a romantic young couple who only want an evening of escapism I must take into account that at this time of no divorce (except for the wealthy) there were a great many more loveless marriages than today. There was no television, either, and for many women marriage meant waiting for her man to get in from pub or speakeasy and then submitting to sexual intercourse carried out with neither love or consideration. For such women, Valentino's chief virtue may have been his lack of aggressive virility – for indeed it was not a quality with which he was overly endowed; and not long before his untimely death in 1926 unfavourable publicity had been growing, culminating in an attack by the *Chicago Tribune* because a dance-hall had installed in the men's room a machine emitting face powder for its clients' powder puffs, apparently because of Valentino's influence.

Equally ambiguous is Erich von Stroheim, though as actor and image he is the antithesis of Valentino. He seemed to be impelled by a fire in his loins, to be assuaged on any female that crossed his path, be it duchess or serving-maid. He could be courtly, if her social standing demanded it, but was prepared to use force if she resisted – which, given his lack of conventional good looks, was more than likely. There is nothing equivocal in his lust and not the least regard for his own sex, yet as director on one film he insisted on mono-grammed silk underwear for the extras playing soldiers, an action which was in keeping with his extravagance and his penchant for that material. Later, when he worked only as an actor, he liked to appear in satin knee breeches and silk stockings – attire hardly called for by his roles as a nightclub ventriloquist or soothsayer; as a butler in *Three Faces East* there is a flash of silken half-hose under his robe instead of the pyjamas or trousers we might more reasonably have expected. In that same film he holds a lady's lace panties to the light before fondly lying them on the bed; in one of the films he directed a chambermaid massages her mistress's silk-stockinged legs. Whether or not von Stroheim was fetishist or narcissist, the image of male sexuality in his films is consistent, either as writer, director and actor, or a combination of any of these. Two of his movies begin with identical scenes, of a servant in the morning gathering up his master's clothes, deposited around the room after the previous night's debaucheries. And the clothes are invariably uniforms, for whether he was aristocrat or parvenu the von Stroheim hero owned a panoply of uniforms which made those of the Hohenzollern emperors look dowdy. The von Stroheim hero seldom has a friend, though if he does he will have a foot fetish or a collection of naughty postcards; and he will be his companion in visiting ornate high-class brothels, where

Above: Erich von Stroheim and Mae Busch in what may be the best-known still of a scene *not* in the release version of the film, the film in this case being *Foolish Wives*. Equally well-known are the stories of the ways in which the producers and then the censors whittled the movie down from its enormous length to a running time of two hours. It is not known which was responsible for the removal of this sequence.

the objective would seem to be drunkenness rather than sexual consummation. The von Stroheim woman has more variety, and it may be stressed at this point that he made his name with *Blind Husbands* (1919) and *Foolish Wives* (1922), in which the ladies were married Americans, tempted by European decadence in the person of von Stroheim's uniformed seducer. On occasion the women, though not the heroines, are as lecherous as he; in this case they will probably smoke cigars – and the presence of a stub in a bedside ashtray may not have the expected significance, since the lady may have smoked it herself. When the queen in *Queen Kelly* walks past her guardsmen half-naked it may be because she is insolent and half-mad or just provocative – or then again it may perhaps be that they have already seen her wholly naked.

Below: Von Stroheim, up to no good again, in *The Wedding March*, an acceptable enough tale of an aristocratic soldier who loves a simple, poor, pretty girl but who is forced to become engaged to a plain, wealthy one. Before becoming involved with either, he has designs on the maid who is clearing up the clothes left around his room after the previous evening's debauchery.

Hollywood executives did not consider the sexual attitudes of von Stroheim's films usual, but he was acclaimed as a great director by urban critics, which meant that his films could arrive in hick towns trailing a certain glory; and the controversy stirred up by local bluenoses did not harm the box office. On balance, these 'decadent' movies brought respectability to an industry whose parvenu bosses longed for it with a passion; to them, there was no paradox, for if the critics said they were art they were art. So was Heironymous Bosch. However, as for von Stroheim himself, his arrogance and extravagance alienated so many producers that he rarely worked for the same one twice. Circumstances dictated that his last two Silent pictures (the second part of *The Wedding March* and *Queen Kelly*) were not shown in the US, which may have contributed to Hollywood's losing interest in him as a director; and the changes that occurred when Talkies came in turned him into an old-fashioned figure.

It would be too simple to say that sex was the making of von Stroheim for his films remain impressive today; but it was certainly the unmaking of him. He became famous, as I've said, with stories of blind husbands and foolish wives, their very titles promising adultery; the intervening film, now lost – *The Devil's Pass Key* – was set among a corrupt Paris aristocracy and its American friends. During the making of *Foolish Wives* Carl Laemmle, the head of Universal, appointed Irving Thalberg as head of production. Thalberg battled with von Stroheim over expenditure and lost – since von

M-G-M envisaged *The Merry Widow* as a star vehicle for Mae Murray, one of the studio's leading stars and a major exponent of glamour of the period. Von Stroheim had other ideas, and there was accordingly much friction between them; he also was concerned in making the story considerably more steamy, adding several sequences set in a high class Paris bordello. Somewhat surprisingly, M-G-M executives sanctioned the changes.

Stroheim stated that if he was sacked as director he would quit as star, and he was in far too many scenes to be replaced. When the film opened in New York despite the controversy over length and content the critics acclaim established von Stroheim as the outstanding figure in the industry, which was no less than he had expected. He was publicised as a Viennese aristocrat, which was what he claimed to be; but another Viennese, Paul Kohner, a relative and employee of Laemmle, remarked upon his lower-class Viennese accent and ignorance of Austrian and German literature. When von Stroheim embarked upon a tale set in Vienna, it emerged as not unlike the plot of *Old Heidleberg*, a film in which he had once appeared, and those who know the piece under that name or as *The Student Prince* will not expect much sophistication. That quality stems entirely from the degradation of the principals, the Count and his fiancée, the Countess. He may be sleeping off last night's revels, but the corsets and stockings retrieved by his valet are not necessarily hers: and she in time is

208-

found to be having a relationship with her groom. The resemblance to *The Student Prince* begins when the Count falls for a girl who works in the Prater. Norman Kerry played the role, enabling Thalberg to fire von Stroheim – which he did when five weeks' shooting had resulted in only the first reel. Extravagance was not the sole reason: following De Mille's example with his leading ladies, von Stroheim had photographed Kerry disrobing to get into his bath. Von Stroheim claimed that he planned to cut the nudity, but his letter of dismissal spoke of his 'flagrant disregard of the principles of censorship and . . . repeated and insistent attempts to include scenes photographed by you, situations and incidents so reprehensible that they could not by any reasonable possibility be expected to meet with the approval of the Board of Censorship.'

It is difficult now to know what the studio junked, and certainly that part of *Merry-Go-Round* not directed by von Stroheim is innocuous enough; but a novelisation of the script – to which he was party after being fired – is, according to his biographer Richard Koszarski, 'mild pornography permitting the detailing of obsessions forbidden on film' and the relationship between the Countess and her groom has become sadomasochistic. Thalberg again inherited von Stroheim when he moved over to the company that would shortly become Metro-Goldwyn-Mayer, but despite more difficulties (over the length of *Greed*) he was happy enough to keep him for *The Merry Widow* (1925), perhaps because Thalberg had matured as a film-maker. By now Thalberg was apt to stress that films must appeal to 'here and here and here', pointing successively to head, heart and groin. When the star, Mae Murray, complained of von Stroheim's 'degeneracy' Thalberg defended him as a genius, adding that he was giving the story dimension – though some might call it deviation – inasmuch as Danilo (John Gilbert) now has an elderly friend, a baron who is content enough to fondle high-heeled shoes. One of von Stroheim's own friends, publicising the picture in a fan magazine, noted that 'his penchant is Freud, with trimmings by Havelock-Ellis and sauce by Krafft-Ebbing. Some of the characters he has composed . . . will be recognisable only by those who have pursued a similar bent.'

Despite the film's popularity, M-G-M was not inclined to retain von Stroheim's services, and nor was Pat Powers, who next employed von Stroheim to direct and star in *The Wedding March*. However, von Stroheim remained a towering figure in the industry, and as such was sought by Gloria Swanson, now an independent producer, encouraged by her financier and lover, Joseph P. Kennedy. *Sadie Thompson* had given her career a much-needed fillip, and she felt that von Stroheim would come up with something equally *risqué*. They agreed upon *Queen Kelly* – a story about a schoolgirl (Swanson) who attracts the attention of the queen's fiancé (Walter Byron) when she loses her bloomers; in the second part of the story the girl goes to Africa to look after a sick aunt, who runs a hotel – an establishment whose real function can be ascertained by the fact that some men dance with men, while others drift to the rooms upstairs with the girls from the bar. It

was while filming one of these sequences that Swanson, already alarmed at the expenditure, telephoned Kennedy, who ordered the film to close down while the script was re-examined.

The film as its stands is the usual von Stroheim mixture: the thoroughly reprehensible couple, one of whom – the man – is saved by the love of a good woman. The queen and prince are drunken and dissolute (in the script but not now in the film is a scene where the prince waves from the balcony to the crowd who cannot see that he has not bothered to don his trousers). He uses an aphrodisiac when he first wines and dines the girl and the queen seems to derive some sexual satisfaction when she beats her with a whip. But the second, unfilmed, part has other refinements which although not entirely original are new to von Stroheim. There was to have been an intermission: just before it, Swanson, who has succeeded to her aunt's position, gazes upon a cigarette and a glass of whisky. On returning to their seats, audiences would have found Miss Swanson queening it over the other inhabitants of the hotel, obviously enjoying a life as colourful as they. She has also married – though the union has not been consummated – her aunt's choice of husband, a lecherous, ugly old cripple, played by Tully Marshall. It was while von Stroheim was instructing Marshall in the art of dribbling tobacco juice on to Swanson's hand as he fitted the wedding-ring that she got up and made that telephone call. Kennedy was appalled when he saw the film: his prominent position in the Roman Catholic community meant that he could not be associated with a salacious movie. Several attempts were made to salvage the project, which was not abandoned, as has been claimed, because of the coming of Sound for at one time it was to have been issued as a part-Talkie*, still a common enough practice at the beginning of 1929. The screenplay was rewritten on more than one occasion, tests were made and filming recommenced; but after many setbacks the project was abandoned. In 1931 a musical score and a few scenes were added to von Stroheim's footage as shown in Europe, but United Artists declined to release a Silent film in the American market.

Von Stroheim was involved in none of the salvage attempts. Following the débâcle of *The Wedding March* (which was so long that it was issued in two parts, the second part being insufficiently successful on its European release to justify any attempt to distribute it in the US) no studio now wanted to employ him. Miss Swanson, however, must take some of the blame. Having triumphed as Sadie Thompson she must have thought that she could get away with the African sequences of *Queen Kelly*. She had been alarmed when after losing her panties the prince had picked them up and wafted them in front of his face before stuffing them into his uniform, but she had passed the sequence on seeing the

* *The public's rejection of Silents was such that no company really wanted to release those they had. There was not time to convert all existing scripts, so the more interesting scenes were shot (or hastily re-shot) with Sound, while intertitles carried the rest of the plot, accompanied by a music track and sound effects.*

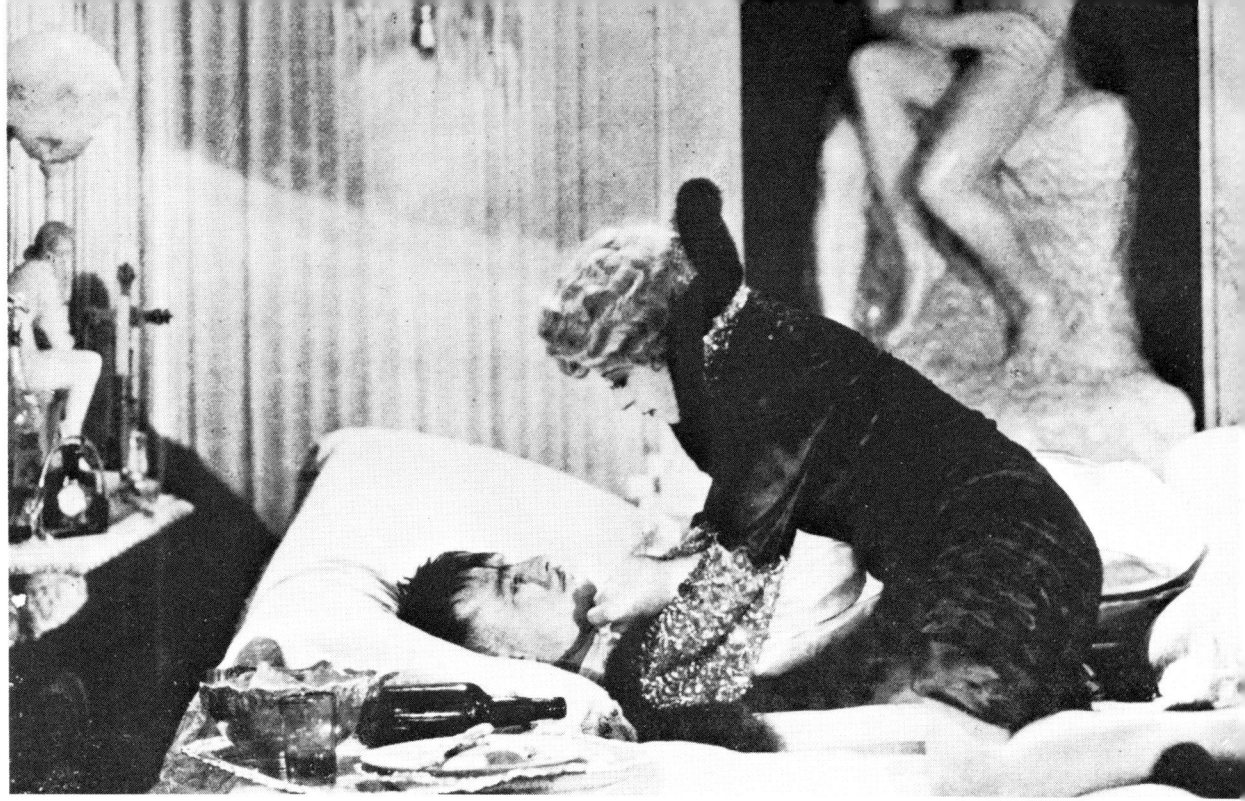

More von Stroheim debauchery, but this time it is not he but Walter Byron who returns home at dawn after a night on the town. Trying to waken him is his fiancée, the Queen (Seena Owen), and the film is *Queen Kelly*, which features Gloria Swanson in the title role, so called after becoming owner-manageress of a sleazy African dive. For many reasons filming was abandoned when only a few of the African scenes had been shot: this is one of them, below, and in 1984 it was added to the existing footage to replace a 'false' ending not shot by von Stroheim.

rushes. Besides, nothing in the African scenes seems to have been as quaint as an idea in *West of Zanzibar*, a film also made at that time, in which a cripple (Lon Chaney) gets revenge on the man who had wounded him by having the man's daughter brought up in the stews of Zanzibar – and subsequently getting her so hooked on drugs that to obtain them she continues her life of sin. The film was adapted from a 1924 Broadway play, *Kongo*, and it seems to have been von Stroheim's inspiration for the second part of *Queen Kelly*. Swanson's memoir does not mention the Hays Office as contributing to the film's difficulties, though she does say that the script, which the office would certainly have read, specified a dance-hall rather than a bordello, 'steamy and filthy'.

As it happened, the Hays Office had been formed while *Foolish Wives* was in production, and as newspapers were then accusing Hollywood of being the new Sodom, Universal had expected the film to be eloquent witness of that – and indeed the New York Censorship Board was forced to demand a second set of cuts after the newspapers had fulminated. The Hays Office itself does not seem to have come into confrontation with von Stroheim, but this is probably because for its first decade it was little more than a front for the industry's hypocrisies and did not become effective till 1934. Its stated intent was to control the content of motion pictures, but it had come into existence in response to press criticism – directed at personalities rather than pictures, and then reaching a crescendo.

The world had not before known anything like the idolisation of movie stars, who could not be seen outside Los Angeles – or indeed anywhere in the world – without being mobbed. Many of them did not know how to behave. Charles Ray, known for his boyish roles, was prone to throwing his cigarette stubs on the floor, just for the pleasure obtained in ordering his servants to pick them up. 'To place in the limelight a great number of people who ordinarily would be chambermaids and chauffeurs, and give them unlimited power and wealth, is bound to produce lively results' remarked Anita Loos, one of the few literary people to enjoy their company. The writers and the European film-makers who would raise the tone were yet to come. Hollywood's aristocracy consisted of a dozen directors and stars, with Douglas Fairbanks and Mary Pickford as the undisputed king and queen. Their fans and lovers of romance may have revelled in their fairy-tale marriage, but each had to divorce before they could be united, with both divorces immeasurably covered by reporters. Show business people were not exactly expected to behave like your great-aunt Florence, but they managed, by and large, to keep private their irregularities, sexual and otherwise: but the whole world now took an intense interest in this young community in California which was blessed with much more wealth than their talents actually deserved. The chief victim was Roscoe 'Fatty' Arbuckle, a genial comic whose blubbery face and figure made him an ideal embodiment of the new Sodom. In 1921 he participated in a weekend party held in a San Francisco hotel which resulted in the death of a party girl, Virginia Rappe. Some of the other partygoers immediately realised that it was to their financial advantage to claim to the press, with

its cheque-books ready, that the girl had been sexually assaulted by Arbuckle, and that was what, in Prohibition America, most people wanted to believe. But despite dishonest police reports, unscrupulous lawyers, prejudiced jurors and perjured evidence Arbuckle's first two trials ended with hung juries and an acquittal and exoneration at the third. Thus he became Hollywood's scapegoat at a time when the drug addiction of, in particular, Wallace Reid, Mabel Normand and Barbara La Marr was rumoured if not reported. And not long after the Hays Office was set up a director, William Desmond Taylor, was found dead in mysterious circumstances. No one was apprehended, but Taylor's private life came under minute scrutiny by the press, with disastrous consequences to the careers of Mabel Normand and especially Mary Miles Minter, whose screen roles had suggested not only she was a virgin but that she was unaware that sex existed. Hollywood executives feared federal interference in their affairs and selected the impeccable Will H. Hays, a political organiser, to put them in order – that is, to be their spokesman with the press and Washington. The ten industry figures who issued the invitation to Hays spoke of 'the necessity of attaining and maintaining the highest possible standard of motion picture production in this country' and Hays in return told them (in a speech at the Hollywood Bowl) that their 'industry must have towards that sacred thing, the mind of a child, towards that clean virgin thing, that unmarked slate, the same care about impressions made upon it, that the best clergyman or most inspired teacher of youth would have'. It was not, however, the unsullied minds of children which had made the industry profitable and powerful so quickly, and the lecture was couched in such terms as to indicate that the more sophisticated writers and directors could outwit the Hays Office when they wanted to present situations for older, more tarnished minds. Hays' first action, prompted by the Taylor murder, was to propose a morality clause in contracts, which could be suspended or terminated should it be transgressed, and since the public had so completely rejected Arbuckle, despite his innocence, there was no objection. The existence of the Hays Office prevented some states from setting up their own censorship boards, to the satisfaction of the industry which, ungratefully, paid little attention to a list of guidelines issued by Hays in 1927. Prior to that, Hays had proposed that screenplays and novels be submitted for approval, but most of the objections that they raised were circumvented. If a book achieved notoriety, and what we now call bestsellerdom, Hollywood was going to buy it regardless, and just as euphemism was common in presenting unsavoury facts in writing so movies had developed a similar code.

Few novels of the period were as notorious as Michael Arlen's *The Green Hat*, which is the story of an Englishwoman, Iris March, whose mainly amorous exploits are a means of wreaking revenge on society for having taken her husband on their wedding night – after telling her, in Deauville, that he has syphilis, he jumps to his death. The Silent film version, made in 1929, follows Arlen's original by referring to the fact that he died from 'purity' or from 'decency'. It is assumed that she drove him to his

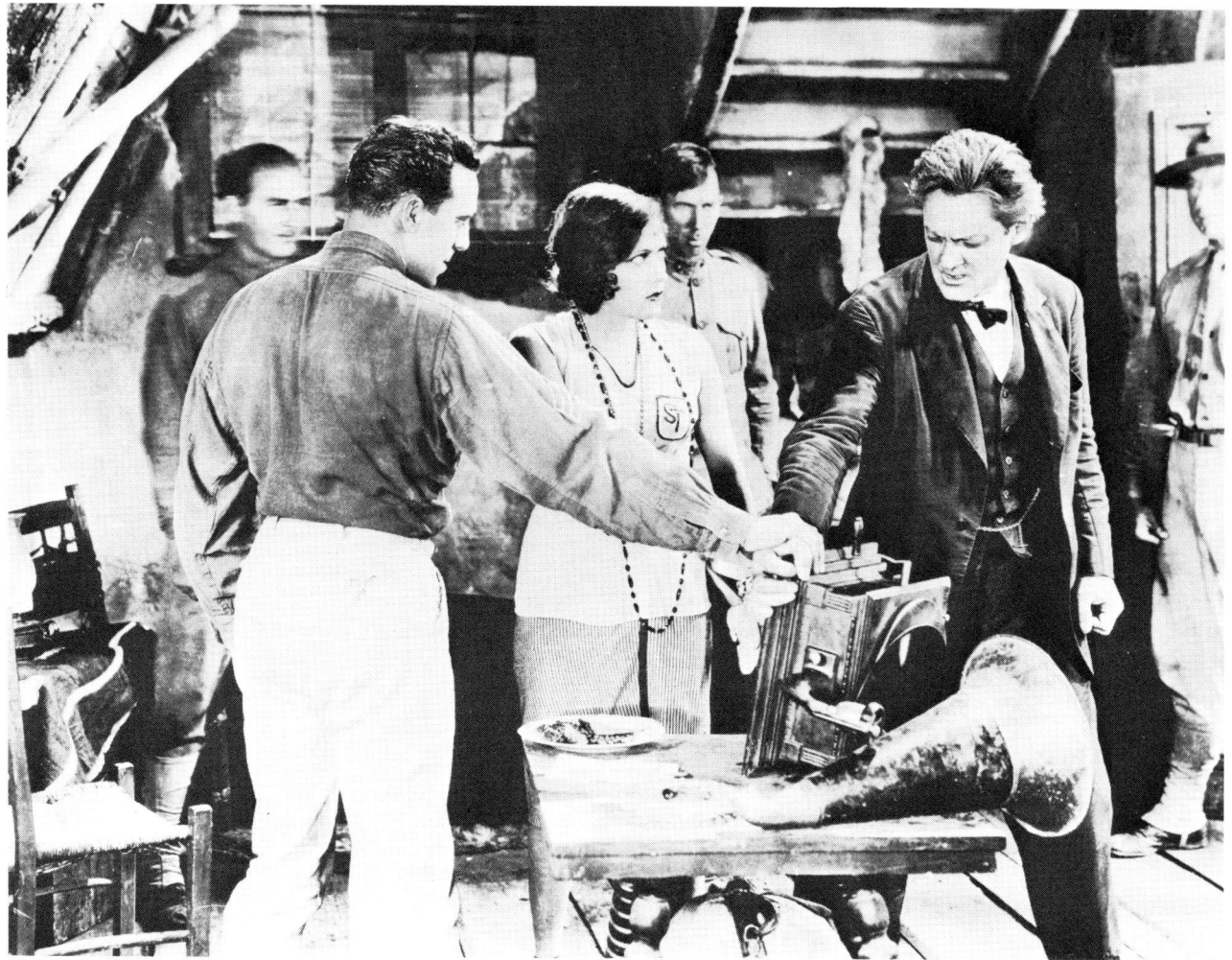

Prostitutes in Silent movies were always sinners and a sympathetic view often depended on the size of the part. When Gloria Swanson decided to film Maugham's story 'Rain', the role required her to be sympathetic and yet – for plot purposes – anything but repentant at the end, and that is one reason why this lady is unique for the time. Here is Swanson as Sadie Thompson and Lionel Barrymore, right, as the 'reformer', while at left is Raoul Walsh as her marine admirer.

death, and her reputation is thereby tarnished. The film adds a sequence in which, shortly after his suicide, two men arrive to arrest him for embezzlement, giving us the option of believing that that was the subject of his confession: but since his friends refuse to believe that he was a thief Iris' reputation suffers anyway. The conjunction of the wedding night and suicide, taken with Iris' refusal to explain fully, makes her the guilty party: and since society believes her to be loose her subsequent behaviour only conforms to her reputation. She gets a chance of redemption when her childhood sweetheart proposes, but his father, disapproving of her, sends him off to Africa, thereby providing a further reason for her bitterness. Marriage – to his best friend – doesn't cure her, and she becomes Europe's most 'talked-of' woman. All we know of her sins first-hand is that she tries to seduce the said childhood sweetheart on his return: and since that is true love every member of the audience can sympathise. The film is about honour and reputation, which was not entirely what Arlen intended, but as directed by Clarence Brown it remains compulsively watchable, whereas the book is now virtually unreadable. The Hays Office insisted the film be retitled, so it became *A Woman of Affairs*; and also that

the infamous Iris be renamed Diana Merrick. But so avid were the public for news of movies and their favourite stars (in this case Greta Garbo and John Gilbert, to whom I shall return) that M-G-M did not need to stress the Arlen connection in its publicity: that would be done by columnists and critics. The Hays Office and respectability, however, were satisfied.

The Hays Office also took objection to the title 'Rain', so it came to the screen as *Sadie Thompson* although this also had little effect since everyone knew who *she* was. Somerset Maugham's short story had acquired instant notoriety when published in 1920, telling as it does of a clergyman whose carnal feelings get the better of him. He is the Rev. Davidson who, with his wife and another couple, is quarantined because of an epidemic at a small hotel in Pago Pago. The four of them are disgusted by the presence in the same hotel of Sadie, an unrepentant whore. The Rev. Davidson undertakes to convert her, which he does successfully although at the same succumbing to her sexual charms. Maugham conveys his fall subtly enough, for the Rev. Davidson is found on the beach, a suicide, and Sadie is back in her familiar gladrags and make-up, yelling 'You men! You filthy, dirty pigs! You're all the same, all of you. Pigs! Pigs!'

Four years after publication of the story Maugham approved a dramatic version which was a success throughout the world, and one much imitated. Indeed, some of the less notorious copies came to the screen with their original titles but the Hays Office was adamant in the case of 'Rain', as 'Miss Thompson' had been renamed for the stage. At first, in fact, Will H. Hays gave Swanson his personal permission to produce and star in the film, though according to her account of the meeting he seems to have been vague about its reputation. With the encouragement of Joseph Schenck, who ran United Artists, she purchased both story and play clandestinely. The roof fell in, as Swanson herself put it, when the press announced the project, and she and Schenck were bombarded with a two-page telegram signed by the fifteen leading studio heads and/or chiefs of the huge cinema circuits, claiming that no 'individual member has the right to jeopardize the interests of all the members'. They also obtained Hays's backing, after pointing out to him that the play had been banned and that 'we all have in our possession material bought and paid for in times gone by which we have refrained from making and there are also in the market many plays no more offensive than this one that there can be no justification for refusing to make if this one goes through'. Swanson in response not unsubtly pointed out that Hays would be on the spot if the press learnt that she had only committed her money to the project after Hays gave her the go-ahead. This ploy brought to her side Marcus Loew, the head of Loew's circuit and M-G-M, with the other signatories thereafter remaining silent and, where applicable, planning similar stories if this one was successful.

The change of title was agreed; and the Rev. Davidson is not a man of the cloth but 'a leading reformer' – and not even called Davidson, but either Miller (in the only extant print) or Hamilton or Atkinson, depending on which printed source one uses. Maugham's tale was an indictment of this man, arrogant rather than hypocritical, without a notion of Christian charity while deluding himself that he has been sent on earth to spread God's word. The film concentrates on Sadie and introduces Sgt O'Brien of the US Marines, played by Raoul Walsh, who had suggested the project to Swanson in the first place. Walsh also directed, from his own adaptation (neither the sergeant nor the Marines are in the story, but they reappear in the two subsequent film versions). Sadie and the sergeant fall in love, and although the film is as equivocal as Maugham on Sadie's past we may feel that she had also truly loved all those men of whom she has kept momentoes: and since, in movie fashion, the sergeant offers redemption with love there is no reason why she should fall under the spell of the 'leading reformer'. The only surviving, incomplete, print concludes with this gentleman about to take Sadie in his arms, his prayers to resist temptation clearly having failed. According to the *Kine Weekly*, he 'follows her into her room at night. In the morning she appears with her good resolutions shattered, her mood defiant. She has been shocked to learn that Hamilton has been found on the beach with his throat cut. She is consoled by the faithful marine, who renews his offer of marriage.' Pre-sumably she accepts, but Maugham's Sadie returned to being unrepentant, emphatically not the marrying kind.

In that respect Sadie was no different from other movie heroines, but the stage had made her notorious. Further, she was an exception to the usual movie rule that sex only occurred in Europe – Maugham's Sadie came from Honolulu, and this one from San Francisco (although that did not necessarily make her an American). The spate of films looking back to the War gave great impetus to this conception, for it was widely believed that continental girls, doubtless prompted by gratitude, forced the noble doughboys to forget their parents' warnings, allowing themselves to be initiated into the wicked ritual of fornication. As Eddie Cantor sang, 'How Ya Gonna Keep 'Em Down on the Farm (After They've Seen Paree)?'. In *The Big Parade* (1925), the mademoiselle is demure and motivated by true love, but in *What Price Glory?* (1926), adapted from a Broadway play of 1924, she has become the sort of woman who has followed armies since time immemorial. In *Wings* (1927) she has been replaced by an American ambulance driver (Clara Bow), but we notice that the film, directed by William. A. Wellman, was written by John Monk Saunders, whose bitter experience of the War survives in a handful of movies no less trenchant now than when they were made. Back home, Miss Bow had been the girl next door; in Paris, she's just someone else in uniform till she dons a frock. Her motive may be consolation or it may be true love: the worst is thought of her, however, even though he passes out. At the end, the boy (Charles 'Buddy' Rogers) realises that he does love her, after all, so that's all right then. In his later films Saunders was to be one of the most powerful chroniclers of the lost generation, but here his aviators are neither whoring nor despairing. They regard Paris as somewhere to drink – into oblivion because of the horrors they have seen at the front. At the Folies-Bergère the camera passes a lady who is fondling the cheek of another lady; two of these perverse creatures may be glimpsed kissing in *The Red Dance* (1928), set in pre-Revolutionary Russia.

The influence of the European cinema is apparent in both films, and if celluloid orgies could cross the Atlantic and not cause the ceilings of New York cinemas to cave in there seemed no reason why Hollywood should not produce a few of its own. Not only were audiences growing more sophisticated, they were also growing more demanding. The 'language' of the Silent screen had become rich and complex and so while American film-makers argued about the merits of Sound there were few other technical problems to overcome; haunted, as ever, by the prospect of falling audiences (defecting, this time, to the wireless) they added richness and complexity to their movies. For a brief while, till the coming of Talkies, they examined the temperament of mankind, with the consequent allusions to sexual variety. This did not necessarily result in stories less absurd than usual, as you will find if you chance upon two of the early films of Howard Hawks, *Paid to Love* (1927) and *Fazil* (1928), both made for Fox.

In *Paid to Love* Crown Prince Michael (George O'Brien) is much more interested in cars than in girls, so

In the late twenties radio began to keep audiences at home. Hollywood responded by offering tales of often bizarre sexual content. *Paid to Love*, with William Powell and Virginia Valli, is one of them.

an apache dancer, Dolores (Virginia Valli), is hired in Paris to seduce him. On the way to him, her car runs into a storm and she tumbles into his home. She doesn't know who he is, and they fall in love. His cousin, Prince Eric (William Powell), knows of the scheme and impersonates him. We may suppose that Prince Eric and Dolores share some wild nights, for when the Crown Prince overhears him boasting about Dolores he rushes to her, forgetting their declarations of everlasting – and presumably pure – love. He crushes her to him, causing her knife to fall from her garter; his boot steps on it as her pearls fall around it. When the camera returns to her she is dishevelled, clutching the remains of her necklace. 'Forgive me' he says.

Fazil is the name of an Arab prince (Charles Farrell) who in Venice gazes out over the canal and sees 'child of caprice' Fabienne (Greta Nissen). Their married life in Paris is ecstatically happy till his concept of female subservience returns, and when he realises the effect on her he does the decent thing and deserts her. She pursues him, into the harem, whose inmates she scorns: 'You brought these empty mockeries of me to forget – but how could you?' she asks, and he ditches them, only to take another wife later. Such things only happen to apache dancers and children of caprice, and it serves them right, even if in the last reel True Love triumphs.

The vile hero of *Yellow Lily* (1928), directed for First National by Alexander Korda, is a Hungarian archduke (Clive Brook), who meets the village doctor's sister (Billie Dove) when his mistress takes poison because he has tired of her. He has now found the one to replace her, and spends most of the film plotting to get her into his bedroom or himself into hers. 'No wonder people call you a contemptible cad!' she cries, almost succumbing. She shoots him accidentally, and the experience of near death makes him realise that this was True Love – and consequently he will face 'centuries of tradition' to bed her honestly.

The unequally-matched lovers in *Laugh, Clown, Laugh* (1928) are an Italian count (Nils Asther) and a bareback-rider (Loretta Young). Encountering her on the border of his estate he asks her to meet his friends, though his true intention is seduction – and he might have succeeded if his ladyfriend hadn't turned up. Two years later he runs across the girl's guardian, a circus clown (Lon Chaney) suffering from melancholia; the count's complaint is exactly the reverse, for he is a manic who cannot stop laughing. If that is due to a life of self-indulgence, the self-indulgence does not yet include the girl, loved also, if chastely, by her guardian. Both men are suffering from sexual frustration, and that is the pivot on which the plot turns. Herbert Brenon directed for M-G-M, shooting alternative endings (one in which Chaney fails to defy death during a death-defying stunt, and one in which he smiles on the Young–Asther nuptials). This was a ploy at this studio, particularly in the case of Greta Garbo. European audiences did not mind her ending unhappily, so in *The Temptress* she pays for her transgressions by becoming a street-walker and in *Love* by suicide. In the American endings she is reunited with her true love, in the second case having changed her mind about that train in St Petersburg station – for this is a modernised *Anna Karenina* and with a leap and a bound we learn that Count Karenin

is dead and that Alexei's new riding master is Count Vronsky.

The Garbo films constitute a remarkable canon in the expression of screen sexuality, and that is entirely because of her personality if not her performances. Her unique ability to convey sexuality through the smallest gestures is seen in the opening sequence of *The Mysterious Lady*, directed in 1928 by Fred Niblo. At the Vienna Opera House she watches *Tosca*, languid but intense, occasionally stretching out her arms. An officer (Conrad Nagel) has eyes only for her, and cannot believe his luck when she accepts his offer of a lift home in his hansom. He escorts her to the door. She goes inside, to lean against the door. Why? Because that was Garbo's way? But there is a knock on the door: she has forgotten her gloves. This time she invites him in for cognac or a coffee. She is elated but at ease – happy, anyway. He, carried away, grabs her from behind. She fights him off. He apologises and prepares to leave. She holds out her hand and as he advances her hand clasps her breast and stays there as he kisses her. Is she moved, bored, or excited? Who and what is she? Mysterious lady indeed. We can read her thoughts, when she wants us to; it is her reactions which are extraordinary. She clutches her lovers to her, feeling the material of their clothes, fondling the chairs in which they have sat. In love she is exultant, a girl who is becoming a woman. Strictly speaking, this was by chance: when M-G-M found that this twenty-year-old girl could play a simple Spanish peasant they had to hope that her European persona would rub off later when the peasant has become a world-famous and sophisticated opera singer. Thereafter Garbo eased herself into a series of roles playing *femmes fatales*, *demi-mondaines*, courtesans, women whose pasts are unknown to the youthful suitor smitten in the first reel. He has spied her, if not in the opera house, in a garden. She must, because of her beauty, break his heart, and in reel two he will find that she has a lover, a husband, or a protector who is much, much older than herself. She will be denied happiness because she earlier settled for – well, what? Of course she is wealthy, but we cannot suppose that baubles matter to her; on a couple of occasions her older man is impotent, so she didn't marry for *that*, either. When, in *Flesh and the Devil* and *A Woman of Affairs* she marries her beloved's best friend (in both cases John Gilbert), not waiting for his return from foreign parts, no explanation is given. The conclusion has to be that *femmes fatales* would find it difficult to go several reels without sexual intercourse. Innocently amorous in reel one, she is now experienced and erotic. M-G-M were fully aware of the public interest in Garbo and Gilbert, who were supposed to have had a passionate affair off-screen; and Gilbert, a magnetic actor in Silents, responded cinematically to the 'mature' Garbo now that she wanted to seduce him.

A succession of men lies strewn behind this long-limbed girlish figure, and yet we do not find her shallow or unprincipled, but intensely vulnerable. We do not blame the men for taking leave of their senses. We should like the opportunity to do so ourselves. We would not forget her as quickly as do Gilbert and Lars

It was a long while before M-G-M could see Greta Garbo as anything but a seductress, and since she was so beautiful how could any man resist her? Here, in *Flesh and the Devil*, is John Gilbert trying to, left, and here he is again, above, after the flesh has succumbed. You probably do not need to be told that the intruder is her husband (George Fawcett).

Hanson in *Flesh and the Devil*. The mistress of one, the wife of another, she had destroyed their friendship, and the marriage. She had seemed to exult in the duel they were about to fight till the last minute – when she went through the ice in an attempt to stop it. The two men are again united, at peace with the world and each other. The kid sister of one grows up quickly to claim the heart of the other for a perfunctory ending, meant perhaps to imply that the two men are not in love with each other. It is clear that this was not, as has been claimed, the movies' age of innocence, and the last scenes are distinctly bizarre.

After *Flesh and the Devil* Garbo was to have made *Women Love Diamonds* (1927), but she preferred to go on suspension, partly for an increased salary and partly because her sensible Swedish mind had not yet accomodated itself to the thinking of M-G-M, which was unable to see her in anything but variations of the same role. *Women Love Diamonds* would have been one of her rare roles as an American – and accordingly it is one of the few films about American sinners. Matters for them hadn't changed: they were still in the redemption business – in the age of the 'new' woman and Clara Bow. Mavis Ray (Pauline Starke) is a sophisticated and worldly woman, in love with a wealthy Long Island scion (Douglas Fairbanks Jr); her 'uncle' (Lionel Barrymore) asks to meet him and the silly biddy agrees. We are not party to the conversation between the two men, but Long Island society turns on Mavis, indignant that she dared aspire to their circle. It's only on the return trip that we learn of Mavis's true relationship with uncle, and she doesn't go sour on him till she gets caught up in the troubles of her chauffeur's family. In the course of this she falls in love with the chauffeur (Matt Moore), causing her to confess (he hadn't guessed?), after which she rushes out into the night. However, they meet again . . . a fallen woman is not good enough for a well-born young man, but she's acceptable for one from the working-class. Kept and wealthy, Mavis's wardrobe and way of life can be guiltily admired by every woman in the audience, while every man may fantasise about owning one like her: and the fascination of both will turn to sympathy as she realises what a rotten life she is leading and finds True Values. She makes amends, not by packing parcels at Macy's, but by a real hard job, nursing. And not just for a few weeks. It takes a year for the faithful chauffeur to find Mavis – a year in which she hasn't for an instant regretted swopping sex, luxury and diamonds for a life of drudgery. Naturally.

4.
Bad Old Europe

So far the reader may have noticed only passing references to homosexuality, and it may be fair to assume that that was something that Silent moviegoers did not want to know about. Indeed, one might suppose that it was something not known to exist, at least in the middle reaches of the social scale. It was not discussed; the awkward references in Shakespeare's sonnets or the writing of the Ancient Greeks were ignored by commentators and there were few literary incidences for the curious other than a hint or two in *The Portrait of Dorian Gray*. Older people may have remembered the newspaper reports of the trials of Oscar Wilde, but the subject was considered so repellent that press reporting of court cases – male homosexuality was against the law in Britain (till 1967) and other Western countries – was circumspect.

Otherwise the only public acknowledgement of 'deviation' or 'perversion' was to be found in music halls, where there was a long tradition of bawdy jokes and sketches. Probably the first screen reference is in a filmed version of one of the latter; the earliest that I know is in Charlie Chaplin's *Behind the Screen* (1916), and we do know that he utilised in movies situations learnt in his days on the halls. In a movie studio an actress (Edna Purviance) disguises herself as a stage-hand and Charlie raises his eyebrows when he sees 'him' powdering 'his' nose: when he discovers the truth he kisses 'him', only to be seen by his fierce boss, who cries 'Oh you naughty boys!' and minces across the set in the supposed manner of homosexuals.

There was a similar theatrical tradition in Germany, with ladies getting dragged up and then wishing they hadn't. In *Das Liebes ABC* (1916) Asta Nielsen decides that her fiancé isn't man enough for her so she disguises herself as a chap so she can take him out for a night on the town. He then becomes too much of a man, and appears to be having an affair with another woman: Nielsen gets back into pants, as a waiter, and sees him kissing the woman, who turns out to be a man in drag. In Ernst Lubitsch's *Ich Mochte kein Mann Sein* (1919) Ossi Oswalda dons an evening suit because she's bored with being a girl. Another night on the town follows, this time with a guardian as unwitting as Nielsen's fiancé, and ends with the two of them getting so drunk together that the guardian gives 'him' a kiss. That's all right, though, because he kisses her again when he knows she's a she. In Lubitsch's *Ein Fideles Gefängnis* (1917) a drunken jailer (Emil Jannings) kisses other men, because he is drunk, so we may be sure that such shenanigans tickled the German sense of humour, even if one man is a

woman, or vice versa: but in most comedies of transvestism, from Shakespeare onwards, physical contact was usually avoided. The humour here is often Germanic and not typical of Lubitsch. ('The Lubitsch Touch' belongs to his American period, but there is a good gag in *Der Bergkatze* when the preening lieutenant is being watched in his drawers through a keyhole by his fiancée, who is angrily pushed aside by her mother.)

We should also note that Miss Nielsen's screen *Hamlet* was revealed after death as being of the fair sex. Drawing on sources which include Danish legends and a German play, *Fratricide Unpunished*, Miss Nielsen plays an heiress who for reasons of state is brought up a boy. She conceives an impossible love for Horatio and it is not until she is dying that she receives that longed-for kiss from him. I should say that I have never considered that homosexuality is concomitant with transvestism – not in life, anyway, though films (and the theatre) often found a link. Censorship forbade overt homosexual expression, but *something* might be hinted at with men in drag, which was permissible. The free climate of the Weimar Republic did produce three films with homosexual themes, of which the most discreet is Carl Th. Dreyer's *Michael* (1924), for it is quite possible to believe that Michael (Walter Slezak) is the adopted son of the painter Zoret (Benjamin Christensen). The film concludes with an image of woman as predator, for one has stolen young Michael away; it is also as much about Zoret's artistic circle as it is about relationships, but it is only for Zoret that the film has much admiration – handsome and masculine and the only one of this group of friends to show no heterosexual inclinations.

Such feelings were more acceptable among artists and Paul (Conrad Veidt) in *Anders Als die Andern* (1919) is a violinist. His path to depravity is demonstrated by his putting his arm round a schoolchum – to the wrath of their teacher – and by his detestation of female kisses at student parties. The film makes no bones about his preferences, for he haunts the bars where men dance with men. Otherwise there is nothing more shocking to be seen than a caress on the cheek – and that leads to blackmail, which is the film's true subject, spelling out at the end that the Penal Code must be amended, so that men like Paul may not be driven to suicide. The director, Richard Oswald, also made notable crusading films on prostitution and venereal disease.

Suicide also provides the solution in *Geschlecht in Fesseln* (1928), which concerns several sorts of sexuality, including the inability to put it to use. Wilhelm (later, in Hollywood, William) Dieterle, who also directed, plays

Franz, who is glad to get through the Depression by selling vacuum cleaners door to door, but that comes to an end when he accidentally kills a man making persistent advances to his wife. His fellow prisoners are all frustrated: as one of them exclaims, why can they eat, sleep and drink but not *that*? One reputedly could not sleep and has castrated himself; others make models of female bodies, drooling and quarrelling over them; Franz and his wife fantasise about each other in bed, till one night in frustration she goes to the home of her boss, whose propositions she has hitherto turned down. For his part Franz is not angry when a fellow-prisoner shows him a fly-leaf of a book with their names written intertwined. A few nights later neither man can sleep and Franz asks the other what he is honestly thinking. The intertitles do not translate his reply till he concludes that Franz must now despise him. Franz, on the contrary, reaches out for his hand and the sequence ends

Conrad Veidt in *Anders Als die Andern*, the pioneering work about homosexuality. But no matter how favourably it viewed Veidt's activities these could not to be said to be beneficial to his health – and thus the eye-shadow that he customarily wore is even heavier than usual, denoting real degeneracy.

with the suggestion of movement, of Franz leaving his bed. When husband and wife are reunited, she at first understands that his refusal to remain with her is due to her adultery, but she realises, on seeing Franz's lover, that he too has been unfaithful.

Geschlecht in Fesseln is one of many Silent movies in which feelings are expressed by symbols and Dieterle (as writer, actor and director) used them again to express Ludwig II's homosexuality in *Ludwig der Zweite, Konig von Bayern* (1930), which is in fact one of the last German Silents. One of the footmen is found sitting in the presence of the king, who is admiring a statuette of a naked man; after the footman has been asked to pose (clothed) in the same stance, the two men slip to the floor and the screen is ablaze with nude male statuettes, one of which is discernable as a couple making love. The image is shattered as the king smashes his own statuette and calls for the footman to be arrested – which may indicate guilt or merely his madness. This time, of course, the tragic ending of the film bows to historical force, but the sympathies of both films are extraordinary – at least by the standards operating in the English-speaking cinema at this time. As we shall see, however, Germany's movies would have compassion for all the sexually lost and strayed, though their behaviour was more orthodox.

In the meantime we move to Sweden for the remarkable *Häxan* (1922) or *Witchcraft Through the Ages*, made by the Danish director, Benjamin Christensen – the same man who had played the artist in *Michael*, and he appears here, if fleetingly, also imposingly, as the Devil. This semi-documentary (as we would now call it) imaginatively blends ancient prints and live action for its interpretation of one facet of history. Its first re-told tale concerns a friar's housekeeper who successfully feeds him a love potion; and the longest is about a party of prim and evil-minded monks whose accusations of witchcraft and torture destroy a nobleman's family before moving on to equally wicked business elsewhere. The piece is surely confirmation of the nordic distrust of clerics, but the conclusion, that they have been replaced by psychiatrists, could not have been convincing, even at that time.

Not that many had a chance of testing that suggestion, since the film was banned in most countries. *L'Atlantide* (1921) directed in France by Jacques Feyder also ran into trouble, although Pierre Benoît's novel – however it looks on the screen – was respectable and in the honourable French tradition of fascination with Africa and the East. After some convoluting plot twists to establish mystery, Lieutenant Saint-Avit (Georges Melchior) and Captain Morhange (Jean Angelo) find themselves inspecting a Greek carving in an African cave. The hashish smoked by a native companion makes them pass out, and they find themselves in all that survived of Atlantis when the rest was submerged in a flood in 9,000 BC. Its ruler is Queen Antinea, who enslaves all white men who gaze upon her: they perish, says the archivist, of love, madness or hashish – and there, clearly dying of all three, is a fellow-officer thought to have perished in the desert months before. He jumps off a cliff, and our heroes see his body, mummified into metal, brought

Many a nude or semi-nude may be glimpsed (if no more) in *Häxan*. The film itself was anti-clerical, but was still able to take the Church's view that witchcraft was evil and therefore practised by sinners who preferred to be unclothed.

into the Hall of Red Marble, the twenty-fourth of Antinea's victims. They realise that they are to be numbers twenty-five and twenty-six. 'From the moment you see her' says the archivist, 'you will renounce friends, honour, country – everything.' Who else ever had such a build-up?

When found, Antinea (Stacia Napierkowska) is lolling on a sea of cushions surrounded by her handmaidens, her pet cheetah by her side. She inspects Saint-Avit but chooses Morhange, who resists her, but only by becoming a zombie. Saint-Avit, however, is crazed with desire and after accepting a drugged cigarette from Antinea agrees to her demand that he murder his friend. And that is not all. This was a very popular entertainment in those countries permitted to see it, but then few of its patrons could have known that hashish is supposed to increase sexual desire. The film is really a variation on the themes of the divismo movies and the central idea – of men slavering around an all-powerful sex goddess – was too good not to be imitated.

But not in Germany. This was a country in dire economic circumstances, but with a vital, expanding film industry, the result, partly, of the international success of *Das Cabinett des Doktor Caligari* in 1920. This became the most celebrated of the so-called* Expressionist films, but the movement had begun in the theatre in 1918 with George Kaiser's play *Von Morgens bis Mitternacht*, which was filmed in the wake of the delirious reception accorded *Caligari*, using similarly stylised sets. So many other movies adopted this device, and the public tired of it so quickly that some went unreleased, including this one. However, the director, Karl Grune, was able to resume the theme in *Die Strasse* three years later. In both cases the protagonist seeks forgetfulness from the daily round by sneaking away from his wife for a night on the town, only to find himself in the midst of a nightmare in which a street-

---

* *So they have always been called: I have argued elsewhere that they are, rather, Surrealist.*

Mutter Krausen's Fahrt ins Gluck portrays working-class life in Berlin, in 1929. Its sexual interests begin with the lodger at the right (Gerhardt Bienert), who brings into the apartment a prostitute (Vera Sacharowa) – and the family is so poor they cannot object. The daughter, (Ilse Trautschold), left, had already been deflowered by him. She finds a boyfriend (Friedrich Gnass) with high ideals, though you would not perhaps think so from this picture. The director was Phil Jutzi.

walker plays a prominent part. Neither film is about prostitution, but *Die Strasse* led to a school of films named after it – the 'street' films, in which prostitutes were not just acceptable but essential. The two films are about lonely men and if these protagonists represent a lost and hopeless Germany the prostitute stands supreme, a representative in turn of desperation, poverty, and where everything is for sale. Young love and idealised love have been all but banished, at least after the first reel where they are shown in contrast to what follows; marital love no longer exists, for the husbands are turning to whores and the wives to young men, often students; adulterous love exists, but only prostitutes seem to have beds – and by the end of the decade will be seen in them with their clients.

Since the German film industry was not organised on the factory-like assembly line of Hollywood, which was geared to supply the circuits owned by the studios, the product it turned out has more diversity. The film that obviously calls for discussion is *Unter der Laterne*, for we all know what happens under the lantern, don't we? It is one of Gerhard Lamprecht's valuable series on Berlin low life, each one of which highlights the economic situation; when the intertitles need to use the word *arbeiten* (work) they do so in larger letters than the rest of the 'dialogue'. Else (Lissi Arna) is a slave to a tyrannical father, who disapproves of her boyfriend Hans

(Mathias Wiemann) – so much so that he locks her out after she has sneaked away to be with Hans. A drunk on the stairway makes a pass, and she walks the streets all night, in the morning going to Hans, who introduces her to his flatmate, Max, as his sister. Max in time proposes, causing Hans to do likewise, even though he cannot marry her without her father's consent. At this point she goes to his room, throws herself on him and extinguishes the candle.

Since she has been the initiator, we may suppose that she brings her eventual fate on herself. For the moment she is tainted by the theatre: just as Else's father is trying to get her back, an agent, Gustav Nevin, agrees to take on Max if Else is part of the act. She turns to Gustav for help, and he opens the champagne. His jealous mistress tells Hans, and although Else is actually struggling when he walks in he prefers to believe otherwise. When the act is cancelled Else has no choice but to move in with Gustav, at which point the movie has a long montage of the things which constitute Else's high life – jewels, champagne, a lapdog, dancing and a maid laying out her scanty underwear. But none of it is paid for, and when Gustav is accused of fraud he shoots himself. Else becomes a *tanzmädchen*, but is sacked on her first evening when she dislikes a customer pawing her. He follows her, and since she has no home she goes with him. We are led to understand that he doesn't put her on

48

the game till he sees her under the lantern in a café. Hans and Max have been trying to find her, but she scorns them, blaming Hans for what has happened to her. He later returns to give her money so she can escape to the country but her pimp steals it. 'Look upon this picture and on this' says the final intertitle as we see Hans happily married and Else about to succumb to an unnamed fatal illness.

Had Else lived she would have become like Asta Nielsen, still playing fallen women, as in Bruno Rahn's powerful *Dirnentragödie* (1927). Nielsen is the ageing Auguste, sharing her apartment with an Else, or herself when young, in the shapely person of Clarissa (Hilde Jennings), who is new to the game. Clarissa gets asked to stag parties, but Auguste uses the street – and it is there that she meets a drunken mother's boy, Felix (Werner Pittschau), for whom she conceives an almighty passion. She dips into her nest-egg to bribe her 'protector' Anton (Oscar Homolka) to leave and uses the rest for a down payment on a shop where she and Felix will regain respectability and be happy ever after. Anton introduces Felix to Clarissa, who wastes no time getting him into the bedroom, and Auguste returns to hear herself being described as old and laughable. In revenge she begs Anton to kill Clarissa, though changes her mind after discovering that Felix truly loves Clarissa: but it is too late. Anton is arrested and we learn from an item in a newspaper that Auguste has committed suicide, because of unhappiness at the death of Clarissa: the crowd gathering to read it includes another ageing whore and her very young one friend. The landlady puts up a notice, 'Furnished room to let'.

Both films – indeed, all these movies – take a romantic view of the whore's life. They are pathetic, pitiable women, seldom hard or mercenary. Only occasionally do we glimpse the mechanics of the life – and the dangers – as a customer climbs the stairways in her wake. The one consistent image throughout is of bachelor parties, with the men grotesque, fat and bald, in heavy three-piece suits, and the girls – except the dubious debutante – keen to flash smiles and glimpses of silk stockings, as the procuresses nod them on. These over-stuffed apartments are in contrast to the homes of the whores – Miss Nielsen's room in *Dirnentragödie* was hardly furnished at all. The gathering places of sinners in American movies tended to be in exotic locales, allowing

Leo Mittler's *Jenseits der Strasse* is one of the most realistic of the German 'street' films, often set in the whores' dives – and it is one of the few which show the punters climbing the stairs or even in bed with them. These gentleman invariably looked like this unnamed actor; the lady is Lissi Arna, who may be thinking about the unemployed country boy who truly loves her – for a while.

art directors full play with fans, shutters and the palms outside, but those in Germany tend to be bare, uncluttered dives, where you're more likely to be offered a quick stand-up job in the alley round the corner than be taken back to a bed of silks and satins. If these films are erotic, it is because of the patently honest account of the milieu.

In *Asphalt* (1929) the heroine, also called Else, does have a luxurious bed with dozens of silk cushions, but her rooms are otherwise virtually bare – and that is our chief clue as to her profession, for we had supposed her to thieve for a living. Else (Betty Amman) is arrested, and she persuades the young policeman (Gustav Fröhlich) to let her stop off at her apartment for her identity papers. We know what she has in mind, but the point is, does he? And if he does, will the flesh weaken? In fact, she gets into bed and immediately pleads illness when he doesn't respond. This is one of the few convincingly erotic scenes in cinema at the time because both participants are young and comely. Reason says he might as well take what she is offering and still march her down to the station afterwards – and reason also knows that policemen can be corrupt, if that is the word to use for what would seem to be a healthy release of his sexual drive. The longer the two stay there, the more susceptible he becomes, and in the end he decides for the best. He had just rejected her attempt at an embrace when she takes a running jump and throws herself on him – the one mistake in Joe May's direction, for audiences today laugh at this point. Presumably the most convincing swift action she might have attempted was an attack on his trouser buttons, which would have had the film banned the world over. We do not see him in the act of betraying his uniform, and we only know that the leap was successful because the film cuts to him crying on his bed, almost dying of remorse. Even worse – depending, of course, on your point of view – the two have fallen in love and plan to marry when she leaves jail.

The situation of May's *Heimkehr* (1928) is equally simple, as taken from Leonhard Frank's once-famous novel *Karl und Anna*. Karl (Gustav Fröhlich) arrives in Hamburg to see Anna (Dita Parlo), the wife of his fellow POW, Richard (Lars Hanson), who has not yet managed to return from Russia. Anna is so excited on hearing about Richard that she lets the potatoes burn; she and Karl have such a wonderful time together that neither can sleep, after she has offered him a bed in the other room. Three days later, still delighted with each other, and heady with wine and music from the café below, they kiss, but Karl retreats to his own room on remembering his old comrade. By the time this last named returns they are miserable, in love but conscience-free, which may give you a clue to the eventual outcome.

Nor do the lovers consummate their love in *Die Wunderbare Lüge der Nina Petrowna* (1929) – not at first, anyway – which is surprising in view of the fact that Nina (Brigitte Helm) is a kept woman, a fact the man undoubtedly knows. He accepts, and uses, her doorkey; but they talk and dance for so long that he falls asleep on merely sighting a bed. She has plied him with champagne and longs to see his door open, but she has such

Of all the German Silent movies about loose living ladies, *Die Büchse der Pandora* is the most famous – due chiefly to Louise Brooks's enchanting performance as Lulu. Right, she is flirting with the lesbian countess (Alice Roberts) and, above, confronted by her husband (Fritz Kortner).

respect for him that that is where she sleeps, outside his door. Thus the purity of love-at-first-sight will permit them to be happy – if only for a while and in poverty, for the lieutenant (Franz Lederer) hasn't sufficient finances to marry. The director, Hannes Schwarz, seems to have liked this situation, for it recurs in *Ungarische Rhapsodie* (1928), though both tales are in the European tradition of pure love vs. the jaded, the innocent vs. the roué. In this case the dashing, licentious officer (Willy Fritsch) cannot afford to marry the girl and refuses to resign from the army so that he can. She observes that while he will give up nothing for her he expects her to give up everything for him; and in view of his ardour it is not difficult to know what she means by 'everything'.

It is unlikely that birth control had reached this small Hungarian garrison town; but any family in the so-called civilised world could have told you stories of great-aunts or distant cousins who were never seen again after having surrendered 'everything' and who presumably descended to a life of destitution. Most sexual situations in movies do connect with life, if at three or four removes, but I don't know what we are to make of Fräulein Else in Paul Czinner's film of that name, made in 1929. Else (Elisabeth Bergner) is on vacation in St Moritz when she receives a letter from her mother begging her to request a loan from Von Dorsday (Albert

Steinrück), who is staying at the same hotel. This friend of her father's is lined and corpulent, but seems so sympathetic that it's difficult to understand why Else takes so long to approach him. He would be only too happy to help her father, he says, adding as an afterthought that he would like to see Else . . . and he nods towards a statue of a naked woman. Else, disgusted, is packing when another letter from her mother again entreats her to request a loan, on the grounds that her father is to be arrested. Else dons a fur wrap, and when she cannot find Von Dorsday in his room, stalks him in the public rooms: calling his name, she exposes herself and promptly expires from a large dose of veronal. It is hard to understand how this humiliation of Von Dorsday could be of help to her father, and equally difficult to find in this is the 'voice' of Arthur Schnitzler, who wrote the original story; but whatever we feel today about Else's behaviour, the facts tell too strongly against us. Girls were brought up to believe that sex was evil, and only a few daft romantic novelists thought otherwise.

The one wholly unrepentant sinner is Louise Brooks in the two films Pabst directed in 1929, *Die Büchse von Pandora* and *Tagebuch einer Verlorenen*. The films themselves end morally: Miss Brooks's sexual adventures end with her either married or dead, but we must conclude that they were fun while they lasted. Faced with seduction or ravishment she reacts like an amoral child, basking in the attention, admiration or just the other's lust, an innocent who moves instinctively and wholeheartedly into a milieu founded on the exploitation of sex for money. It is all a game to her – the champagne, the life in the bordel, the embrace of a lesbian countess (a role, incidentally, cut to nothing when the film was first shown in Britain), even the reversals. Miss Brooks dazzles: she is not heartless but the films are – and cruel, witty and erotic. Pabst, who made one of the best 'street' films, *Die Freudlose Gasse*, no longer sees fit to find prostitution caused by poverty but by man's need for same. In these two films people unashamedly enjoy sex and its trimmings, which to our eyes puts them above most of the films so far discussed.

It is not to be expected that prostitution was to be found in post-Revolution Russia, but that presented no problems to the Soviet film-makers, who were busy making dramas showing how beastly the aristocrats used to be to the serfs – or comedies ridiculing the bourgeoisie which had not adapted to the marvellous new ways. The bourgeoise wives are vain, selfish and grasping, often coveting young men and so sexually indifferent to their husbands that the husbands lecherously eye young girls, and unsuccessfully scheme to get them in their power. There is a famous comedy which we know as *Bed and Sofa* (1927), but the Russian title translates as '3 Meschanskaya Street', an address which shelters a *ménage à trois*, which is the film's entire subject. Volodya (Vladimir Vogel) cannot find a room in Moscow till he meets a friend from his army days, Kolya (Nikolai Batalov), who invites him to sleep on the sofa. When Kolya is sent to Rostov for three months, Volodya takes Kolya's wife on an air trip and to the cinema. That night the inevitable happens and Kolya is told when he returns. He walks out, but is invited back when he can find no lodgings. He then sets out to win back his wife, since Volodya has begun to take her for granted just as he once had. But when he refuses to be the father of another man's child, she walks out to start a life of her own. We may suppose the men have used her for sex and their own comforts, and that she leaves them because they are not good enough for her: but since we leave her on a train to the country with dubious prospects we may feel instead that this is the conventional movie punishment for adultery.

It would be hard to say whether the film expresses Soviet ideology, which, outside the great propaganda films, is largely absent from Russian cinema till the 1930s. Certainly the film is not daring, and much less fun than Fedor Ozep's *The Yellow Passport* – and in this case the Russian title translates as 'Earth in Captivity', just to give its audience an idea how rotten it was for the serfs in the old days. Poverty forces Maria (Anna Sten) to leave for Moscow to wet-nurse the landowner's grandson, and since she cannot read she does not learn that her husband and children have been evicted in her absence. Her husband arrives for help just as she is fighting off her employer (Mr Vogel), a dapper man whose lust and drunkenness is indicated by a sock come apart from its supporter: the doorman, whom she has also repulsed, tells her husband that she is 'carrying on', which accords with his apparent refusal to respond to her pleas for help. The shock of the ensuing mêlée causes Maria's milk to dry up and she is shown the door. Accidentally rounded up with some whores, she is too simple to understand why she has been issued with a yellow passport and she becomes a prostitute, though we may be forgiven for thinking her rather stupid for believing that she must become a prostitute just because she has been classified as one. For all the film's melodrama and special pleading – qualities common to many Russian films of the period – it is clear that no other option was open to girls like Maria. She has not got the fare home and the employment agency (she had supposed the yellow passport to be a ticket to a job) was crowded with applicants. Whether the real Marias had happy endings is open to doubt, but this one does: plying her trade in a low dive she meets a villager (Mr Batalov) from back home, and in response to what he tells her she finds a way of returning to the bosom of her family.

It is not to be supposed that the British contributed much to the case of sex on the screen, though their films featured the usual quota of bounders and unwed mothers. The matinee idol, Ivor Novello, had a great success in the title-role of *The Rat* (there were two sequels), as king of the Paris apaches, sexually inconstant, consorting with the society women who come slumming but truly in love with a waif (Mabel Poulton). Though it could just as well have been set in Huddersfield the Paris setting may have given it some appeal, for the British public failed to respond to the two film versions of Noël Coward's 'shocking' plays, *Easy Virtue* and *The Vortex*, made by the same company and released the following year, in 1927, one of them also starring Mr Novello. Both see sin in high society in terms of tennis parties and artists' studios. The problems concerned – a woman with a past, and another who refuses to grow old gracefully – could not have had much reality for audiences in the factory towns of the north. Perhaps their trouble – apart from the fact that neither film is as polished as Hollywood films were at this time – is that there was no one with whom the majority of spectators could identify. Much more popular were those movies in which working girls and the like get caught up in high society and teach it true values, like Henry Edwards's *A Girl of London* (1925), in which a factory girl (Genevieve Townsend) sets a young wastrel (Ian Hunter) back on the straight and narrow. He's the spoilt son of a wealthy Member of Parliament, spending his nights in opium dens and nightclubs; but when he's down and out he doesn't try and get a job for which his upbringing might have trained him, but one as a docker, porter, or manual labourer. Wealthy movie heroes were ever thus, even when they deserted their riches for a bet or a dare. This heroine, incidentally, survives an attempt at rape, finding the strength of ten men – a fond tribute to British womanhood, whose American counterpart often fainted in horror. In *Palais de Danse* (1928), directed by Maurice Elvey, the heroine is a waif

They are married, so whether she (Lya de Putti) is showing him (Emil Jannings) the hole in her stocking or being provocative it's all right. The film is E. A. Dupont's *Varieté*, a triangle drama set among trapeze artists which was the most imitated movie of its time. The foreigner who is invited to join the act cuckolds the husband when his back is turned.

who gets a job in the establishment which gives the film its title, and the hero is the usual wealthy scion: it's not he who is vile, but his mother, carrying on with a gigolo (John Longden). She gets her come-uppance by learning that he's not the aristocrat she supposed, but a professional dancing partner, and that she is just the latest of a long line of older ladies.

The film itself is one of the many imitations of E. A. Dupont's heavily influential *Varieté*, made in Germany in 1925. Dupont himself churned out numerous versions of this tale, all with but slight variations, usually with a show business background, most of them made in Britain. Alfred Hitchcock did one imitation, *The Ring*, with a boxing background, and *Shooting Stars* (1928),

written by Anthony Asquith and directed by A. V. Bramble, was another. In this case the predator is the wife (Annette Benson), a movie star whose eyes stray away from her husband and leading man (Brian Aherne), to the slapstick clown (Donald Calthrop), who of course is a slick dresser when he is not in baggy pants. She gives him the key to the apartment when she thinks her husband is away. A divorce would ruin her – we are constantly shown the scandal clause in her contract – so she puts real bullets in the gun to be fired at her husband on the next day's shooting. But matters go hideously wrong, and the husband ends as an acclaimed director and she a forlorn, forgotten extra. Serves her right, of course.

5.
The New Woman and the Oldest Profession

We have already noted how well Gloria Swanson represented the women of the postwar generation. These were the women with a freer, less submissive attitude to men and we may take it they only married after looking over the field. Swanson, however, almost always played a married woman, and that was because she had made her name in De Mille's marital comedies; the studios were so loth to tamper with success that few stars were able to escape typecasting. But when she became one of the *Prodigal Daughters* in 1923 the title capitalised on

It, right, was the quintessential Clara Bow tale, all about a clerk who sets her sights on the boss, Antonio Moreno, right. *Red Hair*, above, capitalised on another of Clara's famous assets. Indeed, the film had one reel in Technicolor so that audiences could appreciate it. Once again she was a gold digger, though True Love makes her see the error of her ways.

the fact. Gloria's nickname in the film is Swifty and she horrifies her parents by offering her sister cigarettes and preferring golf on Sunday to church – in an outfit that reveals her knees. *Photoplay* regarded the movie as 'another tirade against the jazz babies of 1923', since Swifty does return repentant to the family manse at the end. Her successors would not do that. As Leatrice Joy says in *Manslaughter* 'Modern girls do not sit by the fire and knit', while her proudest boast is 'that speed never stopped her'.

Not only were women apeing men by smoking and driving motor-cars (if they were rich enough), their appearance was also changing: the War had inadvertently led the way towards shorter skirts and bobbed hair. Young men with cars were able to take their girls away from the jurisdiction of parents, to parties where dancing to jazz records had taken the place, as far as the young were concerned, of the family sing-song round the piano. The introduction of the cocktail made drinking more acceptable for women in society, as beer and hard liquor had not been for their sex, and any man who plied a girl with cocktails might have in his possession an even newer invention, one of the new safe contraceptives. It is no wonder that parents worried what their children were up to. Sin moved lower down the social scale in movies, and the Swanson–Negri hunting ground of boudoir and opera house gave way to the department stores and tenements of Clara Bow – chief of the flappers or jazz babies – and Joan Crawford, who in *Our Dancing Daughters* cannot even keep her Charlestoning feet still as she draws on her panties.

The motives of both might be misunderstood, but the attitude of the thoroughly working-class Miss Bow was unequivocal: she has only to see a handsome man to want him, and she is supremely self-confident of her ability to get him. 'Miss Van Cortland seems rather lacking in reserve, doesn't she?' someone observes of her in *It* – that someone being the stuffy fiancée of the man whom Miss Bow is after. His first suggestion is refused, indignantly, so no matter how much this flapper ogles, primps, flatters and undulates her body she is not, in the end, so different from Mary Pickford.

Though the lecherous William Powell may be tempting Miss Bow with a wicked cocktail in *The Runaway* it would not have been unfamiliar to her on this occasion, for she played a movie star who longed for the simple life.

Many of Joan Crawford's pictures showed what the new generation got up to when their parents were safely tucked up in bed: as *Dance, Fools, Dance* appeared to prove, the worst fears were justified. Lester Vail and she prepare for a midnight dip.

Miss Crawford, an echelon or so higher up the social ladder was to find – as she did throughout her long career – the going much harder. 'Wild' or 'dangerous' she may have been, according to the intertitles, but whereas her friends used any means to get their men, be it concupiscence or its opposite, faking virginity (we are not told how) she is decent underneath, as she constantly reminds us. With the advent of Jean Harlow the pretence stopped. 'Would you be shocked if I put on something more comfortable?' she says to her fiancé's brother (Ben Lyon) in *Hell's Angels* (1930). The 'something' is something in slinky black, revealing much of breast and leg. She observes to Lyon that his brother wouldn't really like her 'if he knew what I really like', adding 'I want to be free. I want to be gay and happy. I want to live while I'm alive' – which sounds less like an Oxford girl of 1914 (which she is supposed to be) than Bow or Crawford, and then not too much like them, yet. However: Lyon, lust satiated, sits with his face buried in his hand, full of remorse. 'Cold in here now' she says, to which he replies, 'God, I'm rotten.' 'I can't see it' she remonstrates. 'Then you're rotten, too' he says. The film was produced and directed by Howard Hughes, the tycoon whose conquest of many famous stars were probably never accompanied by regret.

Clearly what was needed was a new sort of leading man, and he was found a year later in a movie featuring Mr Lyon called *Night Nurse*, which starred Barbara Stanwyck in the title-role. At one point Stanwyck becomes nurse to two little girls. The family chauffeur is a sinister but powerful figure, having gained that power, we may suppose, because their mistress spends her time stoned with her lover on her bed. The lover at one point attempts to rape Stanwyck, but she is rescued by the chauffeur, who just for good measure bops her on the chin. And thus audiences first came to know Clark Gable, who looked tough and acted tough. He remained tough when he became the most dashing of leading men, never taking himself seriously and taking his pratfalls with a will. Burt Reynolds, though by no means as charismatic or charming, is as close as we can get today, and it's no surprise to find Reynolds confessing that he watches a Gable film at least once a week. Gable did not give a damn about his image, and seems to have been happiest in conservative double-breasted suits; by all accounts he did enjoy hunting, shooting and fishing,

Another lady who did exactly what she pleased was Jean Harlow, who in *Hell's Angels* had seduced the brother (Ben Lyon, far right) of her fiancé (James Hall). That was back in Oxford before the War; meeting up with her in bistro near the Front she's not remotely abashed at being discovered in the arms of yet another (Douglas Gilmore).

and M-G-M capitalised on that by issuing stills of him so doing, in tweeds and pullovers. After his arrival the dandified leading men graduated to playing lounge lizards or other less admirable species. Gable's appeal was well expressed by one of his directors, Clarence Brown: 'Yeah, Gable was the greatest male ever on the screen. Valentino may have been the greatest women's actor. But men liked Gable and women liked Gable. He had them all.'

However, since Gable first appeared as an unsavoury character we may turn to Norma Shearer for an explanation of the transformation: 'Gable made villains popular. Instead of the audiences wanting the good man to get the girl, they wanted the bad man to get her.' She was referring to *A Free Soul*, in which she tells him 'You're a new kind of man in a new kind of world', probably referring to the beatings he gives her. The flapper was amoral in thought if not in deed, but in the case of the 'new woman' her dresses are in his closet. 'You're swine walking with swine' she observes, to which he cheerfully retorts 'You're talking to the man you love'.

Miss Shearer represented the new woman better than anyone. Meeting an English aristocrat in *Riptide* (1934), written and directed by Edmund Goulding, she immediately begins an affair with this milord and they disport themselves at every pleasure centre between Palm Springs and the Côte d'Azur. As all good things come to an end, so does this, and she is floored to find it followed by an offer of marriage, it being axiomatic that mistresses were never rewarded with wedlock. Her subsequent sufferings may be due to her having taken that affair so lightly, but she remains chic and *soignée* through scandal and divorce; and at one point consummates her liaison with a playboy (Robert Montgomery)

A Free Soul referred to Norma Shearer, the daughter of respectable criminal lawyer: she was another who got what she wanted and what she wanted was a gangster, Clark Gable, a client of her father.

The Blue Angel is perhaps *the* classic tale of sexual obsession. A schoolteacher (Emil Jannings) goes to the nightclub of that name to discover why his pupils frequent the place – and his aim is to stop them. But from the moment Lola-Lola (Marlene Dietrich) slips off her panties on the stairs and slings them on his shoulder he is as enslaved as his pupils – in fact, more so, allowing himself to be publicly humiliated while also condoning her affair with a younger man. His degradation is so powerfully demonstrated that many spectators forget he escapes at the end.

on the grounds that her husband already thinks she has.

In *A Free Soul* Shearer's greatest thrill is to jump in her roadster and speed – and that was a similar symptom of restlessness in *The Single Standard*, in which Garbo stopped vamping for a while. The foreword sets it out: 'For generations men have done as they pleased . . . and women have done as men pleased . . .' The film begins on her musing on some men kissing their girlfriends good-bye as they prepare to go to a party with their wives, and she subsequently lets men kiss her on the least acquaintance. When a painter (Nils Asther) invites her to the South Seas on his yacht, we do not suppose they have separate cabins. She swims, wears his clothes and the wind ruffles her hair – it's a tropic wind, which like the harbour lights and palm trees is an indication of romantic yearnings, a desire to be away from it all, to be free.

Garbo was not to be a free woman for long. M-G-M soon returned her to the customary plot, in which bad luck or bad judgement brought her to the wrong man too soon, so that she is thoroughly tarnished by the time the right one hoves into view. The point about *Anna Christie*, her first Talkie, is whether the right man will find out about her past and what he will do when he

does. In the famous opening scene Marie Dressler says 'I got your number the moment you came in', to which Garbo wearily replies 'I got yours too. You're me, forty years on' – and you may well wonder why the exchange was excised from the German-language version which Garbo made simultaneously. This was a full-scale major movie about a harlot, but she was a repentant one, wanting to be rid of her sordid life: the subject was permissible because the source was a play by the highly esteemed dramatist Eugene O'Neill. It had also been filmed before – with Blanche Sweet in 1923 – as had *Romance*, in which Garbo is adored by a young clergyman, who is disillusioned when he learns the truth about her: however, when that knowledge fires him to take what he wants without the sanctity of the wedding band, it is she who is disillusioned. What is taken by the man who keeps her may not be given to the man she loves so purely. It was an old-fashioned film, and although Garbo was faced with similar problems in *Inspiration* she and her young admirer move in a world of aged lovers and their young mistresses, a world in which liaisons are much discussed and marriage never mentioned. But then, this was Paris.

59

In her first American film Marlene Dietrich played a cabaret entertainer in *Morocco*. The café's proprietor (Paul Porcasi, above) required her to entertain his clientele in other ways, too, but when she falls in love with a handsome legionnaire (Gary Cooper, right) the purity of their emotions is bewildering – at least to modern audiences.

The extraordinary popularity of Garbo counterbalanced the steps towards sexual honesty made in the names of Bow, Shearer and, to an extent, Crawford: since her personality made her an unlikely person to enjoy flirting or being slapped around, she led men to their doom. In *The Blue Angel* Marlene Dietrich teased her way into the pants of every man who came near her, but by the time she arrived in Hollywood a few months later her bosses had decided that she was a tawdrier, brasher version of Garbo, in the tradition of European vice which included Miss Bara (by implication) and Pola Negri. The American girls might fondle, but they would fall only temporarily: for the European ladies love was so all-consuming that they destroyed for it and were destroyed by it.

That seldom meant sexual love, which traditionally was connected with the giving (or selling) of favours, with riches and rewards. 'Every time a man has helped me there has been a price. What's yours?' Dietrich demands of Adolphe Menjou without preliminary in *Morocco*. His passion is such that he is prepared to marry or buy this cabaret artist on her own terms – which means covering her with wealth and accepting that, though he can have her body, that that is all he can

have. There is another kind of love, and she is victim of it: after one look at Gary Cooper, playing a penniless legionnaire, she tosses her key to him, his looks and/or virility being preferable to the more obviously wealthy men at the other tables. Because of his virility he uses the key, but they do not even kiss: if their passion is to be pure and lasting – True Love – they can do nothing so cheap as to tumble into bed. In response to her boldness he preserves his independence – both qualities being essential to their sexuality and hence their relationship, she very much aware of where her body has been in the past and he apparently acknowledging independence as the chief concern of his masculinity.

In her next four films, Dietrich played whores, usually in an exotic setting. She is already on the game in those set in some faraway place, but has to go through the hoops to sink so low in the one set in the US. The Depression caused Hollywood to look at prostitution, but the industry was not yet prepared to admit that the two were synonymous. Paramount launched Tallulah Bankhead in one such role, perhaps because she was being publicised as the first American sex star, but that publicity was also reminding picturegoers that she had been the toast of London while playing wildly sophisticated roles in the West End. In *Tarnished Lady* she is one of New York's elite, but she is also impoverished, so she marries for money. She decides that this was a mistake just after he has learned that his company has crashed, rushing off to the poor writer she had loved before: but he has comforted himself with another woman – the husband's ex-fiancée – so Tallulah goes

drinking in a low dive with a (male) chum, and when the husband sees them together he makes the inevitable conclusion and never wants to see her again. After months of unsuccessfully seeking work the only recourse is to the streets: and if no cinemagoer failed to recognise the 'shorthand' – a girl's legs strolling on the side-walk – it was comparatively new in an American movie.

In *Susan Lenox: Her Fall and Rise* Garbo starts out as Helga, a Swedish-American, distrusted by her uncle, who thinks she will grow up as 'sinful' as her mother. She is the object of an attempted rape by her fiancé (Alan Hale), who has drunk too much schnapps, but she escapes into the arms of Clark Gable, and they make an extraordinarily winning team, his huge and comforting masculinity in contrast to her insecurity and fragility. Not long graduated from playing slap-em-around gangsters, he is unfailingly courteous, but this was Garbo, to whom no red-blooded man could be immune. He does knock on the bedroom door and try the handle, but that is all. After a happy day fishing she says she will cook his supper, which encourages him to take this bird-like creature in his arms. Thus audiences, cheated of sexual intercourse the night before, could now be assured that it took place later in the day. The film might have finished there, but it is only minutes old. She leaves Gable's neck-of-the-woods when uncle and fiancé come searching for her and becomes a cooch-dancer in a carnival. Gable comes for her – just as its owner tells her that he expects to see her in his tent: Gable refuses to listen to her side of things, and when we next see her a stranger is proposing a meal in the restaurant car and she

Above: By 1931 everyone concurred in the opinion that Garbo was a great actress but M-G-M still couldn't see her as anything but a scarlet woman – on film, that is. There were numerous plot ploys to keep her a sinner but sympathetic, and most of them were used in *Susan Lenox: Her Rise and Fall*. It is also one of the few films in which she is seen to walk the streets – or in this case to ply her trade in a tropical tavern. But ah! there she will meet up again with her true love . . .

Right and far right: Scandal had ruined Clara Bow's career. Fox tried to resuscitate it with *Call Her Savage*, which was packed with as many scandalous elements as its 90-minute running-time would allow. Clara's exploits are such that she eventually takes to the bottle in an attempt to forget the past, but naturally she suffers in luxury.

responds with a wry smile and 'Why not?' When she
next meets Gable she is the mistress of a shady politician. As in *Inspiration* promiscuity is as natural as
breathing, yet the heroine's loss of purity must keep her
separated from the hero.

Dietrich, in *Blonde Venus*, goes back to work to pay
for the serious hospital operation needed by her husband (Herbert Marshall): work is singing in a nightclub,
where she gains several wealthy admirers. One looks
like Cary Grant (for the obvious reason) and with admirable good taste she chooses him; she accepts payment
for the operation from him, and she really shouldn't
have moved in with him while it is being carried out.
When her husband arrives home unexpectedly, she
prefers to disappear rather than give up their child. It
cannot be said, later, that she becomes a whore, because
she is had up for vagrancy, but she *looks* like a whore and
the 'nightclub' looks much like a brothel. These three
films have happy endings – a good way after the
heroine's low point – and of the forgiving men only
Gable takes a long time about it. If the oddysseys of
these ladies are curious, they are as nothing to the fate
meted out to Clara Bow in *Call Her Savage*, one of the

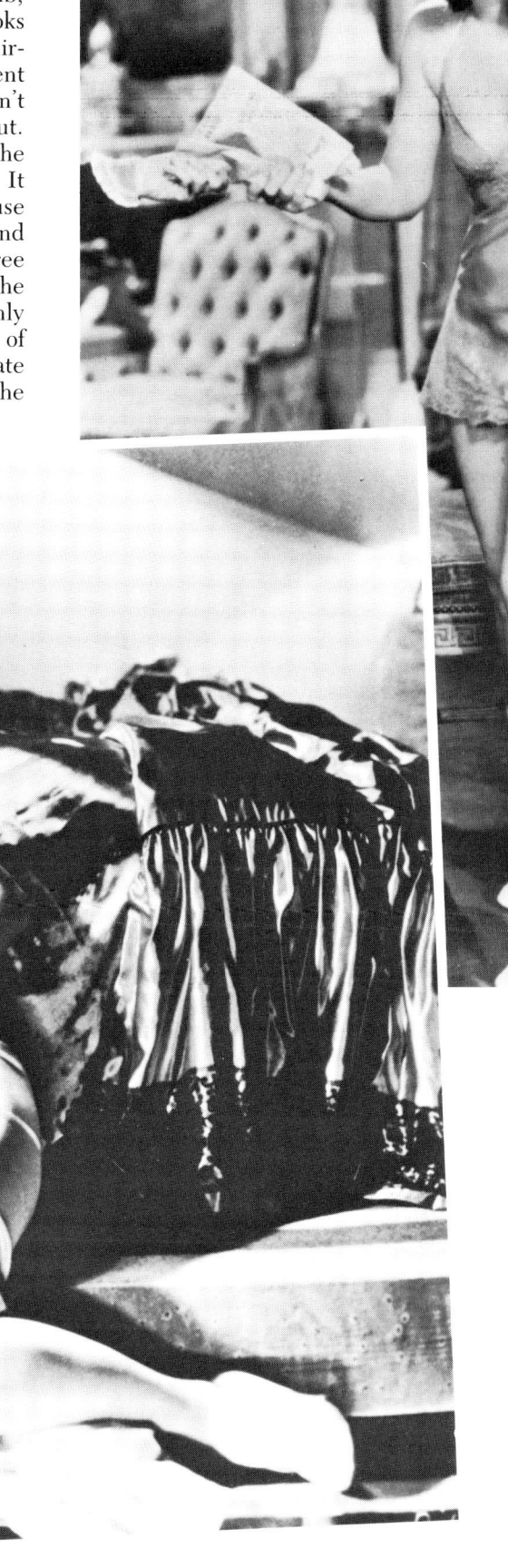

63

two films with which Fox tried to revive her career. She is a handful and a half, complaining to her Indian childhood friend Moonglow (Gilbert Roland): 'Why can't I be like other girls?' To tend to his snake-bite she appears to tear off her brassière; she turns from whipping the snake to whipping him, and when her father asks why she replies 'I was practising in case I got married'. When she does marry, her husband deserts her on the wedding day, since his motive was revenge on his mistress. Nevertheless, dying, he tries to rape her – and both he and her father (although he has disowned her) have put unlimited funds at her disposal. She

gambles them away and, needing medicine for her baby, has no recourse other than streetwalking: but the babe dies that night in a fire, while Moonglow arrives to tell her that her aunt has left her another small fortune. With that she moves into New York society for further exploits, including hiring a gigolo and demonstrating dipsomania, before deciding that she loves Moonglow after all.

There is one very good film about a prostitute – the version of *Waterloo Bridge* made in 1931. However, since its fame has been overshadowed by the 1940 film we may well ask who knows *Waterloo Bridge* who only

Waterloo Bridge know? The later, M-G-M version may be a romantic tale, but it is also absurd. Set in the First World War, it concerns a dancer (Vivien Leigh) who takes to streetwalking, believing her well-born officer fiancé (Robert Taylor) to be dead. When he reappears she cannot tell him the level to which she has sunk and she decides to sacrifice her happiness for the sake of society and his regiment. The 1931 version is also a tall story but charmingly directed by James Whale and not altogether implausible. A prologue added to Robert E. Sherwood's original play establishes Myra (Mae Clarke) as the sort of chorus girl who accepts a fox fur from a

casual admirer; two years later, unable to get a job, she is pounding the pavements when she meets a naive Canadian (Kent Douglass, later known as Douglass Montgomery). He does not realise why she has picked him up, which so bemuses her that they converse platonically, during which he is so enthralled that he wants her to meet his family, which amuses her: so (unlike Miss Leigh later) she has to be tricked into doing so. And there is no nonsense about the regiment.

It takes no perspicacity to realise that *Waterloo Bridge* is not about sex at all, though it may be a love story because two people are attracted to each other. One of them is a prostitute, a profession the American film industry was now endorsing: but not, from these patently dishonest accounts, in a plea for sympathy, but to titillate audiences. Women as ever were supposed to feel 'There but for the grace of God go I' – and men too, for these were the women whose favours they could purchase if, that is, they could afford world-famous movie stars.

Another lady who made sex movies without sex in them was Constance Bennett, who for a while was cast in tales about unmarried mothers. Things had moved on somewhat by the time she became the *Lady with a Past* in 1932, but the title proved to be ironic: she is wealthy, beautiful and intelligent but insufficiently 'shopworn' to attract the men of Manhattan. When one proposes to her, drunk, and reneges the following morning, she goes off to Paris to buy herself a gigolo or so, followed by the American, who decides to wed her 'before she gets worse'. A year later, in 1933, Miss Bennett turned up in *Bed of Roses* as a reformatory schoolgirl desperate for a life of wealth. To that end she picks a sugar daddy (John Halliday), claims to be a reporter and requests a drink for medicinal purposes only: when we next see them he is dead drunk in his apartment and she is scattering their clothes about the place before making for the bedroom – a not uncommon movie manoeuvre. We may be sure that Miss Bennett did not even have to offer herself to get her penthouse: like Dietrich in *Morocco* she is aggressive, but for the time being unsullied. However, where Dietrich moved quickly to true love, Miss Bennett has still to find him: and when she does – a river-boat captain (Joel McCrea) quite as poor as Dietrich's legionnaire – it is probable that his body appeals to her more than all the rich guy's geegaws. 'Why can't I have a guy like that in a place like this?' she moans, looking round her luxurious apartment. 'Why not?' responds her pal (Pert Kelton), 'You got doors, ain't you?', it being the purpose of heroine's friends to be wholly amoral, while heroines themselves had qualms and consciences – at least from time to time.

Constance Bennett was another of the screen's leading sinners, foolishly putting her trust in men who later reneged on their promise to lead her to the alter. Tired of playing drab unwed mothers, she changed her image – as in *Lady With a Past*, but found herself too 'pure' for New York's philanderers. One of them, David Manners, is standing beside her.

6.
A Man in the House is Worth Two in the Street

Above: Mae West in *She Done Him Wrong*, sharing a joke with her maid (Louise Beavers) while preparing for the latest man she has invited to come up and see her. It may have been Cary Grant who, in the course of the film, did not appear to accept the extended invitation. So, since Mae wrote her own scripts, she ensured that he did in the next film they made together, *I'm No Angel*, left.

'All I've got is a body. Made of flesh and blood. I'm not ashamed of it. It got me where I am today': this is not the heroine's friend speaking, but the heroine's rival, and the film is De Mille's *Madame Satan* (1930). Deciding to beat that lady at her own game, the heroine (Kay Johnson) says 'He wants 'em hot, does he? Well, I'll give him a volcano. It'll take the whole fire department to put it out', whereupon the film moves from De Mille's old preoccupations to that plot of Boccaccio's that Shakespeare used in *All's Well That Ends Well*. The climate, anyway, was now free: and when the virginal heroine (Sydney Fox) of *Strictly Dishonorable* decides to throw herself at a famous opera singer (Paul Lukas) she observes 'Maybe good women are good because it takes two to be bad and they can't find a ——' She is interrupted but the point has been made.

It was in this climate that Mae West could at last transfer her stage persona to the screen. Because Diamond Lil was too infamous as both a title and character, these became, respectively, *She Done Him Wrong* (1932) and Lady Lou. It was the first of a series of films in which Mae sashayed into the salon, sizing up the men, and though she didn't pause as her eyes gazed at the crotch she gave the impression that that was where her interest chiefly lay. Her preferred period was the turn of the century, because the gowns revealed the snowy ample bosom which would move as she placed her hand on her hip and slithered. 'Why don't you come up some time and see me? I'm home every evening', she says to Cary Grant in *She Done Him Wrong*, 'Come up sometime, I'll tell your fortune', and it's blatant, confident, even without the afterthought, 'You can be had'. Later she indicates her diamonds, 'It was a toss-up whether I went in for all this or sang in the choir. The choir lost.' He: 'Didn't you ever meet a man who could make you happy?' She: 'Sure, lots of times.' Her *double entendres* have passed into folklore and are too well-known to be repeated here. Her enjoyment of her shamelessness was (and remains) refreshing: this was one screen lady who had never suffered for sex. She gives this chapter its title.

Something similar may be said of Maurice Chevalier, and as, like Mae West, he was at Paramount, it could be assumed that sex was fun at this studio. Chevalier could make passes at the opposite sex which, despite her appearance, seemed so outrageous coming from Miss West – and he was indeed more courtly and somewhat more circumspect. There was the further great difference that sex in the Chevalier films was usually of the marital kind, and that he was inevitably guided by Ernst

Lubitsch, whose witty visual style could take the sting out of potentially *risqué* situations. Lubitsch did not mind *double entendre*, as in Chevalier's song, ostensibly about a sofa, in *The Love Parade*, 'Nobody's Using it Now', and there can be unsubtle moments, as in the denouement of this same movie, when the Queen (Jeanette MacDonald) acknowledges that her husband (Chevalier) is the boss about the palace, promising to be submissive 'from morning to night' but correcting herself, 'from night to morning'. Chevalier and MacDonald were ideal exponents of the Lubitschian view of humanity, he with his darting 'cheeky' looks at the camera and she with her yielding glances. There seemed to be (though in life there wasn't) a sexual attraction between them which Lubitsch utilised, so that the fully-clothed love scenes in *The Merry Widow* (1934, made at M-G-M) have a rare erotic charge. Each of these films is a box of delights, and we should include *Love Me Tonight*, directed by Rouben Mamoulian, and *Trouble in Paradise*, in which the stars are Herbert Marshall, Kay Francis and Miriam Hopkins. If I had to choose a favourite moment I would probably plump for the whispering women (MacDonald and Genevieve Tobin) in *One Hour with You*, of which the audience can only hear 'He can?' 'He can!', eventually revealed to be referring to his ability to make a face like an owl. Or the moment in that same film when Roland Young happily watches his wife leave with bag and baggage and the camera moves to show the maid beside him, smiling as happily as he. That is the Lubitsch touch.

Chevalier the playboy replaced Menjou the ageing rake; John Gilbert and Ramon Novarro – the most successful of Valentino's successors – would also soon disappear, their voices in Talkies at odds with their masculine appearances (though that is stretching the adjective a little in Novarro's case). This was the time of the Depression and audiences demanded new heroes: Chevalier to wink and look the other way, and tougher, more gritty leading men capable of triumphing over it. The Gables and James Cagneys – if we may pluralise such individual actors – were not the equivalent of the new woman, for the gangsters and con-men they played do not represent any movement in society – outside, that is, gangsters and con-men. Their morals were easy, and not only where sex was concerned. The gangster heroes were accompanied by ladies in négligés, but love was only a sideline – and the least of their evils. The Hollywood tycoons believed that love was woman's whole existence but to a man a thing apart, whereas for gangsters bootlegging was their business and drinking their hobby. Now it was shared with women. Mae Clarke in *Lady Killer* is swept into a hotel room by a man saying 'Just you and me, lapping up good liquor all the time', while a gang boss (Spencer Tracy) says to his girl in *Quick Millions* 'Let's get blotto'; he later adds 'And before we get blotto I'm gonna make another suggestion', which may not have been necessary, since for most audiences, after years of conditioning by movies, drink was associated with sex and the fast life.

Curiously enough, over-indulgence often resulted in marriage: any number of men got blotto and proposed, not able in the morning to remember anything – cer-

When Jeanette MacDonald played in the famous series of movie operettas with Nelson Eddy she experienced only the most noble of emotions towards him. Earlier, Lubitsch had co-starred her with Maurice Chevalier in which his yen for her was equalled by hers for him – even if sanctioned by marriage. Here she prepares for the first night of that in *The Love Parade*, though it's really just an excuse to let us see her in her lingerie.

tainly in *The Docks of New York* and *Anybody's Woman*. In *Two Seconds* a dance-hostess (Vivienne Osborne) has designs on a kindly workman (Edward G. Robinson) and though they start out the evening by intending to go to a lecture he is soon falling down drunk in a nightclub. In the morning he is married – and a good thing, too, since he appeared to have a crush a yard high and a mile wide on his fellow-worker (Preston Foster). To an extent this was typecasting, for Robinson was fond of Douglas Fairbanks Jr in *Little Caesar* and would be 'close' to Richard Arlen in *Tiger Shark*; but in *Two Seconds* Robinson shares a small room with his mate, with a double bed, and he specifically mentions that he's hoping for a win on the horses so that he can buy him some neck-ties. This *may* mean nothing, but what can be said for certain is that the whole tone of the film is misogynist. Homosexuality was acknowledged, at last, in *Call*

Her Savage and *Wonder bar*, in each case by a couple of waiters camping it up like mad. In *Quick Millions*, some girls are rounded up from a brothel and as we watch their thighs flashing as they hurry into the paddy-wagon a man's voice is heard saying 'But officer, I've got a wife and kiddies': and when we see the girls in court one of them is a man in drag. Obviously, if homosexuality had to exist at all, it had to be comic; lesbianism was not acknowledged, although a woman is seen reading *The Well of Loneliness* (see p. 81) in *Big City Blues*, and we may be surprised that it did not creep into *Call Her Savage* (since it has everything else). As I have said, it was glimpsed in a European context in the late Silent period, but during the early 1930s America had enough problems of its own and Europe was largely forgotten. It can be assumed that the Hollywood moguls thought lesbianism un-American, but other forms of sexual aberration also crept into movies. For instance what is to be made of Frances Dee in *Blood Money* (1933), as a socialite who gets her kicks from consorting with gangsters? Having been slapped and pushed about by one, she walks away and meets a girl crying because a prospective employer had insulted her and knocked her around. 'What's his name, honey?' asks Miss Dee, brightening and making off in that direction. When in *The Beast of the City* the cop (Wallace Ford) observes to a gangster's moll (Jean Harlow) that if she's not careful he'll beat her up and she wouldn't like that she replies 'Oh, I don't know, depends if it's done in the right sort of way'. Later she tells him, 'I never thought I'd have a yen for a copper. Are you going to reform me?' 'What for?' he replies, but then he is a corrupt cop.

There was no doubt of Warren William's dishonorable intentions in *The Mouthpiece*. Sydney Fox played the secretary enticed to his flat, above. On other occasions, right, one woman was not enough for him. Such heroes went out of style with the advent of a new breed of leading men and William became a supporting actor.

Obviously such men in other circumstances are unlikely to be respecters of women and in *The Mouthpiece* (1932) the corrupt lawyer (Warren William) covets anything in silk stockings. The whole mood of the film is towards vice and luxury. William makes clandestine dates with married women and for days on end goes on a bender, visiting underworld parties where the drinking is heavy and every man is mauling his moll. Most of all he wants to seduce the new typist (Sydney Fox), and he tries every trick in the book, including cajolery, flattery, persuasion and pretended reform. She is tempted, after being fooled into coming to his apartment, where he wears a silk dressing-gown and pours peach brandy into her. This same actor is more successful in *Employees Entrance* (1933), as the manager of a department store, but then the girl (Loretta Young) is a victim of the Depression. He offers her a job and a meal, in that order, and as she prepares to leave he says 'You don't have to go, you know' and she doesn't. It was unprecedented to find the same thing happening later, after the staff party, as by this time she is not badly off and is also married. Doubtless there was something about Mr William's screen personality which suited him for such roles for the equally dapper William Powell was also playing them at this time. Powell is a gigolo in *Ladies' Man*, telling the woman (Kay Francis) who wants to reform him, 'Norma, since I can remember anything, I can remember being picked up by women'.

It has to be said that that particular film made vice very dull, probably because the moguls felt that that was the best way to present male sexuality. As I said, it's only inferred that the tough guys used the girls who adorned their entourage. Today's macho heroes cannot get through a movie without one girl a reel throwing themselves at them. They only have to breathe to be irresistible. Clint Eastwood may feel that he's not the type to be the pursuer, though since so many of the women who bed him turn out to be treacherous he may feel that he's James Bond. The Warren Williams and William Powells are anything but macho, and when *Downstairs* required a hero with the morals of a rabbit he was played by a star well down the lists of the moguls' favourites. As the chauffeur, John Gilbert has to work his way through the female members of the household regardless of their physical aspect. His true goal is the butler's new bride, who after succumbing explains to her husband that love with Gilbert 'is something so dizzying that you don't know what is happening'. To an extent, Gilbert was the Eastwood of the 1920s, enormously popular and as a

William Powell in the title-role of *Ladies' Man*. The lady pleading with him is Carole Lombard, who wants him to render the same service to her as he does to her mother. Since those were more circumspect times the nature of the service was left to audiences' imagination.

movie hero bold, intrepid and a ladies' man; he had since fallen from grace and is here pictured in a most unflattering light – and precisely so that his conduct may not be confused with that of American men the film is another set, for no good reason, in Europe (in fact, in Vienna).

Gilbert's former Silent rival, Ronald Colman, on the other hand had become even more popular and admired with the coming of Talkies. Because of his accent he usually played an Englishman, so it can hardly be claimed that *Cynara* is set in Britain because he plays an adulterer; but arriving in cinemas just a few weeks after *Downstairs*, in 1932, it must still have reassured American puritans that illicit sexual relations were more common in Europe. Colman plays a wealthy lawyer who

drives his mistress to suicide. At least, that is one interpretation of what happens. When Colman's wife (Kay Francis) goes abroad, his best friend encourages him to have an affair with a working-class girl who has indicated she is 'willing'. They have an idyll in the country and he has told her kindly that it cannot last; but he does not appear to suffer and is happily reunited with his wife at the end.

It was not only in the big cities and because of the Depression that morals were easy. According to *Hot Saturday* the teenage kids of this small country town spent their weekends downing bootleg gin at picnics or in the mansion of the local playboy (Cary Grant) who – by implication – doesn't care who slips off to the bedrooms. Scott Fitzgerald had put this view of America's youth a decade earlier, but movies had not reflected it till now. Sex is the sole topic of conversation in Gregory LaCava's *Age of Consent* (1932). 'Don't they ever talk about anything else?' asks the hero (Richard Cromwell), who in the script's parlance is too 'honourable' to go further with his girl than kissing. However, when a friendly waitress (Arline Judge) asks him home for a drink, a boy's only human, isn't he? In movies honesty is always relative: when they wake from their drunken stupor he is still wearing his pants and she her dress. Appearances, however, are much against them, which is the film's true subject. Honesty of sorts wins through at the end, for the boy chooses copulation over college when faced with the choice: but only within the sanctity of marriage.

The film nevertheless conforms to the norm by making the woman the predator (as does *Cynara*, for the girl invites Colman to be her lover, adding that he would not be the first). By glossing over the promiscuity of men and concentrating on that of the women, films could take safety in the still-prevalent view that most women – ordinary women, that is – did not really enjoy sex; alternatively, despite the fact that these come-hither ladies were played by immensely wealthy women, the myth was maintained that for the female sex their bodies provided their sole means of survival. Since Garbo and Dietrich never *initially* sold themselves willingly, whatever followed was deemed forgivable; and the accompanying luxuries, as everyone knew, were women's prerogative. As the Depression wore on, the American gals trod the same path, their aims a square meal rather than silks and satins – and there was not one of them, whatever their iniquities and final fate, who could not be rehabilitated by the love of a Good Man.

These glimpses of delicious sin must have made many a man and maid wonder whether the path of virtue was the most rewarding one. The actual inroads into audience consciousness had been impeded by the lack of Sound: there was nothing subtle about the image of an ankle or a champagne glass, but it could be rendered so by an intertitle at odds with the picture. That way the censors would be as much satisfied as the sophisticates who favoured ambiguity, while for all audiences the 'language' of the Silent screen was so strong that each member would give as much credence to the images and intertitles as temperament dictated. The Talkies arrived with the Depression, but to a great extent audiences turned their back on the kind of subjects they had earlier admired. They demanded 'reality', which meant speakeasies, slang and easy morality. Cops were pitted against gangsters, and movie-makers found the mobster's molls more colourful than the formers' wives.

Wives (*Cynara* apart) got a raw deal, especially those in society. They tended to be stout, crisp, middle-aged, selfish and generally unattractive. Thus the one in *Chained* (1934) who turns up in just one scene to refuse handsome Otto Kruger a divorce. He wants to marry Joan Crawford, his secretary and subsequently his mistress, who, on a transatlantic trip, is romanced by Clark Gable. Poor Joan at this period was constantly having to choose between two men – two ideals, sort of. If she was

a society girl the choice was between a rake and a good man; if she was a working girl the choice was between true love and a sugar daddy. In *Possessed* (1931), like *Chained* directed by Clarence Brown from a story by Edgar Selwyn, the man was again Gable. She is first seen as a working girl looking longingly at a train stopped at the station, seeing through the windows a couple in evening dress dancing, the silhouette of a man shaving, a black maid ironing a pair of scanties, two couples dining. 'I mean to get away' she tells the drunken swell (Skeets Gallagher) on the observation platform. 'Off to the big city to be done wrong?' he asks, handing her his card. But when she rings his bell at 890 Park Avenue he refuses to clasp her to his 'bosom', in his words, so she bats her big eyes at his friend Gable and tells him that she is hungry. Without formality he asks her whether she is interested in his money and she replies that she would be foolish if she wasn't. In the restaurant she cannot read the menu, which is in French; but several diamond bracelets later she is selecting the menu in an impeccable accent, having acquired a *je ne sais quoi* and *quoi*! Marriage is not in their plans, but they are delighted when a friend appears to confer respectability by bringing up his wife – who turns out to be his latest bit of fluff, telling Joan that she 'sure picked herself a swell sugar daddy'. Like *Susan Lenox* this film suggests an American *demi-monde* equal to the French one in *Inspiration*, but consisting of attorneys and executives rather than writers and artists – and more discreetly portrayed.

At one point Gable asks Crawford 'Where's that girl who came to New York demanding everything from life and willing to risk everything for it?', which maybe why the film was banned by the British Board of Film Censors, which took an equally unsympathetic attitude to *Red-Headed Woman* as played by Jean Harlow, whose approach to sex made Clara Bow seem like Little Nell. (Later a goodish comedienne, she was hardly more adept at this time than in *Hell's Angels*.) When at one point she follows her prey into a telephone booth she has all the allure of a two-bit hooker. If she was popular with women it must have been because of her brazenness. She wore loose-fitting satins and no underwear; she attracted men with her pouts and her directness – this latter being the sole quality which fitted her for the role of the new 'independent' woman as envisaged by Katherine Brush in her novel. Its notoriety was such that M-G-M were determined to film it, and they commissioned Anita Loos to write the screenplay so that it might pass as a comedy. So the author of *Gentlemen Prefer Blondes* has Harlow questioning this philosophy in her very first line and then putting it to the test with her boss (Chester Morris), who resists till, drunk and frustrated, she breaks into his house one night. He divorces his wife and marries Harlow; neither custom nor their frequent rows change the way he reacts when she kisses him. He is putty. No one in town will accept her till his best friend (Henry Stephenson) arrives, and it turns out that he and she have met before – and recently; the whys and wherefores have to be conjectured. And so on, till she finishes triumphant, the richest woman in France, with a very aged companion and the handsome

Jean Harlow, pre- and post-Code. In both *Red Dust* (1932), below and right, and *China Seas* (1935) she has the hots for Clark Gable, and in the earlier film her crush is expressed in some very salty dialogue. In both movies they had been past lovers, and it takes him several reels pursuing more ladylike creatures before he realises that she is, after all, his sort of woman. Scorned in *China Seas*, left, she has a consoling drink with Wallace Beery.

young chauffeur (Charles Boyer) who had been comforting her some reels back.

Established as a tramp without a single inhibition, Harlow managed to make sex almost as amusing as Mae West; she had not a qualm of conscience either, but could be very touching when fixated on Gable in *Red Dust* and *China Seas*, with eyes for no other man. Another lady steadfast in sexual resolve was Barbara Stanwyck, encouraged in *Baby Face* by her success as an amateur hooker in the cheap speakeasy next to the factory. In the big city she smiles at the doorman and although the personnel clerk says that there are no jobs he suggests that since the boss is out they go into his office . . . Some reels later she is in the office of one of the bosses, and then he in her apartment; but one evening he cannot wait till later and he follows her into the washroom. We do not see them there, but an executive does and the man is sacked on the spot – an incident, however, which does not impede her upwardly mobile progress, since that executive is himself soon at home in her apartment. Vice, she finds, is not only

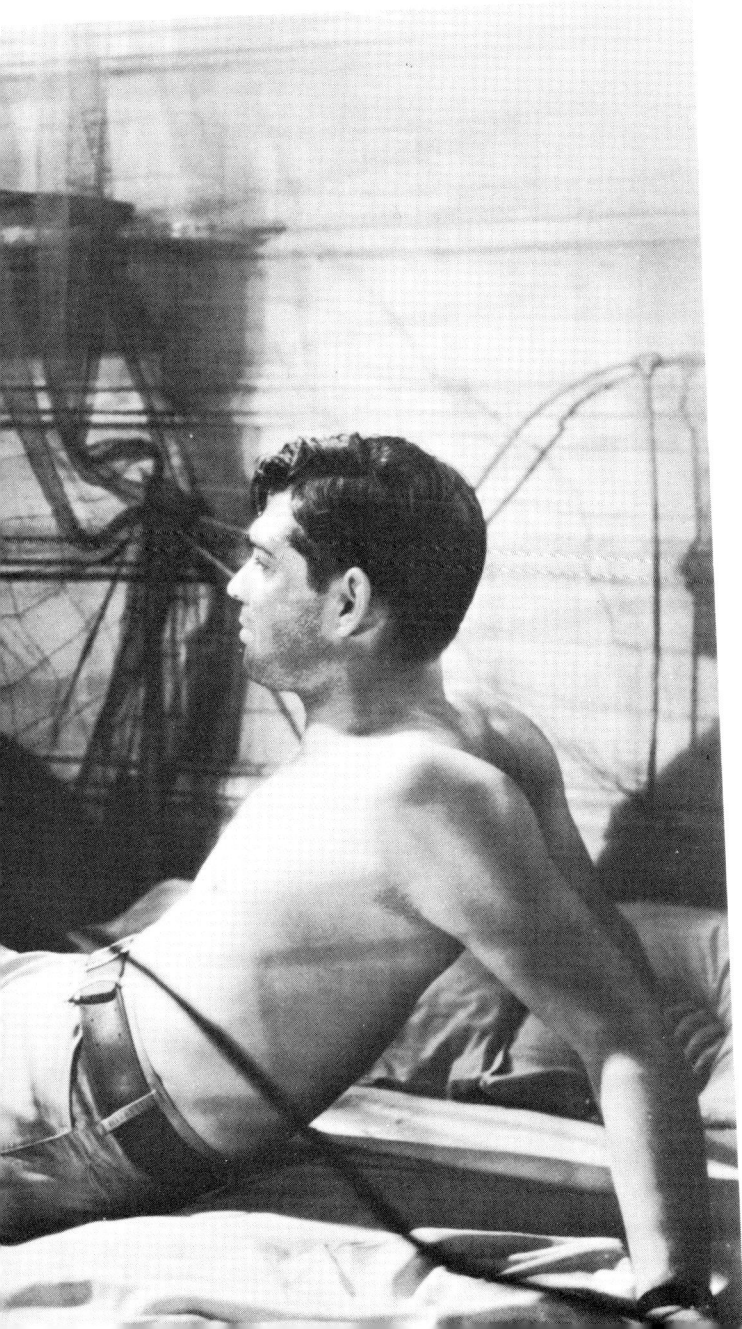

nice but profitable: and Stanwyck has to work harder at it, because she does not have Harlow's contours.

Such vice, of course, could not go unchecked, and editorials throughout the US thundered against Hollywood's attitude. Chastity was as old hat as the victim falling down drunk in *A Fool There Was*. In *Bureau of Missing Persons* Pat O'Brien strolls into Bette Davis's hotel room, lies on her bed and suggests breakfast together on the morrow. Like most of the best of these movies, this was made by Warner Bros, whose writers were the most cynical: in *The Keyhole*, as the hotel telephonist warns several Mr Smiths that the place is being raided, a whole hoard of middle-aged men emerge guiltily from as many rooms (and in the plot, Kay Francis is revealed as not really married to her elderly husband, whose suspicions of her conduct are good enough reason for her to ditch him for someone else). There was no more rape and repentance. To the dismay of bluenoses, couples went to bed together, although they were never seen to do so: would that be next? Among the other ladies revelling in pre- or extra-marital sex were Claudette Colbert, Carole Lombard, Margaret Sullavan, Myrna Loy, Katharine Hepburn, Irene Dunne, Ann Harding, Bette Davis, Ginger Rogers, Joan Blondell, Dolores Del Rio, Helen Hayes and Sylvia Sidney. Marion Davies even played herself, in *Blondie of the Follies*, a showgirl kept by an older man – though in the film, unlike life, she rejected him for a younger man. In *Frisco Jenny* Ruth Chatterton, seduced and abandoned, avenges herself by running an expensive bordello and becoming the power behind the politicians; in *The Story of Temple Drake* Miriam Hopkins is imprisoned in one and finds she likes it. Clara Bow, once using 'It' to attract men's interest, was now openly selling it. As for Mae West . . . She was the chief target for abuse, but those thundering against her were also remembering the red-headed women and baby faces.

It was not that the Hays Office had done nothing. For years its officers refused to sanction a film of Theodore Dreiser's *An American Tragedy* because the chief protagonist gets a girl pregnant and murders her when he meets a richer one. They finally gave in to Paramount, but were adamant when that studio wanted to film William Faulkner's *Sanctuary* – well, under that name, anyway. Those who have read it will know that the heroine's name is Temple Drake. As we shall see, a Production Code existed – and as demands for its implementation grew Ginger Rogers and her fellow chorus girls were singing 'Shake Your Powder Puff' in *Upper World*, a song peddling a message much like those of the gold diggers who sang and hoofed so memorably for the same studio, Warner Bros. These wicked ladies and their lecherous suitors were swept away. The films enshrining them were swept under the carpet, not to be revived – or if they were, like *A Farewell to Arms* and *State Fair*, the offending passages were excised. New lies were required, far more heinous than the old – and, alas, much less interesting.

7.
With One Foot on the Floor

The Hays Office, created out of fear and scandal in 1922, had wielded power wisely enough, in view of its purpose, which was to prevent the confusion liable to be caused by hundreds of local censorship boards. The morality clause of artists' contracts threatened the career of Clara Bow in 1930 when she was involved in two scandals: she confessed to having paid off the wife of a Dallas doctor who sued her for alienation of affection and she was sued by a casino in Nevada after stopping some cheques to pay for gambling debts. Miss Bow was far too important to Hollywood – and Paramount in particular – to be dropped, and the Hays Office responded the only way it knew how, in the circumstances: it drew up a Production Code outlining what might and might not be shown in movies. Its existence, however, had even less effect than the guide lines issued seven years earlier. In 1931 a new scandal dwarfed Miss Bow's previous peccadilloes, when she sued her former

Dante always provided an excuse for getting naked bodies on the screen, even after the implementation of the Production Code in 1934. A year later Fox offered *Dante's Inferno*, which had nothing in common with the Divine Comedy and only a little with the film with the same name produced by the studio a decade earlier.

secretary for embezzlement – actually in retaliation for an attempt at blackmail. Daisy de Voe faced thirty-seven charges but went to jail for only one, and the picture she painted of Miss Bow's life was a lurid one involving paid lovers, drugs and drunkenness. The press had a field day, demanding that Paramount cast Clara out into the wilderness – which is what they did, but only after two of her films failed completely at the box-office.

Thus the public in a fit of self-righteousness reassured

Garbo in *Camille*, with Robert Taylor as her unworthy Armand. Note the way she clutches him while dying: the way she held her leading men was one of the factors that made her so erotic a screen presence.

the industry of its contempt for Hollywood's loose living – albeit that Miss Bow's follies were only in keeping with her image. The Hays Office saw no reason to implement the Production Code till 1934, and then in response to the content of movies. Mae West may have been the individual chiefly blamed, but as far as anyone knew her private life was beyond reproach. The Code was put into effect on 1 July 1934, without much publicity: as far as the general public was concerned it now knew that in movies crime must be punished as night follows day. It was just, ennobling, and moral to see murders and robbers take the rap; and far better to know nothing of such other criminals as fornicators and homosexuals.

The Code was not entirely explicit on the depiction of violence, but sex was another matter, viz:

'The sanctity of the institution of marriage and the home shall be upheld. Pictures shall not infer that low forms of sex relationships are the accepted or common thing.'

'Scenes of passion should not be introduced when not essential to the plot.'

'Excessive and lustful kissing, lustful embracing, suggestive postures and gestures, are not to be shown.'

'Seduction or rape should be never more than suggested . . . they are never the subject of comedy.'

'Sex perversion or any inference to it is forbidden.'

'Miscegenation (sex relationships between the black and white races) is forbidden.'

'Sex hygiene and venereal diseases are not subjects for motion pictures.'

'Children's sex organs are never to be exposed.'

'Indecent or undue exposure is forbidden.'

Since the industry did not change overnight, the public hardly noticed. Scriptwriters were working on material already purchased in the freer climate and it was easy enough to infer that bed was not the only logical place to end up for a couple in love. In any case the Hays Office did not demand the immediate banishment of all human frailty. It was feeling its power. The films of late 1934 and early 1935 are not so different in tone from the pre-Code era. M-G-M released two movies with Jean Harlow in the spring and summer of 1935, *Reckless* and *China Seas*, in both of which she wisecracks in familiar manner, in the one as a scandal-prone Broadway star and in the other as an adventuress on the high seas known as China Doll. In the latter Gable is her co-star and their relationship is much like that in *Red Dust*; but by the time they were reunited in *Wife vs. Secretary* (1936) and *Saratoga* (1937) the toning down was remarkable – or is to us now. Harlow's hair has been darkened somewhat; she enunciates her words more carefully and uses infinitely less slang. In the first film she is Gable's secretary and the plot has him tempted by her while away on a conference, but tempted only, whatever his wife (Myrna Loy) believes; in *Saratoga* their mutual attraction is conveyed by dialogue without either zing or innuendo. For Miss Loy, too, there was no innuendo in the later sequels to *The Thin Man*, and in the general scrubbing job the characters of Nick and Nora Charles lost their once considerable penchant for boozing. The personalities of Miss Loy and William Powell were strong enough to see them through the change and if the later Harlow is uninteresting compared to her younger self the only artist to suffer was unquestionably Mae West. In the first three films she made after the introduction of the Code she could still joke about her past, her somewhat unreal quest for social position, her penchant for men and money but only the last of these was possible in the two 1937 movies; and since she had apparently run out of good jokes about greed the films are dull. Miss West filmed again in 1939 and 1943, but was very much a back number.

Garbo played an adulteress in *Anna Karenina* (1935), a courtesan in *Camille* (1936) and Napoleon's mistress in *Conquest* (1938), but the films, unlike her earlier ones, have no erotic charge beyond what she brings to them. The Hays Office passed the script of what turned out to be Garbo's last film, *Two-Faced Woman* (1941), in which she impersonates an imaginary twin sister, more frivolous and glamorous than herself, in order to reawaken her husband's interest in her. This means that he, Melvyn Douglas, has to commit adultery, and that caused an uproar – not least with the Legion of Decency, moral brother to the Hays Office and founded at the time of the implementation of the Code by a group of American Roman Catholic bishops. The Legion in this case bought sufficient influence to bear on M-G-M to insert an extra scene in which Douglas discovers his wife's scheme. The fact that this brouhaha caused Garbo to retire makes her a candidate as another victim of the movies' new moralism.

Harlow died after *Saratoga* (in fact, during its making; a double replaced her in some scenes); Clara Bow had retired; the other actresses of their era soldiered on, usually as brittle women of the world. Adultery was not exactly excluded from their pastimes, but increasingly had to be assumed by audiences. Margaret Sullavan appeared in two remakes of early Talkies, *The Shopworn Angel* (1938) and *Back Street* (1941), in both of which she is a kept woman. In the first instance True Love transforms her, humanising her and making her realise the error of her ways; in the second the man is married and since they cannot wed she has to snatch at happiness in the odd moments when he can visit, finally becoming an embittered old lady. The plot of *Love Affair* (1939) also requires Irene Dunne to be a kept woman and it is implied that that is why it takes so long for Charles Boyer to find her again – and crippled at that, nature's way of paying for illicit love. In *Another Dawn* (1937) Kay Francis has an affair with one of her husband's fellow-officers (Errol Flynn), but eventually decides that she is unworthy of either man. In *The Rains Came* (1939) Myrna Loy atones for her adultery – with an Indian prince (Tyrone Power) – by redemption in tending the sick and wounded.

The Rains Came had been such a successful book that the Hays Office had to bow to the inevitable. The most famous instance is *Gone With the Wind* (1939) when Hays finally gave in and permitted Rhett Butler (Clark Gable) to say that banned word, 'Frankly, my dear, I don't give a damn'. The popularity of Margaret Mitchell's book meant the retention of Rhett's friend Belle Watling, and though her profession wasn't exactly mentioned it wasn't transformed into a dance hostess, as were most movie hookers at the time; and of course *Gone With the Wind* contained the only rape in a Hollywood movie in years, when Rhett, finally exasperated by Scarlett's excuses, carries her upstairs to assert his marital right. Scarlett O'Hara (Vivien Leigh) is probably the most famous movie baggage of all time; she also – we assume – only makes love with the men she marries, though she would undoubtedly have given her All to Ashley Wilkes if he had given her more encouragement.

Bette Davis's earlier run-through for Scarlett, in *Jezebel* (1938), had been equally discriminating. She had shocked Southern society by going to the ball in a red dress, wanting to appear, literally, a scarlet woman; but her scheming ultimately was to reclaim her fiancé (Henry Fonda), now married, and sex didn't come into it – except incidentally. Davis had made her reputation as the slut in *Of Human Bondage* (1934), based on Somerset Maugham's novel of the obsession of a medical student (in the film, Leslie Howard) with a waitress. Davis was neither conventionally pretty nor glamorous; but she was a considerable actress and able to play sexual circumstances without incurring the wrath of the Legion of Decency (the Hays Office approved or vetoed all scripts, and often advised on which novels or plays were likely to run into difficulties with the Office). To be entirely accurate, Davis did not have to play the situations, which happened off-screen, but she had to face the consequences: in *The Old Maid* (1939), based on a novel by Edith Wharton and a Broadway dramatisation, she has an illegitimate baby and suffers because she cannot bring it up as her own; in *All This and Heaven Too* (1940) she is a governess who loves her charges' father (Charles Boyer), but suffers when he is arrested and guillotined for the murder of his insane wife; and in *The Letter* (1940), based on Maugham's play, she murders her lover and endures the torment of arrest and trial. That is a simplification: the twist of Maugham's original short story and the play is that the woman is believed when she claims that she killed an intruder in self-defence but both her lawyer and husband learn the truth. To remove the acquittal is to destroy the whole point of the tale, but the Hays Office refused to sanction an adulteress-murderess going unpunished. In the original the lover had tired of the affair because he also has a Chinese mistress, and this film finishes with this lady, dagger in hand, preparing to revenge herself on the woman who had killed her beloved.

Movie adultery was never more attractive than when the beloved was Ingrid Bergman, fresh, young, girlish and radiant. In *Intermezzo: a Love Story* (1939) she is different from every other star of her time, apparently wearing no make-up and her hair simply combed – curiously, she looked somewhat more artificial in the original Swedish version, which she was brought to Hollywood to repeat. In the American version the wife (Edna Best) is smart and attractive, though she gets insufficient footage for audiences to care much about her. The straying husband is played by Leslie Howard at his most casual and charming; he is a violinist and Bergman is his daughter's piano tutor, invited to accompany him on a tour. We know they are in love before

That's a bordello, that is, and its madame is the lady with Clark Gable. The Hays Office refused to allow such words to be mentioned in *Gone With the Wind* but reasoned that those millions who had read the book would know about such things, while other spectators would think of dance halls and hostesses. Ona Munson played Belle Watling, the lady in question.

they leave. The progress of that love is not charted but suddenly they are together in a small hotel on the Riviera. How much together? We honestly don't know, till he leaves early one morning for a fishing trip and calls out goodbye, implying – doubtless this was a Hays Office requirement – that they have separate rooms. That night he comes back to find her gone. She had observed 'that love like ours is wrong. It drags us down into remorse and fear.' Earlier a mutual friend had said that 'no happiness can be built on the unhappiness of others'. As far as we can tell neither of the lovers is caused much distress by the parting and the husband returns, apparently unchanged, to a forgiving wife. Few people at the time, we may be sure, considered this anything but a happy ending.

Miss Bergman's natural appearance and manner qualified her to play ladies of doubtful virtue. Today, at least, when we see *Casablanca* we do not suppose her love affair with Bogart – in the Paris flashback sequences – to have been platonic; but it is still difficult to discover what happens in *For Whom the Bell Tolls* (1943). The fame of the book and the prestige of its author, Ernest Hemingway, caused the Hays Office to cede to Para-

mount, though not without many battles and not all the way. Bergman does share a sleeping-bag with Gary Cooper and she does cheerfully admit to being shameless. When he leaves to go to certain death he says 'I am you and you are me. You're all there'll be of me', but you would have had to have read the novel to know that he was referring to her pregnancy.

Those who have read Conrad's novel *Victory* will know that the all-women orchestra supplemented its income by assignations with the customers, and so they do in the 1918 version, and that of 1931, retitled *Dangerous Paradise*. After all, they would hardly have turned up unmarried in Sourabaya without having been around a bit. The heroine, Alma, is helped by the loner, Heyst, because she is trying to avoid the lecherous attentions of the hotel proprietor, Schomberg. As a psychological thriller John Cromwell's 1940 version is the equal of the earlier ones; but the raunchiness they had has gone, with nothing to replace it. Alma's own past, sufficiently evident for her to imply that she would accommodate Heyst if he will help her, has become in the 1940 version one weak statement, 'I'm not twenty'; while the most curious (because unnecessary) change required by the Hays Office was Schomberg's offer to send his wife back to Germany if Alma will become his mistress.

'It would not have seemed normal if Joe Breen [of the Hays Office] had not complained about our script' said Hal Wallis, who produced *The Maltese Falcon*. Those who know only the classic 1941 version may be astonished to find Sam Spade sleeping with Miss Wunderly in the one made ten years earlier, but Breen wouldn't allow this; he would not allow Sam to say to his secretary, 'You'll come tonight'; and the implication that Joel Cairo is homosexual was changed from 'Just smell those gardenias' to 'Hmm! Gardenias'. Since Breen also objected to the characters' hard drinking and to Mr Guttman's 'By God, sir!' (it became 'By gad, sir!') we may well wonder how much better Hollywood's good films might have been.

Anyway, sex did not go underground in the pre-Code era; it was merely seen through a dark mirror. The coming of Talkies had reduced the age of children in cinemas, since the tots could listen if they were not yet able to read. Before long it was the era of the child star – Deanna Durbin, Judy Garland, Shirley Temple and Mickey Rooney, and one or other of the last two of these always prevented Gable, the 'King' of Hollywood, from taking his place at the head of the annual official box-office poll. Though a few critics pined when Mae West's fangs were cut, I can find no printed regrets about the end of the great demotic movies. Audiences had enjoyed those sinning shopgirls and soiled showgirls – but vicariously, it now seemed. Hollywood had reasserted the traditional and only view now possible of sex, that it was best left undiscussed and, except when necessary, undone. Beds, seldom hitherto used in movies, were now seen and used all the time: but they were single beds with reading lamps – reading seeming to be the chief occupation for which they were used, with maybe some conversation. The habit was so all-pervading that it spread to British films – even the very few about the working-classes – and that was because their producers were hoping for distribution in the US. Any double-bed glimpsed had only one occupant, and should this be a she, about to be kissed, the camera ensured that we remarked the man's foot planted firmly on the floor.

It was quickly recognised that romantic comedy was impossible without the pursuit of the sexes, and if there is one theme of the 1930s and 1940s which was staggeringly over-exposed it is one we have already examined – that of the married couple each of whom flirt with another in order to rekindle the spark of marital love. It's useless to complain that no one gets hurt, but I am at least always hopeful that they will – because most variations on this theme are so banal. The other most frequently employed themes are probably: the girl in pursuit of a wealthy husband but who settles for the poor boy who loves her in reel one; the honest, decent girl wrongly thought to be an old man's darling; the career woman who eventually rejects her stuffy fiancé in favour of a man completely her opposite; the in-name-only married couple who take several reels to realise that they are in love; and the non-consummation of marriage – due to family, housing or hotel problems. These are

not the comedies of the period you will recall, for the memorable ones are those with original plots – give or take something like Leo McCarey's *The Awful Truth* (1937), in which Irene Dunne and Cary Grant divorce and do not remarry till the penultimate reel; the last reel itself keeps us theoretically in suspense as to when or whether they'll sleep together again.

There is, however, hardly a spark of sex in these films: their writers did not use euphemisms nor did their directors require what we might feel to be the requisite expressions – but most of the players were masters of their craft, bringing wit to situations sexual *au fond* but desexed in the handling. At the beginning of this period a shared apartment for an unmarried couple meant showing sofas, settees, spare-beds, eiderdowns, or any other such paraphernalia, but so complete was the conditioning that by the early 1940s few spectators would suspect any impropriety. The props were no longer needed. In 1934 Frank Capra had a memorably funny scene in *It Happened One Night*, when a blanket is hung, in a motel room, between the beds of Clark Gable and Claudette Colbert; in *The Devil and Miss Jones* (1941) Jean Arthur agrees to let her boyfriend (Robert Cummings) spend the night at her place – though admittedly we later see him sleeping on a rooftop. Two years later this same actress shares her apartment with either or both Charles Coburn and Joel McCrea, in *The More the Merrier*: that is the central situation and later, in the plot, a threat to her reputation. But only for a fleeting second is it suggested that she may be in danger.

If then, heterosexual couples could be safely left together, what of homosexuals? Of course, there weren't any, beyond the 'camp' valets and hotel managers of the Astaire-Rogers films. Yet I know of three homosexual reference in the films of the late 1930s: in *The King Steps Out* (1936) Raymond Walburn orders the ballet girls not to flirt with the soldiers, adding to the ballet master that he trusts that he won't, either; in *Never Say Die* (1939) an innkeeper spies on Bob Hope and Andy Devine in compromising positions in one of his beds (in fact Hope has joined their toes by a string because he believes Devine can prevent him from being murdered); and in *East Side of Heaven* (1939) Joan Blondell bursts into tears when she overhears Bing Crosby and Mischa Auer murmuring endearments (she doesn't know they're talking to a baby). The two last of these are variations on old vaudeville routines, but no matter how innocent they are more explicit than references in the pre-Code films.

Male homosexuality remained the great taboo, except for two British plays, one about Oscar Wilde (which due to censorship had to be done in a club theatre) and *The Green Bay Tree*, which had a similar plot to *Michael* and was just as lacking in explicitness. Lesbianism was more acceptable, at least in America, which permitted the publication of a British novel on the subject, *The Well of Loneliness*, banned in 1928 in its country of origin after the successful prosecution of the author, Radclyffe Hall. In 1934 the Broadway critics admired a play by Lillian Hellman, *The Children's Hour*, in which a spiteful child accuses two of her teachers of having an affair. Sam

Rita Hayworth laying the blame on Mame (or so she sang) in *Gilda*, while attempting a modest striptease.

Goldwyn bought the screen rights and the (doubtless apocryphal) story goes that when told it was about lesbians he replied 'We'll change their nationality'. The Hays Office made him change the title, to *These Three*, and the plot now concerns a child who accuses one teacher (Miriam Hopkins) of having an affair with the fiancé (Joel McCrea) of another (Merle Oberon).

And there the matter ought to rest; but there is a handful of Hollywood movies which parade homosexual references which, at that time, would only have been apparent to the cognoscenti – or, at least, were not recognised as such by either the Hays Office or studio executives. The sophisticated newspapermen who came into movies as writers at the coming of Sound loved to get the better of the executives, whom they despised; with the rules now so firm as to what they could and could not do they played the game more keenly. Take, for instance, *Spawn of the North*, directed in 1938 by Henry Hathaway and co-written by Jules Furthman, who contributed to some of the buddy-buddy movies directed by Howard Hawks. Henry Fonda and George Raft are boyhood friends, so it's natural enough for them to get drunk when they're reunited. Hearing their drunken singing Dorothy Lamour observes 'I hope they've got their clothes on', an enigmatic remark till we see them undressing in order to throw themselves in the creek. So that's all right then, till we see them soaping each other, which is all right, too, if a situation not found in a John Wayne movie. The matter has an added piquancy if you know that the script was written for Cary Grant and Randolph Scott, whose house-sharing had been celebrated by Paramount by the issuing of publicity pictures showing them in cosy domesticity. But time went by and the world became somewhat less innocent, causing Paramount to think twice about this particular teaming.

When Robert Montgomery meets George Sanders in *Rage in Heaven*, they become so inseparable that Montgomery's mother sarcastically refers to Sanders as 'your beloved Ward Andrews' (the character's name); Montgomery admits that he's the only person who made his years at university bearable. He throws Ingrid Bergman at him, but then perversely decides to marry her himself. But she notices: 'Why must you always drag Ward into everything?' Montgomery later goes mad with jealousy, suspecting them of infidelity, but it is Sanders's picture, not Bergman's, that he has in his desk drawer at work.

That film was made at M-G-M, which also put out *Johnny Eager* around the same time. Reviewers of this film remarked that the source of Van Heflin's alcoholism was caused by a crush on his buddy Robert Taylor: but I can find no contemporary acknowledgement of the cause of Montgomery's paranoia or the relationship between Glenn Ford and George Macready in *Gilda*. Rita Hayworth is Gilda, the epitome of the screen sex goddess – and in her songs is as close to eroticism as the screen dared get. In a limpid black satin dress that starts (or stops) low on her bosom, she intones (she was in fact dubbed) 'Put the Blame on Mame', removing long black gloves in the manner of the famous striptease artist Gypsy Rose Lee (who made some films at this time,

originally under her real name, Louise Hovick, as her stage name was considered too notorious). Hayworth also invites the assembled nightclub crowd to undress her, explaining that she is a —— but the Hays Office had Ford slap her before she could get the word out. Most of the *femmes fatales* and wicked ladies of the 1940s yearned for a succession of men. Those who knew the word, which wasn't then much used, would call this nymphomania, but there wouldn't be much to be seen on the screen beyond a kiss or so. Gilda does, we gather, slip off to hotel rooms with men whom she's just picked up, so we assume that she is indeed a whore: and men only have to see her to want her. As Ford loved her Back Then and as Macready marries her, how *could* there be anything between the two of them? Yet, Macready the toff gives Ford the sailor his card instantly on meeting and makes him his right-hand man in his nightclub. 'You've no idea how faithful and obedient I can be' says Ford with feeling. When Macready returns with Hayworth in tow, Ford shows an antagonism hardly justified by the revelation of their earlier relationship, and he hands his door key to Macready, who is nonplussed. 'What's this?' he asks. 'Tact' rejoins Ford. These matters are ambiguous and by no means daring today, but in movies then men didn't give other men keys to their apartments.

One film focussed the spotlight on male effeminacy if not homosexuality, and it was produced, not surprisingly, by Hal Roach, whose two-reel comedies had been getting occasional laughs from that subject since the Silent days. Roach's first feature had been based on one of Thorne Smith's racy novels, *Topper*, and it had been followed by two sequels. Adapting Thorne Smith created long discussions with the Hays Office, which allowed very little of the raciness. Topper himself, played by Roland Young, is a respectable banker plagued by ghosts or a ghost, Marion (Constance Bennett, in the first two of the trio), whose sense of humour is somewhat off-colour: in *Topper*, she leaves behind a pair of her panties so that his wife shall find them; in *Topper Takes a Trip* she tugs off the swimming trunks of Topper's rival – under the sand, but women, even spectral ones, pulling off men's pants or leaving their own around were rare gags at this time. To digress further, there is a strange, irrelevant scene in Roach's *The Housekeeper's Daughter*, in which Joan Bennett looks at a chastity belt in the shape of two metal jewel-studded garters. The professor explains that men fitted these to their wives in times of war, sufficient information for those spectators who knew the function of a chastity belt. Miss Bennett fixes the garters round her thighs and then can only walk with difficulty – and as she does so, a bell rings. Anyone who could get that past the censor was unlikely to balk at filming Thorne Smith's *Turnabout*, which Roach directed in 1940. A husband (John Hubbard) and wife (Carole Landis) go to bed after a quarrel, each wishing to be in the others' shoes: that night their wish is granted, though we only know this physically because he speaks with her voice and vice-versa. So when he goes to the office his colleagues are shocked by his effeminacy, while her friends think that she has turned butch. At the end of the day they admit the experiment has been a disaster, and that's almost all there is to that aspect of the plot except for the appearance of Franklin Pangborn, who specialised in pompous but camp hotel clerks and managers for over two decades. His finest hour may have been the Silent, *Exit Smiling*, where as the *jeune premier* of a touring company he screams at Beatrice Lillie, who has entered his sleeper by mistake, 'I never gave you the least encouragement'. If not, it is here, as an irate buyer charmed by the wife in the husband's body: they are found cooing together and at the end he says something about getting better acquainted – which may be the only overt homosexual line Pangborn spoke in a long and prolific career.

Scandalous heterosexuality made a brief comeback during this time, initially with *Tobacco Road* in 1941. Erskine Caldwell's novel about the dirt-poor and ignorant folks of the backwoods of Georgia had been dramatised by Jack Kirkland in 1933 and had been running ever since, creating a reputation for salaciousness that was not entirely unjustified, particularly in the scene where the ageing sharecropper, accompanied by his daughter, looks through the window of the shack to see his son consummate his marriage to his sexy bride. This is not in the movie, which was bought by 20th Century-Fox and assigned to the director John Ford, who at that point had just finished his much admired and serious film of John Steinbeck's *The Grapes of Wrath*, which was also about the problems of America's rural poor. Further merit was conferred on *Tobacco Road* by the absence of stars, suggesting both serious purpose (very, very few films without stars returned a profit) and an unwillingness to draw crowds to the box-office. The film's sole concessions to the play's notoriety are in two lines spoken by Ward Bond as Lov, who takes Ellie May (Gene Tierney) as mistress or girlfriend when her sister Pearl runs away from him. He cannot understand why Pearl ran off, 'I wasn't doin' nothin' to her but tying her up with some rope', and her replacement, he is permitted to say, is at twenty-three far too old for him (Bond was just under forty at the time).

A posed publicity still from *The Outlaw*. Howard Hughes planned the film as a showcase for his big-bosomed discovery, Jane Russell, and so it was, but these other denizens of the Old West seemed often to be less taken with her than with each other. They are, from left to right, Thomas Mitchell, Walter Huston and Jack Buetel.

It was possible to claim that *Tobacco Road* was an accurate portrait of people who behaved as they did because they knew no better; it was also possible to reconstruct Caldwell's material, because its main subject was poverty. Neither element prevailed with *The Outlaw*, a screen original whose *raison d'être* was sex. Ben Hecht wrote the screenplay, a new version of the adventure of Billy the Kid, which came into the hands of Howard Hughes, who was looking for a subject with which to make his return to the film industry. He also regarded the chief female role as one to launch a new sex-queen as he had launched Jean Harlow, who had had no replacement – though at the time Hughes read Hecht's script Warner Bros were promoting the warm and witty Ann Sheridan as 'The "Oomph" Girl', issuing photographs of her in sweaters or smiling seductively from a pile of cushions. Hughes started a search for his own sweater girl, and at a dentist's he found her – the receptionist, whom he described as 'the most beautiful pair of knockers I've seen in my life'. This was Jane Russell; for her leading man he chose a small-part actor, Jack Beutel, whose name he promptly changed to Jack Buetel. Howard Hawks was engaged to direct, at which time the script was completely rewritten by Jules Furthman. Hawks envisaged a budget of under $500,000 and began filming in Arizona, but quit after three weeks of Hughes's interference. Hughes took over direction, and filming dragged on for nine months, mainly in attempts to bring the two new players to the level of the two veterans in the cast, Thomas Mitchell and Walter Huston. Meanwhile the publicist Russell Birdwell, who had masterminded the search for Scarlett O'Hara, was engaged to make a star out of the lady's knockers; while Hughes himself waged a battle with the Hays Office, which insisted on 108 cuts in the script. It was agreed to waive 105 of these after Hughes had hired a mathematician to prove that other stars had been allowed to show more inches of cleavage. Hughes refused to make the other three, and when the film was finished – at a total cost of $3,400,000 – he decided to show it without Code approval, choosing San Francisco for the world première, hoping that the approval of that worthy city would force Hays's officers to see the errors of their ways. It opened there in February 1943 and quickly closed. Hughes lost interest, and the film remained on the shelf till 1947 (as Hughes was preparing to launch another sex-queen, Faith Domergue) when it was released abroad and in some major American cities. It was not widely seen in the US till 1950 when RKO Radio, by this time owned by Hughes, showed it widely, and then it attracted many curiosity seekers to the box-office.

The advertising campaign centred on Miss Russell, leaning back on a pile of straw – and piles of straw were at this point more associated with sex, willingly enacted or not, than beds, which were where mummies and daddies slept. Farmboys, everyone knew, took milkmaids into barns, and Miss Russell was inviting every male who saw her to join her there. She was also, according to the slogan, 'Mean! Moody! Magnificent!', meaning that although she played hard to get she would eventually make it worth your while. That, however, does not reflect the plot of the film in which Russell plays a subsidiary character, Rio, the mistress of the much older Doc Holliday (Walter Huston). Holliday is in uneasy alliance with the sheriff Pat Garrett (Thomas Mitchell) and some way into the plot the men take as protégé a young horse thief Billy the Kid (Buetel). Rio tries to kill Billy in revenge for his murdering her brother, in exchange for which he discreetly rapes her, after which she becomes so crazy about him she jumps into bed just to keep him warm. She starts to wear his ring in the belief that they are married, a considerable delusion but conceivably one to prevent the Hays Office from becoming too agitated. She also begins to show much more décolletage, but that may be Hughes's device to prevent audiences leaving in droves. The film does attempt to make points about sexuality, but whether that includes the on-off relationship between Billy and Doc isn't clear. At one point they are prepared to jettison Russell and ride off together in the sunset; at another point there are tears in Garrett's eyes as Doc deserts him for Billy. These are odd emotions to be found in a movie whose *raison d'être* was a lady's knockers but, as already noted, such emotions did occur in the films Furthman wrote. In this case they may have been his revenge on Hughes for submitting him to the horrible experience of working with him.

Freudian analyses are in order for other wartime movies as well. Some symbols were almost as old as movies themselves, and many of those associated with sexual intercourse were resurrected after the implementation of the Code, having laid dormant since the Silent days (when symbols were an essential in story telling). Among them are: fireworks; crackling fires and their concommitant, smoke emerging from a chimney; waves; thunderstorms; guns, preferably cannon; the popping of champagne corks; sunrise or sunset; a train entering a tunnel; and probably a volcano or so. Among those occasioning some new (to movies) symbols was a Brazilian singer of vitality but limited ability called Carmen Miranda, whose fame was associated with outrageous costumes, including head-dresses modelled from exotic fruit. This led to a number in *The Gang's All Here* (1943) called 'The Lady in the Tutti-Frutti Hat', in which serried rows of showgirls raise and lower giant bananas; and given that musicals were the preferred entertainment of servicemen this paid them the dubious compliment of suggesting mutual masturbation sessions. The fountains that spring up from the swimming pool in *Bathing Beauty* (1944) are phallic by definition: but what in my opinion places them alongside those bananas in any sexual thesaurus are the jets of fire which shoot forth from them at full height. I mention these as examples of what those minds out on the West Coast could dream up, perhaps subconsciously; and of what movies could show in all innocence.

The GIs' preference for musicals may have been due to a desire for mindless escapism, but was not unconnected with the fact that pretty girls strutted around in the musical numbers displaying legs, shoulders, arms and in some cases bare midriffs. Betty Grable was without dispute the leading pin-up girl, ordinary enough to have represented all the girls back home. She was what we would later call a sex symbol, and so were

Some wartime pin-ups. The morale of the troops was considered so important that the studios happily obliged by turning out thousands of stills like these. They had been doing so for years in any case, but now they didn't need the excuse of sea and sand to get the stars and starlets into bathing-suits. Even some of the classy ladies disrobed and when Greer Garson (the classiest of all and then a very big star indeed) appeared in tights in *Random Harvest* there was much discussion as to whether she would be offering further examples of leg-art. The British studios also got their girls into pin-up poses, but we thought we would spare you those. From left, Betty Grable, Veronica Lake, Rita Hayworth. Overleaf: Hedy Lamarr and Jane Russell.

87

Ann Sheridan, Hedy Lamarr, Dorothy Lamour, Rita Hayworth and dozens of others. None of them were ever put into the sort of sexual situations which earlier and later stars coped with – unless they could not sing or dance, in which case there were some mild ones in the comedies and dramas in which they appeared. Sex was still left to real actresses such as Joan Bennett in mac and beret in *Man Hunt* in 1940, and everyone knew what her profession was, though no one ever mentioned it; Barbara Stanwyck as an adulteress in *Double Indemnity*; Miss Bennett again, picking up Edward G. Robinson in *The Woman in the Window* ('I'm not married, I've no designs on you. One drink is all I require') and *Scarlet Street*; Lauren Bacall telling Bogey in *To Have and Have Not* that if he wanted anything to just whistle. These were thrillers, traditional home of dubious morals, though audiences had usually to draw their own conclusions.

Ingrid Bergman had a celebrated long kiss, sanctioned by the Breen Office as the Code Administration Office became known when the Hays regime came to an end in 1945; so for the sake of simplicity let us hereafter refer to it as the Motion Picture Association of America or MPAA. These people, anyway, allowed Bergman her kiss with Cary Grant in Hitchcock's *Notorious* and a couple of years later she was in the mac and beret in *Arch of Triumph*, but these were only permissible because she and the film were very prestigious. When the producer Pandro S. Berman indicated that he wished to make a film about adultery in the European manner he was advised that the concept was more likely to be passed with an actress like Jennifer Jones, rather than one with a 'sexy' image like Lana Turner: which is why Miss Jones became Madame Bovary at Miss Turner's studio. She had made her name as the French peasant girl who would be canonised as Saint Bernadette, so was only showing her versatility in essaying a half-caste of uncertain parentage and ambition in *Duel in the Sun* (1946), directed by King Vidor and produced by David O. Selznick in a half-hearted attempt to top *Gone With the Wind*. If we add the movies' new dream hero, Gregory Peck, who had made his name playing a priest, we have four names of the utmost probity: so there were few objections when Peck and Jones lusted after each other over half the rocks of New Mexico. To all those recovering from the World War there was a need for more honesty in all matters, including those sexual: but this idiotic movie did not provide it – and indeed, probably set the cause of sex on the screen back several years.

Those American directors who had served in the War returned with new purpose. Frank Capra's first postwar movie was called *It's a Wonderful Life*, a declaration supported by the film's content: to prove his point he needed a hooker, played by Gloria Grahame. The MPAA let him get away with that, but then he was Capra. They were much less helpful with other prestigious names and the infidelities caused by wartime separations were touched on in only a couple of films (*The Best Years of Our Lives*, and *The Unfaithful*). Inertia seems to have set in among film-makers, and with cinema admissions at an all-time high in 1946 there

seemed little enough reason to change things. The MPAA was certainly in no mood to relax its restrictions and in the five years which completed the decade there were hardly more movies with sexual themes. Only respected actresses were permitted to transgress: Katharine Hepburn committed adultery in *The Sea of Grass*, though married at the time to Spencer Tracy; while neither of the feuding sisters (in real life) Olivia de Havilland and Joan Fontaine were content to wait for wedding bells (in respectively *To Each His Own* and *Letter from an Unknown Woman*). And Jane Wyman's illegitimate child in *Johnny Belinda* was conceived not

by seduction but rape, a matter as tactfully handled as all such matters in these movies.

On Broadway Claudia had been a Connecticut waif who had landed a husband because he found her as sexy as she was naïve: and so is Claudia still, in the 1943 film of that name, though they underplayed it a bit. The movie, though prepared by Selznick, was produced and released by 20th Century-Fox, run by Darryl F. Zanuck who saw all women as whores or saints. And his favourite

actress, Linda Darnell, played either one or the other but never both at once. We shall return shortly to her, but should glance first at the problems caused by the polarisation of women. This became acute in the postwar period as Hollywood was invaded by stars resembling the boy or girl next door, and nice girls still didn't – even though Deanna Durbin in *Nice Girl?* in 1941 had wanted to, going to Franchot Tone's apartment while in her adolescence: though it may be that her adolescent

Billy Wilder's *Double Idemnity* centred on an adulterous couple (Barbara Stanwyck, Fred MacMurray, right) who murder her husband (Tom Powers). MacMurray played an insurance salesman, not given to subtlety and when she calmly responds to his pass with a satisfied 'There's a speed limit in this state' we know the inevitable.

fans thought she wanted just a kiss. Of course Mr Tone sent her packing, but you do wonder why Universal and the Hays Office let the impure thought enter the head of this beloved former child star.

No such thoughts entered the heads of Janet Leigh, June Allyson or Jeanne Crain – or, though she is completely forgotten now, if not then, Allene Roberts. She and the equally anodyne Lon McAllister supported Edward G. Robinson in *The Red House*, written and directed by Delmer Daves in 1947. They are the juvenile leads and they have a happy ending, in contrast to Julie London and Rory Calhoun, who emphatically do not. Miss London is long-haired, soft lipped and round-bosomed in low-cut blouses; Calhoun wears the blue jeans and check shirts of he-men. They tussle a bit on their first meeting and she allows him to kiss her on the

Cary Grant and Ingrid Bergman in *Notorious*, indulging in what was described as 'the longest kiss in screen history' – and so it was, if you include the nuzzling while Grant was speaking on the telephone. The director was Alfred Hitchcock, and this was his first major instance of challenging the limits of movie permissiveness. It helped that Miss Bergman was considered a great actress and a respectably married woman: why, in life it was said, there were times when she didn't bother to wear lipstick!

second, even though he is drunk – real hussy behaviour. He: 'I can't get you out of my mind.' She: 'Same thing with me.' He is unsuccessful in persuading her to run away with him, so he changes his tactics: 'We'll have a honeymoon that'll top any honeymoon that anyone ever had', to which she agrees with alacrity. They don't, as I implied, get it, but the spectator's baser emotions have been stirred.

Even Clark Gable was affected: returning from the War in *The Hucksters* (1947), directed by Jack Conway, he prefers prissy widow Deborah Kerr to lush and sexy old flame Ava Gardner. Ah, but in Frederick Wakeman's original novel the Gardner role is small and the Kerr not a widow but an unfaithful war wife who is so swept with passion for the Gable character that she enjoys going with him to a sleazy whore-infested hotel – a situation turned upside down in the movie. The couple do go to such a hotel, but it was not used for such purposes when he had known it earlier, and she is not remotely understanding about his mistake. Other examples of bowdlerisation, not necessarily demanded by the Code (but because studios did not want to offend fans), include *Christmas Holiday*, in which Deanna Durbin is a roadshow singer instead of a whorehouse inmate, as required by Somerset Maugham's novel: that was set in Paris and the film in New Orleans, where brothels are unknown (or at least unacknowledged). The alcoholic protagonist of Billy Wilder's *The Lost Weekend* has descended so low because of writer's block: but in Charles Jackson's original novel he drank to block out homosexual tendencies. The homosexual victim of Richard Brooks's novel *The Brick Foxhole* has become a Jew when filmed by Edward Dmytryk in 1947 as *Crossfire*, a matter given much prominence since Jews were hardly more welcome in movies than perverts. The piece was much praised for its daring and we may suppose that it was easier for audiences to loathe a Jew-baiter than a fag-hater.

The most famous case of censorship belongs to the most infamous book of the decade, *Forever Amber*, in which Kathleen Winsor had set down the adventures of an imaginary mistress of Charles II, who doesn't seem to mind that she had made the rounds of the courtiers before arriving at him. (Perhaps the most famous of the many Amber jokes was this exchange: 'What happened to Amber in Chapter 16?' 'The same as Chapter 15, only twice'.) The book's bestseller status made it valuable to Hollywood and Zanuck bought it, promising to drastically reduce the number of Amber's ravishers and conquests. After a false start with the British actress Peggy Cummins, the film was recast with Linda Darnell, who had once been the vision of the Virgin for Zanuck (in *The Song of Bernadette*). Miss Darnell's Amber is seen only once near a bed, and then she is administering to the sick: doubtless that might be misinterpreted, for Amber's exploits now inevitably arise because her noble motives were misunderstood – by such as the Legion of Decency, which had campaigned vigorously against the film being made in the first place. The result, thundered the Legion, 'is a glorification of immorality and licentiousness', a fine example of those seeing only what they want to see. Had it been otherwise, the piece might surely have attracted a larger public, for reports quickly indicated that it was not a movie anyone might be ashamed of being seen at (except on artistic grounds) – unlike the book, which had generally been loaned and read in plain brown covers.

It was followed in notoriety and chronology by Norman Mailer's *The Naked and the Dead* and James E. Jones's *From Here to Eternity*, different kettles of fish entirely, being both about the experiences of men in war – and both, unlike Miss Winsor's opus, being critically esteemed, if not highly. Each is a realistic novel, using much army slang (if euphemistically, with Mailer substituting 'fug' for 'fuck') and treating women as soldiers have ever treated women, as fit only for a quick shag. An exception is Jones's Pvt Prewitt, who falls deliriously and passionately in love with a Honolulu hooker. In the 1953 film version directed by Fred Zinnemann, she has become a dance hostess who – rather oddly, one feels – refuses to give up her job to marry him. In the book their heartsearching takes place in the bedrooms of a brothel, which means that the film's dance hall has to have quiet sitting rooms where they can talk. The MPAA did permit the captain's wife (Deborah Kerr) to continue her affair with a non-comm (Burt Lancaster), with the inference that her unhappiness is tied to an incipient nymphomania. And the film deserves its place in the annals of sex films because of the famous beach scene, where the couple embrace on the sand, seemingly unaware that the waves are rippling around them. The scene stood for something, even if it is more romantic than erotic. Even those who had not read the novel recognised the film as backward in its portrayal of sexual matters but the piece was so powerful in other ways that the bowdlerisation did not raise too much comment (unlike *Forever Amber*, but in that case there was little else to say). Movies had been all-pervading, all so much part of everyone's lives that the changes to Jones's intentions were accepted without demur. Movies were, at the time, a force for good – unlike Tallulah Bankhead, who unwittingly pointed to their future direction when she met Mailer for the first time and said 'So you're the young man who can't spell "fuck"'.

Another famous movie clinch, and we had moved on a bit, since the lovers – Burt Lancaster and Deborah Kerr – in *From Here To Eternity* were involved in an adulterous affair.

8.

The Days of the Furtive Brigade

During the 1930s and 40s the Continental cinema continued to do its bit on behalf of sex maniacs – and I use this expression advisedly, for it was used indiscriminately about anyone foolish enough to show an interest in sex. It was one thing to know about the facts of life and quite another to believe them necessary to the ordinary business of living. Any further interest in sex was by definition abnormal. The intellectuals had, as they had always had, Boccaccio, Rabelais and *The Golden Ass*, while back street shops which sold trusses and athletic supports stocked manuals for married couples and books with titles like 'The Red Light'. If you searched hard enough in the industrial regions of large cities you would find bookshops displaying paperbacks with lurid covers – and by the standards of the offerings in respectable bookshops their contents were often colourful: there was a lexicon of words to describe the lady's contours and it was easy enough to know what was going on when her partner 'thrust in' or 'plunged in'. Under the counter these shops may also have had poorly printed copies of 19th century pornography – and if they did, it was most likely to be either *The Autobiography of a Flea* or *Fanny Hill*.

Naturally these shops also stocked naturist magazines, but these were also found on most railway bookshops, though only behind the counter so that they had to be asked for by the reckless and the intrepid. Schoolboys, if lucky enough, sniggered over photographs of men and women playing tennis, naked except for socks and plimsolls, the men invariably photographed from behind (or the waist up). If the people in the pictures were suspect, what of the men who posed in swimming trunks or G-strings in the muscle magazines? These were almost certainly drooled over by those gentlemen who preferred gentlemen; they were also freer than the others with strangely worded letters and answers (by 'a doctor'), which could – just – be interpreted as a desire to have wankers' guilt exorcised and an assurance that it was all right if practised in moderation. Virtually the only printed references to a practice passed on by conversations in the school playground noted that 'until recently' it was thought to cause blindness/insanity/hair to grow on the palm of the hands. If most British schoolboys referred to it as 'tossing off' that wasn't known to the readers at the British Broadcasting Corporation, who passed a joke of Max Miller's to the effect that he met a sexy lady on a narrow bridge and didn't know whether to squeeze past or toss himself off. Miller was immediately banned from broadcasting for several years.

It was healthy and normal to pursue the opposite sex and demand a kiss, especially if you were a boy. Anyone who wanted more or something else was a sex maniac. So were those who masturbated, looked at nude photographs or read 'dirty' books – or, rather, those who boasted or even confessed to doing any of these things. Anyone who did was likely to be a patron of the more dubious movie fare programmed in small cinemas – flea-pits – which only got the films the grander houses did not want. Depending on the attitude of the police or the local authority they turned themselves into clubs for the occasion: whatever, it was a bold patron who did not arrive with his hat pulled down and his coat collar well up. Until the proliferation of naturist movies in the 1950s the flea-pits' most notable and notorious attractions were those few Continental movies passed for screening by the local authority after being banned by the national censor. These were sometimes of an ethnic nature, with nothing on view more outlandish than the breast of a native girl. The first, foremost and most famous of all the other films was a little number which started out as *Symphonie d'Amour*.

It was not exactly a French film, but one of several curiosities made at this time aimed at different nationalities. The film industries in the US and Europe – especially Germany – had been afraid of losing their foreign markets with the arrival of Talkies and had for a time prepared multi-lingual versions. The practice ceased as dubbing was so much cheaper and didn't seem to be a barrier to European acceptance of their Hollywood favourites. The Continental film industries saw their export market contract, as their pictures were being shown only in large cities where the population could support a cinema specialising in subtitled films (or those with a large ethnic population, like New York, which would support films from the old country without subtitles). By 1932 a few dreamers, chiefly from Central Europe, were trying to find a way of making movies with such little dialogue that the few speaking sequences could be filmed cheaply in several languages. One of these was a Czech named Gustav Machaty, whose experience as von Stroheim's assistant in Hollywood in the early 1920s had taught him that audiences of all nationalities enjoyed seeing sex on the screen. He was not, however, a maker of exploitation films, and the evidence of this particular one suggests that he was much influenced by the Russian film-maker, Dovzhenko. Technically, this movie is Czech, and it seems to have been made only in German and French versions. Common to both are a podgy Austrian actress, Hedy Kiesler, who

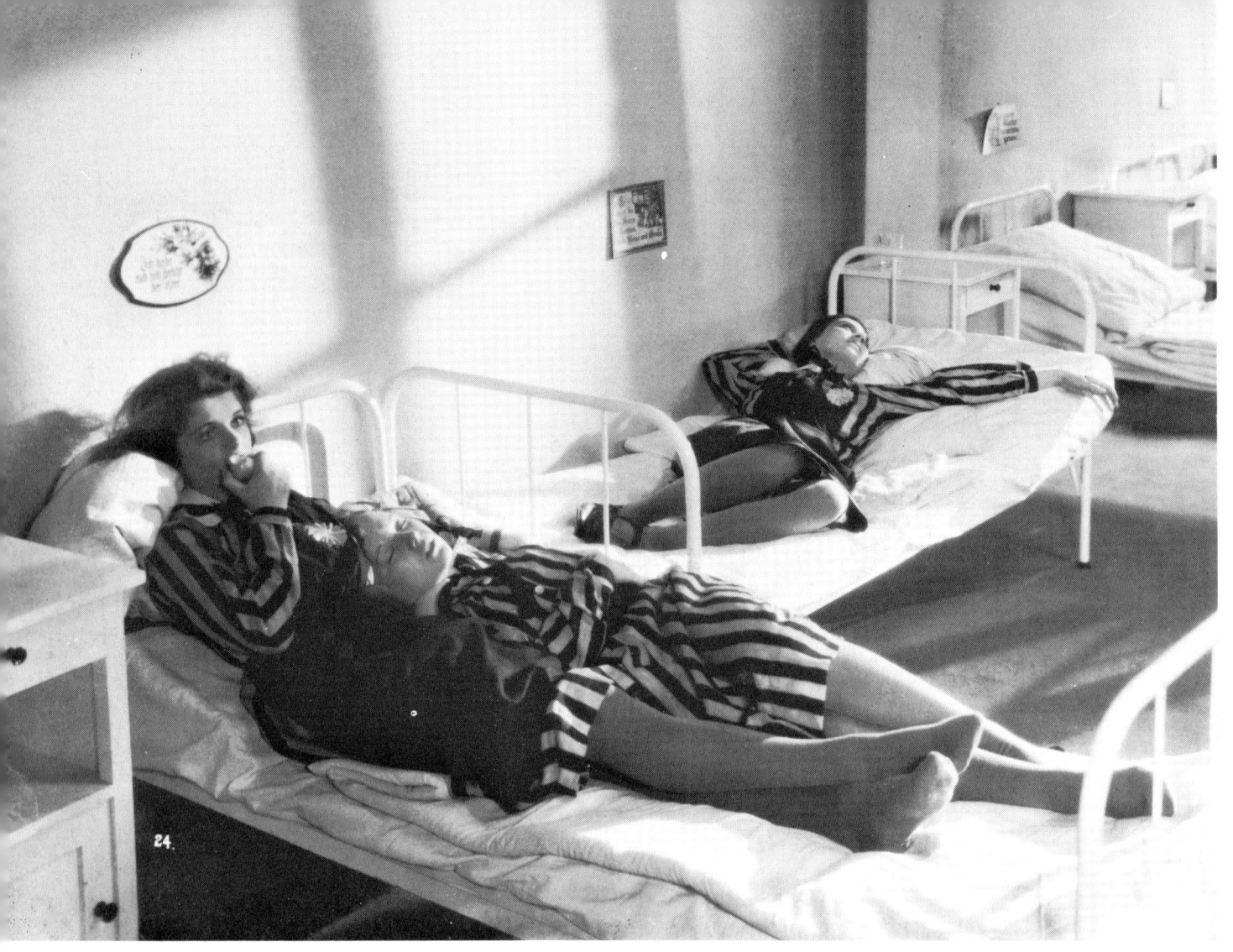

The sombre *Mädchen in Uniform* seethed with unsuppressed passions, as experienced by a teacher, Dorothea Wieck, and a pupil, Hertha Thiele. There were those who claimed that such emotions were not unknown in real life, but they did so not with great assertion – and in any case, were only supported in print by small-circulation, highbrow journals.

had played ingenues in some German films, and the German actor Aribert Mog; the elderly Czech actor Zvonimir Rogoz was replaced by Pierre Nay in the French version. There are only about twenty lines of dialogue, offering no explanations of Kiesler's conduct, if needed.

She plays a young girl who marries an old man. On their wedding night she lies back on the bed waiting for him, but he falls asleep in the bathroom. When we next see them, they are at an open-air restaurant where young couples dance to a sensuous waltz; the husband is engrossed in a newspaper and the wife looks very bored. A year, apparently, passes: she tells her father that she wants a divorce because the marriage has not been consummated. In the country, she is riding when she sees a lake, which induces her to take a dip. While doing so, her horse bolts, so she chases through the woods after him, naked. He is stopped by a handsome young surveyor, working on a building site. He also hands her her clothes. Dressed, she runs away, but stumbles. The surveyor binds her bruised foot. That night she goes to his cabin and there is a close-up of her face whilst love making. She returns home to find her husband waiting.

She then leaves for town by train; the husband cadges a lift from the surveyor, each unaware of the other's identity. In a café, as wife and lover are reunited, the husband commits suicide. An epilogue depicts the coming of summer, with the surveyor lustily in command again while the wife fondles her baby.

At the film's première in Paris, one spectator cried out 'L'extase' as Kiesler ran through the wood, and the word was taken up by others when the movie finished. Machaty promptly renamed the film *Extase*. He was fond of other people's ideas: his 1929 movie *Erotikon* had been named after Mauritz Stiller's more famous 1920 film, though it was by no means a remake. Miss Kiesler was renamed, too – by M-G-M, for whom she became Hedy Lamarr – partly because of her connection with this notorious movie. Nobody, but nobody, appeared in the nude in movies in those days, except in stag films, and to our porn-jaundiced eyes Miss Kiesler/ Lamarr is no exception: undoubtedly what we see through the trees is a naked woman, but we glimpse her so fleetingly that there is no chance to admire the curve of her breast or buttocks or appreciate a titillating nipple. Equally surely the surveyor was able to do just that. The film is simplistic, schoolboyish, romantic, a masturbatory fantasy, for he has seen this desired woman, who then takes the initiative by coming to him in the night. Woman, deprived of satisfaction at the hearth, seeks it with a handsome stranger. Machaty's thesis is that all impotent husbands deserve to be cuckolded and that all beautiful young females should be serviced by equally handsome young studs. The lover is in the Rusian tradition of handsome labourers – muscular, ruddy, keen-eyed, open-necked – while the husband is in the tradition of French farce – bald, pincenezed, slight, frock-coated. In life the roles would have been reversed: *that* would have made a film.

The general air of triteness is accentuated by the shots of rearing horses – an obvious symbol of sexual potency – and of statuettes of horses. The result is hardly, or even softly, erotic but the film became very famous, if largely unseen. It was imported into the US in 1934, and destroyed as obscene by the US Marshal on 5 July the following year. The distributing company appealed, importing another copy which was passed by the Circuit Court of Appeals, but fearful of the publicity few cinemas would book the film. The less scrupulous exhibitors made their own cuts, and the situation of prints became hazardous when Miss Kiesler married a millionaire who tried to buy all that existed. Pirated prints abounded, especially in Britain, where it was shown in cinema clubs throughout the 1940s, eventually being passed for adult viewing only in 1950. It had been shown to New York's critics a decade earlier, but the reviews came out on Christmas Day and little attention was paid. In any case, Hollywood's sleeker, more glamorous Lamarr could be currently seen with Clark Gable in *Comrade X*; *Extase* was not the sort of film her current fans went to see.

Other films from Europe with a relatively high sexual frankness attracted little attention, for they were shown only in subtitled versions, in art cinemas, and were accordingly seen only by highbrows and intellectuals. Until the Nazis took power, the Germans continued to make their admirably honest films set among the working-classes. In 1931 Leontine Sagan directed a version of a play by Christa Winsloe, called as a movie *Mädchen in Uniform*, and for more than two decades it was a film spoken of chiefly in whispers, except by lesbians, for whom it was a byword. It was the only film 'about' them, and what is more, sympathetic. Any minority group must want public discussion of its problems and especially since the trial (in Britain) and publication (in America) of *The Well of Loneliness* many homosexuals of both sexes had privately decided that they weren't so different after all: those who went to the cinema may

Hedy Lamarr – or Hedy Keisler, as she then was – in a scene from the most famous and least seen of films *maudits*, *Extase*, a Czech film which had caused censorship battles throughout the world. The reason, of course, was that she indulged in a little skinny-dipping before meeting, still naked, the young man who could give her what her husband was too old and/or too tired to supply.

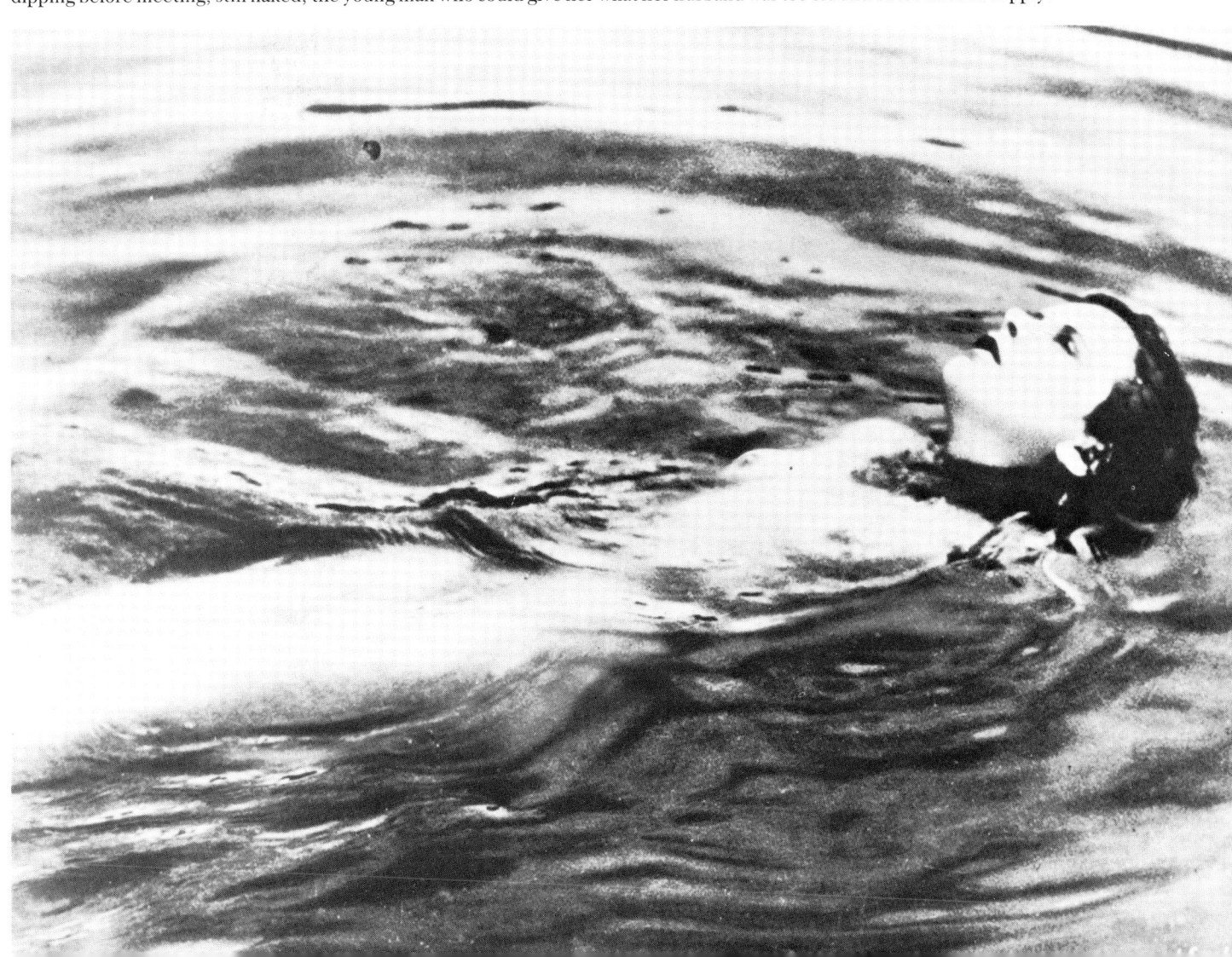

have supposed that they would be represented by mannish women or womenish men till doomsday. More rounded portraits had appeared in literature but with the specifics ommitted: the fact that the wretched character eventually committed suicide invariably meant that he or she was not happy with his or her human lot. The schoolteacher protagonist of *Mädchen in Uniform* (Dorothea Wieck) is not only sensible and thoroughly likeable, but she gives as good as she gets when reprimanded and isn't forced to suicide – that, or an attempt at it, is reserved for the schoolgirl object of her affections. Since their friendship is platonic or at least represents no betrayal of a teacher's principles we might say that the film is no less decorous than *The Fifth Form at St Hilda's*, but there is no misinterpreting the scene in which the teacher goes round the dormitory kissing the girls goodnight – with more fervour than is proper.

The German enthusiasm for transvestism was maintained by *Viktor und Viktoria*, a cheerful musical directed by Reinhold Schunzel in 1933 and centered on two unemployed performers, played by Herman Thimig and Renate Muller. When he tells her he once saved himself from starving by becoming a female impersonator, that is what she becomes (except the other way round), though not without some embarrassing moments when she's expected to change into costume in the men's dressing-room. The plot has only one way to go and it goes it: as the toast of London Muller meets a playboy (Anton Walbrook), whose friendship soon turns into something stronger. Beyond some giggling among his pals, no one concerned seems to know how to handle this situation, including Walbrook, who feels no panic or guilt at turning gay – nor surprise on discovering that the beloved is, after all, of the required sex. At that, the homosexual references are wittier and more subtle than in the 1982 American remake, *Victor/Victoria*. The material seems to have an abiding appeal, for there was a German remake in 1957, and a British film of 1935, *First a Girl*, borrowed the initial premise. So does *Fanfaren der Liebe*, a German film of 1951, inasmuch as two out-of-work musicians find, after several false starts, that they can find a permanent job, if suitably attired, in an all-girl orchestra. That is all that it has in common with the best of all transvestite films, but we may be grateful that Billy Wilder had the acumen to buy the remake rights.

By the time *Viktor und Viktoria* was completed the Nazis were in power. With Goebbels keeping strict control over the industry there were no more lesbians or transvestites – curiously, for you might have expected the Nazis to add degeneracy to the faults of the Jews and communists they ridiculed in so many of their films. These were always lazy, dishonest, moneygrabbing and licentious in a weary sort of way. Conceivably sex was something the Nazi mentality could not comprehend: certainly Nazi youth as seen in the films had no thought of it after marching hither, thither and yon, while the scrubbed-apple-face girls admire them in nice hearty fashion. Like other totalitarian states, Nazi Germany did not wish to acknowledge sexual licence within its borders, but then Jews and communists did not belong within those borders either. However, Goebbels was sufficiently realistic to know that Nazism could not banish adultery, which turns up in several German films in the middle and late 1930s – most memorably in some sad period romances in traditional fashion, of handsome hussars, neglected wives and elderly husbands.

Like its contemporary, *Mädchen in Uniform, Le Rosier de Madame Husson* had censorship problems in some countries. Its source in a story by Guy de Maupassant gave it a certain acceptability, as did the fact that it was witty about sex. Because of that, many considered it the sort of film only the French could make; others thought it the sort of film only the French would want to make. Of course, at this time, 1931, sexual matters were not rare on the screen, and although France was more immune than most countries from Hollywood's all-pervading influence this film remained for many years the most daring to be seen in art-houses. Mme Husson (Françoise Rosay) has long been in the habit of donating a cheque for 500 francs to the girl chosen to be the annual rose queen – and chosen as such for her virtue. When no woman is found to be suitable by the town council one member suggests a rose king: thus is selected the grocer's idiot son Isidore (Fernandel) who uses the money to go to the nearest town, where he instantly visits a prostitute's bar, and soon winds up in bed with one of its inmates.

Less explicit but more piquant are the situations in *La Kermesse Heroïque*, again concerning the tribulations of a town council, this time in 1616 in Flanders, in the line of the approaching Spanish army. The Burgomaster (André Alerme) envisages rape, torture and looting, which he feels can be avoided if the town is in mourning – for him. This leaves his 'widow' (Mme Rosay) in charge, and since we see others of the townswomen offering themselves to the gallant Spanish soldiers we may suppose her equally compliant with their handsome commander (Jean Murat). The director was Jacques Feyder, who made one of the best of the many atmospheric movies about the French in Africa, *Le Grand Jeu*, which has a memorably erotic sequence in which the legionnaire hero (Pierre Richard Willm) removes the shoes of his sleeping mistress and then bends to kiss her toes, at which point she rises from sleep to embrace him and he throws himself upon her.

I cannot say that such scenes are common in the films made by the French at this time, but they did not banish the double bed. They did have a distressing tendency towards euphemism, so that in *L'Alibi* and *La Maison du Maltais*, both directed by Pierre Chenal, the 'girls' are dance hostesses working in a dance hall but their attitudes are those of whores – as are their situations in the plots, being used by some men and falling truly in love with others who will remove them to a less sordid life. The stereotyped characters now banned from American movies remain – the lady with the past, the lecherous villain, often given flesh and blood by superior playing, directing and writing. The most consistent figure is the loner, the role always played by France's biggest star, Jean Gabin, who in a series of doomed romances never had one which was later sanctified by marriage, and in none of them could we suppose that he only kissed or kept one foot on the floor. Many of the ladies he loved were shopsoiled, even if just out of their teens – and they were sometimes played by Michèle Morgan, who in the film which made her famous, *Gribouille*, played an adolescent who had murdered her lover. She was poor and he was wealthy; she had taken some time to succumb to him after accepting his favours, and she had killed him in self-defence. She attracts the sympathy of one of the jurors (Raimu), who after her acquittal takes her into his home, which becomes the chief strand of the film's plots. She attracts our sympathy too, wholeheartedly; and although the movie itself, directed by Marc Allégret, is now likeable but old-fashioned, the heroine stands in complete contrast to those then appearing in the films made elsewhere at the time.

When, after the War, French movies returned to the screens of British and American art-houses, there was relief among aficionados that they had not lost their sexual frankness. In Clouzot's *Le Corbeau*, made during the War, the doctor hero (Pierre Fresnay) is attracted to two women, one of whom is married but virtuous and the other (Ginette Leclerc) cheap and trampy but unmarried. Our first view of this lady is memorable, sitting on a bed with cigarette dangling from her lips, painting

her toenails. She sets her sights for the doctor, even pretending illness to get him into her room. He balances his lust for her against his purer feelings for the other woman, and when lust wins he discovers that she is a cripple. Among the characters in the same director's *Quai des Orfèvres*, made in 1947, are a pseudo-sophisticated woman photographer (Simone Renant), who enjoys photographing female nudes, and an aged man (Charles Dullin), who drools over her pictures; there is also the heroine, Jenny (Suzy Delair), who receives men without donning a peignoir over her black underwear (but then she is on the stage). It is only towards the end that we realise why the photographer risks so much for this lady.

Les Maudits, directed by René Clément the same year, is hardly more explicit about the relationship between the self-appointed leader (Jo Dest) of a group of Nazis fleeing Europe, and his 'adjutant' (Michel Auclair). We must make assumptions about their relationship when the latter pauses before introducing himself as such; and on the fact that the much older other man slaps him across the face when he finds him chatting up a blonde. This portrait of a fascist as a deviate may have been influenced by *Roma Città Aperta*, in which one of the women collaborating with the Germans is

In depicting the degeneracies of collaborators and occupiers in wartime Rome, Roberto Rossellini resorted to a spot of lesbianism, as represented by Giovanna Galletti, right. Her companion was Maria Michi, who was much less interested in her than the fur coat that such circles could provide. The film was *Roma, Città Aperta*, better known as *Open City*.

unquestionably a lesbian, while an amateur whore is
attracted to their circle for the ill-gotten luxuries. The
actress who played this role, Maria Michi, had a more
significant role in *Paisà*, also directed as the war ended
by Roberto Rossellini. She picks up a GI (Gar Moore) in
a bar, but we assume that she is only a part-time whore
because she has to borrow a room from a friend. Very
drunk, he tells her – in flashback – of the pure young girl
he had met as the Americans had first entered Rome;
and he adds that he intends to go searching for her. The
whore tells him where to find the girl and leaves him
quickly; she scrubs off her make-up and dons her old
clothes: but he doesn't bother to turn up, presumably
because he too has been changed by the War.

Audiences had been changed by the War and foreign-
language films were being more widely seen. Rossellini's two films (as well as being influential) proved that
Italy could stand with France in dealing with more
mature matters, while for the first time in more than two
decades a Swedish film attracted more than passing
attention in the international market. The Scandinavian
cinema had never abandoned its tales of deserted unmarried mothers, but the view of adolescent sexuality in
this new film does concern a wanton girl. Its title is *Hets*
(1945), which the Americans translated as *Torment* and
the British as *Frenzy*, and these are both emotions

Below: Signorina Michi again,
in the second of the amazing
realistic dramas with which
Rossellini depicted the end of
hostilities in Europe. *Paisà*
consisted of six episodes, and in
this one Michi has brought back
a GI (Gar Moore), who fails to
recognise in her the pure girl he
had encountered on his last
furlough.

Sex, Swedish-style *always* meant nights like this one from *One Summer of Happiness*, when a young couple got carried away after a naked swim in the lake . . .

experienced by the schoolboy hero (Alf Kjellin). The girl (Mai Zetterling) says that she has a tormentor, but that remains a matter for conjecture. The boy meets her late at night and takes her home because she is very drunk – which disgusts him, but he finds that he cannot refuse her offer of sexual intercourse. They begin an affair; and he gets drunk one night when he knows that her lover is visiting her, wondering why he got mixed up in all this. Her visitor (Stig Jarrel) is the teacher who treats him vilely at school and since, we gather, he treats her similarly we may use the word 'sadist' of him. The film was directed by Alf Sjöberg and its writer was Ingmar Bergman, whose films would subsequently help to

break down many barriers as to what could be shown on the screen. Those he directed in the 1940s were not widely known outside Sweden till much later, but we might note that one of them, *Thirst*, does contain a fairly rounded portrait of a lesbian among its characters.

The British cinema also made a huge leap forward in quality during the War and with it went not greater sexual frankness but a higher sexual content – though, as it happened, in some of its worst efforts. Despite Charles Laughton's Henry VIII and a number of melodramas in which adultery was a minor element, George Formby was the leading exponent of sex in British movies of the 1930s, and should receive due ack-

Sex, British-style, was most likely to be a period melodrama such as *The Wicked Lady*, in which passions of all sorts ran very high. It starred James Mason and Margaret Lockwood, in the title role.

nowledgment for reminding audiences of its existence. He frequently lost his trousers, but as the least comely of comics that could hardly have excited any of the female spectators; even in singing his *double entendre* songs to his ukelele he is only like a small boy who has discovered that babies are not brought by the stork. *Turned Out Nice Again* gives him plenty of underwear jokes, as he works in a factory manufacturing them. Sent to London to inspect some new yarn, he is instructed by the city's beauties not to say knickers, bloomers or drawers, but step-ins, panties or scanties. Anyway, he wants a pair for his wife but the price is too high; well, I'll wait for them to come down is the obvious answer. This film also has a typical Formby song, as his assistants parade in their step-ins (or panties or scanties), 'You Can't Go Wrong in These'.

Within a few years Formby had been replaced by James Mason as Britain's favourite male star, and that was partly because of a period melodrama, *The Man in Grey*, in which Mason has an affair with the best friend (Margaret Lockwood) of his wife (Phyllis Calvert) but later horsewhips her because she has murdered that

lady. There followed a series of such films, now known as the Gainsborough melodramas after the company which produced them and usually starring one or more of these players, plus or minus such as Stewart Granger and Patricia Roc. The men were as likely to be as mean, moody and magnificent as the ladies, with rape often their weapon. When the popularity of Mason and Granger made both of them demand better material Gainsborough searched for replacements, including Maxwell Reed. The public didn't respond, but Reed represents the British movie ideal male of the postwar period – at least in *The Brothers*, because he glowers a lot, especially at Miss Roc, who plays a city orphan girl come to be housekeeper on a remote island in the Hebrides. Reed's brother lusts after her but hands her over to Reed when a beating needs administering: she, who until then had scorned him, responds at once to his embrace, whereupon the loss of her virginity is indicated by a shot of her hand opening and closing.

The best of these Gainsborough films is *Fanny By Gaslight*, though it can hardly show what was such a feature of Michael Sadleir's original novel – the sexual underworld of late 19th century London, in which milords consorted with prostitutes and kept love-nests in St John's Wood. And the most famous is *The Wicked Lady*, in which Miss Lockwood lusts after several men, including a highwayman (Mr Mason), who deserts his 'doxie' (Jean Kent), as he calls her, for her. Both films failed to meet the requirements of the Code in the US, which apparently could not accommodate, respectively, the garter-belt attachments of the can-can dancers or Miss Lockwood's milky breasts (though no more revealing than the beauties painted by Lely and Kneller). Gainsborough reshot the offending sequences, adding yards of tulle to the neckline of Miss Lockwood's original costumes. But the cost was hardly justified, for the films failed to even echo their sensational success on their home territory. Thereafter the MPAA worried less about British movies in the US, confident that they were unlikely to be widely seen.

Nevertheless, when Launder and Gilliat decided to film *The Blue Lagoon* in 1949 there were protracted negotiations with that body. De Vere Stacpoole's novel had been a bestseller on publication in 1908 and was still in print. The two narratives, however, have little in common beyond the central situation: two children are shipwrecked on a South Sea island and grow up there; one day, well into their teens, they 'discover' each other

and a baby eventually arrives. In the film the youngsters (Jean Simmons and Donald Houston) are no longer cousins and amongst the baggage washed up with them is a handbook containing the marriage service, which they read to each other. It is precisely because of that that audiences could anticipate the baby, and because of it there was nothing in the film to which anyone could object, beyond some semi-nudity.

Much objection was taken to *No Orchids for Miss Blandish*, a title at the time to rank with *Tobacco Road*, *The Outlaw* and *Forever Amber* (the book), at least as far as the British were concerned. Although a dramatised version of James Hadley Chase's novel had been passed by the Lord Chamberlain, the British Board of Film Censors made it known that it was unlikely to sanction a film. In 1948 the otherwise forgotten St John L. Clowes decided to have a go, and is credited with production, direction and script. The BBFC did cut the movie, though it is impossible to tell where, so innocuous is the film today. Chase's plot, borrowed from *Sanctuary*, tells of a New York gangster who kidnaps for ransom the daughter (Linden Travers) of a meat king. He decides to let her go, but we hear a door reopen and after a long-held shot of an orchid he says 'I'm glad you came back'. When next we see her she has a new hairstyle, is in a robe, with a whisky in her hand, saying 'This is

You wouldn't believe what the adolescent lovers (Donald Houston, Jean Simmons) had to get up to to justify her pregnancy in *The Blue Lagoon* – or perhaps you might, in view of the bra she has fashioned on that otherwise deserted South Sea island. Brooke Shields in the 1980 version wasn't clever enough to make a bra, but most of the time long hair covered that area.

freedom to what I've known . . . You're the first man I've ever had.' The film sunk into well-deserved oblivion (it played a few test engagements in the US in 1951), and it is in an equally obscure film that I find one of the few honest sexual situations in any English-speaking film of this period. Its title is *No Room at the Inn*, directed (not well) for a minor company by Daniel Birt. Joan Temple's play (in which the situation originated) concerned a household of evacuees cared for by a woman (Freda Jackson) as sexually liberal as she is rapacious. Salvation for one little girl seems to lie in the arrival of her father (Niall McGinnis) but he is so entranced by the woman's skills as a drinking companion and her subsequent offer of sex that he not only disbelieves his daughter but gives the woman his dead wife's watch. It was a long time since any movie had suggested that one night of bliss could blind one of its participants to what was, in any case, self-evident.

The reader may have noticed that none of these films had dealt with postwar problems. The changes in morality wrought by the War went unrecorded, except indirectly in the columns of the agony aunts in women's magazines, dealing with love affairs which had resulted from wartime separations. No one was prepared to admit publicly that many of these casual affairs had resulted in people being hurt. In Britain, the 'Yanks' played havoc with womenfolk wherever they were stationed, being better-paid and better-uniformed than British tommies, as well as representing exotica. British women expected to find counterparts of Gable, Tyrone Power and Robert Taylor in their local USAF unit and they weren't disappointed. The re-adjustments of married couples after separation were the subject of two British movies, *Perfect Strangers* and *The Captive Heart* and one American one, *The Best Years of Our Lives*, which was so successful that most people felt that there was nothing more to say on the subject.

Otherwise, only a handful of movies touched on the problems that their audiences were facing. In any case, a movie on marital sexual difficulties would hardly have brought a stampede to the box-office, although postwar sinful sex was dealt with, after a fashion, in *Good Time Girl*, directed in Britain in 1948 by David Macdonald. In the US during the Depression, they were called party girls; in Britain, after the War, they were the good time girls. They were not whores and they no longer exist, since few women today think twice about conferring sexual favours and few men, consequently, have to consider the gifts traded in return. In Depression America and postwar Britain times were bleak: a number of young girls sought to escape discomfort and misery at home by flocking to the bright lights, aware that there were enough men – if not Yanks, for whom the movement started – prepared to offer them a good time. Arthur La Bern's original novel, based on the trial for murder of Betty Jones and a GI deserter, showed this particular good time girl using her body for advancement, but the film – hoping for American distribution – doesn't. Just a kiss or so. And it's not in the milieu of petty hoods and spivs that she gets 'corrupted', but reform school.

Still, if the British remained sensible on the matter of

sex they could also manage that odd scene in *No Room at the Inn*, and if they could manage that it was only to be expected that matters were getting out of hand on the Continent, where they were always so much more excitable. The re-establishment of the Venice and Cannes film festivals resulted in some movies achieving international notoriety, and temperatures began rising in Albion at the thought of these iniquitous artefacts crossing the Channel. As the critics of the responsible press reported favourably, it was soon clear to the British censor that, like King Canute, he could not stop the unstoppable. His problem was the young – or, alternatively, those parents who could not be trusted as to what was fit fodder for their offspring. Under the classification system no one under sixteen was allowed under any circumstances to see a film with an H certificate – but since H stood for Horror and since such

Manon was a hussy as she ever was – since the Abbé Prevost first published his highly moral account of her exploits in 1731. There is no immediate parallel between the France of that time and 1944, in which Henri-Georges Clouzot set his modernised version, but it worked well enough, since Manon's adventures ensured that she was involved in the black market activities of Paris. She remained an easy lay, and here are Manon (Cecile Aubrey) and her des Grieux (Michel Auclair) getting down to it.

movies were rarer, then, than cobras in the countryside the H was associated with double-bills of the antique Hollywood appointments with fear which played the flea-pits. An H was clearly unsuitable for the admired new European productions, so the Board in its wisdom instituted an X certificate, subconsciously choosing the one letter of the alphabet which rhymed with the word 'sex'. The popular press, enraged at the imminent undermining of British morals, constantly hammered home the equation, as did some exhibitors, patiently explaining that they only displayed the X in huge letters for the sake of children, who would not therefore turn up for films to be turned away.

When the X certificate was introduced in 1950 some previously banned films were resubmitted, but those which had been passed with cuts were not. They were deemed to have exhausted their commercial life, and

since family audiences were still the vital factor in cinemagoing the market for X films was expected to be small. (One reason for its existence, incidentally, had been certificates granted to individual films by local authorities after the Board had turned them down, and those same authorities still had the right to disagree with the Board's findings and ban the X movies.)

Among the films causing all the fuss was Clouzot's *Manon* (1949), a modernisation of the Abbé Prevost's novel, with an adolescent Manon (Cecile Aubrey), now up to her neck in wartime black marketeering, but still with a taste for luxury *'plus fort que moi'* – and that takes her at one point to work in a brothel. Amélie (Danielle Darrieux) in Claude Autant-Lara's *Occupe-toi d'Amélie* (1949) is a Paris cocotte who encourages a number of suitors, one of whom waits trouserless because, as he says, it saves time. The source of this glittering comedy

was one of the *belle époque* farces written by Georges Feydeau, now a staple of our theatre but then considered unsuitable to make the channel crossing. Max Ophuls's *La Ronde* (1950) was also based on an old play, by Schnitzler, first produced in Berlin in 1920: it caused a scandal then, since it is a roundelay in which one lover passes on to the next until the last of them is coupling with the whore in the first scene. Since ten people are involved, that means nine couplings, a matter or matters about which Schnitzler was cynical – and Ophuls and his collaborators, by changing the emphasis slightly, witty. Almost all the lovers seduce and copulate for entirely

Below: Of the four film versions (two American, one French, one Italian) of *The Postman Always Rings Twice* this remains the most famous, perhaps because it was the only time the adulterous wife was played by an actress whose name was synonymous with sex: but Lana Turner, here with John Garfield, was never an inspired actress and is, ironically, the least satisfactory of the four screen actresses who have played the role.

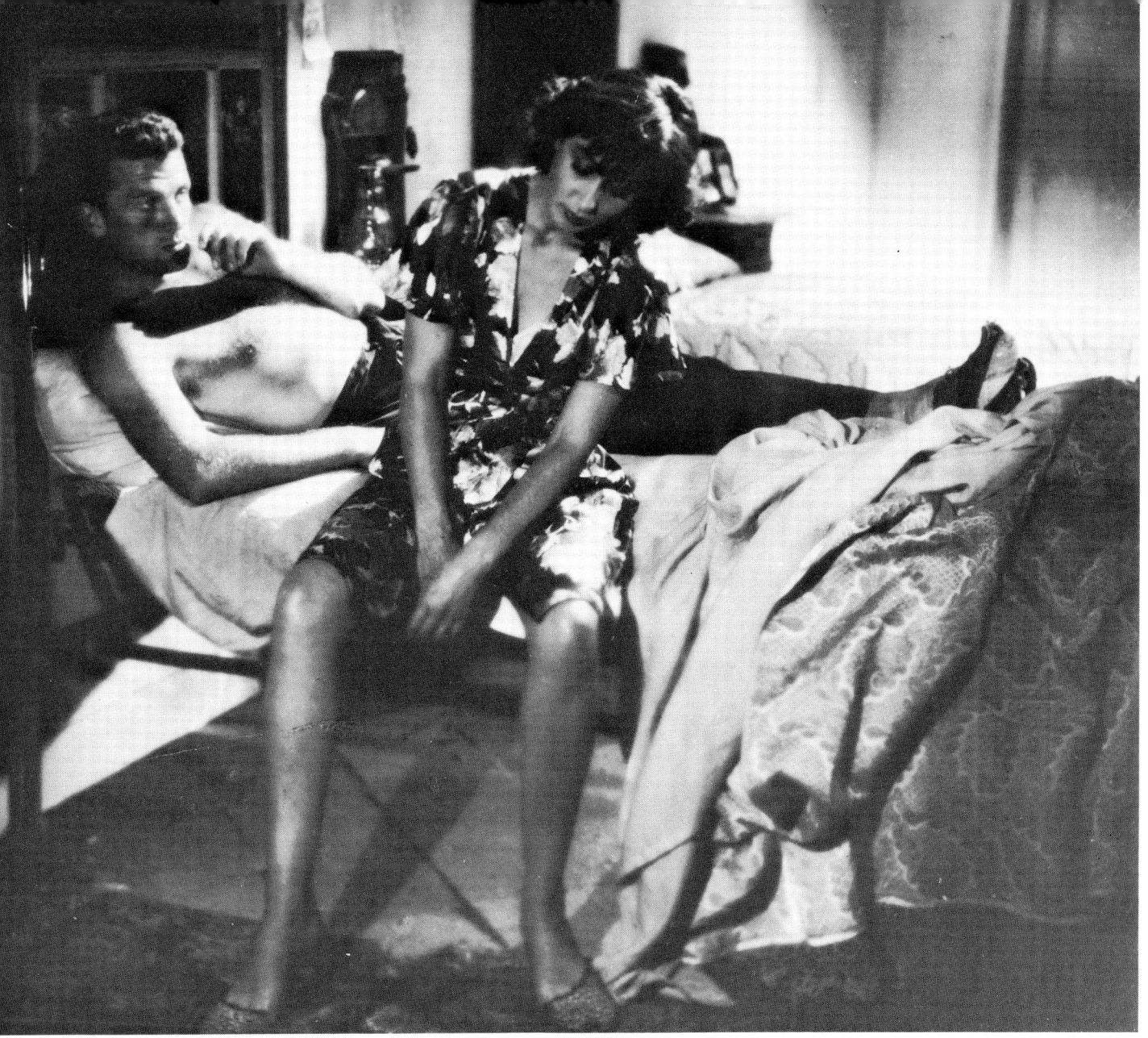

Above: *Ossessione* is Visconti's version of *The Postman Always Rings Twice*. Jean Renoir had suggested the subject to him after seeing the 1939 version directed by Pierre Chenal, *Le Dernier Tournant*, from which Visconti borrowed a number of details, including this scene of the lovers on the bed. In the French film they were Fernand Gravet and Corinne Luchaire; here they are Massimo Girotti and Clara Calamai.

selfish reasons, and since this is all they do except talk about same either before or after it can confidently be said that there had never been a movie remotely like this. There was, of course, no nudity, precious little disrobing and, following the stage directions, the actual intercourse is left to the imagination. Ophuls's stylish handling and the prestigious cast (including Danielle Darrieux, Jean-Louis Barrault, Anton Walbrook, Simone Simon, Daniel Gélin, Gérard Philipe, Simone Signoret and Serge Reggiani) were among the factors which made the film so admired.

Then there was Silvana Mangano in *Riso Amaro*, or *Bitter Rice*, the title by which most people knew it. There she was indeed, standing in the rice-field, head up, lips pouted provocatively, bosom thrusting at her sweater and thighs exposed above her black stockings.

The pictures of her far exceeded any sexual content within the movie – though two men pursue her and she has a spot of nooky with one of them (we suppose) – but they were so widely disseminated that the film was as notorious as any of the time. To this group I want to add a film made six years earlier, in 1942, but not seen publicly in Britain or the US till the 1960s for copyright reasons – for it was based on James M. Cain's novel *The Postman Always Rings Twice*. This is Luchino Visconti's *Ossessione*, which with *La Ronde* marks the most significant advance then made in the depiction of sexual relations on the screen. Visconti was influenced by a film made a year earlier, *Fari nella Nebbia*, which was about a disintegrating marriage, between a truck-driver and his wife; when he takes up with another woman we see them in bed together – which is not the case with

Visconti's lovers. The lovers, the married woman (Clara Calamai) and the rolling stone (Massimo Girotti) who turns up at her husband's *trattoria*, have several scenes with an erotic charge rare for the time. These consist partly of looks – that which passes between them when they first set eyes on each other, and hers an hour or so later when her husband's impending absence means that the two of them can make for the bedroom; and there is a sequence later when, reconciled in the open air, their looks tell us that they are not going to wait till they can get back to the bedroom.

Nothing in cinema quite prepares us for this view of sexuality; that it can be enjoyed with a stranger no matter where. The film is about the relationship of this couple, who since they conspire to murder her husband are unadmirable. What with lust and murder the Italian government banned the film; what it also has is a suggestion of homosexuality, when the man leaves his mistress and falls in with a strolling player – whose equivalent in the novel is a woman. If the suggestion is slight it is also gratuitous, possibly inserted because Visconti himself was homosexual; he was to deal with homosexuality in several more films, always, as here, equating it with violence.

This was a subject now being tentatively handled in literature – at least in the United States, in *The Fall of Valour* by Charles Jackson (the author of *The Lost Weekend*) and *The City and the Pillar* by Gore Vidal, the first being about a married man who plucks up the courage to tell another that he is attracted to him, and the second set in a homosexual milieu. There were two novels on ladies, Dorothy Baker's *Trio*, published in New York in 1943, and in Europe, *Olivia* by Olivia, originally published in French but translated into English in 1948. The author was later revealed to be Dorothy Bussy, Lytton Strachey's sister, and since it was a more or less factual account of her experiences at a French school it was appropriate that it was filmed in France, directed in 1951 by Jacqueline Audrey. The movie was all tenderness and sentiment but indicated that little had changed for deviates, for they usually ended up dead, and by their own hand. In this case the headmistress (Edwige Feuillère) has an affair with one of her teachers (Simone Simon) who, however, suspects her of liaisons with some of the pupils – and an English girl, Olivia, does come between them.

Leaving aside *Ossessione* as a special case, these films all took time to cross the Atlantic – though the least noxious, *Bitter Rice*, took the least time (one year). *Olivia*, rechristened *The Pit of Loneliness* – which in no way describes its contents – did not arrive till 1954, nor did *La Ronde*, by then four years old, and that was only after a battle in the Supreme Court to get a copy into the country in the first place. The fury aroused among the guardians of morality by this whole group of films was as nothing compared to the furore surrounding *Il Miracolo*. This quite short film (it originally formed part of a longer one, supported by another story altogether)

was dedicated to the art of Anna Magnani, who was at the time the mistress of the director, Roberto Rossellini, both highly esteemed by critics (and the screen writer, Federico Fellini, later would be – at least as a director). Magnani played a village outcast, a shepherdess who, after too much wine beds down with her drinking companion, a passing stranger. She thought he looked like Saint Joseph, so when she becomes pregnant she believes that she will give birth to the Messiah, and is thus reviled by the villagers, proving that they are not true Christians. Well, there: not only sex but blasphemy, and the film was rejected outright by the censors in both Britain and the US. However after battles lasting throughout 1949 the local authority of London allowed it to be shown, with a few cuts, in January 1950. New York's authority followed suit, despite the opposition of the American Legion of Decency, and the film opened in that city at the end of the year. The Legion recommended that no Catholic go near the film, but just in case they hadn't heard out there, its condemnation was joined by Cardinal Spellman and other Catholic groups. There were ugly scenes with pickets outside the cinema, causing the state censorship board to think again, after which the matter went to court; but in February 1952 the Supreme Court decided that Americans would not be sullied if exposed to the sad adventure of that peasant woman. So in two infamous cases the judiciary had supported the licentious, giving pause to both the Legion and the MPAA.

Their chagrin was the worse because the film had been made by the world's most immoral man, Rossellini, though since he was a man he was probably not quite as evil as his inamorata, Ingrid Bergman. After seeing *Roma Città Aperta* and *Paisà* she had asked him, by mail, whether he had a film subject for her. She simply wanted to escape the synthetic stuff that she was doing in Hollywood – and he, once she was working with him, decided to make a conquest. Or vice versa. He would not have been the first director to sleep with his star, but alas for her she held a special place in the affections of the American public. All of us may understand Rossellini's desire to make love to her, but she was not one of Hollywood's 'sexy' stars: and hadn't she played a nun? And Joan of Arc? Few people would have known of their affair if she had not decided to have Rossellini's baby. That wasn't the first time that a movie star had become a mother out of wedlock, but it was the first time the world's press were on to the matter. Daily, the headlines screamed. Fortunately for Hollywood, she was Swedish and her misdemeanours had occurred in Italy. With the films that Europe was now exporting, the Bergman affair only went to confirm the decadence of the old world. What happened in the Supreme Court and some art cinemas was decidely worrying, but it affected few Americans. The MPAA reacted to a star's wrongdoing as it had in the past, by looking at Hollywood's movies more keenly. The end was nearer than anyone realised.

9.
Getting to Letting It All Hang Out

One of the first films in English to be granted the British censor's X certificate was *A Streetcar Named Desire*, which in 1951 brought blatant nymphomania to the screen. Hollywood had been progressing slowly, urged on by its leading directors. In 1950 Billy Wilder has a sales clerk say 'As long as the lady's paying . . .' in *Sunset Boulevard* to the young unemployed screenwriter (William Holden), indicating his status vis-à-vis the dotty ageing movie star (Gloria Swanson) who is buying him clothes; and the following year the sweet heroine (Jeanne Crain) of Joseph L. Mankiewicz's *People Will Talk* is a pregnant student when for the purposes of the plot she might just as well have been a pregnant student widow. The father, another student, has gone away and that is all there is to it. There is much more to that streetcar, whose very title was enticing to those who didn't know that Desire is a district in New Orleans.

Tennessee Williams's play had opened in New York in

When in *Sunset Boulevard* an unemployed screenwriter (William Holden) goes to live with a wealthy ex-movie star (Gloria Swanson) it's clear that he's not merely preparing the script for her proposed comeback.

Caught in the Act

The acclaim which greeted *A Streetcar Named Desire* did much to change attitudes to the depiction of sexual matters on stage and in film. Tennessee Williams's florid, poetic dialogue was one reason for the wide acceptance, so was the fact that the nymphomaniac Blanche Dubois was not the sort who lived next door, nor was her brutish brother-in-law Stanley – who rapes her, and notice, below, that he has donned his best pajamas to do so. The artists are Vivien Leigh and Marlon Brando, and that is Brando, right, with Kim Hunter, giving him a wifely kiss. We sensed, rather than knew, that theirs was a torrid marriage, and to that extent *Streetcar* was the more insidious in its effectiveness.

December 1947 and as with the two novels by Mailer and Jones there was no going back – though Williams's play is better bracketed with Arthur Miller's *Death of a Salesman*, produced in February 1949, as the two plays with which the Broadway theatre matured. The keynote of both is compassion, in Miller's case towards a failed travelling salesman and in Williams's case towards a woman who has granted her favours to too many men. She is Blanche Dubois, who puts on such airs while staying with her sister and her slob of a brother-in-law that the latter understandably taunts her when he learns of her less than snow-white past. Blanche's past was not entirely shocking since no one expected the best of faded Southern belles. Williams handled it in such a way that no one was offended: Blanche had been sacked as a teacher for frequenting the Flamingo Hotel and he merely inferred that she went there less for money than because she liked to be around men. Stanley – the slob –

not only takes Blanche down a peg or two by ridiculing her, but while his wife is away having a baby he dons his best silk pajamas and rapes her.

Despite the quality of the play and superlative acting and production, it is doubtful whether it would have been so warmly received if Blanche had not wanted to erase her past by becoming respectably married. Equally integral is her eventual descent into insanity. In London the play was presented by the West End's leading production company, starring Vivien Leigh as Blanche and directed by her husband, Laurence Olivier, acknowledged as Britain's premier actor manager. Miss Leigh was called to Hollywood for the film version, being co-produced by the agent Charles K. Feldman and Warner Bros, with three of the players from the New York cast – Marlon Brando as Stanley, Kim Hunter as his wife and Karl Malden as the nice bachelor Blanche hoped to marry. Elia Kazan, who had directed them on

Broadway, felt that he had nothing new to bring to the material and agreed to do the film only at the behest of Williams, but his ranking as a Hollywood director was another reason the MPAA had to bow to the inevitable. Despite petitions from the Legion of Decency, there was no stopping *Streetcar*. The battles were many and the MPAA lost nearly all of them though they had some victories: Stanley no longer says 'We've had this date together from the beginning' as he rapes Blanche, which is an improvement on the play (if valid behaviour, in view of her coquettish manner towards him); the Hotel Flamingo is no longer 'Out of Bounds' to troops, which made it really raunchy; and Blanche's reference to the discovery of her husband's homosexuality is even more oblique than it was on the stage – and in any case few spectators could have thought that Blanche's weakness for men was caused by coming into a room 'with two people in it' and the boy husband's subsequent suicide. The MPAA also won in one vital matter. After Blanche has been led away at the end her sister says with great firmness 'I am never going back to him – ever', to punish him for his violation of Blanche. But till that moment she had shown enormous enjoyment in Stanley's company – and since she had so clearly married beneath her we may suppose that that had much to do with his personality. It would be too easy to say that he was good in bed, although Brando's performance radiates sexuality. Whatever his shortcomings Stella obviously regards them as equal partners in their emotional relationship. No matter what the rest of the content of the film, the American screen had never before seen a marriage depicted with such sexual honesty.

Warner Bros were very careful with *Streetcar*. Following the precedent of Hollywood's last full scale attempt at a sex film, *Duel in the Sun*, the advertisements were what the trade calls 'dignified'. A pre-title credit defensively announces 'The Pulitzer Prize-Winning Play and Recipient of the New York critics award'. Despite, later, several Academy awards, the film did only moderate business in cinemas. Those spectators who had gone seeking sensationalism quickly disabused their friends, for *Streetcar* deglamorised sex. Not only is the loose lady led off to the loony bin, but before ravishing her Stanley holds a naked lamp-bulb near her face to expose the ravages of time. This wasn't Lana Turner or Betty Grable. Those in the MPAA Office breathed again: filmed Broadway plays of this nature were only caviar to the general and not wanted by the great unwashed.

The intellectual buffs in the cities remarked this step in Hollywood's growing-up process and returned to their foreign-language films. The French exported Jacques Becker's beautiful *Casque d'Or*, in which a *poule* (Simone Signoret) attempts to leave the milieu when she meets and falls in love with a carpenter (Serge Reggiani) who is not part of it; in Max Ophuls's three-

Casque d'Or is a love story set in the Paris underworld of the *belle epoque*, where big and small time crooks are involved in theft, prostitution and other unlawful activities. The mistress (Simone Signoret) of one criminal finds a sudden but overwhelming love for a mild-mannered carpenter, and they flee together to a rustic idyll, both more honest and more convincing than most in many movies of the time.

part movie *Le Plaisir*, based on stories by de Maupassant, the jolly inmates of a bordello go to spend a day in the country; in René Clément's *Knave of Hearts* a young Frenchman (Gérard Philipe) living in London sets out to discover successfully that British women are not as frigid as reputed; and in Claude Autant-Lara's *Le Blé en Herbe*, based on a story by Colette, a fortyish woman (Edwige Feuillère) initiates an adolescent boy into the mysteries of sex. There were many lesser films, including a version of Sartre's play *Huis Clos* (1955), directed by Jacqueline Audrey, in which one of the three leading characters is a lesbian (Arletty) – and the reason that she is so is because they are doomed to spend eternity together, making each other unhappy. Added to their other problems, the man cannot have her and she cannot have the other woman. France was also beginning its long run of underworld thrillers, where at best the female characters were nightclub dancers and at worst streetwalkers.

Mostly from France (but also from Italy and Germany) were the 'Red Light' films, so-called despite the fact that the light that glowed from the lamp, in the advertisements, was yellow. Under the lamp stood a woman in mac and beret, often with a cigarette dangling from her lips. In the really bold ads the shadowy figure of a man loomed nearby, even if there was no such sequence in the film itself. The movies themselves varied from the underworld thrillers mentioned above to cheap exploitation jobs; they were usually dubbed and played at the sleazier 'art' cinemas and the small independents whose old reliables, B Westerns, had now dried up. The British produced *Women of Twilight* which, if not the sort of movie booked by the circuits, could claim some merit in being based on a 'crusading' West End play. There was little sex in the movie, whose thesis was that the women of twilight led rotten lives. But there it was: the title was enticing.

Those ads for the Red Light films played a part in our emancipation, along with *A Streetcar Named Desire* and *La Ronde*. There were a number of other factors, equally small but crucial, including the novels mentioned in the last chapter. Only sociologists and sex maniacs had actually read the Kinsey Reports on male and female sexual behaviour (published respectively in 1948 and 1953), but most people knew that the bedroom activity of others was not confined to straight-A heterosexual intercourse. Hugh Hefner started *Playboy* magazine, and although his formula of interspersing serious articles and supposedly highbrow fiction with pin-ups was borrowed from *Esquire*, it probably owed more to a British magazine, *Men Only*, which removed the bras and bathing-suits. No one any longer pretended that nudes were only for naturists. The introduction of the two-piece bikini bathing costume led to other brief beachwear as well as underwear for both sexes which covered only the bare necessities. Starlets whipped off their bras for publicity at the Cannes Film Festival, and although the pictures in the press showed the ladies with hands over their nipples no one was much scandalised.

In Britain a number of homosexual scandals featuring prominent people brought that subject into the open.

Many bachelors no longer blushed when asked when they were going to marry, and their penchant for after-shave lotions and more colourful clothes was soon common, too, with straight men. Contraceptives came up from under the counter, and many a young man and youth carried one in his pocket (alas, sometimes for years) as a badge of honour. More girls went away to college, and as more and more youngsters moved away from home before marriage there were more opportunities to be alone and unchaperoned with a member of the opposite sex. At the same time the 1950s was probably the last decade (and the first) in which a couple could indulge for hours in heavy petting and below-the-belt conversation and yet part amicably when the girl decided that they shouldn't, after all.

None of these freer attitudes were reflected by the American cinema. During both world wars it was expected that much would change afterwards, but as far as sex was concerned the old hypocrisies were too strong in 1919. After the Second World War the movies were too strong. Before it, once the Depression was over, very few movies were set in any real world, but particularly towards the end of the War some good films (from both Britain and Hollywood) did try to grapple with the problems that audiences were facing. And from 1946 onward Italy exported a series of impressive topical films which were expected to revitalise film-making the world over; but Hollywood buried its head in the sand, as did France and Britain, if to a lesser extent. I have already said that there were less than a handful of films about postwar re-adjustment. The American film industry returned to escapism in 1945 and no matter how its critics lambasted it – using the latest European movie as an example – there were few movies on important contemporary subjects in the years that followed.

Traditionally, it was a backward-looking industry and it had always prided itself on providing entertainment first and foremost; but by a paradox movies were not more serious because they were being regarded more seriously. Before the War, only Frank Capra and Charlie Chaplin were highly esteemed among American directors, but by the early 1950s the select group had been expanded to include George Stevens, John Huston, Billy Wilder, William Wyler, Elia Kazan, Joseph L. Mankiewicz, Vincente Minnelli and John Ford. Even the moguls acknowledged these as the leaders of the industry. These directors were individually impatient of the Code's restrictions, but with a couple of exceptions they did not make the sort of movies which challenged our social conceptions. I believe this was coincidence rather than intent, but the fact is that none of them matches the record of Fred Zinnemann, who certainly belongs to the group and who between 1948 and 1951 made three consecutive pictures rooted in postwar problems, *The Search*, *The Men* and *Teresa*. It was not till 1956, when Kazan made *Baby Doll* and *A Face in the Crowd*, that it was apparent that the American cinema had matured: but this was chiefly due to a series of films adapted from television plays and directed by talents arriving fresh from that medium. There is little sexual activity in these films, which include *The Bachelor Party*, *The Young Stranger* and *Edge of the City* but

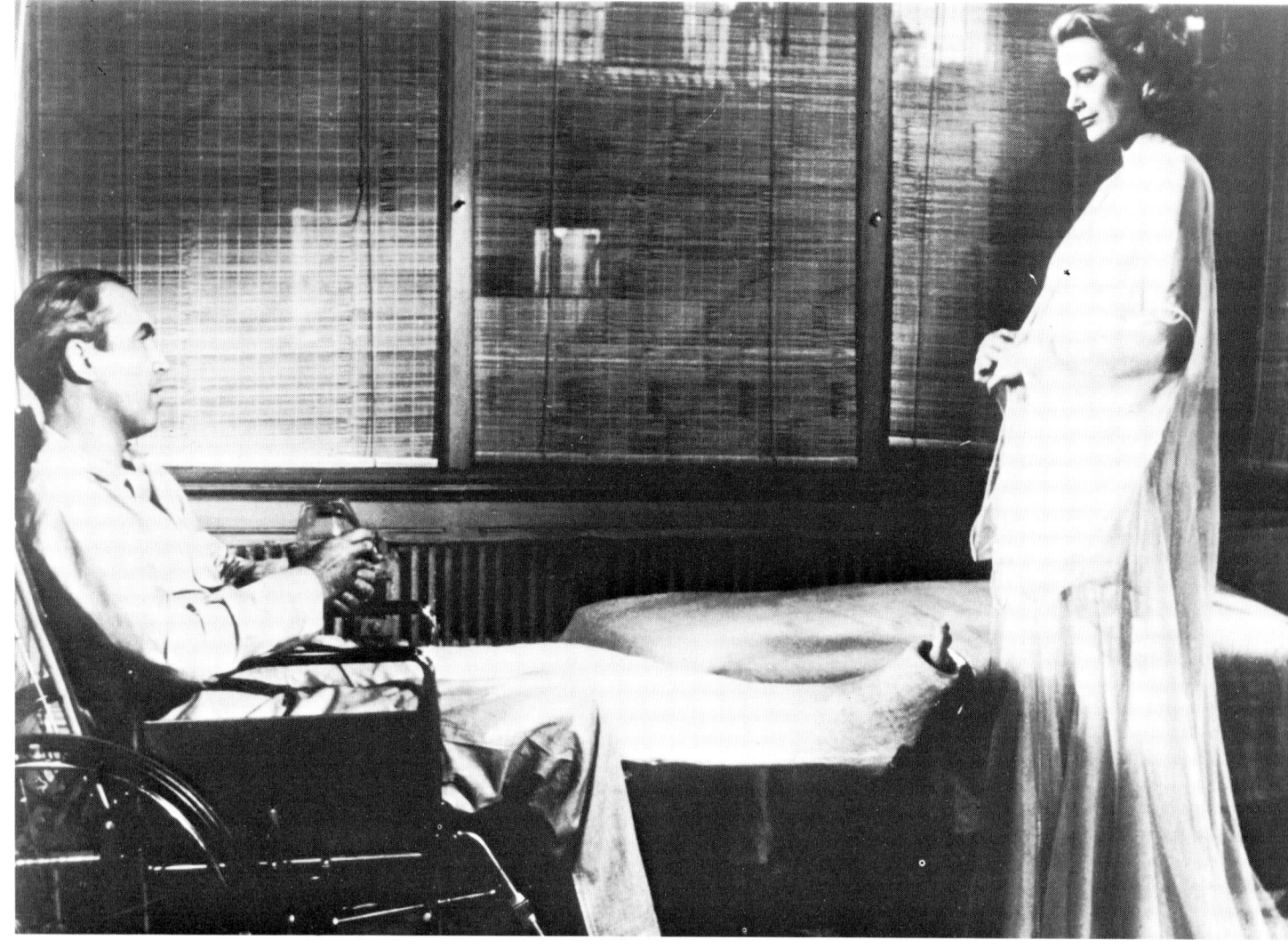

What is happening before the *Rear Window*? Since James Stewart has his leg in plaster his fiancée, Grace Kelly, can spend the night without offending either propriety or the Production Code office; but what is happening across the courtyard more than makes up for the lack of sexual action this side, as the director well knew.

they are attempts to look honestly at contemporary American life. Had they come earlier, the cinema's sexual barriers might have been sooner breached.

As it was, that task was allotted to an idiotic piece of fluff called *The Moon Is Blue*, which startled the industry in 1953 by calling a spade a spade. After a philanderer (William Holden) has picked up a young girl (Maggie McNamara) she asks him whether he intends to seduce her; she announces that she is glad that virgins do not bore him; and once in his flat demands to know whether he has a mistress. The situations – and these forbidden words – were taken from a successful Broadway play by F. Hugh Herbert. The movie director Otto Preminger had been involved in its stage production and resolved to film it, despite assurances by the MPAA that they would not pass the screenplay as it stood. Preminger refused to change a word, claiming integrity. Holden's popularity guaranteed that some cinemas would show the film even if it was denied the Code's seal: and in fact almost all the budget went on Holden's fee. Maverick exhibitors did show the film, despite pickets from the

Legion of Decency, and Preminger gained a reputation as a purveyor of controversy. Six years later he managed to get on to – or, if you like, from – the screen many other words banned hitherto – 'spermatogenis', 'rape' and 'contraceptive', since they were required in *Anatomy of Murder*, a thriller built round a murder trial. The pseudonymous author of the original novel was a judge who had decided that it was time the public was not sold only bromides about life in the courtroom, and it had been a bestseller. The MPAA told Preminger that it would not sanction the words but gave in when he said that he would again go ahead without the Code seal.

Apart from a sequence in *Carmen Jones* in which Carmen (Dorothy Dandridge) dusts down the pants of Joe (Harry Belafonte) after an auto accident, just after they have met, Preminger actually did little for the cause of sex on the screen. Alfred Hitchcock did more, especially in *Rear Window*, which he made in 1954. He believed that there was no suspense 'if sex is too blatant or obvious', adding that he had liked to use 'the drawing-room type, the real ladies who become whores once they're in the bedroom'. He was then speaking with hindsight and thinking of Grace Kelly, who had retired from acting and become Princess Grace of Monaco before entering the marriage bed. She was the most remarkable of his blondes, serene and elegant, keeping in check a tendency to giggle. She was also wonderfully sensual, displaying her nightgown to her fiancé (James Stewart) in *Rear Window*, knowing that she can safely stay the night because his leg is in plaster. 'Preview of coming attractions' she says. He has become a voyeur at the rear window, and what he looks at in his boredom are neighbours up to no sexual good – if we except the newly married couple whose curtains are almost permanently drawn; and when the husband wearily goes to the window for a smoke he is called back to bed. Others include a party girl whose only guests are men, several at a time, and a spinster who, after many tête-à-têtes with imaginary men, plucks up courage to pick one up (and is then outraged when he expects to make love to her). Individually, none of these people is astonishing, but the concentration of them is extraordinary. What was now permissible in one film had been extended – due in part to a movie director's sense of humour.

What was not permissible was Sally Bowles. Christopher Isherwood's promiscuous friend had moved from his stories, *Goodbye to Berlin*, to a Broadway play written by John Van Druten, *I Am a Camera*. Despite its success, Hollywood passed on this one, uncertain of getting a script which would accord with the terms of the Code. A British company took it up, together with Broadway's Sally, Julie Harris. The life led by Broadway's Sally led inevitably to pregnancy, so she had an abortion, but Britain's movie Sally changes her mind about the abortion after arriving in the clinic – and then discovers that she had been mistaken about her period. The change was made to accommodate the MPAA, which nevertheless refused to grant the film a seal. Some American showmen booked it, in the summer of 1955, but it did not attract much attention – unlike *Baby Doll*, which, on the other hand, is primarily a film about sex. This second movie collaboration between Elia Kazan and Tennessee Williams was primarily Kazan's work, though Williams was credited with the screenplay as drawn from two of his one-act plays. In fact, Williams did little more than approve (or disapprove) Kazan's work, though he did contribute some dialogue. The film was made in defiance of the MPAA, which, remembering *Streetcar*, decided at the last minute to grant it a seal: but the indignation of the Legion of Decency rose to new heights – with Cardinal Spellman once more leading the pack, to the extent that many exhibitors were afraid to book the film.

This is what the lady's husband sees in *Baby Doll* – from his secret spyhole; and he has to be content with that for the moment, since he has consented to leave her unviolate till the night of her twentieth birthday. It proves his undoing when an enemy decides to precede him. Carroll Baker was Baby Doll.

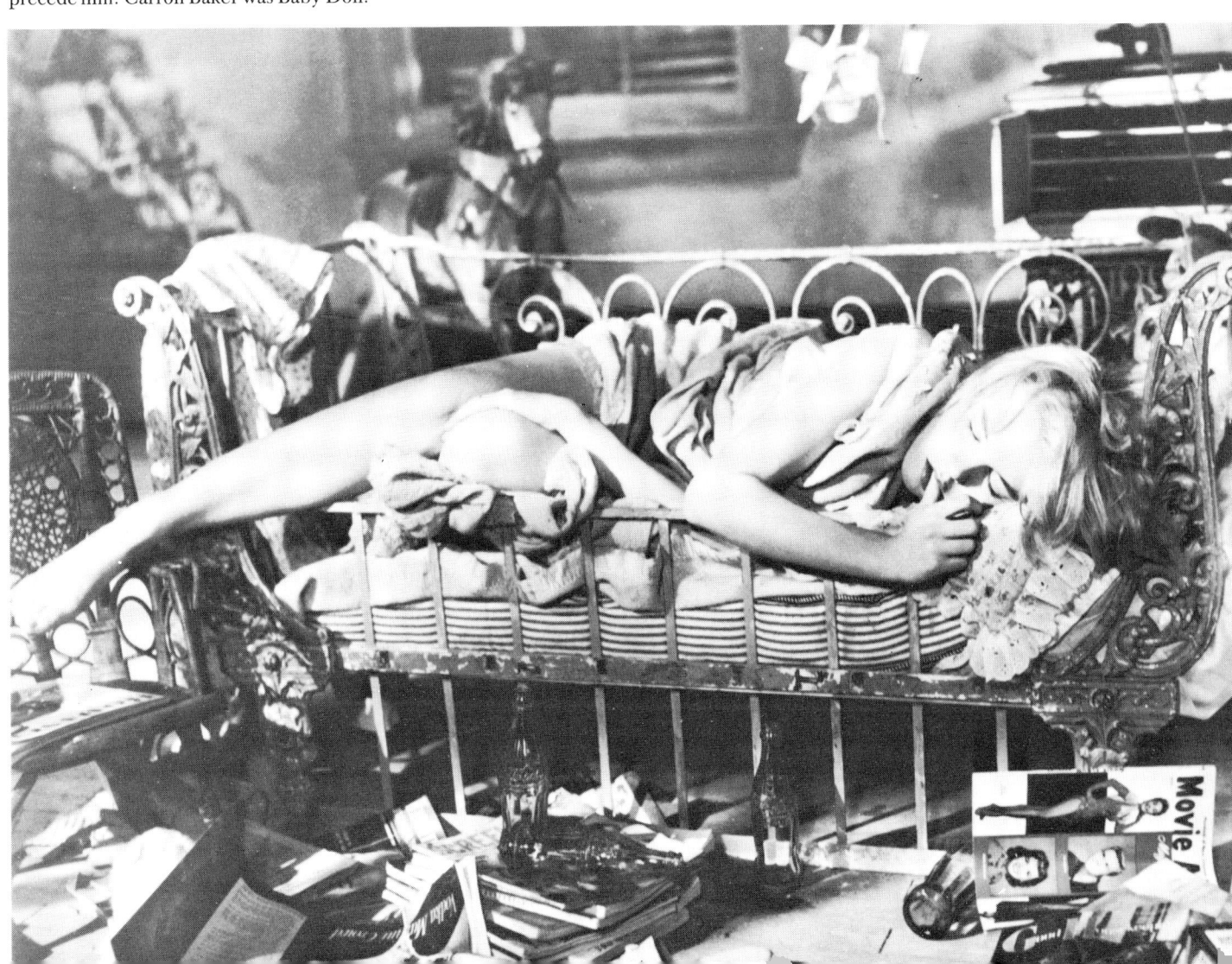

It is set in cotton gin country in the Deep South, and Archie Lee (Karl Malden) loathes Vaccaro (Eli Wallach) because he believes his gin syndicate has put him out of business. Vacarro suspects him of setting fire to the gin and is confirmed in his belief by a remark dropped by Archie Lee's wife Baby Doll (Carroll Baker). She also mentions that her arrangement with her husband is that he shall not possess her till the night of her twentieth birthday (meanwhile he spies on her) and Vaccaro's choice of revenge is that by then she will not be a virgin. She is flattered to have two men now finding her sexually desirable and her contempt for Archie Lee, possibly emanating from his agreeing to the 'arrangement' in the first place, is compounded by his having been discovered in his crime. While Archie Lee is away she and Vaccaro play a cat and mouse game which concludes when she invites him into the nursery where she sleeps. We do not see what ensues, and when we return to them he is on the bed, fully clothed with a blanket over him;

she is kneeling on the floor, her head in his lap in the position of fellatio. Whatever has happened she has developed an uncharacteristic tenderness towards him, and she smooches with him in front of Archie Lee, with the purpose of infuriating the latter.

Those audiences who were able to see the film were not apparently overimpressed, for the piece had little of the success envisaged for it by the press. Unlike *Streetcar*, the sex scenes were erotic, if in a rather odd way. Miss Baker assumed, if briefly, the mantle of sex symbol, of whom the most glorious example, then, since and ever, is Marilyn Monroe. Like Harlow and Mae West, Monroe made sex funny. There was some hesitation in the industry's regard for her when it was known that in her hard-up days she had posed nude for a calendar, but when asked whether she really had nothing on she replied 'The radio' or/and 'Chanel Number Five' – which made the world laugh, and the industry breathed again. Maybe the press agents made up her jokes, but as

Marilyn Monroe remains the ultimate among the screen's sex symbols. She said that she didn't understand it or like it, because 'a symbol becomes a thing – I hate to be a thing. But if I'm going to be a symbol of something I'd rather have it sex.' She never looked more beautiful than in *The Prince and the Showgirl*, below, with Laurence Olivier, though perhaps our fondest memory is of her trying to get cool on a hot New York night, in *The Seven Year Itch*, right.

she emerged from supporting roles as a sexy secretary to stardom – despite the hostility of Darryl F. Zanuck, who held her contract – the public embraced her to its collective bosom, never refusing her its love, despite revelations of mental illness and, after her untimely suicide, of being just another party girl on the studio lot available to visiting firemen. She is at her most provocative in a cod melodrama, *Niagara*, obviously wearing no underwear and wiggling her behind as she walks; at her most enticing in *The Seven Year Itch*, letting her skirt be blown above her head as she stands over an air duct and elsewhere seemingly unaware that the grass widower downstairs lusts after her; at her most beautiful in *The Prince and the Showgirl*, as a plaything for a lascivious European royal (Laurence Olivier); at her most ethereal in *Let's Make Love*, a showgirl helping a man she thinks a theatre aspirant; at her most endearing (and amusing) in *Some Like It Hot*, driving two guys (Jack Lemmon, Tony Curtis) wild while they are dragged up in her all-girl orchestra; and at her most vulnerable in *Bus Stop* and her last completed movie, *The Misfits*, in both cases as a lost soul bringing comfort to males out there in the wilds of Arizona.

In *The Misfits*, made in 1961, she is unequivocally Clark Gable's mistress. Earlier, in 1956, she had serviced Olivier and in 1959 she offered to cure Curtis of his (pretended) impotence. She was allowed so much rope because of her air of innocence. Hefner had started *Playboy* magazine not long after she wiggled her way into our view, and she was a Hefner playmate in the peachy flesh. The magazine was so successful that it removed the nude from under-the-counter: together with Marilyn's calendar poses – which of course it bought to reproduce – it did more to make naked ladies okay than anything since Lady Godiva took that ride through Coventry. Also contributing was decadent old Europe, which sent across the Atlantic a slight, lithe young puss – hardly out of her teens – who in her first important role is first discovered on her stomach, bare-arsed soaking up the sun of St Tropez. She didn't care who saw her, and it was soon clear that she was just as liberal with her body as the views of it. She was restless, as youth is ever restless (though it had not been seen to be so in movies since the time of Clara Bow). She worked in a bookshop, and this being St Tropez, there were yachts in the harbour with rich owners ready to shower

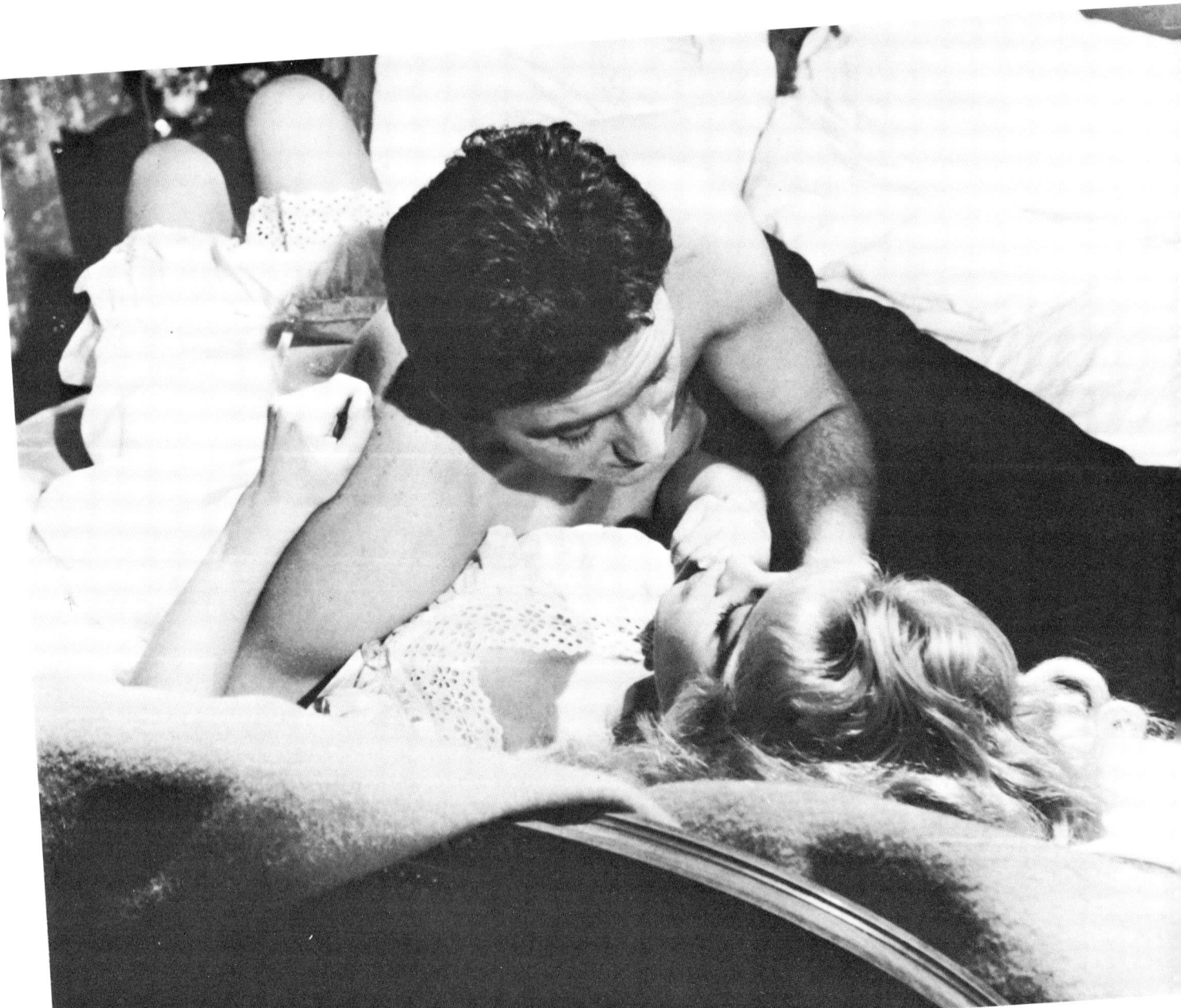

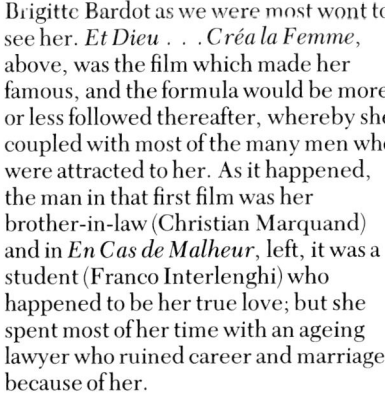

Brigitte Bardot as we were most wont to see her. *Et Dieu . . . Créa la Femme*, above, was the film which made her famous, and the formula would be more or less followed thereafter, whereby she coupled with most of the many men who were attracted to her. As it happened, the man in that first film was her brother-in-law (Christian Marquand) and in *En Cas de Malheur*, left, it was a student (Franco Interlenghi) who happened to be her true love; but she spent most of her time with an ageing lawyer who ruined career and marriage because of her.

luxuries – though these were less important than having the means and time to spend all night dancing the cha cha cha in a small boîte. Sex is secondary, but once embarked upon to be enjoyed to the full, even as the wedding guests sit at the reception lunch downstairs, embarrassed at the absence of bride and groom. Sex becomes primary just a few days later with the handsome brother-in-law: they are on a wide, open beach, not bothering to move away to the sheltering bushes. There is no one about, but you are certain that they wouldn't have cared if there were. The girl is Brigitte Bardot and the film *Et Dieu . . . Créa la Femme*, directed in 1956 by her then husband, Roger Vadim.

Whatever Marilyn's languorous looks and desirability, she was not as readily available as Bardot, nor as two bosomy Italians, Gina Lollobrigida and Sophia Loren, both to be annexed by Hollywood. It was difficult to see what Hollywood could do with either, since their speciality was the village flirt or the town tease, and Hollywood was no longer making movies set in Italian villages. The problem was magnificently solved

Though Howard Hughes did succeed in making a star of Jane Russell the cause of bigger bosoms on the screen did not really make headway till the advent of Italians such as Gina Lollobrigida, above in *La Loi* (aka *Where the Hot Wind Blows*).

with *Boy on a Dolphin*, in which Loren was a Greek marine archaeologist given to rising from the sea with her frocks clinging to her splendid body, but the sexual identity of both ladies – till Hollywood tired of Lollobrigida – was only maintained by casting them as kept women. This moviegoing generation, since revivals then were virtually non-existent, knew Harlow only as a name; in any case Bardot's intentions and actions were more explicit than Harlow was ever allowed. This girl wanted to copulate and she enjoyed doing so: it was no wonder that she brought a vast new public to the art houses of America!

She and the two Italians were not the only ladies to project a seemingly new, earthy image of screen womankind, though their imitators – who include Dany Carrel, whose naked upper-half could be glimpsed in 1957 while romping in a double bed with Gérard Philipe in *Pot-Bouille* – were much less successful. The ladies in the films of Sweden's Ingmar Bergman enjoyed their couplings and went away guiltless afterwards, notably in two comedies, *A Lesson in Love* and *Smiles of a Summer Night*, while his earlier *Summer with Monika*, now shown abroad on the strength of his growing reputation, is probably the best movie till then on the subject of young love – when blighted, that is, since as the summer dies Monika no longer feels obliged to be constant to the young man who has given up so much for her. She is, in fact, a tramp, and Harriet Andersson, who played her, enflamed many a male spectator simply because she resembled the girl across the street far more than Bardot and indeed most movie players. Though it wasn't widely seen, Mizoguchi's *Street of Shame* was a full scale portrait of life in a brothel, and, while we didn't know it then in the West, in the tradition of many, many compassionate Japanese movies about geishas and prostitutes. In most of them, including this one – which is specifically about the changes wrought by the War and the Occupation – the ladies are destined to return with a

Sophia Loren in *The Pride and the Passion*. Like La Lollo she wasn't particularly impressive in her first English-speaking films but she went on to have a distinguished career, including an Oscar-winning performance in *La Ciociara/Two Women*.

sigh to their work after hopes of something better. Thus also the prostitute heroine of *Le Notte di Cabiria*, which the Italian director Federico Fellini fashioned as a vehicle for his wife Giulietta Masina, a wry, cute little bird who saves for that rainy day, to be spent with a respectable husband – only he makes off with the boodle before the knot has been tied; but as the piece closes we see that she's not going to be down for long.

On the other hand *Das Mädchen Rosemarie* ends up dead – or, rather, starts out that way, since this movie, based on fact, sets out to discover why someone or several wanted her out of the way. It would seem that she had been blackmailing some of the tycoons who had engineered the economic miracle – tycoons who had telephoned her for assignations. For callgirl Rosemarie was the descendant of the hookers of the German movies of the 1920s, and this was one of the few German movies widely seen abroad since that time. Similarly *Anders Als Du und Ich* was meant to remind the cognoscenti of Oswald's 1919 movie on male homosexuality, a subject almost wholly ignored by the cinema in the thirty-five-year interim. Viet Harlan's young hero, Klauss, is more interested in paintings than the opposite sex; he creeps away from his cousin's hetero party to be with his best friend, Manfred, who, it so happens, is one of several teenagers 'collected' by a middle-aged antique dealer, who entertains them with *musique concrète* and demonstrations of Greek wrestling by youths in satin swimming-trunks. The film tugs at every family's heartstrings by inferring that there's always a queer in its midst, and naturally the father brings charges against the antique dealer. At which point Klauss suddenly discovers that he's straight after all, chasing the maid round the lawn till the passion of her kisses causes him to Give In. And since Mother had insinuated to the maid that a bit of nookey with Klauss wouldn't be amiss, the antique dealer malevolently brings charges against her.

The film, a mild thing indeed, attempts seriousness by wheeling on a number of medical and legal authorities, and it was later retitled *Das Dritte Geschlect* (*The Third Sex*) in the hope of drumming up some interest. As such it was shown in London and New York in 1959, respectively by virtue of the local authority and a courageous exhibitor: the British censor, like most American cinema owners, was still trying to prevent the world at large from knowing that homosexuals existed. When Warner Bros filmed James M. Cain's novel *Serenade* in 1956 they were confronted with a hero, an opera singer, who is the lover of his impresario: rather than render the affair platonic they turned the impresario into a woman. One who wanted the world to know was the playwright Robert Anderson, who in *Tea and Sympathy* wrote of a boy who worries, if not much, about his lack of virility till he is seduced by the housemaster's wife. Anderson wrote to Vincente Minnelli, who directed the M-G-M's film version in 1956, that the chief meaning of the piece was 'that we must understand and respect the differences in people . . . Along with this is the whole concept of what manliness is . . . Another point, of course, is the tendency for any mass of individuals to gang up on anyone who differs from it.' The piece is not really about a homosexual at all – and

that word is not in the screenplay, having been banished by the MPAA, along with its various pejoratives (and they are what made Britain's Lord Chamberlain ban the play, so that it had to be presented at a club theatre). You can't help thinking that the boy was responsible for his own troubles, what with accepting the role of Lady Teazle in the school play and teaching one of the faculty wives in broad daylight how to sew on a button. He has to be taught to walk in more masculine fashion and when his date with the town tart doesn't work out he thinks of suicide. If there is a homosexual in the film, he is both repressed and villainous – the hearty housemaster, so vehement about the boy and 'long-hair' music. At the end, it is *he* who is listening to long-hair music, doubtless brought on by weekends away with the boys and his wife's comment, 'Bill, we don't touch any more', a not uncommon euphemism during this period for the breakdown of marital relations. The MPAA, incidentally, insisted that the wife pay for her infidelity, so she writes the boy a letter saying that since she left her husband she has had a miserable life because what they did was 'wrong' – but, enigmatically, she sends it to him not via his publisher but her husband.

Only a few months later the MPAA did not seem to have noticed the homosexual implications of *The Strange One* – implications not in Calder Willingham's novel *End As a Man*, but which had crept in when dramatised for New York under that title. The setting is a military academy where the students touch each other more than seems necessary, though the only real weirdo is the one prepared to be a slave to the gentleman who gives the film its title and who is also writing a book about him. Except, of course, there is Jocko himself (Ben Gazzara), a congenital sadist who goes about bullying in socks and garters and forces one of his most despised fellow-students into dating the girlfriend in whom he shows no interest. Otherwise, homosexuality disappeared – except by implication – from *Compulsion*, based on Meyer Levin's novel about the Leopold-Loeb case, and Tennessee Williams's *Cat on a Hot Tin Roof* had to be restructured, so that the chief protagonist (Paul Newman) drank and neglected his wife (Elizabeth Taylor) not because he had had a crush on his dead friend but because she had had an affair with him.

Straight-A sex, prompted by Broadway, did get a better deal. The two couples in Williams's *The Rose Tattoo*, middle-aged and young, did come to the screen with most of their mutual lust unimpaired, while in both *The Rainmaker* and *Summertime/Summer Madness* Katharine Hepburn was an ageing spinster whose life is changed after having been encountered by ships more or less passing in the night. Of course she was Miss Hepburn, Hollywood monument and associated usually with class products, and of course there was much more to these two very romantic films than that: what was new was the spectator's certainty that Hepburn's eventual satisfaction was due to something more than handholding in the moonlight. And the sad situation of the phoney major who played footy-footy with ladies in cinemas was allowed to remain in the Hollywood film of Terence Rattigan's British play, *Separate Tables*.

There were few Hollywood originals at this time, and

Elizabeth Taylor in *Cat on a Hot Tin Roof* appearing to find more comfort from the bedstead than her impotent husband.

After *A Streetcar Named Desire* and *Baby Doll* Tennessee Williams wrote a number of other steamy dramas which were filmed after their success on Broadway. All of them were somewhat bowdlerised for the screen, but there remained no doubt that sex was the main preoccupation of their characters. In *Sweet Bird of Youth*, below, an ageing movie star (Geraldine Page) worried about holding on to the younger man (Paul Newman) she kept. Ava Gardner didn't exactly keep these beach boys, left, in *The Night of the Iguana* but, it was implied, they kept her happy at nights.

In *Peyton Place* one half of the population (Terry Moore and Barry Coe) had no trouble controlling their sex urges and gave expression to them in public, while the other half (Russ Tamblyn here) suffered from frustration.

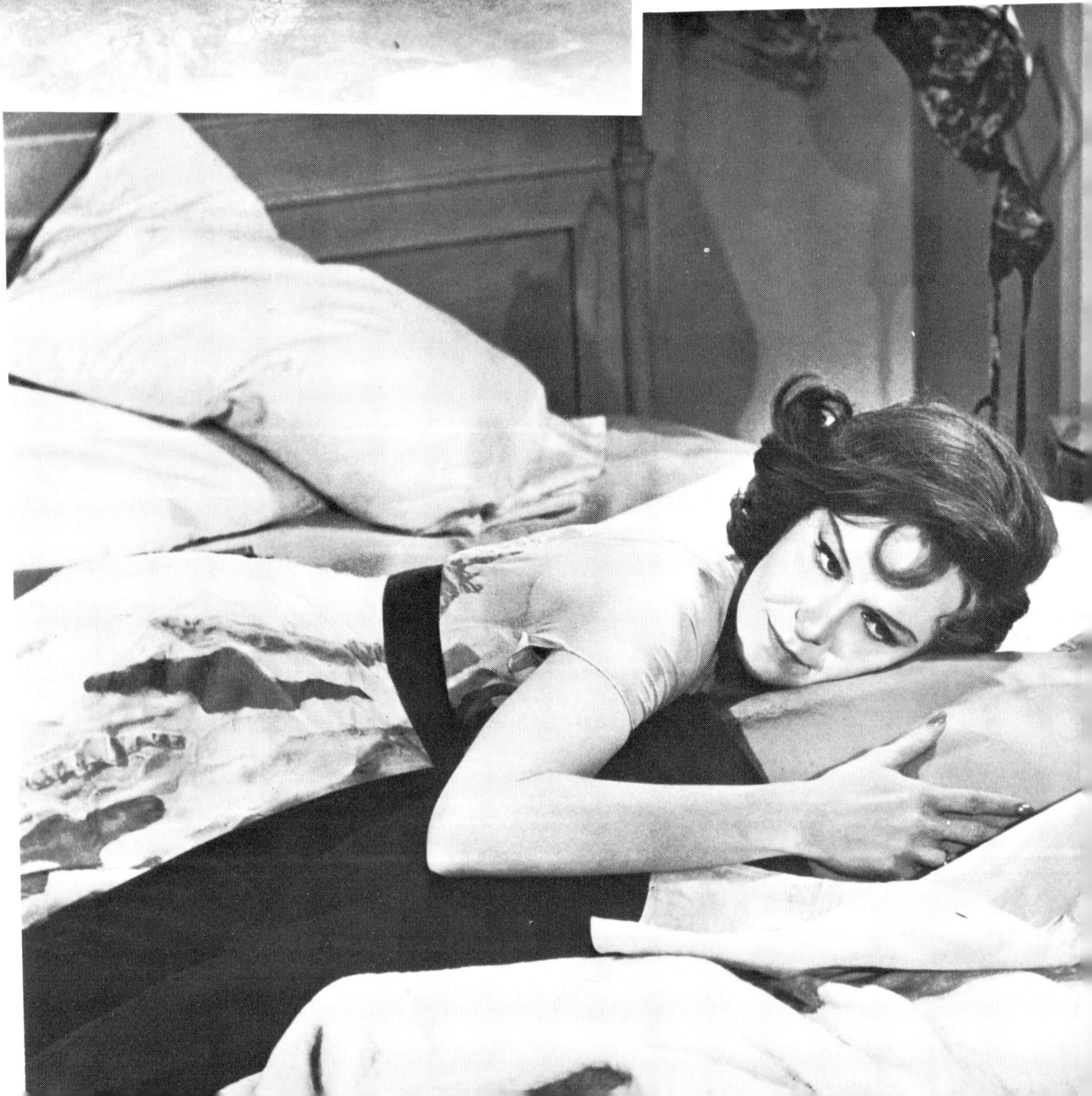

indeed Ernest Lehmann's screenplay for *Sweet Smell of Success* was an extension of one of his short stories; but it does use one situation not seen since the pre-Code era, in which the ambitious but fawning press agent (Tony Curtis) tries to sweet-talk his girlfriend into obliging a client. Further helping the growing-up process were two novels, of differing quality, but in both cases 20th Century-Fox used their status as bestsellers in their arguments with the MPAA. These 'daring' elements, hitherto unseen on the American screen, were used in the exploitation of these movies, unlike those in the films adapted from Broadway plays. New York theatre-goers, probably sophisticates, did not represent the country as a whole and could not therefore be accepted as a guide to what provincial audiences would like. Bestsellerdom allied to the escalating sales of paperbacks had further conferred a certain respectability on Alec Waugh's *Island in the Sun* and Grace Metalious's *Peyton Place*, both filmed in 1957. In the first, a white woman (Joan Fontaine) goes around holding hands with a black man (Harry Belafonte). At least, this was what all the fuss was about. No one seemed to bother that a white man (John Justin) went into a clinch with a black girl

Although its central theme was a reworking of Dreiser's *An American Tragedy*, *Room at the Top* was set so firmly in contemporary Britain that it seemed almost revolutionary, telling as it did of the grammar school educated Laurence Harvey ruthless in his determination to achieve the highest executive jobs. In so doing, he sacrifices his mistress (Simone Signoret, here) for the boss's daughter. The film gained much force from the deliberate contrast between the sensual, touching Signoret and the English rose pallor of the other actress.

(Dorothy Dandridge), a sequence equally revolutionary. Whites had ever gone off the rails in the tropics, but the dusky maidens of past amours had always been played by white actresses blacked-up. Miss Dandridge was black. Diplomat Justin's dilemma is solved by resigning, marrying and going to Britain to write, while Fontaine decides that her friendship with the politician is a bar to his ambitions. The film has in common with *Peyton Place* and others of their genre several sensational elements, including rape – in this 'mature' era not to be thwarted at the last minute. We can partially discount the rape in *Island*, because the couple are husband and wife, but in *Place* the violator is a stepfather, and a drunk into the bargain. Miss Metalious departed this world not long after her book made her very rich, but in the words 'Peyton Place' she left a synonym for all sleepy small towns (meaning every one of them) where passions seeth behind the curtains and closed doors. An adolescent couple discuss the purchase of a manual which will arrive by post in a plain wrapper and the girl says 'Norman, it's time you knew girls want to do the same thing as boys' – but then they don't, perhaps taking their cue from the film's star, Lana Turner, playing a frigid widow. (The casting was opportunism, since Miss Turner was known to lead a colourful life, details of which were made public as this film went the rounds, when her daughter stabbed Turner's gangster lover. With the exception of some messy deaths – from drugs, suicide, murder – and a guilty verdict brought against the director Roman Polanski for sexual relations with a thirteen-year-old girl this was the last great scandal involving a major figure in the movie industry.)

A British bestseller, *Room at the Top*, became a much admired film, chiefly because of Simone Signoret as an older, 'experienced' woman resigned to losing her ambitious lover (Laurence Harvey) to a rich man's daughter whom he has (deliberately?) made pregnant. It is certainly more honest than a curious item released a few months earlier, *The Key* (1958), directed by Carol Reed from a screenplay by the producer, Carl Foreman, taken in turn from a novel by Jan de Hartog. The key of the title pertains to an apartment, with which goes a luscious beauty, played by Sophia Loren. The time is the War, and the key is passed on by various tugboat captains before being killed, till she has quite a collection of their jackets in her wardrobe. The latest 'fiancé' is an American seaman, William Holden, who refers contemptuously to his predecessors. Her attitude is expressed thus: 'I didn't think those rules were so important, after all. People are so busy killing each other.' But since he – the first of many? – offers True Love she walks out on him on discovering that he had passed on the key in a weak moment, not expecting to return from his current mission. That is the highly moral ending. As for Loren, she wears pyjamas and not négligés; she never goes out and is seen cleaning the chimney; and naturally she is bitter about her role as a sailor's comforter.

So: Sophia was awarded the Code seal by the MPAA and Signoret wasn't, and when the latter won the Best Actress Oscar that was another nail in the coffin of the Code. The British, meanwhile, were turning their attention to homosexuals, after a parliamentary report in 1957 which recommended that what two of them did together should no longer be illegal. The enlightened British censor observed that he would not look unfavourably on a 'responsible' handling of the subject, which in effect meant prior consultation with him. First off the mark was *Serious Charge*, based on a West End play, about the effect on the vicarage when the vicar is accused, falsely, of assaulting a boy in the youth club. Next were the two rival films about Oscar Wilde which, reasonably enough, gave not the lowdown on Oscar's low life but concentrated on his arrogance and misfortune: but by quoting direct from transcripts of his trials did manage the sort of dialogue never before heard from the screen. Then there was *Victim* (1961), made by the producer-director (Michael Relph/Basil Dearden) team who had recently had a certain prestige success with *Sapphire*, a thriller set against a background of racial prejudice. Hence, here: 'They make me sick' (barman in gay pub), 'Poor devils, they don't have much of a life' (customer), 'They should all be locked up' (young copper), 'There but for the grace of God . . .' (old copper). Every now and then someone says of the law, 'They call it the blackmailer's charter' and it is a barrister (Dirk Bogarde) who sets out to find out who had driven a young friend of his to suicide. You may well wonder why the blackmailer picked on the poor boy instead of this wealthy, married lawyer, who eventually decides to handle the case at whatever risk to his career and marriage – though not much to the latter, presumably, since he and his wife have 'no secrets from each other' and the film finishes as they go upstairs to bed. Gays of various persuasions are revealed as such during the course of the action including, to his astonishment, the lawyer's best friend: but none of them is the blackmailer. A woman is.

Even the MPAA had conceded that there was such a thing as the love that dare not speak its name – and it didn't, either, in *Suddenly Last Summer*, but it was lurking somewhere within this baroque film. On this occasion the MPAA had to contend with a powerful producer (Sam Spiegel), a prestigious director (Joseph L. Mankiewicz) and, once again Tennessee Williams, who had written the original play. The gay man is dead to start with. The question of what happened during that summer is much debated and it is clear that after the mother (Katharine Hepburn) grew too old to pimp for Sebastian the job was taken over by his cousin (Elizabeth Taylor). That information prevents the necessity of telling us which sex Sebastian preferred, and since he is dead we do not see him preferring it. A flashback at the end reveals that his prey got so sick of his goings-on that they rose up and ate him, causing the film to be known, after its contemporary, *Please Don't Eat the Daisies*, as 'Please Don't Eat the Pansies'. Since Williams was by all accounts, including his own, cheerful about his own homosexuality, we may not suppose that he thought Sebastian got his just rewards. We may consider, however, that the MPAA took that view and that the Board only passed the script because Sebastian seemed to confine his filthy activities to faraway places, not corrupting redblooded American boys.

The title *Never on Sunday* referred to the one day a week when a happy hooker (Melina Mercouri) did not receive her clients. Made in Greece on a minute budget by a blacklisted American director, Jules Dassin, its technical deficiencies and subject-matter should have restricted the showings to art-houses, but it was so popular on its initial showings that the big circuits were happy to book it – and thus general audiences had their first experience of a wholly unrepentant whore.

Jules Dassin could hardly be described thus, but he is an American tourist from Middletown, USA in *Never on Sunday* (1960), arriving in Athens to find 'the purity that was once Greece' but spending most of his time with a prostitute – played by Melina Mercouri (whom Dassin married; he also wrote and directed, playing the male lead since the budget wouldn't run to another player). The Dassin character is enchanted to find that Mercouri's favourite way of relaxing is to watch the tragedies – and that she speaks several languages. Amazed, he asks where she learnt them. 'In bed' she replies laconically. 'A whore can't be happy' he insists, but she is – insistently and relentlessly. He has his values up-ended, while she is seen in bed with a sailor, assuring him that he'll make it. Partly because of Hadjidakis's score and partly because of the film's sweetness and robust humour it was a success the world over, despite the fact that most of the dialogue was in Greek, requiring subtitles.

If *Never on Sunday* is revolutionary in wholly approving of prostitution then so is Louis Malle's *Les Amants* (1958) in its view of adultery. When a bored and restless wife (Jeanne Moreau) wanders downstairs in the moonlight she meets a house guest (Jean-Marc Bory) who, she tells him, irritates her. A moment later she changes her mind and lets him kiss her. They take a boat on to a lake, kissing all the while. She tells him that she will leave her husband for him and they go to her room so that she can pack. Instead of packing she unbuttons his shirt and lowers her nightgown . . . Afterwards, they take a bath together.

Above right: *Les Amants* was another film which revolutionised what was permissible on the screen, as a bored wife (Jeanne Moreau) and a house guest (Jean-Marc Bory) spend one moonlit night together. Advance reports from France suggested that the film would have censorship difficulties abroad, but it was of such quality (as directed by Louis Malle) that it was passed in most countries with no cuts.

Right: Apart from a few German films homosexuality remained outside the scope of those made elsewhere. There was nothing ambiguous, however, about this pioneering scene in Bolognini's *La Notte Brava*, as a wealthy young man (Tomas Milian) offers money to a poor boy (Laurent Terzieff).

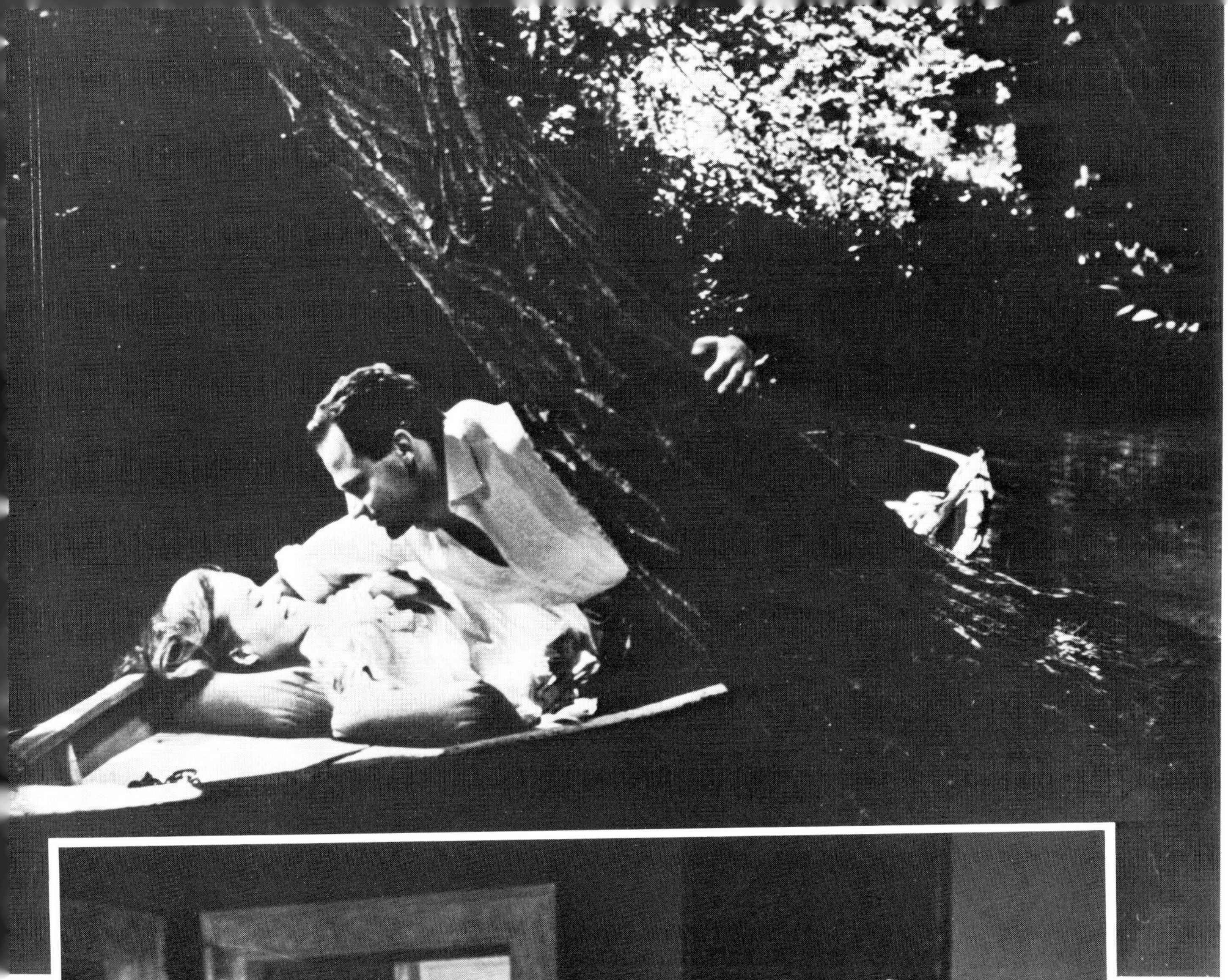
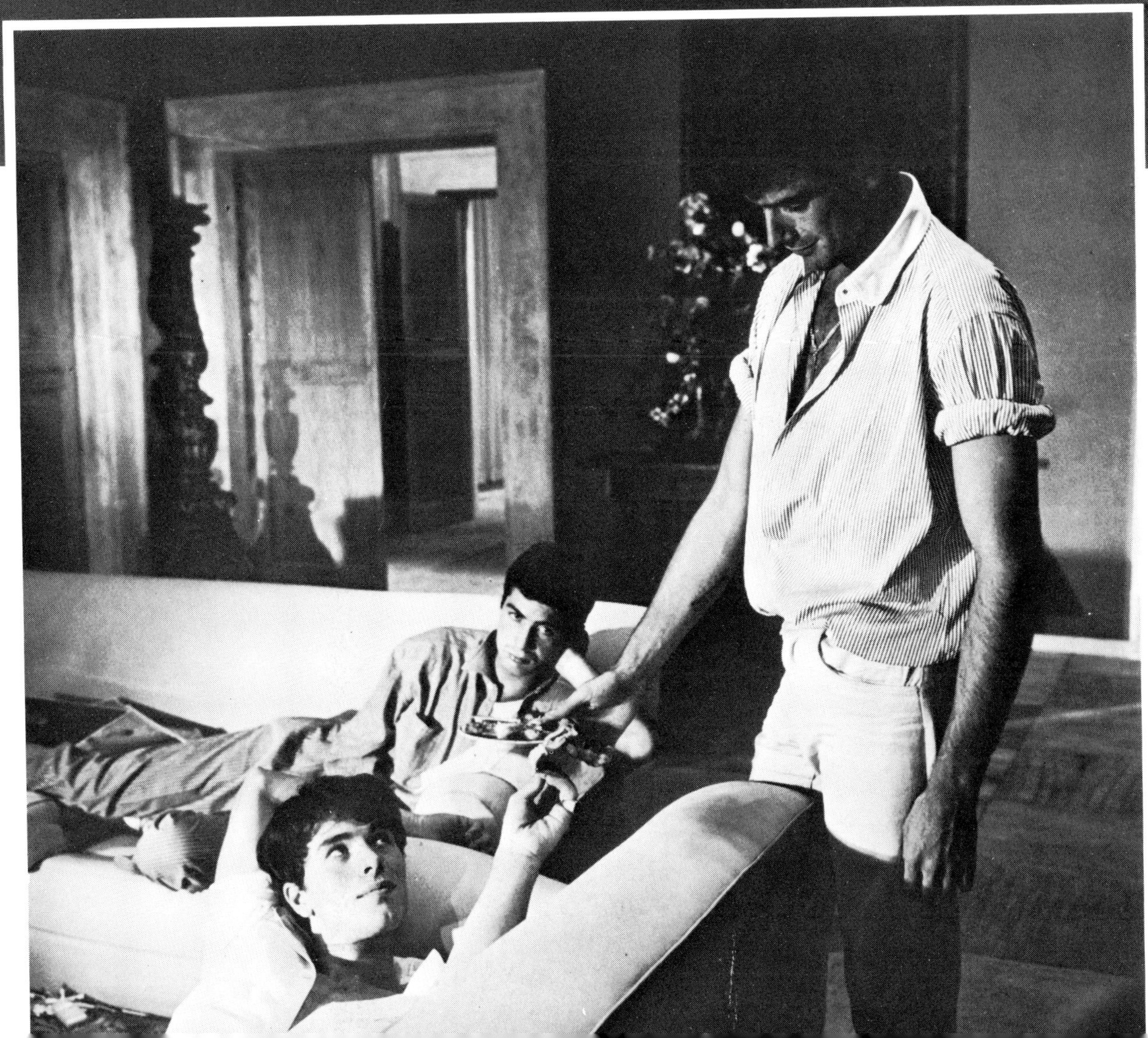

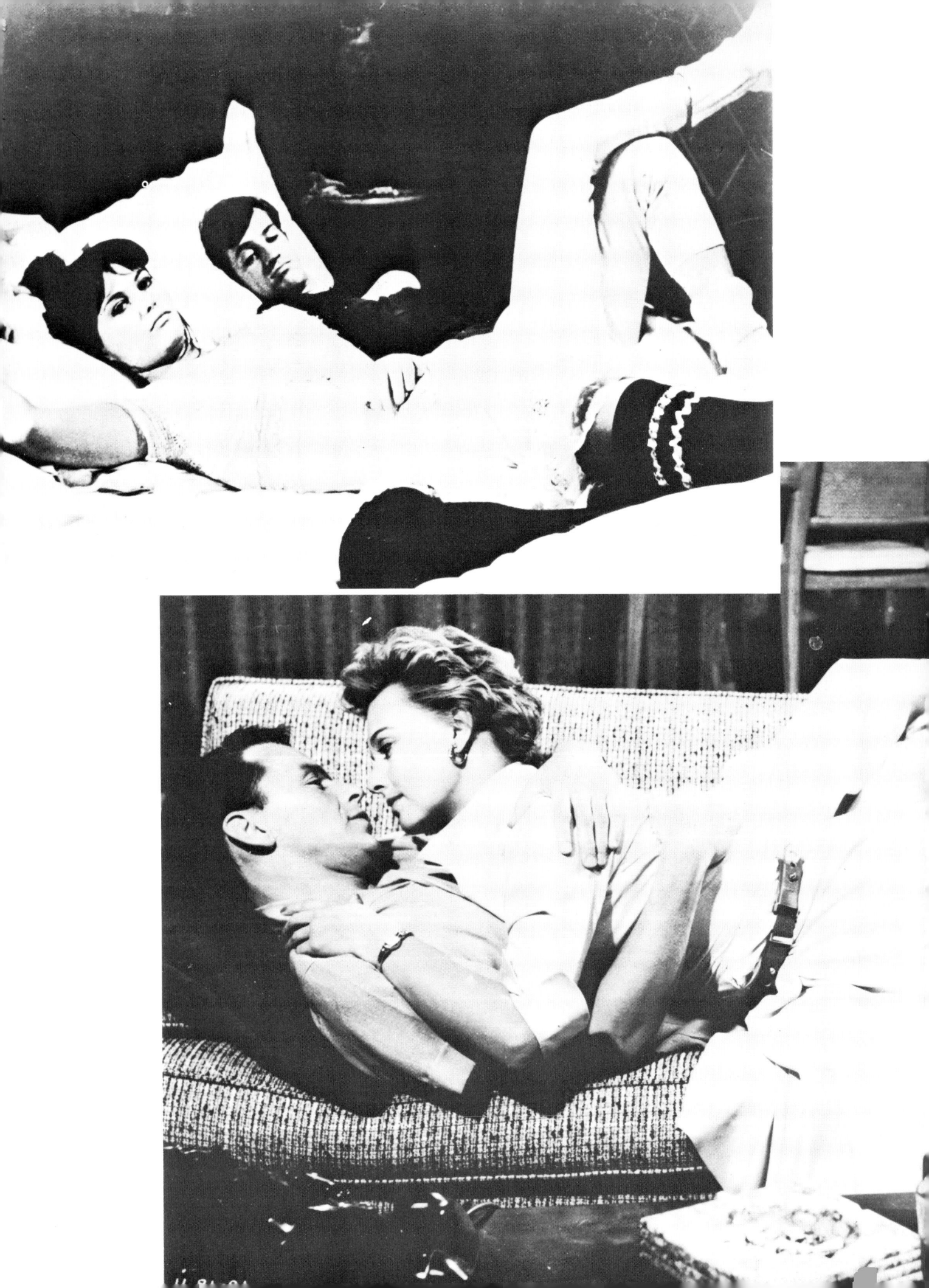

Sexual intercourse was indicated by some hand-holding, but the feeling behind the film – that love is all and marriage secondary – was so strong that most countries were expected to ban the film: few did, probably because it was recognised as one of the key products of the *nouvelle vague*, the movement of young French film-makers acclaimed as bringing a new honesty to the cinema. Another key *nouvelle vague* film, *Hiroshima Mon Amour*, began with a tour of post-coital naked

Left: *La Viaccia* (1961) is set chiefly in a 1880s bordello, for once this landowner's son (Jean-Paul Belmondo) has become attracted to the establishment's prettiest girl (Claudia Cardinale) he is not interested in much else.

Below: *The Tender Trap* was about a bachelor (Frank Sinatra) who kept postponing his wedding because a number of ladies (including, here, Jarma Lewis) proved more willing than his fiancée to hop in the sack with him. The subject was not new, but not since the days of Adolphe Menjou had philanderers had so much licence – and such a luxurious life-style.

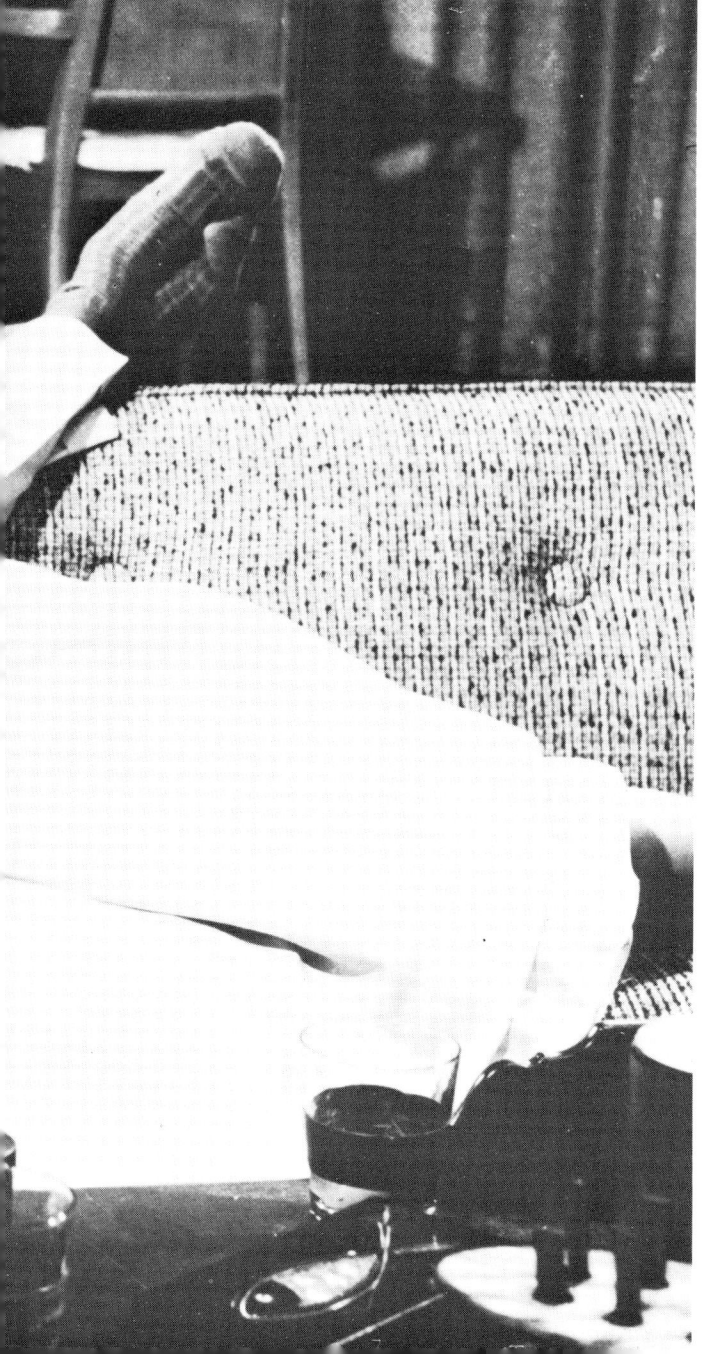

limbs, while another, *Une Femme est une Femme*, celebrates a young lady (Anna Karina) who decides to have a baby by another man when her lover refuses the honour. The young film-makers of France 'spoke' to young audiences with a force unprecedented in cinema, and at the same time three Italian directors – Antonioni with *L'Avventura*, Visconti with *Rocco e i suoi Fratelli* and Fellini with *La Dolce Vita* – offered three extended essays on contemporary life in which, overall, the only form of love excluded was the marital. Less admired but more significant was one of the many studies of youth emanating from Italy (France was making them too), *La Notte Brava* (1959), in which a gang of rich boys pal up with some at the other end of the social scale: and when one of the former gives a wad of lire to one of the latter we can guess the reason. It's a considerable advance on *Anders Als Du und Ich*. The film's director, Mauro Bolognini, went on to direct *Il Bell'Antonio*, about a man suffering from impotence; *La Viaccia*, about a farmboy enthralled by a whore; and *Agostino* (from a novel by Moravia), about a pre-pubescent boy whose friendship with a fisherman is thought to be not unlike that of his mother with a playboy. The writer of *La Notte Brava*, Pier Paolo Pasolini, became a director and made an admiring portrait of a pimp, in *Accattone*, the first of his many studies of rampant sexuality of all persuasions.

Whatever their merits, these films were mightily refreshing after a series of Hollywood comedies as salacious in tone as they were innocent of consummation. Starting in 1955 with *The Tender Trap*, based on a Broadway play, Frank Sinatra – followed by a host of others including Rock Hudson and Jack Lemmon – played a swinging bachelor who hoped to bed the girl without wedding her. The girls pursued used every weapon in their armoury short of actually complying. Not since the days of Adolphe Menjou had there been so many Hollywood philanderers, and as the films became ever more desperate for laughs the heroes feigned impotency or effeminacy to retain their quarry's interest. This situation was used in Billy Wilder's *Some Like It Hot*, which otherwise towers above Hollywood comedies of this period. Wilder had constantly chipped away at the movies' permitted view of sexual relations and, finally, in *The Apartment* (1960), he made a statement which the world endorsed. His starting point was the 1945 British film, *Brief Encounter*, and the flat which was borrowed – but not in the event used – for adultery. Wilder's apartment is used by executives hurrying, once sex is over, to get the 8.14 train, and moronic girls with a penchant for 'Easy Listening' records and resentful of not being put into a taxi. The apartment is owned by Jack Lemmon, a clerk who regards its key as his pass to the executive suite, and one of its clients is Shirley MacLaine. By prevailing standards they made an unappetising couple but the personal qualities of these players – aided by the master director and his fellow screenwriter, I. A. L. Diamond – made them both funny and poignant. Miss Mercouri's Piraeus whore had been nominated for an Academy Award; *The Apartment* was nominated in several categories and took some of the big ones, including Best Picture, Best Direction and Best Story and Screenplay.

10.
Heaven Knows, Anything Goes

The battle was won with *The Apartment*. Wilder, as we shall see, continued to test the screen's areas of permissiveness and in 1964 did so with such bile (and wit) that *Kiss Me, Stupid* drew forth more editorials attacking Hollywood's standards of morality than any movie since Mae West's big successes in the 1930s. By this time the world's screens were awash with hitherto forbidden subjects and few people outside puritan America gave a damn. Changes were afoot in other fields and movies were not, for a while, in the vanguard. When in 1955 Vladimir Nabokov submitted a novel about a middle-aged man obsessed with a twelve-year-old whom he makes his mistress, his publisher did not dare risk prosecution by issuing it. In desperation Nabokov offered *Lolita* to The Olympia Press in Paris, which specialised in hard-core pornography in English for

You don't need to be told the profession of either Jack Lemmon or Shirley MacLaine in *Irma la Douce*. It was the first Hollywood movie set in a brothel – and even at the time the notion seemed unthinkable.

tourists (if they knew where to find it). Championed by Graham Greene, it was published in the US in 1958 and in Britain two years later (despite a prolonged attack on Greene and this 'filfth' by the editor of the *Sunday Express*, who had sent for the book after reading Greene's praise). Encouraged by this, Penguin Books in 1961 decided to issue an unexpurgated edition of D. H. Lawrence's *Lady Chatterley's Lover* in Britain, and in the obscenity trial which followed they were supported by the entire literary establishment. The fact that it was an immediate bestseller was not lost on its opponents, who realised that it would have sold relatively few copies without the publicity. Halfway through the decade the distinguished critic Kenneth Tynan used the most common four-letter word to denote fornication for the first time on television, while elsewhere he was extolling – if in small-circulation, highbrow journals – the joys of pornography, erections and masturbation.

He was one of the eloquent critics of the Lord Chamberlain, who for centuries had decreed what was permissable on the London stage. As late as 1965 the Royal Court Theatre had to turn itself temporarily into a club in order to present John Osborne's play *A Patriot For Me* because its central character is the Austrian traitor Redl and it was Osborne's contention that his treachery was inseparable from his homosexuality. The play was later produced on Broadway without difficulty, just as the unexpurgated version of the Lawrence novel had been on sale in the US for years: the interaction of British and American culture was now so strong and so much known and accepted that it was only a matter of time before London's theatres were granted the freedom of New York's. In New York a musical about youngsters defying the draft and choosing flower power became respectable because it was initially presented by a cultural group, the New York Public Theatre; but *Hair* was unquestionably successful and fashionable because of the scene of hippies writhing naked behind a net – as well as its songs, including a hymn to masturbation.

Tynan did not consider *Hair* went far enough in its depiction of nudity and with some well-known contributors devised *Oh, Calcutta!*, a revue in which chiefly naked players were involved in sexual situations: it opened in New York in 1969, two years after *Hair*. Both shows opened in London the year following their Broadway opening, with *Hair* being the first show to benefit from the abolition of the Lord Chamberlain's office as stage censor. If London audiences were curious about *Hair* it had infinitely less relevance for them, as the hippie movement was one of the few American youth movements not to attract a large following in other countries. The movement grew not only from the violent anti-Vietnam feeling and the cult of loving your fellow creatures (which was considered by some to mean that you had sex with whoever was nearest to you) but was the most extreme reaction against parental values since the 1920s. And subconsciously or not, hippies were reacting against the forced, dishonest, antiseptic television pap on which they had been reared. Television had replaced movies as the world's favourite leisure pursuit and was even less honest on the matter of

sex than the cinema had ever been – if it mentioned it at all. The situation was more acute in the US than elsewhere, for the commercial companies were both more powerful and more timid than the state chains operating in most other countries. By refusing to offend anyone, they lost the respect of an entire generation. Hollywood's* hold on world entertainment remained so strong, however, that American television shows were exported to almost every country outside the Soviet bloc.

The rivalry between television and the movies was the chief reason why the MPAA had begun to sanction more adult themes, for it was apparent that the public would venture out to see elements not permitted on the home screen. The public, after all, was buying novels about promiscuity and homosexuality; it was also not only buying *Playboy* and the by-now myriad imitations, but leaving them about the home; and it was discussing such topics as abortion and the contraceptive pill for youngsters. Gingerly the cinema entered these murky waters and in the early 1960s moviegoers found themselves participating in such topics as pre-marital sex in *Splendor in the Grass* (if, however, set in the 1920s) and a youth's initiation into sex by a much older woman in *A Cold Wind in August*. Audrey Hepburn was a happy call girl in *Breakfast at Tiffany's*, and the man she fell in love with was kept by an older woman; and thanks – yet again – to Tennessee Williams, gigolos featured in *The Roman Spring of Mrs Stone* and *Sweet Bird of Youth*. Even *Lolita* was filmed, in 1962, though only by making the nymphette somewhat older and the man somewhat younger than in the book. In Britain the heroine's best friend in *A Taste of Honey* was a gay man (and she, unmarried, was pregnant by a black sailor). The hero's best friend in *The Leather Boys* was also gay and the hero goes off with him at the end when he leaves his squabbling wife. In two political dramas, *Advise and Consent* and *The Best Man*, a homosexual past proved grounds for blackmail but was otherwise unexceptional, perhaps because both deviants were now contentedly married. Lesbians were treated sympathetically, more or less, in the British *The Greengage Summer* and *The L-Shaped Room*, in the French *La Fille aux Yeux d'Or* and *Phaedra* (which was chiefly about a mother in love with her stepson), as well as in *The Haunting*, while William Wyler remade *These Three*, restoring the original plot. Unwanted pregnancies were the subject of *The L-Shaped Room* (again) and *Love With a Proper Stranger*, and only at the last minute (in the latter) does Natalie Wood decide not to go through with an abortion. Rape was not a last-minute idea in *Cape Fear* but one nurtured, for revenge, throughout the entire film. And there was little doubt (at least to any adult) of what those horrid Turks had in mind for Lawrence of Arabia when they had him in prison.

Beside this catalogue, the adulteries of *Saturday Night and Sunday Morning* and *The Entertainer* seem commonplace. A relatively high proportion of these

---

* *By this time all the movie studios were making television programmes as well as films.*

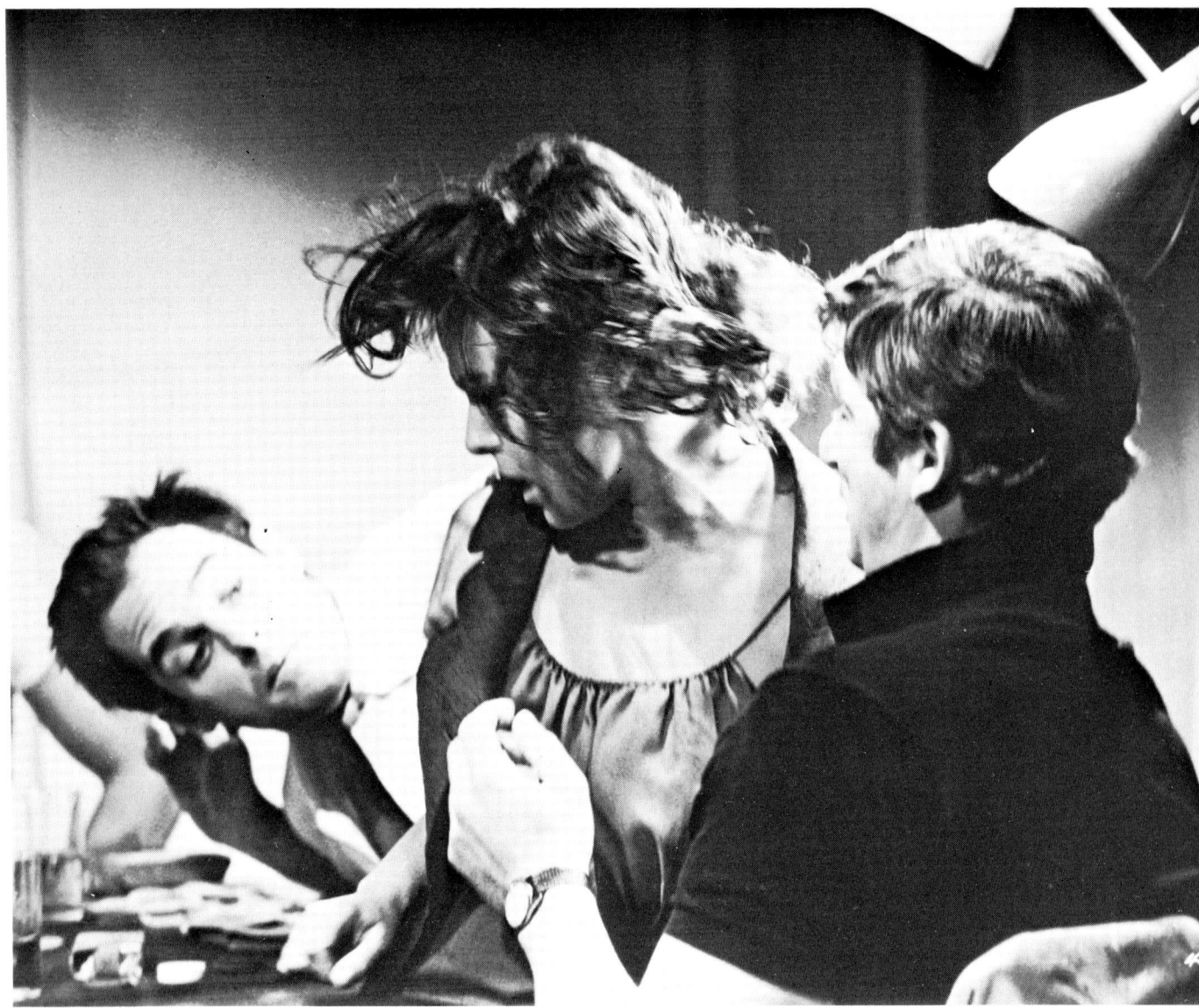

The Chapman Report was pretty daring in its day – concerning as it did the private lives of four ladies. The one played by Claire Bloom liked men much too much, so she got what were her just deserts by the standards of the time: gang rape – but it was a first in American cinema.

films were British, and it could not be said that the American films treated their hitherto-taboo subjects with much vigour. The British movies were further examples of the benevolent censorship there, and their influence and relative popularity in the US were factors in further relaxations by the MPAA – though with results like *The Chapman Report* (1962) they were of doubtful benefit, at least artistically. In this case the MPAA only conceded ground because 20th Century-Fox argued, as in the past, that Irving Wallace's bestseller had been loved by too many to be tampered with. In the event the Association demanded further cuts in the finished movie and others were made both by Darryl F. Zanuck, the producer, and Warner Bros (who for complicated reasons eventually released it). The book was a mild satire on the sort of people who answer questionnaires on their sex lives in the many surveys published since the Kinsey Reports. The film reduces the ladies

with problems to four, including two wives (Glynis Johns and Shelley Winters) who guiltlessly embark on extra-marital affairs and a woman (Jane Fonda) whose unfortunate frigidity derives from guilt over letting boys go too far in adolescence. The director, George Cukor, managed to inject a modicum of satire into these three tales while the fourth is the same old tosh despite introducing gang rape to the American cinema. Nymphomaniacs were not exactly uncommon in movies, but you usually had to guess at their sexual appetites from their habits. Claire Bloom's character in *The Chapman Report* is typical in that she both drinks a lot, and hates herself. Blanche duBois had tried to seduce a delivery boy and he wasn't interested: the delivery boy in *The Chapman Report* can't believe his luck and it is she, unaccountably, who has second thoughts. One day a scruffy musician invites himself in and soon she's a groupie. Drunk one night, his pals rape her; assuming that she's

The James Bond thrillers shattered box-office records, while Bond himself may well have broken records for the number of baddies he killed and the number of girls who jumped into his bed. Their popularity was a contributory factor in movies becoming more permissive: certainly Bond had less ladies in the first of them, *Dr No*, than later. Sean Connery is Bond; the playmate is Zena Marshall.

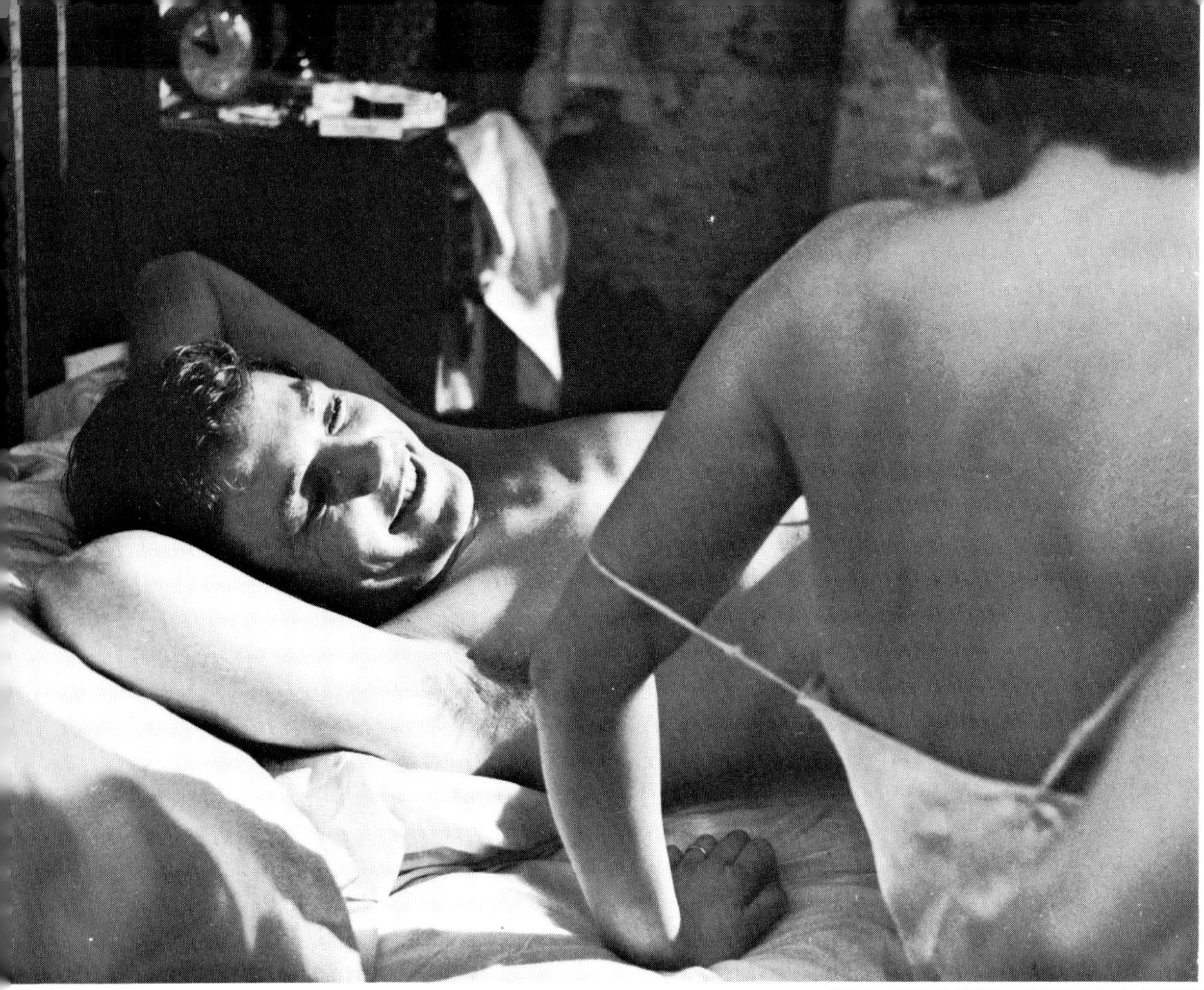

Among the founders of Woodfall Films was the playwright
John Osborne and the theatre director Tony Richardson. After
filming two of Osborne's plays, Woodfall turned to *Saturday
Night and Sunday Morning*, above, about a Nottingham
factory-worker (Albert Finney) having an affair with the wife
(Rachel Roberts) of one of his colleagues. Woodfall had its
biggest success with *Tom Jones*, right. Finney was Tom,
involved in any number of sexual exploits, and Susannah York
was his true love.

the guilty party the musician drops her but she's soon
desperately trying to get him back – and it's a sign of her
utter degradation that she should want a man with
friends like that. Perhaps that is why she eventually
commits suicide.

An American movie set chiefly in an establishment
where men went to purchase sex still seemed unlikely,
and in fact *The Balcony* (1963), produced by a small
independent New York company, was intended for art
house distribution; also, it was based on a play by Jean
Genet whose works, when translated into English, were
staged by avant-garde theatre groups. However, later in
the year, there was *Irma La Douce*, which also originated in a Paris stage piece. Peopled exclusively by
flics, pimps, whores and their punters, *Irma* would
never have made the sea crossings had her exploits not
been accompanied by its attractive, very Parisian songs.
They made palatable such unlikely situations as the men
impatiently queueing at the brothel door. Billy Wilder
argued with the MPAA that what was acceptable for
family audiences in Paris, New York and London was
ipso facto suitable for movie houses and the MPAA

capitulated, though not without demanding changes. One factor in conceding was that Wilder was reuniting Jack Lemmon and Shirley MacLaine, the three of them fresh from the international acclaim for *The Apartment*. The result is vastly inferior, partly because Wilder jettisoned the score and despite the fact (or because?) he adopted a comic-strip style. It is many people's least favourite Wilder picture, including Wilder's; but as its popularity far exceeded both *Some Like It Hot* and *The Apartment* it was clear that Americans were far more interested in brothels than bad notices. Emboldened by a third box-office success, Wilder made *Kiss Me, Stupid*, a story based on the premise that a small town song-writer (Ray Walston) would offer his wife to a lecherous television star (Dean Martin) for a chance at success. This brilliant film, as I said, brought forth wrathful comments recalling the heyday of Miss West, and the film received relatively few bookings, at least in America. Perhaps Wilder should have set it in Europe – where, incidentally, it offended no one and occasioned much admiration.

Perhaps many Americans were still not ready to acknowledge that they were sexual creatures. If *Irma La Douce* was sanctioned by its Paris setting and its international success on the stage, the next film with a high sex quotient, *Tom Jones*, sanctioned itself by its

137

English setting and its source, a classic 18th-century novel. Tom, like Irma, is good-natured in his various beddings, including one celebrated preliminary when he and his lady dine together, mouthing and sucking on their food in a way intended later for each other. No one in either tale (except the villains) got hurt; Irma even had her baby on the church steps. Her adventures and Tom's misdeeds drew laughter the world over and he got some Oscars into the bargain (other Oscars around this time went to Elizabeth Taylor's call girl in *Butterfield 8* and Lila Kedrova's unrepentant whore in *Zorba the Greek*). The MPAA and the Legion of Decency were being defanged and there was nothing they could do about it.

Once again it should be noted that most of these films were adaptations of novels or plays of note if not of quality. There was no gainsaying their reputation as there was no denying that of Luis Buñuel, who profited from the new leniency to film two aged novels, *Le Journal d'une Femme de Chambre* in 1964 and *Belle de Jour* in 1967 (although made in France, where the material would not have raised eyebrows, the production costs were such that the financiers would have expected lucrative export sales in order to get into profit). Respectively, Buñuel's heroines* are a house-maid who is desired by all the male members of a bourgeois household, including a foot fetishist (although all he wants to do is look) and a respectable housewife who moonlights in the afternoon by working (because she enjoys it) in a Paris bordel. This director's most complex sexual tale is *Tristana* which, since it was made in 1970, belongs to the age of permissiveness; but I mention it here because he had despaired of ever getting a censor-free script from the novel by Benito Perez Galdos and had incorporated several of its themes in *Viridiana*, which had restored, if not made, his reputation in 1961.

Buñuel's amused examinations of the human condition included its sexuality and its relationship with God, preoccupations also of another great director, Ingmar Bergman, though his films are less cynical than analytical. *The Silence* is one of his most profound and astonishing films, centered on two sisters who are travelling apathetically through a country which may (or may not) be in the midst of Civil War. There may (or may

* *When Jean Renoir filmed Octave Mirbeau's novel in America in 1945, as* Diary of a Chambermaid, *he was able to retain much of its pungency without being as explicit as Buñuel in sexual matters.*

The brothel in *Belle de Jour* is almost unique among such establishments in movies because it is not ornate or plush. The girls are Françoise Fabian and Maria Latour, the customer Francis Blanche.

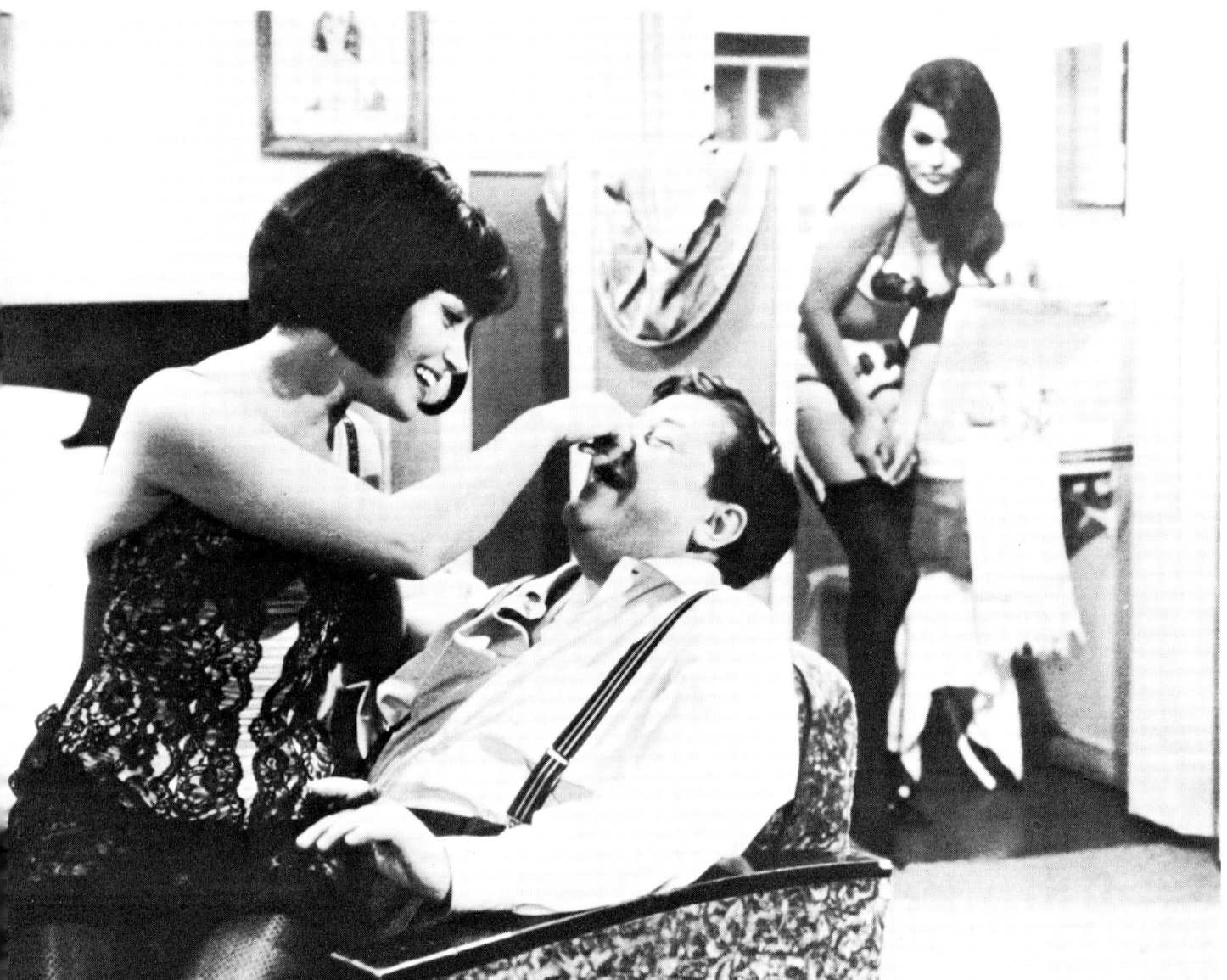

not) be a lesbian, and hence incestuous, relationship between the women; one goes out and meets a stranger, a waiter, and forthwith has animalistic sex with him; the other, alone, drinks some wine preparatory to masturbation, which we experience via close-ups of her face. I do not wish to belittle Bergman's standing by discussing him only in this context, but this sequence was an amazing element to find then in a movie. He told the foreign art-house distributors who bought the film that the sequence should not be removed, and in every country the censor respected his wishes.

The film was first shown in Stockholm in September 1963, and so was *A Sunday in September*, directed by Jörn Donner. This study of a marriage is to my knowledge the first movie to record a couple in the process of the sexual act itself (apart, that is, from that fleeting moment in *Extase*). Seen only in profile and from the waist up, because they are standing, the camera nevertheless stays on them till the man orgasms and slides out. The trouble is, he doesn't seem to have enjoyed himself much. The joylessness of sex in this and other Swedish films was such that it was unlikely to incite even the most excitable foreigners to imitation, which is doubtless why such scenes were not banned elsewhere – even granted that such pessimistic entertain-

ments were unlikely to be seen outside the art-houses.

It was a Danish film, *Seventeen* (1965), which introduced moviegoers to male masturbation – if only in conversation. An older man invites the adolescent hero to join him as they look at a book of nudes showing pubic hair: 'We needn't touch each other' he states, adding that they can pray together afterwards. As a good hetero, the boy refuses to indulge in what a pamphlet on the table calls 'The Secret Vice'; we may be surprised, however, that he exercises the same self-control when looking at a book of erotic prints – since he is shown as overwhelmed by frustration, writhing about in bed unable to sleep. Alas, he doesn't know how to respond to the maid's advances, but after experimenting with his pretty cousin he finds both confidence and several domestics wanting to further his experience. 'There is another way of doing it' says one girl, as they are about to start again, and she leans over in an invitation to sodomy. This wasn't the first time that we had seen a girl's naked breasts nor a boy's bare buttocks but it was the first time they had been an offer in a film whose whole *raison d'etre* was sex. Thus this sexual fantasy – directed, incidentally, by a woman, Annelise Meineche – did break new cinematic ground in several areas. The fantastic element was furthered by the fact that these

I Am Curious – Yellow, in which Lena Nyman played a political activist called Lena, who embarks on an affair with Börje Ahlstedt, playing a lusty man called Börje. Since the director also appeared as himself, some conclusions can be drawn.

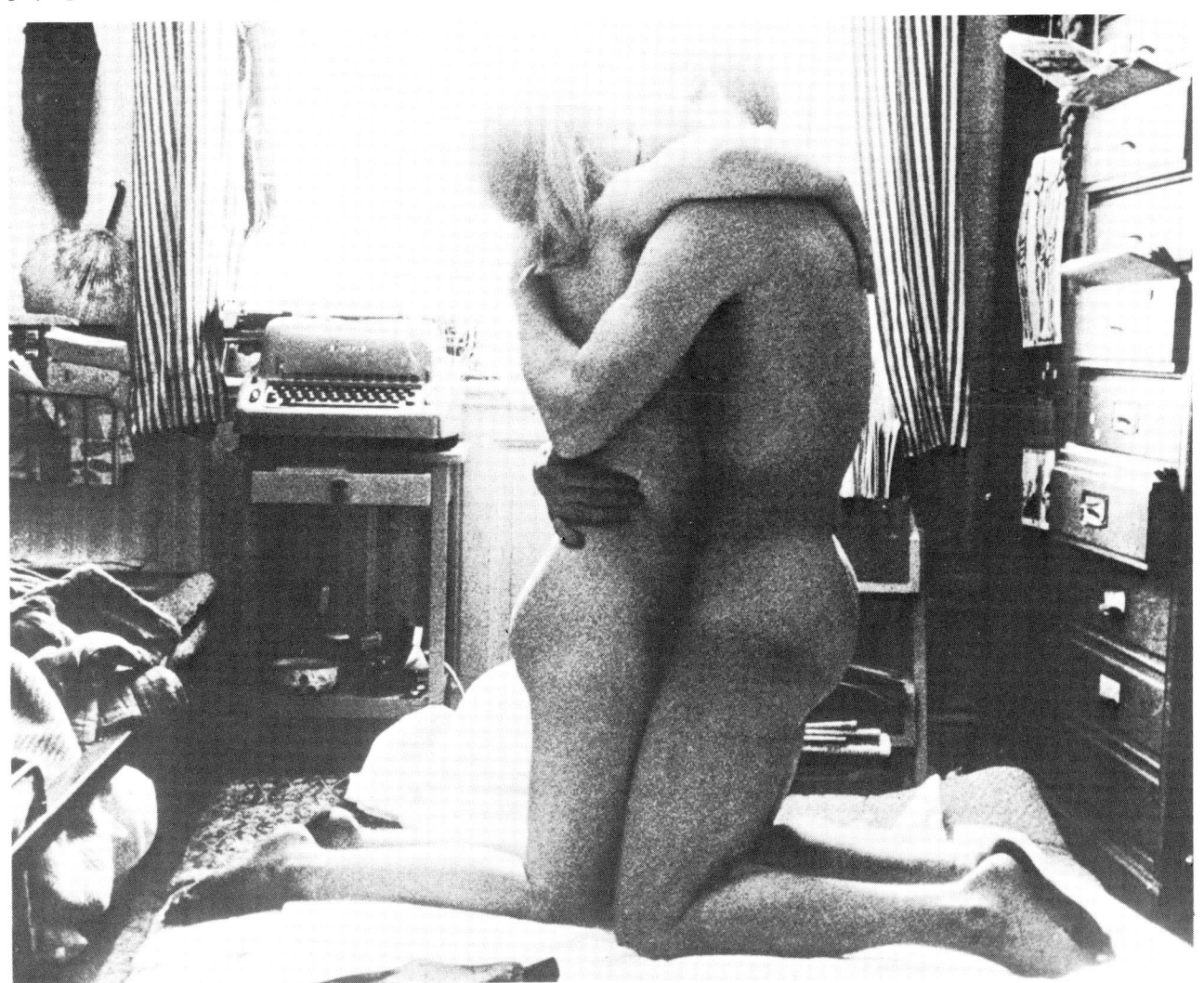

Elliott Gould and Natalie Wood in *Bob and Carol and Ted and Alice*. Note his trousers and her underwear: in the age of movie permissiveness these stayed on remarkably often – for the ladies always seemed dressed for a movie set rather than for bed or against the cold.

events were supposed to take place in 1913, suggesting that the way youngsters then behaved had little to do with today's morals, while knowing that these had not yet been set down so explicitly. Since the film reflected the cheerier nature of the Danes it had few censorship difficulties overseas, reflecting further relaxation of the moral climate.

It ran for months in the less responsible art cinemas, but its daring looked tame just two years later when *I Am Curious – Yellow* arrived from Sweden. The director, Vilgot Sjöman, had already dealt with such topics as perversion and incest on the screen and his theme on this occasion was sexual liberation – as practised by a girl and her lovers who weren't afraid to display their all to the camera. Nor did any of them have any inhibitions

about making love, which included anal intercourse. In Britain the censor who, unlike his American counterpart, was not yet ready to sanction nudity, cut the sequence and others, with a loss of eleven minutes overall; accordingly it did not equal its transatlantic success in Britain.

Clearly, the Scandinavians were not the only people capable of making love in a movie studio. Independent American producers, working on a small budget, were constantly trying to go further and further. At one end of the scale were the anti-cant exploitation guys who sensed that the time had finally come when pornographers could get as rich as they always should have been, while at the other, supposedly, were idealists like the pop painter Andy Warhol, who thought the world was

In *Rachel, Rachel* Joanne Woodward played a schoolteacher who has been so busy looking after her pupils and her parents that she suddenly realises that she will probably never marry. So when an old schoolfriend (James Olson) shows interest in having an affair she goes into it with her eyes wide open.

ready for the truth about the transsexuals, transvestites and hustlers who were denizens of his world. The results, made with minimum funds and minimal technique by amateurs, were as lavish with naked flesh as they were meagre on plot or documentary detail. Perhaps only those who took Warhol's paintings seriously were not bored by these fatuous tombstones, but once again the uninitiated had cause to be grateful to New York's culture vultures. *The Sound of Music* was one thing, but many another family film was failing to find patrons. Exhibitors were prepared to book anything which would draw spectators from their television screens. The industry was in turmoil. The line between what was acceptable and what was not had become blurred. In 1965, for the first time since *Tabu* thirty-four years earlier, a woman's bare breasts were seen in an American film. *Tabu*, photographed in Polynesia, had been regarded as an ethnic movie; the plot of *The Pawnbroker* required a black woman to tear away her blouse. There was no real reason for this, as far as I could see, but this was a serious film (about contemporary New York malaise, as experienced by the pawnbroker himself, comparing it with his years in Auschwitz) directed by Sidney Lumet, who hitherto (and since) had shown no interest in sensationalism. Doubtless that was one reason why the MPAA passed the sequence (as did the Italian censor, despite grim forebodings in the Vatican newspaper).

In 1966, in response to demands from exhibitors the Code was revised, and two years later the MPAA issued a ratings system such as long been practised in Britain. No one under seventeen was allowed to see a film with an X certificate, but by this time many of the less established film-makers and exhibitors were not bothering about classifications. During this period audiences were endorsing movies which couldn't have been made just a few years ago. In 1967 a woman seduced her friends' adolescent son in *The Graduate* and a photographer beds two women at the same time in *Blow Up*; in 1968 the trouble in a lesbian ménage is worsened when a newcomer seduces one of the couple in *The Killing of Sister George*, while in *The Secret Life of an American Wife* a Connecticut commuter's wife decides to put into practice her favourite fantasy of sleeping with a movie star by pretending to be one of the call girls she knows he fancies.

That year, too, *The Sergeant* plucked up courage to tell an enlisted man that he was in love with him, and the spinster in *Rachel, Rachel* decided upon an affair when one presented itself – before, she thought, it was too late. But it was in 1969 that movie people really threw away their inhibitions, especially in *Bob and Carol and Ted and Alice*, in which the young suburban executive set blazed new trails in movie adultery. Bob and Carol may look Ivy League, but they are into Group Therapy, i.e. understanding the 1960s. When Bob, away on a trip, has a casual affair he decides to tell Carol who discovers that she doesn't really mind. Bob has to take a firmer grip on himself when he discovers that Carol now believes that what is good for the gander is good for the goose and is putting the concept into practice. Discussing their adulteries with their best friends, another

couple, they discuss wife-swapping (a phrase unknown to earlier generations) but when all four end up in bed together they have second thoughts. Some inhibitions clearly aren't thrown off that easily.

In *Women in Love* there is a nude wrestling scene between the leading male characters. In *Easy Rider* the hippie heroes are usually stoned when they make love, and invariably do it standing up – on one occasion in a cemetery. In *Goodbye Columbus* a young couple embark on an explicit affair, with some discussion on contraception aids and a word or two new to the screen (when the heroine is asked how she spent her summer, she replies 'Growing a penis'). And in *Midnight Cowboy* a small time hustler arrives in New York convinced that his physical gifts will make him irresistible to women, and hence wealthy; but he's soon reduced to servicing a middle-aged, out of town homosexual in a 42nd Street cinema.

'You can't have two kinds of love' says Rupert's wife towards the end of *Women in Love*, when he laments his failure to come closer to Gerald. Earlier, the two men (Oliver Reed, Alan Bates) had discussed the extent to which they should take their relationship; they decide to wrestle, stripping completely to the buff. Extraordinary.

Above: When Andy
Warhol began to dabble
with movie-making the
result was minimal
cinema. *Flesh*, which
showed how Joe,
played by Joe
d'Allesandro, hustled
on the streets to pay for
the needs of his wife
and her girlfriend.
Despite an abundance
of male nudity, the
combination of
Warhol's reputation
and numbing boredom
made the film admired
in some quarters.

By the time *Midnight Cowboy* had won its several
Academy Awards there were few American cities which
did not have movie houses specialising in hard core
pornography (then being legalised in a number of European countries). By 1972 such movies as *Deep Throat*
and *Devil in Miss Jones* were attracting audiences large
enough to indicate that sexual mania was not confined to
the minority but had most of the nation in its grip. If the
sudden change in public morality was causing confusion
in the movie industry it also had the press in turmoil.
There were pros and cons on advertising these products,
till it was generally decided that the title plus the
description 'Adult Film' and 'Male Film' was all that
prospective patrons needed to know.

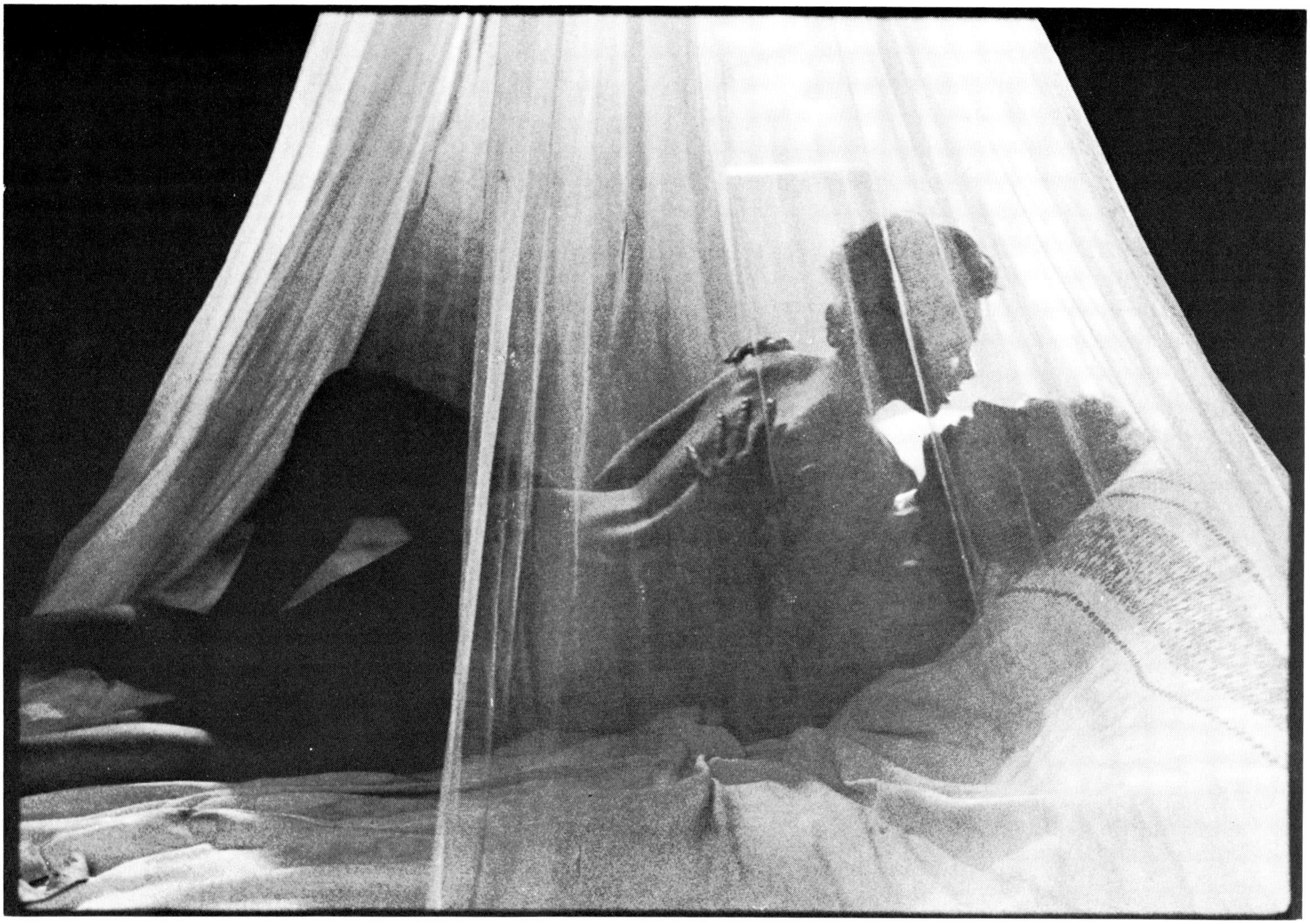

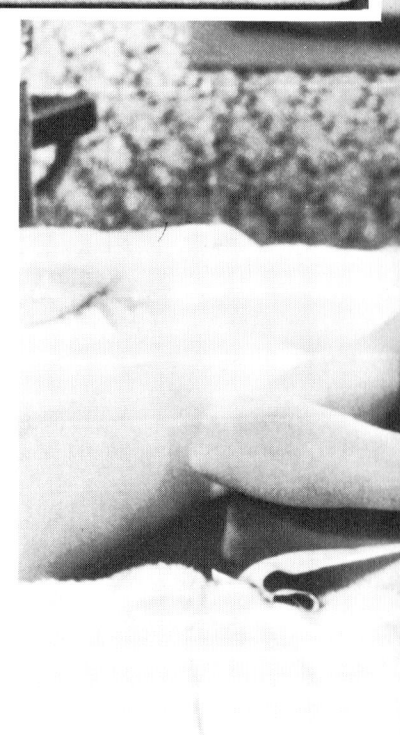

After a while, also, the trade press ceased to review these movies, which was a pity for the plot summaries were often funny, inasmuch as the plotting was chiefly or only concerned with getting sex acts on the screen: and as these had only one purpose the reviewers were cagey, being naturally disinclined to say whether this had been achieved in their own case. *The* classic plot is this: a honeymoon couple's car breaks down and they have to seek shelter in a lonely mansion where they become separated and accordingly assuage their sexual frustration with its many naked inmates – in her case by some of the ladies who have already enjoyed him. This plot was satirised, if that's the word, both in a British stage musical, filmed in 1975 as *The Rocky Horror Picture Show* which is chiefly notable (for our purpose) for the fact that no one seemed to think it odd that some strapping young men are clad only in garter belts and the necessary accoutrements, and again in *Thunder-crack!*, which surfaced a year later. The latter film received a respectful summary in *Sight & Sound*, and although that august and austere journal didn't exactly endorse it, it was rare enough that it even noticed a cheap exploitation movie – in this case so cheap that it looked as though it had cost all of fifty-six bucks. *Variety*, which tended to ignore porno flicks, did review this one,

Above: *Emmanuelle* was the familiar tale of a bored wife – of an official at the French embassy in Bangkok – who finds that there are many people (of both sexes) only too willing to help her relieve her boredom. Sylvia Kristal was Emmanuelle, and has played the role since in the many sequels – some of which have only a tenuous connection with the original.

Right: Brigitte Bardot with Jane Birkin in *Don Juan 1973 ou Si Don Etait une Femme*, an absurd vehicle dreamed up for her by her discoverer and former husband, Roger Vadim. Both their careers were faltering at this point, and she retired after only one more film.

which is nothing if not pornographic – and since this is amateur night run riot any satiric intent does rather fall by the wayside.

The sex scenes are eclectic, for the makers have not bothered with a honeymoon couple: those who are stranded are two lesbians and their male hitchhiker, and two men, one of whom has turned gay after experiencing marriage, and his pick-up. They are welcomed by the mistress of the house and a female neighbour, as randy as they. The hard porno sequences come in three batches, presumably so that only six excisions were required to turn this into a soft porn movie (after 30 minutes of exposition there are ten or so minutes of assorted sex, then another hour of plot, which is followed by more sex, and after more plot there is more graphic action just before the wind-up). The various permutations prove that there *is* something for everyone, but the straight sex couplings are much less enthusiastic than the buddy-buddy scenes. Someone, somewhere, is inevitably watching, through a keyhole or a peephole, so there's a deal of masturbation – to prove, unless the lady has a handy salami or vibrator, that the male participants have something to show. If this is not a gay movie masquerading as a straight one it is still unpleasingly misogynistic; but it does, I think, demon-

strate why screen eroticism was not the liberating thing many hoped for: God imposed physical limitations on both actors and players in porn movies which could only be overcome by imaginative movie-makers – who, if working in main-stream Hollywood, were chary of this form of expression. Audiences for pornography had begun to decline, at least in cinemas: its patrons, after all, have one predominant reason in wanting to see it, and that is perhaps best not achieved in public, even in the dark. 'Adult Films' were soon just as likely to be found on video. As more people acquired VCRs so increased the number of porno films that could be hired from the local Video shop, along with *The Sound of Music*, but to be viewed after the kids had gone to bed.

In the first fine careless rapture of freedom, mainstream Hollywood, or at least 20th Century-Fox, came up with two films that exploited the situation. One was based on Gore Vidal's much-applauded comic novel, *Myra Breckinridge*, which certainly could not have been filmed while the Code was in practice. Myra, in the movie, is a man who, after a sex-change operation arrives in Hollywood seeking revenge on all the male gender, which she exacts by raping a Hollywood stud with a dildo. Many considered the piece one of the worst ever to emerge from an American movie studio, because of quality rather than content; and it wasn't helped by Mae West's return to the screen, for her familiar humour had become too explicit and unattractive from a lady in her seventies. *Beyond the Valley of the Dolls*, also on the surface a satire, a big word to hide behind, was little better. The studio wanted a sequel to its successful *Valley of the Dolls*, but for various and chiefly financial reasons could not reach agreement with the author Jacqueline Susann: so the project was handed to a Chicago film critic, Roger Ebert, who wrote a script, and the off-centre producer-director Russ Meyer, whose soft porno movie, *The Immoral Mr Teas*, made in 1959, had returned over a million dollars for its $24,000 cost. Ebert and Meyer kept Susann's view of the pop-music world, in which its female stars are sexually voracious and their (male) hangers-on ever eager to oblige – even if, in this manifestation, the men are not overly endowed with virility. One character is a nymphomaniac, who boasts that she's even done it swinging from a chandelier; there are several orgies, some explicit girl-girl caressing, and a sequence in which a probably gay man tries to arouse a certainly straight one by playing with him under the bedcovers.

The studio's motives were unquestionably financial, having incurred a loss of over $100 million in the financial year 1969–70. Among the films contributing to that figure, however, were one about a romance between a gambler and a showgirl of doubtful morals (*The Only Game in Town*), one about a homosexual ménage (*Staircase*) and yet another in which most of the characters were promiscuous or of dubious sexuality or both (*Justine*). On the other hand the public had enthusiastically endorsed two other love stories, both with a high sexual content: *Goodbye Columbus*, already mentioned, in which the Jewish hero recommends his girlfriend to buy a diaphragm because she doesn't bother to take the pill, and *Summer of '42*, in which the sex-obsessed and youthful hero goes to buy a condom because an older woman, a war wife, is going to teach him to make love. 20th Century-Fox's experiments with *Beyond the Valley of the Dolls* and *Myra Breckinridge* followed several years of expensive failures and many executive changes – including the return of Darryl F. Zanuck, who thirty years earlier had been chiefly responsible for making this one of Hollywood's great studios. Almost all the movie companies were in turmoil, confronting heavy losses and internal quarrels and

shifts in power. These two fiascos hastened Zaunck's departure from the industry to which he had contributed so much, and he was gone within a few months of their release.

He was the last of the famous studio heads. Doubtless he reflected that such contemporaries as Louis B. Mayer and Harry Cohn were lucky to be gone before permissiveness came to the cinema. If they were spinning in their graves at the sequences he had sanctioned in *Beyond the Valley of the Dolls* and *Myra Breckinridge*

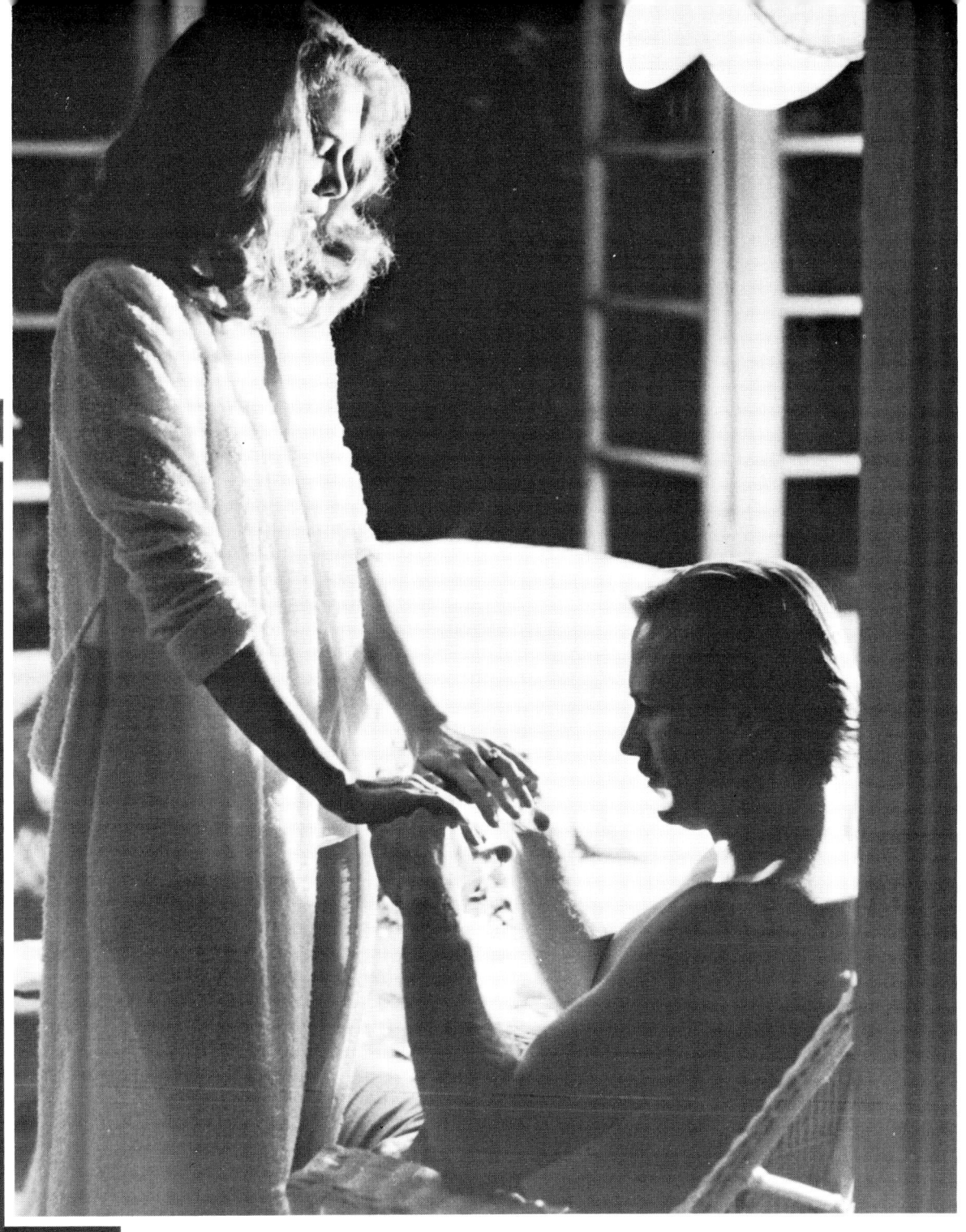

118-15A

Above: *Body Heat* told of a woman (Kathleen Turner) and her lover (William Hurt) who conspire to murder her husband. The writer-director Lawrence Kasdan's avowed inspiration was the *films noirs* of the 1940s, but he took amusing and exciting occasion to show couplings not permitted then.

Left: Keith Carradine and Brooke Shields in *Pretty Baby*, the tale of a nice man who goes to live in a New Orleans brothel and finds himself drawn to a twelve-year-old about to enter her profession.

there were many more to come. Here, in more or less chronological order, are some other things that Mayer's generation would never have dreamed of experiencing in a movie-house: the hooker (Jane Fonda) in *Klute* saying 'Wow, sounds like fun' to an elderly client with deviate tastes, and another in *Carnal Knowledge* telling her client (Jack Nicholson) how 'it' is getting up, as she prepares for fellatio; in *Such Good Friends* a man who ejaculates prematurely on the face of the lady servicing him, and the discussion of butter as a means of lubrication, for heterosexual sodomy, in *Last Tango in Paris*; the dentist (Michel Piccoli) who in *Grandeur Nature* becomes so obsessed with a life-size plastic doll that his marriage and then his job succumb to this fetish;

147

the lady (Julie Christie) who at a party in *Shampoo* kneels under the table to fellatio her boyfriend (Warren Beatty) and the man (seen from behind) in the Greek film, *The Travelling Players*, who masturbates as a half-naked girl sings to him; the girl prostitutes in *Taxi Driver* and *Pretty Baby* and the adolescent in *Hardcore* who deserts a respectable home to appear in pornographic/bondage movies; the hockey-player in *Slap Shot* who does a public striptease (as far as his jockstrap) and the hidden husband (Marcello Mastroianni) who in *Mogliamante* is able to watch his wife's sex-life (as she well knows) and that includes a succession of lovers, kissing another woman and masturbating; the teenage hero (John Travolta) of *Saturday Night Fever* telling his girl that he wants 'a blow-job' since he doesn't have a rubber; the paraplegic war veteran (Jon Voight) bringing his mistress (Miss Fonda) to orgasm by cunnilingus; the wife (Shirley MacLaine) in *Being There* who tries to get the mentally retarded newcomer (Peter Sellers) to become sexually interested in her by masturbating herself – or simulating same; and the lover in *Body Heat* who looks down at his organ and comments that it's so red and shrivelled from overuse that he wants to give it a rest.

For a while in the early 1970s it was virtually impossible to see a movie without sex in it. It was obviously time to call a halt on naked figures humping on beds, though it is probable that the movie-makers only decided to do so when it was clear that such scenes no longer guaranteed box-office success. *Carnal Knowledge*, which was entirely a study of sexual ethics, disappointed commercially in spite of its quartet of star attractions; *Last Tango in Paris*, despite Marlon Brando, the much-touted Italian director Bernardo Bertolucci and considerable notoriety, came nowhere near breaking movie records, as predicted by United Artists. *Pretty Baby*, with equally high expectations, went unremarked by the public at large: here was another admired European director, Louis Malle, making his first American film – and the first serious major American one set almost wholly in a bordello (in New Orleans, c. 1917). The subject, moreover, was child prostitution, with a plotline about a twelve-year-old preparing to enter her mama's profession.

Perhaps those who have seen any of the manifold Japanese films set in geisha houses, or Mauro Bolognini's *La Viaccia* made fifteen years earlier, would feel they had seen this all before; but only one scene in *Pretty Baby* engenders the sort of wonder and indignation we are supposed to feel, and that is when the mother takes a client to her room and makes ready as he quickly pulls down his pants and waits: and the child walks in obviously expecting something to involve the three of them. The dialogue tells us that brothels corrupt, degrade or drive their inmates mad, but we don't see it. Their clients, save a drunk or so, are seemly enough and they themselves are the same sentimentalised whores we've seen in movies from the beginning.

Previously, Malle's films had been sympathetic on the matter of sexual love, not only in *Les Amants* but in *Le Souffle au Coeur* (1971), which says as much as anyone might want to know about reaching puberty in the summer of '54. The theme is a boy growing up, learning

to share himself, the variety of life and the enormity of literature. At one point he settles down to masturbate while reading *J'Irais Cracher sur Vos Tombes*, and he confesses to his priest that he had also masturbated on occasion with his brothers, who introduce him to the real thing by taking him to a brothel. Later, when he is in a sanatorium, he becomes his mother's comforter when her lover leaves her. Their subsequent copulation seems natural enough, and as far as I know there was little adverse comment among the rapturous notices the movie received. It may be supposed, however, that the situation would have been unacceptable in the days when all mothers (except those of very young children) were played by white-haired old ladies. In this case the actress concerned – Lea Massari – was such a knock-out that few spectators could have forgotten that she was a glamorous movie star enacting a role.

If ridicule had greeted the two Fox movies *Beyond the Valley of the Dolls* and *Myra Breckinridge*, Paramount found public indifference awaiting *Pretty Baby* as well as

its contemporary, *Looking for Mr Goodbar* (1977). Richard Brooks adapted and directed Judith Rossner's novel, managing along the way to either show or mention every aspect of sexuality except those which might be an audience turn-off. A nice Catholic girl, Theresa (Diane Keaton), says 'Thank God' after being deflowered by her teacher, who subsequently reveals his true character by brutally telling her that he will not leave his wife for her; she can still reduce him to jelly by raising her skirt to reveal that she is not wearing panties, but she is further disillusioned by his silence, explained thus, 'I just can't stand a woman's company after I've fucked her'. In New York her sister introduces her to porno movies, smoking pot and, though she doesn't participate, group sex. By day Theresa teaches handicapped children; by night she haunts Singles bars and picks up Tony (Richard Gere), who does a wild dance in just a jockstrap, constantly flashing a knife in her face. When he leaves she cannot hide her delight at what has passed: 'I don't believe it, I don't believe it'. She is impatient of the nice Catholic social worker who wants to marry her and laughs when he produces a condom, saying that she has never even seen one. She goes to a gay club and the man she picks up there is presumably straight, but he's rejected when Tony turns up. Tony subsequently beats her up and threatens to kill her; trying to avoid both him and the social worker on New Year's Eve she joins the transvestites in the Village and when we first see Gary (Tom Berenger) he's dressed in a black bra and panties and quarrelling with his black lover. He's in blue jeans when he's picked up by Theresa, who's delighted to discover that he's an ex-con. He's so angry with his lover that he pretends to be straight ('In my neighbourhood, if you didn't fight, you were a fruit. In prison, if you didn't, you spread ass . . .'); but despite his use of amyl nitrate he cannot get aroused – till she laughs at him, preparing to find someone else. He rapes her and stabs her to death.

Since, as I said, this film is the visual equivalent of a mail-order sex catalogue, I think we can take it that

The 1981 remake of *The Postman Always Rings Twice* took the chance of showing what could not be seen in the 1946 version, with some steamy scenes between wife (Jessica Lange) and lover (Jack Nicholson); but despite the playing and a fine director, Bob Rafelson, the piece did not quite work either as thriller or love story.

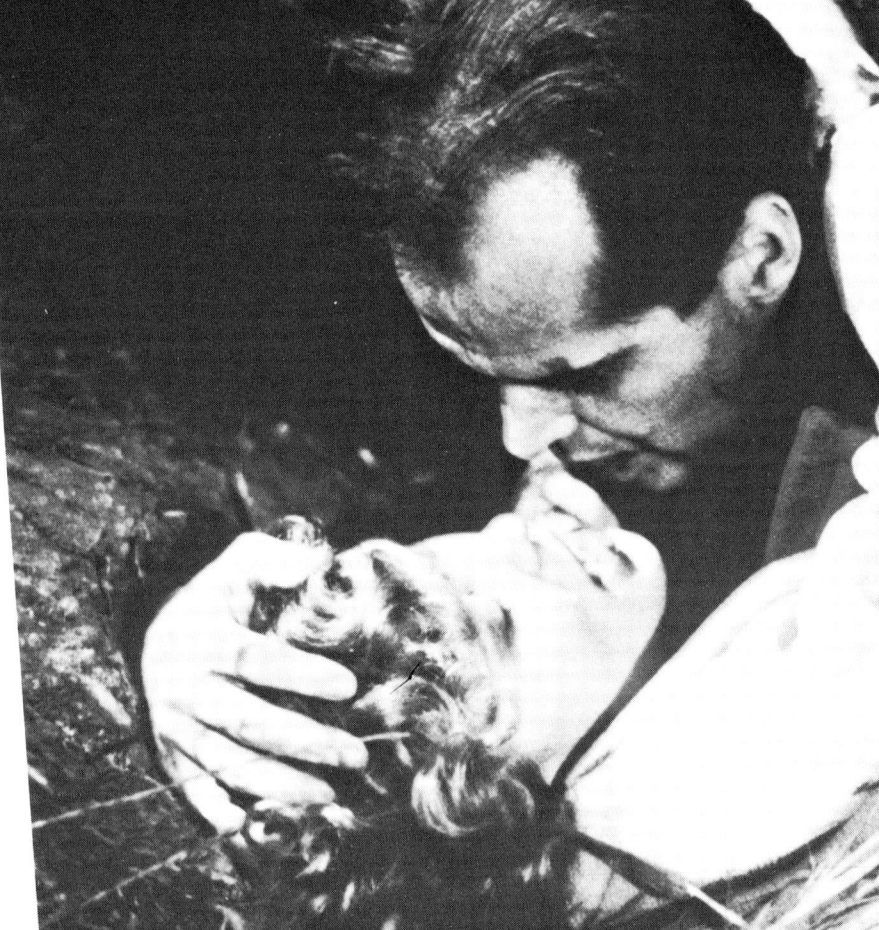

Left: Benoit Ferreux and Lea Massari, mother and son in *Le Souffle au Coeur*. When he goes to a sanatorium she stays nearby, for the sake also of seeing her lover. The boy's acceptance of their meetings and his subsequent pity when her lover leaves leads them to this, which seemed inevitable enough in context.

Right: The white-hot passion of the Lange-Nicholson love scenes in *The Postman Always Rings Twice* remain almost unparalleled in mainstream Hollywood cinema, for the simple reason that most movie-makers prefer a more lyrical approach.

Above: The sequence in *American Gigolo* in which the unworthy hero (Richard Gere) finds himself falling in love for the first time (with Lauren Hutton).

Theresa is not a nymphomaniac. She is certainly not one in the movie tradition, racked with guilt and a lush, but a nice cheerful girl who enjoys sexual congress – and the more so when there's an air of danger. Since she is not depicted as abnormal, Theresa's trouble may have arisen from confusing straight with gay (there is a hint that Tony is a male prostitute; he refers to Theresa and his mother as 'the two biggest cunts in the world'; and he does not appear to have been indulging in any athletic activity when wearing a jockstrap, symbol of the macho male and accordingly a fetish for many gays). Apart from that, the film emerges as moralistic as any Code movie:

the wages of sin are death. Sexuality is shown to be bad and wrong, but along the way we've watched Theresa and others having a marvellous time. Fifty years earlier it was accepted that many young couples in love liked to emulate their screen idols: then, drug-taking was associated with evil but now when Theresa and Tony make love under the influence of cocaine the presentation is lyrical. We are really no distance from Theda Bara.

As much may be said of the same actor, Richard Gere, in *American Gigolo*, a title in itself being a cry of defiance, since the two words could at one time not be presented in conjunction. Gere plays Julian, a Los Angeles hustler whose flashy apartment and large automobile are the results of accommodating older women. He does this in three ways: by acting as guide and interpreter, perhaps more; by having affairs with married women – and Julian's character is supposed to be clear by his pride in being one of the few men willing to spend three hours in bringing one woman to her first orgasm in ten years; and by working for two pimps, one

151

What with his auto, his vast wardrobe and his ease in the best restaurants, many a youth might want to be like Richard Gere in *American Gigolo*.

white and possibly a lesbian, and one black and certainly homosexual. One assignment leads Julian into sado-masochistic sex and when later the woman is found murdered he finds that he is the chief suspect, with no one to help him. In true movie tradition he is too hon-ourable to turn to the woman with whom he has fallen in love; and he refuses the money offered by her hus-band, a Senator, who regards Julian as a blackmailer. The writer-director Paul Schrader proved himself a moralist

in his earlier scripts for *Taxi Driver*, *Hardcore* and *Blue Collar*, so he makes Julian suffer for what he regards as his ignoble life. As a modern movie-maker Schrader is prepared to promise him a happy ending. But even that is hemmed in with the ages-old redemption of true love. When Julian's mistress (who has left her husband) tells him that she loves him he responds – and this is at fade-out – 'My God, Michelle, it's taken me so long to come to it'. The film is much surer than *Looking for Mr Goodbar* of the crossover point: having in his good days refused to 'do fags [or] kinks', Julian in his downfall is whimpering that he will do nothing but; he is as well-known to the doorman of a gay bar as he is to the best *maitre d's*, and his pimp knows that he is not asking the impossible when they have this exchange: 'Got a job for you.' 'Straight?' 'This time of night?'

In 1981 a new version of *The Postman Always Rings Twice* was predicated on the assumption that the cinema could now render James M. Cain's steamy lovers with honesty. And since he created them there is no point in complaining that retribution is built into the story. However, the first sexual encounter is surprisingly joy-less after the looks which have passed between the couple. Indeed, the woman puts up such a struggle as he pushes away her encumbering clothes that this is much like rape; and their subsequent couplings seem hardly more enjoyable to them.

Anyone indulging in screen sex was still, however, likely to wind up very dead. *Star 80* might have been based on fact, but the film is permeated with a feeling that posing for *Playboy* is not the most admirable way to get ahead. Too much sex leads to suicide in *Bad Timing* and *An Officer and a Gentleman*, the last-named being the only film in this *galêre* to achieve wide popularity – and that was due to other factors. And murder muddles events in both *Body Heat*, which was an attempt to return to the *crime passionel* thrillers of yesteryear, and also *American Gigolo*.

These failures made Hollywood wary of sex on the screen. During the late 1970s and so far in the 1980s the big box-office successes have had little or no erotic content – or, indeed, romance in the sense that it would have been recognised by the screen lovers of the past. However, today's predominantly teenage moviegoers have responded warmly to a number of movies on the line of *Porky's* (1981), in which kids of their own age are involved in comic dilemmas chiefly concerned with their attempts to get laid. Since all these movies were dismissed or condemned in the public prints they be-came popular solely by word-of-mouth. Youngsters may be blasé about sex because they are able to make love freely, as earlier generations could not, and it could be argued that they do not derive the same vicarious thrill of watching others do it on screen. The success of *Porky's* is surely due to the fact that the pursuit of sex is amusing and its achievement pleasurable; and the fail-ure of the other films is due to the fact that it is, by and large, punishable. In *Maria's Lovers* (1984) the young husband's trouble is impotency on his wedding night, and since he is not cured of this during the next year he and his wife lead depressing and frustrating lives. He is said to have dreamed about her too much while in the

Now homosexuality is well out of the closet its representatives are likely to be butch types in leather bars, as in *Cruising*.
Different of course from the old Hollywood stereotypes – and probably most gay people.

army. He eventually leaves her and when she arrives to tell him that she is pregnant (by a wayfaring stranger) he angrily rejects her. 'Still crazy about her, kid?' murmurs a colleague. When the dream comes again, the husband is able to exorcise his inability, and he returns for a fine bout of love-making – and seeing this in 1985 was a little like being in a time-wrap, back in the early 1970s when nude bodies moving in unison were inescapable. (I cannot help thinking that the unfortunate young man would have had no trouble in the first place if he had only removed his trousers: the movie is set in 1946, when such scenes were not permissible, but presumably in life young bridegrooms were not so circumspect.)

Elsewhere there is a deal of timidity. *All Of Me* is based on the Thorne Smith-like premise of a man (Steve Martin) who finds half his body taken over by the soul of a dead woman (Lily Tomlin), who is reluctant to let him urinate in the men's room and even more unwilling to let him indulge himself with a compliant and already undressed young lady. On the second occasion he lectures Tomlin (his reflection in the mirror) on the joys of sex, getting her excited about the tingling sensation – which might have led to a mild lesbian joke or so. It doesn't, nor is there a single gay reference to the fact that the Tomlin part of Martin makes that part effeminate. That leaves only one sex joke in the form of a comment of a colleague, having witnessed the contretemps in the men's room, that Martin is a pervert because he talks to, and plays with, himself, in such places.

Ten years after *Bob and Carol and Ted and Alice* the writer-director Paul Mazursky found himself in the same confusion in treating homosexuality as he had had with wife-swapping. *Willie and Phil* confirms his belief that people should share each other, but only coyly. The eponymous heroes are in love with Francois Truffaut's *Jules et Jim*, in which Jules and Jim are in love with the same woman and she with them. Willie and Phil manage to emulate their movie idols, and their lady goes from one to the other. Mazursky, reasonably enough, decided to take the men's affection for each other to its logical conclusion, and when their wife/mistress has turned temporarily against both of them they bed down together. The camera cuts away at once, with Cole Porter's song 'What Is This Thing Called Love?' surging up on the soundtrack. Later the lady is waiting for them while they are in the jacuzzi: 'I'm going to go' they both agree, pausing slightly before the word 'go' and not attempting to move as the scene fades.

Most films about lovers of the same sex are made with the sort of good intentions which cannot be identified in the finished product. In the English-speaking cinema there are commercial pressures: one in six of the world's population may be gay, but they might not necessarily support a movie in which Scarlett pairs up with Melanie and Rhett with Ashley. It was once held that it was natural for heterosexual men to be stimulated by the thought of women making love together; it has since been admitted that women are often drawn to gay men, but (till recently?) they squeamishly didn't want to know who did what to whom. Nobody did anything to anybody in Visconti's *Death in Venice*, a particularly successful transcription of Thomas Mann's novel about the

passion engendered in a man's breast by the sight of an adolescent boy, but elsewhere this director faltered. While Jean Cocteau made allegorical references to his homosexuality in such films as *La Belle et la Bête* and *Orphée*, Visconti inserted unnecessary homosexual references – in *Ossessione*, as we noted, and *La Terra Trema*. Working into the permissive era he blundered, as far as this theme is concerned, in *The Damned* and *Ludwig*.

Conceivably the best film on this subject is *Another Way*, directed in Hungary in 1982 by Károly Makk, who wrote the screenplay with Erzsébet Galgóczi, author of the autobiographical novel on which it is based. If this is another tale in which the protagonists, the lovers, end tragically, we may not for once object since its purpose is to constantly draw parallels with, or make comments on, life in the Soviet bloc countries (and it is one of the more subtle of several such critiques). We know from the opening section that Eva and Livia will become lovers and their lives are contrasted on Christmas Eve when the lesbian Eva sits lonely, disconsolate, waiting, while the married Livia laughs with her husband. Livia, however, is unhappily married and also drawn into a relationship with Eva, who works in the same office. She believes that she can hold this to a tipsy kiss or so but even then is racked with guilt, at one point trying to break off with Eva, since the stronger the emotion the more the furtiveness involved. Free from the restraints of home – they are away on an assignment – Livia tells Eva that she will come to her room, but works herself up to such a nervous pitch that she cannot. Other films on lesbianism omit these steps to physical expression, as well as the suppressed feelings apparent in virtually every scene. Anybody of mature age who changes sexual orientation surely would want to discuss the reasons – and that does happen in the best scene in the otherwise inferior *Making Love* (written, incidentally, by an 'open' gay, Barry Sandler).

Cruising, a murder story, set in New York's gay underworld, had more reason than either *Looking for Mr Goodbar* or *American Gigolo* for showing the vast drinking and dancing caverns where the men shake to loud rock music under strobe lighting, dressed sometimes in little more than leather harnesses, often kissing and inhaling amyl at the same time. The scenes in all three films are so extraordinary as to suggest that the presumably heterosexual writers and directors of all three films felt impelled to tell moviegoers of these emporia discovered while in pre-production research. *Cruising* itself upset many in the gay community, but it seems to me that showing handsome chaps in leather kissing is a vast advance on the old effeminate stereotypes. Despite much strangeness (the surreal ending has the pursued and pursuer – murderer and undercover cop – stripping for either sex or death), this movie is otherwise a traditional thriller, just as *Making Love* is the sort of love story Hollywood has always made. In this eternal triangle the wife is the loser, but she doesn't lose her husband to another woman. No one, including the film's makers, seem to care much about the wife, whose life, after all, has been shattered, but the piece has the rare and positive virtue of ending happily, even if the husband's eventual companion is not the man who caused his homosexuality to surface irrevocably in the first place.

Despite the ending, the film was no more popular than *Cruising*, but by this time one comedy on the subject had been a great international success, leading to a sequel and a long-running Broadway musical version. This is *La Cage aux Folles* (1978), which examines what happens to a middle-aged gay ménage when the son of one of the couple wants to bring his prospective in-laws to dinner. The carryings-on are harmless enough, but what do we make of the German *Taxi zum Klo* in which we watch the hero pulling on his cock-ring and preparing to service an erect penis pushed through the hole in the cubicle wall? As we watch the actor's graphic and varied homosexual encounters we may note the blotches on his skin. His name is Frank Ripploh, who also wrote and directed the film, which is avowedly autobiographical. At the Berlin Film Festival this movie was awarded the Max Ophuls prize for comedy; it went on to the film festivals in Hof, Cannes, Rotterdam, Edinburgh, New York and London. Even in America's redneck country it played for months in the art-houses. The film is not, however, a comedy. It is not a barrel of laughs, and at the end Ripploh's life lies in ruins, due – of course – to his lifestyle.

It seems to me that many of the film's spectators must have speculated on Ripploh's motives in issuing this extreme, self-lacerating comment on his life-style. I conclude these notes on sex in the cinema with his movie because it seems to me that it is as far as movies can go without becoming pornographic. It would be rash to predict that there will not be movie confessionals even more revealing and I daresay the next will be by someone whose fame hitherto was not confined to his own circle. Whatever Ripploh's motives, his film must be considered far healthier than the mutilations, blood-letting and killings which so often are offered as screen entertainment. The equation of sex and violence has been around so long that few can remember when it started. It is a sad comment on our so-called enlightened era that it took so long to separate the two. That we took so long to throw off our inhibitions about sex and our sexuality is, as I've said, proof of the strength of the morals of the last century. However, we should also remember how our civilization was shaped by the myths and legends of one peripetatic Hebrew tribe. If the Bible and the Church had approved of sex (outside marriage, that is) the movie industry would have had many fewer problems. The permissive age has solved only a few of those problems and it has brought a whole crop of new ones. It may be that sex in movies will be surrounded by hypocrisy till it's put there by a generation which does not equate it with sin.

Acknowledgements

Grateful thanks are extended to those who supplied stills and/or gave permission to reproduce: The Cinema Bookshop (p. iv, 75, right, 121), Columbia Pictures, Iéna Films, Lorimar, M-G-M/UA, Nouvelles Editions de Films, Paramount, Paris Films, The Photo Source (p. 117, 120), RKO Radio, Rank, Rex Features (p. 135, 136, 144, top), Sandrews, Speva, Thorn EMI, Titanus, 20th Century-Fox, Universal, Warner Bros and especially the National Film Archive.

Index